THE DIVINING HEART

By the same author

Fiction

A CHANGED MAN
THEN WE FALL
A FAMILY AFFAIR
THE DESTROYER
THE DAM
VERY PERSONAL PROBLEMS
THE CURE
THE DETECTIVE
TALK TO ME ABOUT ENGLAND
A DISTANT COUNTRY
CHILDREN OF DUST

Reporting

THE CITY
THE CHURCH OF ENGLAND
THE DOCTORS
THE NAMELESS: ABORTION IN BRITAIN TODAY
MEN AND MONEY: FINANCIAL EUROPE TODAY
THE NEW MILITANTS: CRISIS IN THE TRADE UNIONS
GENTLEMEN OF FORTUNE: THE WORLD'S INVESTMENT BANKERS
SEX AND THE BRITISH: A TWENTIETH-CENTURY HISTORY

Biography

THE HOUSE OF NORTHCLIFFE: THE HARMSWORTHS OF FLEET STREET
DYLAN THOMAS
RICHARD BURTON
DYLAN THOMAS. THE COLLECTED LETTERS (ED.)
SIR HUGE. THE LIFE OF HUW WHELDON
CAITLIN. THE LIFE OF CAITLIN THOMAS

PAUL FERRIS

The Divining Heart

HarperCollins*Publishers*

HarperCollins*Publishers*
77–85 Fulham Palace Road,
Hammersmith, London w6 8jb

Published by HarperCollins*Publishers* 1995
1 3 5 7 9 8 6 4 2

Copyright © Paul Ferris 1995

Paul Ferris asserts the moral right to
be identified as the author of this work

A catalogue record for this book is
available from the British Library

ISBN 0 246 12977 8

Set in Sabon

Printed in Great Britain by
HarperCollinsManufacturing Glasgow

All rights reserved. No part of this publication may be
reproduced, stored in a retrieval system, or transmitted,
in any form or by any means, electronic, mechanical,
photocopying, recording or otherwise, without the prior
permission of the publishers.

For Daisy and Emily

Let not thy divining heart
Forethinke me any ill . . .

John Donne, 1572–1631

PART I

1919

CHAPTER 1

'Dear Aunt Margaret,' wrote Isabel in gritty school ink, 'this is the night we are supposed to wash our hair, but the pipes have frozen. Several girls are in the San with influenza. A panic broke out in case it was the Spanish Flu again, but all are now eating junket. We are not supposed to read newspapers so I am not sure whether an epidemic is raging outside. I am amazingly healthy, although I sometimes think I will die young. Did you ever think that, when you were fourteen? I am at last reading the life of Queen Victoria you gave me for my birthday, and I have decided to be a model of conformity. This is a pact I have made with the dark gods, whoever *they* are. In return, I have asked them if I can change my name, and they said, OK. Thus from this day in 1919 and henceforth and for all eternity, I, Isabel Rees Buckley, wish to be known as SIBLI Rees Buckley. If you agree, please tell Mrs Mason so they can change it in the registers. The Welsh form is much nicer, don't you think? I write regularly to "Aunt" Aeronwy, but I don't get much in return. With love, I sign myself as the newly hatched *Sibli*!'

The school was on the south coast of England, grey stone under black slate. Each girl had a cubicle. Helen, Sibli's best friend, called them cells. 'Come along, gels,' she would call, tying paper curlers in her hair, 'time you were locked up.' She spoke of the town on whose outskirts the school perched as Bracing-on-Sea. 'O Lord,' she prayed out loud, to make the dormitory laugh, kneeling on the lino, 'bless Thy female convicts at Bracing-on-Sea Prison and grant them remission.'

Helen pretended to be rebellious, but Sibli found her soft-centred, sweet, passionate about ponies on the Downs and snapshots of other girls' brothers. Sibli's experiment with conformity was serious. In the past she had been reticent about her father, saying only that he was 'in business'; most of the school's fathers were in business, unless they were professional men. Now, when Helen next talked about hers, a surgeon-commander in the navy who once removed an earl's appendix, Sibli began boasting about Morgan Buckley the new London publisher.

Helen was suspicious. 'You've never said.'

'I've never talked about him. He's a brilliant man. You should see the people he has at his dinner parties.'

'We thought he was something boring, like a wholesale grocer,' said a square-faced girl called Beatrice.

'He keeps a mistress, as a matter of fact.'

'What?' they all shrieked. 'Your Pa?'

She told them that the mistress was a beauty who dined by candlelight that sparkled on her diamonds and bare shoulders. Anyway, her father was a widower, so why shouldn't he have a lady friend if that was what he wanted? They lapped it up. Sibli hated the idea of showing off about one's father – and the mistress in any case was no more than a guess – but everyone did it, so she demeaned herself like the rest of them. It was all part of the experiment.

At netball, she was suddenly enthusiastic. She went to practices in the freezing gymnasium, waving her goose-pimpled limbs like the rest of the idiots. 'You see?' said the games mistress, addressing the East House seconds. 'If Isabel can do it, so can anyone. Her timing in the circle is exemplary.'

'Sibli, Miss Mills. I have been Sibli for ages.'

'You are down here as Isabel.'

Determined to perfect her methods, she did an about-turn on boiled cabbage. She was famous for liking it. The stewed bitterness on her tongue set off the thin meat and dead potato. Now she fell into line, and resisted attempts by others to smuggle virid forkfuls on to her plate. 'Realized I hate the stuff,' she said. She even gave up temporarily her attempts not to be Isabel.

Hardest of all, in the spring she let Helen kiss her. Fondling, the *idea* of fondling, intrigued Sibli, though it was not to be compared with an incident when she saw Uncle Aubrey lean across Aunt Margaret (in a gazebo, blurred by foliage) to enjoy what she recognized as the 'passionate kiss' of the novels they didn't keep in the school library. Nor did Sibli relish the thought that something was expected of her and Helen, that they were best friends of the bolder kind, with bosoms and secrets, whose friendship was egged on by timider girls to provide them with heroines or villainesses – either would do, thought Sibli.

Still, there it was, you couldn't have a decent shot at conforming to expectations, and then leave out the lying on a bed and nuzzling. Sibli cleaned her teeth furiously beforehand and saw Helen doing the same, flinging the Calox oxygen tooth powder (as recommended by the surgeon-commander) on her brush.

When the moment came, in the dark, in Sibli's cubicle, and their mouths began a strange congress in which teeth and tongues had to be found roles, not just the lips, it was Sibli who went further, opening the neck of Helen's nightdress and stroking the breasts inside.

Soon Helen was whispering, 'I love you' in Sibli's ear, to which Sibli returned a polite 'Me, too,' after which Helen sighed and said, 'Do you think we shall ever love men as much as this?'

The question was ridiculous. In addition, Helen had made no attempt to reciprocate the bosom business. The smell of tooth powder was overwhelming. Sibli pulled out her hand and they lay shoulder to shoulder.

'I shall marry a tall, thin man,' she said chattily, taking

Uncle Aubrey as a model. 'An American? Someone exciting. An actor? An explorer?'

A muffled voice said, 'What are they doing now?' It was Beatrice. Far off, the sea thumbed the beaches, where they were allowed to walk two by two in fine weather, pairs of brown skirts and brown shoes, brushing the edge of vastness.

'Better go,' whispered Sibli.

'Have we done something awful?'

'I shouldn't think so.'

There was nowhere else for conformity to go; it was a dead end. Sibli couldn't escape herself, whatever that self was. The knowledge didn't surprise her. She went back to liking cabbage and let them down at netball.

Nor did she squeal with alarm next term when they were all being terrified at the prowler, that summer's sensation. 'It was probably old Jake,' she said, Jake being the gardener, a wasted man with a tiny head who hadn't seen military service.

Helen was furious that Sibli took it so calmly. 'You'd laugh the other side of your face if you saw him,' she snapped, and described the cruel lips and wild eyes – she had it from Beatrice, who knew Milly Cartwright in the Upper Fifth, a dean's daughter and thus ultra-reliable, who saw the ghastly features pressed to a window-pane when she was making cocoa by special permission at nine PM, there being a thunderstorm, which stopped sensitive girls sleeping.

'Poor man, he must have had a soaking,' said Sibli, and refused to be thrilled with terror like everyone else. *Burglar* and *escaped lunatic* were popular choices. Sibli had other ideas. She put herself in his place, standing in the rain and hearing all those female creatures rustling like beetles on the other side of the walls. It needed no great feat of imagination to reverse the process and put oneself outside a building full of boys in pyjamas. Helen told her not to be disgusting and went on enjoying the danger they were all in. Next day housemistresses were busy telling them to pay no attention to silly rumours, but presently a police-constable was spotted at dusk, looking purposeful behind the rhododendrons, and the scare lingered for weeks. If there really was a man, said Sibli, brushing her friend's hair, what a lark if us girls could catch him. 'You wouldn't dare!' said Helen hopefully.

The weather entered a dry and congenial phase; the art class got up early to paint dawns; it was a while before Bracing-on-Sea had one of its characteristic nights of gale and rain roaring up the Channel, and Sibli, waking with a start, thought immediately that if one happened to be a nocturnal prowler, a downpour would be the thing to prowl in.

She had been dreaming about Pa, who was fastening a string of green stones around her throat and patting her bare shoulder. Pa-dreams made her feel womanly and confident. It wasn't cold. Mackintoshes were kept downstairs, but she borrowed a bicycle cape from the sleeping Helen. The cubicle smelt of tooth powder. Sibli draped the cape over her nightie, stuck her feet into gym shoes and snapped the school-hat elastic under her chin. Her luminous wristwatch showed a few minutes after eleven o'clock.

The way out was through the fire-escape door at the end of the corridor, secured by a bar on the inside that needed a sharp blow to release it. Windows were rattling in the gale, and one more rattle didn't matter. A folded hymn-sheet, brought for the purpose, jammed the door shut from the outside.

Sibli whisked down the iron steps. The lawn had an outline, a lighter grey on a darker. What moon there was sent a few candlepower through the clouds. In the west a lighthouse sparked. With the wind blowing up her legs and rain spattering the cape, she walked slowly around the long rectangle of the school. Once at the rear of the building she was protected from the worst of the wind. In the yard the waste bins reeked of dead food, and something scuttled past her feet. Imaginary conversations kept her going.

'*Weren't you TERRIFIED, Sibby?*'

'*Down to my bones, dear.*'

'*Why ever didn't you put your knickers on?*'

'*I felt like feeling dangerous.*'

By the west wing she was back in the gale. A light burned on the ground floor. Disappointingly it was a store-room, brushes against a wall, buckets, a fire-extinguisher, rolls of linoleum. The mad hope of catching the prowler watching a housemistress in the bath vanished.

By now rain had got under the cape at both ends, making her too wet to care. In a flash Sibli was a goddess of air and storms. She danced across the grass, arms outstretched, the flying water determined to strip her naked, wind shouting in her ears, cape rising up, nightie clinging to skin, nipples outrageous, nymphs and shepherds applauding. The elastic broke under her chin and the hat whirled into space. Free at last, she hopped in the air, wondering if she dare ring the fire-bell and get them all out, three hundred girls, hopping in the rain.

Something emerged from the direction of the rhododendrons, like a bit of the storm detaching itself. A squatness loomed up, shepherd rather than nymph, smelling of pipe and beer. She shivered and it grabbed her. A man's voice said, 'Got yer, yer booger. Saw yer at the winder.'

As Mrs Mason said, it could have been serious. This was a popular view. Sibli spent two days in the sick-bay, where Matron said it could have been very serious *indeed*. Aunt Margaret came, having been advised by telephone that Isabel had walked in her sleep but was fortunately spotted by the gardener, a most reliable man.

'I had better tell my aunt about the prowler,' said Sibli, when she was waiting in the headmistress's sitting-room at four in the afternoon for the taxi to arrive from the station.

'You had better do no such thing. The prowler, as you

call him, was a poor sick soldier from the army hospital whose brain has been damaged by a shell.' Mrs Mason had a summer cold. She blew her nose in a frilly handkerchief. 'I tell you it in confidence because I'm sure you are a sensible girl.'

'So please, Mrs Mason, what was Jake doing when he caught *me*?'

'He was keeping an eye on things.'

'Was he looking for another prowler?'

'I hope you aren't turning into one of those girls with her head full of nonsense,' said Mrs Mason, 'and I think this is Mrs Mappowder's taxi now.'

Her aunt was as calm and beautiful as ever. It had taken her since breakfast-time to come from Wales via London.

'So what was it,' she said, when Mrs Mason had closed the door and left them alone with a pot of tea, 'an illness or an escapade?'

'I was bored.'

'That's hardly a reason. You can't just give way to fancies.'

'Pa always does.'

'Try not to be impertinent all the time, there's a good girl.'

'I'm sorry, I really am. I was only out ten minutes. I'd have had a rub down with a towel and been fine, if old Jake hadn't been wandering about. I'm jolly glad you came, though. I never thought you would, because it wasn't anything really.'

'Come and give me a proper kiss. I have a confession to make,' and she pressed Sibli's face to her dress. 'I had to come up from Wales in any case. There is a funeral tomorrow. You remember I was married once to a man called Henry?'

Sibli nodded. Henry Penbury-Holt was deep water, the English businessman that Aunt Margaret had sworn to love, honour and obey, about the time of Sibli's birth. There had been adultery, that scrumptious word, and cruelty, rather less scrumptious, and Margaret had divorced him before the war and fallen in love with Major Mappowder.

'He has died,' said her aunt. 'The funeral is at Gaddesden, in Essex. I shall stay in London overnight.'

'But . . .'

'But what, little rabbit?'

'Do divorced people have to go to funerals?'

'Not at all, unless they want to. I feel an obligation.'

'Oh, it's a *duty*,' said Sibli with relief, not wanting to think of any rift with Uncle Aubrey.

Her aunt stayed barely an hour. It wasn't long to the summer holidays. The taxi drove off with the sun flashing on its windows. Sibli felt so chastened by death, even the death of an ex-uncle that nobody ever liked very much, she forgot to beg Aunt Margaret to tackle Mrs Mason over the great SIBLI-not-ISABEL question, one of the things that was vital to her future happiness.

CHAPTER 2

Margaret wondered how quickly she should get away after the funeral. Gaddesden church was cool and flowery, its battle flags dangling above the congregation. A regiment raised in the district had been shot to pieces late in the war, so the vicar would have had other congregations to sharpen his grief on. He glanced at his notes as the bearers shuffled down the aisle.

A brass handle glinted and Margaret couldn't spot her orchids among the wreaths on top. It was hardly to be expected. An ex-wife had no rights. She supposed the choice had been tactless, reminding them of Henry's unhappy career as the orchid king, after he left the family firm. But life with Henry had had its moments. A cellophane cone of blooms gave the marriage its due. Two of Henry's brothers, Tristram and Stuart, were at the head of the coffin. Stuart wore uniform, a captain in the Air Force. Tristram, she knew, had stayed behind and kept Penbury-Holt & Co going in the City. She hadn't seen either of them since before the war. The other bearers, big pale boys, must be assorted relatives. The only one she recognized for sure was Tom, Tristram's eldest. The family had been lucky. None of its sons was old enough to be slaughtered.

Only Henry had come to grief. But no one was in a mood for tears, and the singing of 'Abide With Me' bordered on the raucous. Had no one ever loved him except Margaret, and then not for long? Dreadful possibilities about human beings who were dislikeable from birth made her stop singing. It was a relief when the vicar got going, trying to put Henry into an eternal context.

What an irony, he told them, to be gathered for the obsequies of our departed brother on the eve of the Peace celebrations, when the nations were to celebrate the laying down of arms the year before. For Henry was a warrior, *de facto* if not quite *de jure*. Not for him, admittedly (said the vicar), the shrill of bugles, the dawn attack. Like many another of undoubted courage, he served his country by remaining at his post in a reserved occupation. Yet the call, when it came, was answered without flinching.

History, now. The vicar had boned up on Whit Monday 1918. 'Little did we realize then,' he intoned, and Margaret imagined the last wisp of Henry's ghost corkscrewing up to the roof, 'that the war was drawing to its close. The Hun was starving. He sent his bombers over England. Gothas and Giants rained destruction on the capital. It was the last air-raid on London, as it turned out. Henry Penbury-Holt had been to the Paddington area on business,' and the vicar spoke of burning buildings, masonry crashing, women at risk, a dash from the street, a falling beam, a fearful wound, a long illness, the final succumbing last Saturday. 'Dear friends,' said the vicar, 'Henry has no medal. But when the trumpets sound he will be known as a hero.'

Margaret found her eyes watering. It was ridiculous. But it was over. They sang 'Onward, Christian Soldiers', and presently Henry was underground and she was free to go.

She had travelled on the train from London with Esther, the odd one out of the family, the only Penbury-Holt she had stayed in touch with.

'I hope you were not reproaching yourself because you didn't visit him before he died,' Esther said, as they left the graveside.

'I don't think I was.'

'Because I am his sister, and I found him very difficult

at the end. He actually shouted at me. He said, "Esther, it was bad enough when you were one of those blessed Suffragettes. Now you're one of those blessed birth-controllers." He was an impossible man. I shall say it if no one else does. Now here's Tom. Tom, come and greet your Aunt Margaret.'

The boy stopped a yard from Margaret and bowed. 'I would like to express my condolences,' he said. It was almost a shout. He had a red flush over the cheekbones.

When she spoke to him, he stood to attention. He said he would be joining the family firm as soon as he was old enough.

'I have told Tristram to let him go to the university first,' said Esther. 'He's clever enough. But they slap him on the back and tell him the City is the thing.'

Margaret lingered for a moment. Stuart's wife, Virginia, was shepherding a couple of children. She pretended not to see Margaret come towards her, then gave a crooked smile and said, 'What a heavenly day. Have you come straight from Wales?'

'I have a niece at school on the south coast. I was there yesterday.'

'That's Morgan's child, of course. Is he still a spiritualist?'

'He has decided to become a publisher,' said Margaret, resigned to defending him, if she had to. But the woman who was once her closest friend merely said, 'You look very well, Margaret,' and stooped to wipe earth off a boy's shoe.

It might have been easier had they addressed her as 'Mrs Mappowder', but that would have been too explicit. It would have announced that this woman with the return railway ticket from Wales in her purse, who had been privileged to become a Penbury-Holt, had declined, in the end, to put up with Henry. It was bad enough to have divorced him, let alone to have married again. Calling her 'Margaret' kept the lid on all that.

As she turned to go, however, Tristram stood in her path, raising his hat, saying that she was welcome at Old Saracens, and they would be going back across the fields directly.

So the Penbury-Holts had softened. Surprised and pleased, she walked with Esther by the hedges. Pigeons made echoes in the elms, and she glimpsed the lake. Presently she was on the terrace with something on a plate and a glass of sherry, trying to remember where the tennis courts had been. Beyond the strict rectangle of emerald lawn, the grounds looked unkempt. It must be the war.

Everything was 'the war'. Travelling from Carmarthenshire the day before, she found the train already crowded with soldiers when she boarded it at Port Howard – coming on leave from Ireland, she heard someone say. The English hedgerows were as thick and purple as she remembered, but now and then she saw armoured cars outside concrete buildings, and fields full of barbed wire. Near London there were still guns pointing at the sky.

Arthur Penbury-Holt, Tristram's father, in theory still the head of the family, came to talk to her. He seemed to have shrunk. 'I lost my wife three years ago, you know,' he said.

'I'm very sorry. I did hear.'

'You still see Esther, I believe.'

'We have stayed firm friends.'

'I told Tristram to invite you to the house.' He blew his nose. 'We must all forgive and forget.'

She didn't ask who should forgive what, though she was tempted to. Each conversation came up against a brick wall.

Daisy, the youngest, was the last of the brothers and sisters she spoke to. In her late thirties, she was stouter than ever. Was she pregnant yet again by Mr Munro Parton the gynaecologist? That was him, under the cypress, cornered by Esther. Was it possible that the Penbury-Holts were still producing little Englishmen?

She hadn't changed – Dippy Daisy, all excitement, sweat on her upper lip. She whispered that they had to talk. 'Not here!' she breathed. 'It concerns Henry. We have to go indoors.'

Nothing about Henry concerned Margaret any more. But she followed Dippy, whose ankles bulged over her shoes, and was led down a passageway. A maidservant flounced past with cake.

'Upstairs!' hissed Daisy.

Even in summer there was a hint of damp about the place. Margaret had forgotten the geography. She and Henry had slept here from time to time – in a room off this corridor or that one, in a bed that was no doubt still there, between linen sheets that were still in use.

'This was where he died,' said Dippy, and gripped her arm. 'I'll close the door, just in case.'

The windows were shuttered and the electric light was on. The bed was stripped to the springs. A whiff of disinfectant remained in the air.

Dippy was fumbling in a drawer. 'Here,' she said, prising open a rectangular box to reveal a nest of cotton wool, and, within it, a blackened teaspoon. 'Henry spoke to Munro about it, only hours before he passed away. We were here by chance – Munro had a case in the neighbourhood. They were alone for five minutes. Henry said you were to have this – that I was to give it you, and you'd understand.'

Margaret rubbed the clouded metal on her sleeve, and it came to her. The late Henry had suffered from earaches, and the late Margaret used to warm olive oil in a silver spoon and dribble it in. Henry's ghost, screeching upwards, had left something behind after all. She would take what was offered.

As she replaced the spoon, the door opened and Tristram stood there, mouth turned down, his wife Charlotte behind him.

'Perhaps you would care to explain,' he said. He was looking at Dippy, but the tone implied Margaret.

'Munro said it was all right,' squeaked Daisy.

'This room is sacred. I'd have thought better of my sister.'

Charlotte's bosom had crossed the threshold. 'Mrs Mappowder,' she said, 'has something in her hand.'

'. . . dying wish,' came from Daisy.

'Kindly give it to me,' said Tristram, palm outstretched. 'This minute, if you please.'

'What a fuss you make about things,' said Margaret, and put the box on the dresser. 'In due course I expect Munro to swear an affidavit, and I shall look forward to receiving one silver teaspoon, slightly bent. I'm sorry you were embarrassed, Daisy. Don't let them bully you too much.'

Outside, Esther was looking for her. 'I have had enough of my family for one day,' she said. 'I have been attempting to interest Munro Parton in certain matters. It is like talking to a dinosaur. He said, "Don't speak to me of Marie Stopes. The propaganda in that book of hers is an insult to man's finest feelings." I said, "That's all very well, Munro, but what about woman's finest feelings?" He pretended to see a pike in the shallows and changed the subject.'

The village taxi took them to the station. All the way to Liverpool Street, Esther rattled on about the new dawn of womanhood. Margaret couldn't get Henry and the teaspoon out of her mind. What had he meant to convey to her after so many years? That he was sorry? That they should have persevered? That the conjugal bed might finally have yielded up the baby whose absence had nearly destroyed her?

Only memories could harm her now. Margaret blotted them out by attending to her companion. Esther was describing the ideological war being waged in the birth-control movement over the pessary. They sat alone in their Ladies Only compartment, racing towards London, one childless woman listening to another.

CHAPTER 3

The house at Peele Place had grown more comfortable, not less, since pre-war days. Morgan Buckley had his new friend Johnny Cox in the drawing-room drinking whisky when Margaret's taxi was heard in the street. 'Stay and meet her,' he said. 'Owns a tinplate works in her own right. Married pots of money as well.'

He was proud of his sister. 'Maggs!' he said, 'you look ravishing. This is my new partner, Sergeant-Major Cox MM. He prefers not to talk about the war.'

'We are all like that, ma'am,' nodded the soldier, who had a straight back but uncertain eyes.

'My sister's husband came through the Somme unscathed. He dreams about it, she tells me. You should have taken Aubrey with you to the funeral, Maggs. Or would that have been bad taste?'

'You should have gone yourself. Henry worked for you for long enough.'

'You may be right. My sister is famous for being right. She has always been my mentor.' ('Stop talking rubbish.') 'Many years ago I had doubts about my faith. I would have been a minister of religion but for a stroke of bad luck, if you can believe it.' ('I wouldn't if I were you.') 'It was Margaret who kept me going.'

'If I could leave my business card with you, ma'am,' said Cox, 'then should you have any printing needs, I would be happy to give you a quotation. We are an old family firm.' The card had a trace of thumbprint. 'Everything from invoices to luncheon menus.'

'I tell him to forget all that. We plan to publish a wide range of books. Memoirs, the occult, high-class fiction – how does that appeal to you, Maggs?'

'You leave me speechless, as usual.'

'I told you she'd be impressed. The public gobbles up entertainment these days. Look at the cinema. We are entering an era of peace and plenty. People will want to be amused. There will be rewards for men of vision.'

'With respect, ma'am, there isn't much you can tell a Welshman about the power of the word,' said Sergeant-Major Cox, and she saw he was a lost cause already. 'You must excuse me. I have compositors working late.'

She heard them laughing on the steps, and Morgan came back and said, 'One couldn't not like Johnny, could one?'

'They say the country is full of ex-soldiers looking for jobs.'

'Johnny owns the works. His Dadda had a seizure while printing a song-sheet for an Armistice concert. Say you think it's a brilliant idea.'

'What will you do, corrupt him like you corrupted Henry?'

'Henry was a moral coward from the start. You know that.' He ran a finger down the back of her hand as far as the wrist, where he pushed the tip inside the cuff of her blouse. 'You never forgave me for the spiritualism, did you?'

'You could have done better.'

'I used to agonize over what my true level in life should be, till I realized the answer was painfully simple. It's wherever you find yourself. But I had a good run with the spirits.'

'All that's really finished with?'

'Henry looked after the accounts, as you know, and one of the last things he did before he fell in action – was that how the vicar put it? – was report a definite drop in takings. There've been too many mediums cashing in on the slaughter. And the big houses no longer find it fashionable. Time to move on, Maggs.'

'I suppose I should be glad. But books – are you sure?'

'Would you be happier if it was patent medicines or second-hand tanks? It may be, yet. God will pull the puppet-strings as it suits him.'

He was brooding on the past, on his lost vocation as a preacher; or pretending to brood on it, for her benefit. Over a meal served by a middle-aged woman, he wanted to know more about her life in Wales, and she said what she had said a hundred times, that she was happy, that she had never looked back on her decision to marry Aubrey in the middle of the war.

'I hope he's as fond of you as I am,' said Morgan. 'If I'd met a Maggs I'd have married her like a shot. But there it is.' He crumbled a piece of cheese and looked at her sideways. 'Do you mind not having children?'

'I mind you harping on it.'

'I can't help wanting to know your secrets,' he said, and leaned over to kiss her neck.

She told him to stop being silly, but it soothed her; she couldn't help it. She could reach an equilibrium with Morgan, a point of balance between the life she had once led with Henry and the life she now led in Port Howard, in which Margaret was a kind of disembodied Margaret, separated from the outside world, neither married nor unmarried, and Morgan himself was similarly disconnected, neither wicked nor virtuous; they were simply the two together.

It didn't last. In her bedroom, a handsome room at the front of the house with walnut furniture and a fire in the grate, she found her stockings and handkerchiefs put away in tissue paper in a chest. Glancing in another drawer, she found some crêpe de chine knickers with the initials 'VPH' stitched on them. 'Virginia Penbury-Holt,' she supposed: was meant to suppose.

Either it was one of Morgan's jokes or one of Morgan's

hidden messages. It was hardly an accident. He wanted to tease her or annoy her. In the old days, the Henry days, she had noticed Morgan's eyes on Virginia, the prettiest of the sisters-in-law. Not even Morgan would try such a thing, she used to think, with Virginia happily married to Stuart, and busy producing babies.

Ten years later, things like that were less certain. Stuart had been to the war. She knew little of Virginia's life in those years.

Margaret was curt with her brother over breakfast. He wore striped trousers and had a diamond pin in his tie. 'Sleep well?' he said, spearing kidneys for her on a fork.

'Nothing but coffee, thank you. I saw Isabel on Tuesday. She was found wandering in the grounds during a rainstorm, in her nightie.'

'Surely public schools encourage that sort of thing. They are always going on about character and cold baths.'

'You take no interest in her welfare, do you?'

'I pay sixty pounds a term, that's hardly indifference. Don't let's quarrel, Maggs.'

'When she's here in the summer holidays, I hope you're careful who you invite.'

'The house revolves around her. Even Henry mended his ways, God rest his soul. He met her once or twice, you know.'

'Explain "mended his ways".'

'Speak no ill of the dead,' said Morgan, glancing at an article about profiteers in the *Daily Express*.

'Stop playing the goat. If you want to say something unpleasant about Henry, say it.'

'We are what we are, Maggs. I liked Henry. I used to say to him, "Henry, why don't you get married again?" and he'd say, "Once was enough." I know you like the truth.'

To put down the cup and go would be to acknowledge defeat. If only she could hate Morgan all the time, instead of in fits and starts.

'A man who lives on his own is tempted,' he was saying. 'He used to visit an establishment in Paddington. French, so-called. He was there the night the Huns came over. His Whitsun treat, he said. A couple of the women were hurt. He managed to get his clothes on, and in the confusion, who could tell if he was inside coming out, or outside going in? He told me about it in hospital.'

Margaret hoped that her face registered nothing. 'Remember that Isabel *is* only a child, however precocious you like to think she is. She's as much open to influence as anyone of her age.'

'She has you in your Gothic splendour. She has Aeronwy in Swansea. In between she spends a few weeks in the year with her father. No breath of impropriety attaches to my behaviour when she's within twenty miles, I do assure you.' He wiped kipper from his lips. 'How is Aeronwy, by the way? Still feeling sorry for herself?'

'You should know that better than anyone.'

'I shall never be forgiven, shall I? Not ever. I was fallibility. Aeronwy was innocence.' He grinned at his sister; nothing subdued him. 'How goes her typing agency?'

'I believe she wants Isabel to work for it when she leaves school. I've got other ideas for her.'

'You'll find your niece does what she wants to do, *cariad*.'

'Like you, you mean.'

'Like me. She calls herself Sibli now, did you know?'

'One of her fads,' said Margaret. 'I don't believe in fads.'

CHAPTER 4

Port Howard was the place that Margaret understood. The estuary spread out from the railway bridge, the red stack of the copperworks appeared, and then the cluster of tinplate chimneys at the bottom of the town, hers among them. That was her domain.

Since before the Great War it had made her a subject for gossip. A woman didn't run a tinplate works, even if she was a boss's daughter. When David Buckley was killed, and neither of his sons – Morgan the black sheep, Will the almost-socialist – was able or willing to take over the business, she was the one who returned, minus husband, to run Tir Gwyn. Bankruptcy would have brought out the best in everyone. Instead, she prospered. This made her respected. But she never outgrew the original stigma. She had interfered with the natural order.

Some kind person told the *Port Howard News* about the funeral. The *News* had disliked her father and saw no reason to spare his offspring. 'Local interest,' said a sly paragraph, 'was awakened by the presence at a funeral in Gaddesden, Essex, of Mrs Margaret Mappowder, the well-known local mill-owner and wife of Mr Aubrey Mappowder, of Mappowder's Copperworks. Mrs Mappowder was attending the obsequies of her first husband, Mr Henry Penbury-Holt. Her divorce is still remembered in the town.'

Her Aunt Villette had the cutting ready when Margaret called at the old Buckley house, Y Plas, on Saturday, as she always did. 'Far be it from me to say anything about your no doubt excellent intentions in attending the obsequies,' Villette said, wiping her hands on the piece of sacking she wore around her waist when doing housework. 'But I have to ask myself what your dear mother would have said.'

'She was quite fond of Henry. Let's not discuss it.'

'I am well aware of my lowly position, Margaret. My views count for nothing. There is no need to rub it in.'

'You mustn't say such things,' said Margaret, and made a little speech about how nice everything looked. She had given up begging her aunt to leave Y Plas alone. Gaunt, poor and proud, Mrs Lloyd martyred herself every Saturday. 'I may have an artistic temperament,' she would say when threatened, 'but I know my duty when I see it.'

Streaks of polish had dried on the woodwork. Uncle Abraham was in the yard, mercilessly beating a carpet. From the kitchen came a ghastly humming of flies – Villette must have clogged the sink again.

It was all unnecessary. Y Plas didn't belong to the Lloyds. They lived where they had always lived, in Bank Cottages, which Villette refused to leave, where she had caused scenes when Margaret had an inside lavatory put in. Y Plas belonged to Margaret, who kept it for sentimental reasons.

At present it was rented for a trifling sum to Theodore, the son of Villette and Abraham, who was hardly ever there. Theodore was at the root of the Saturday ritual. As a child he had shown a talent for music, and David Buckley paid for piano lessons and examinations. Buckley didn't care for music, and found Theodore an odious lad, but his wife, who was Villette's sister, was a persuasive woman. The boy's talent was the only spark in Villette's life. She complained constantly about Abraham, the kind old potato she had married for romantic reasons long forgotten and ever since regretted. If, against all the odds, a musical artiste had been created out of the nothingness of Bank Cottages, she had a duty of gratitude, had she not?

Thus Y Plas was assaulted weekly by broom and floorcloth in memory of David Buckley Esq.

Aunt Villette had dismantled the framed poster of an early performance by her son, which hung at the foot of the staircase, in order to remove a dead bluebottle from under the glass. Replacing it had defeated her. Margaret screwed it together again.

WIGMORE HALL
36 WIGMORE STREET

A RECITAL BY
THEODORE LLOYD, PIANO.

Bach: Chromatic Fantasia & Fugue in D minor BWV 903.
Schumann: Arabesque in C...

She failed to persuade her aunt to come to the Peace Day supper at Cilfrew and bring Abraham. It was out of the question, said Villette. He was behaving oddly these days, carrying on conversations with Joe.

Joe had been their elder son. He was to have been a Port Howard sea pilot like his father. But in the war he was second officer of a tanker, torpedoed off Ireland one spring evening.

'It is embarrassing,' said Villette. 'Abraham shows no interest in Theodore whatsoever. It was always Joe, Joe, Joe. I tell him, "Joe is dead," but he just looks through me.'

'Come by yourself.'

'It would not be right, Margaret. Now, if you will excuse me, I have things to do in the drawing-room' – no doubt meaning the Bechstein, tuned once a fortnight by a man from Swansea, which wasn't good enough for Villette, who liked to burrow underneath the dust sheet, clean the keys with methylated spirit, and search for reckless insects which might have died among the strings.

Margaret left her to it. She would have given her aunt and uncle everything they needed for a comfortable old age, if they would have taken it. But they were beyond such an obvious solution, no doubt like many in the town, or in any town. Or was that the convenient philosophy of the employer? Questions of that sort whispered behind the walls of her life. She drove hard bargains, paid her workers the rates agreed by the Federation, and was exemplary about sick pay and holidays. What else could one ask of a modern capitalist? She had come late to the role of proprietor, though. She was there by accident. Her doubts were always present, about the system, about herself.

The Peace Day supper was a straightforward affair, nothing to reflect on. We had won the war, boys, and there was sparkling wine by the bucketful and an ox roasting in the summer twilight. Mayor and Mayoress were there, a title or two from Glamorganshire, some military, a clutch of manufacturers, enough foremen and clerks to be democratic, the shopkeeping world, the Harbour Trust world, stuffed aldermen with ladies to match, together with Medicine, Education, the Church and Rugby Football. They ate, they danced, they pretended the clock had gone back to 1914, but they knew it hadn't.

Margaret wasn't in sole charge of the proceedings, only joint hostess with her mother-in-law, Lady Mappowder. Sir Lionel, propped up in his invalid chair, did his share of entertaining the guests – rather more than Aubrey, who preferred his cronies or his own company on these occasions.

At eleven o'clock everyone gathered on the terrace to watch bonfires being lighted on the hills. Soon they were burning all down the spine of Gower, across the estuary. Margaret could see the cronies with their cigars, but there was no sign of Aubrey.

Sir Lionel called to her. A rug was tucked in around his legs. In the dark, in his colonel's uniform, he could have been a younger man. 'Here,' he said, holding out field-glasses. 'You can see them round that fire. Must be five miles away.'

Flames filled the lenses. Margaret made out black marks

that might have been people. Her father-in-law said, 'That was a brave deed, going to the funeral. I met him once. Funny chap.'

'Funny family. Though I suspect most families have that said about them.'

'How is that brother of yours? The one in London, I mean.'

'He plans to publish books.'

'Good God!' said Sir Lionel, and took back the glasses. Two of the fires had merged, as if the hill was starting to burn. 'Must be memories in people's minds tonight. I hope your husband isn't brooding.'

She took the hint and went in search of him. He was in the billiards room, practising cannons.

'Everything all right?'

'I felt like half an hour on my own. But don't go.'

'There are bonfires. We've been saying "Oh, look!" as if we were all blind. Go on playing. I'll watch.'

She stood in the shadows. Suddenly the air rumbled. The pools of light around the table shook.

Aubrey put down the cue. The noise came again.

'Is it a storm?' she said.

'Storm be damned.'

He hurried down a corridor to a side door, Margaret following. His dog Homunculus was barking from the kennels. Rays of light flew across the sky, and the detonations were louder.

'You'd think it was the artillery, laying down a barrage,' he said softly. 'Bloody guns.'

She couldn't make sense of his mood or guess what it was leading to. The garages were nearby. He pushed her into a car, drove fast down to the main road, and out of the town to the west, his face up against the windscreen. People were outside houses, watching the enormous flashes.

'Try not to kill us,' said Margaret.

Down a side road they came to iron fencing, barbed

wire, notices, brick towers, chimneys, waste land. Aubrey slowed, and a ball of flame hurt her eyes.

'Smell the gun-cotton?' His voice had an edge. 'Once met, never forgotten.'

'Of course. It's the munition works.'

The main gates were open, with a pole barrier across. Aubrey crashed through it, and the pole flew in the air. A whistle blew, someone came running after them, floodlights were switched on. A man appeared from an office block. Aubrey stopped the car.

'You're trespassing,' said the man.

Aubrey's bony figure clambered out. 'And what did you do in the war, my friend?'

'Filled shells with the necessary. Who the hell are you?'

'Aubrey Mappowder.'

'Sorry, Major Mappowder, sir. Didn't recognize you.' The man raised his hat, and there was another giant flash and thunder. 'Tom Bowen, assistant manager. Celebrating the peace. Dismantle it is what we do these days, so we thought, instead of burning the old stuff, we'll have some fun. Hear it from the Castle, could you?'

'Have it stopped. Shells were for killing Germans with. They aren't fireworks.'

'I can't stop the men now.'

'Very well.'

Aubrey returned to the car. 'Margaret,' he said, 'please get out and wait for me here.' When she refused, he drove the two of them around the building and on to the waste land.

Men were shouting and running. Flames poured into the sky in front of them. Margaret felt the heat of an explosion, and earth spattered the roof. She thought they were going to die. Then Bowen appeared, dancing up and down, screaming, 'All right, all right, all right.'

Going back, Aubrey pulled in by a hedge and leaned out of the door, vomiting. He lay in her arms, shuddering and tearing at her dress with his fingers.

'I love you,' she said. 'You are the point of everything,' and she wished it was true.

All at once, he was himself again. Margaret, her heart still racing, said that he had never talked to her about the fighting. He put his hand on her thigh and said that he never would.

PART II

1921–1925

CHAPTER 5

Helen's parents, Surgeon-Commander Dorkin and the faintly dotty Mrs Dorkin, lived less than an hour's drive from the school. The house was rural; goats and ponies grazed the field. Up to a point it was the ideal place for a best friend with peculiar domestic arrangements of her own to be invited to for Sundays or brief holidays from school, and Sibli was once referred to by Mrs Dorkin as 'my second daughter'.

Bits of rural England appealed to Sibli; other bits of it repelled her. Without wanting to be unkind, the goat-and-pony department was disappointing. Fortunately Helen had cousins, some of them boys, who came by with their parents in battered motors or now and then on horseback. Some playing the fool went on, mock-brutal in the English way. The house rambled and had black beams – the Commander threatened to turn it into an hotel when he left the navy – and there were useful attics.

Sibli's domestic arrangements were never gone into in any detail at school. They revolved around Pa, now well established in dormitory gossip as a fascinating demon king who very occasionally popped up in a cloud of cigar smoke to take Sibli and friend to a posh hotel, from which the girls returned all smiles and even wobbly; there was a story about champagne. When it came to one of these rare outings, Pa took priority in Helen's eyes as well as Sibli's. She persuaded her mother to let her miss a cousin's wedding because that nice man Mr Buckley was promising tea at the Metropole when he would be en route from A to B one Saturday.

For reasons that were never explained, any more than A and B were ever identified in his itineraries, Pa called off the outing at the last minute. A telegram sent via Mrs Mason spoke of 'unforeseen circumstances'. Sibli took it in her stride; she never doubted her father's affection, and his telegram sent her 'buckets of love', a phrase she enjoyed hearing Mrs Mason have difficulty reading aloud. What upset her was Helen's bursting into tears, followed by a row with the housemistress, Miss Matthews, when Sibli argued that she and Helen should be allowed to go to the Metropole anyway, and send the bill on to Pa. It blighted the weekend. They would have behaved with perfect decorum and brought little cakes back for the dormitory. But Miss Matthews said she must be mad to think that at sixteen years of age, a girl was old enough to start walking into hotels and ordering tea. Perhaps in compensation, Sibli had another of her Pa-and-naked-shoulders dreams that night, this time with red stones round her throat. School was becoming a nuisance.

On Monday morning wind blew the lid off a dustbin with 'East House' painted on it as she was passing. Inside was a newspaper, mixed up with tea-leaves and shrivelled snowdrops. Sibli hid the damp pages under her coat. It was the *News of the World*, a paper no decent family took, so people said. The newsagent had written the name of the customer at the top, 'Miss W. Matthews'.

Sibli saw nothing wrong with that. Why shouldn't the housemistress want to read about a baron's unfaithful wife, or what was going on in the Higgly Piggly Club when police arrived? Alone in her cell after supper, Sibli was riveted by the case of the Archdeacon of Wakefield, accused by the Church of England of immorality with a Mrs X, whose nightdress, a chambermaid said in evidence, still had the shop ticket attached. The Archdeacon was sixty-one. It was amazing. She closed her eyes, visualizing the bedroom.

At that moment Beatrice put her hand around the door and grabbed the newspaper. In seconds it was being torn apart and giggled over by the rest of the dormitory. Inevitably, they made a noise. Inevitably, Miss Matthews walked in.

'I found it in the dustbin,' said Sibli, when the pieces had been collected and handed over.

'We shall discuss your behaviour in my study, while I decide whether this is a matter for the headmistress.'

When a girl was older, Miss Matthews explained carefully, in a tiny room with a coal fire that leaked smoke through the bars, she could distinguish for herself between the wicked and the innocuous. The teacher had bulging eyes. They bulged at Sibli as she said that the *News of the World* was in general unwholesome, but it also printed useful paragraphs about bottling fruit and making chair covers. 'That is why *I* might look at it. *I* can use my judgement.'

Sibli smiled. She heard the woman ask her to promise to stop reading unhealthy newspapers, in return for which she might be allowed to see the Upper Sixth's *Daily Telegraph* when their common-room had finished with it. She refused: she would read what she could lay hands on.

'I also find it deplorable that a young lady should be peering in dustbins,' said Miss Matthews, with surprising venom. 'If you have a grudge against me because of what happened on Saturday, you had better look me in the eye and say so.'

'I wouldn't waste a grudge on you,' said Sibli, and the deadlock was complete.

In Mrs Mason's room next morning, chapel-like with its carved oak and dried flowers, they didn't get as far as the *News of the World*. Sibli had woken up looking for trouble. She frowned when the headmistress called her 'Isabel'. For heaven's sake, most people had come round to 'Sibli' by now, and the records only said 'Isabel' because Aunt Margaret hadn't pulled her weight.

'It would be really nice if you could call me by the Welsh form of my name, Mrs Mason,' she said.

Mrs Mason, who had her usual cold, told her not to be foolish. The school registers said she was Isabel, and Isabel she remained unless her parents decreed otherwise.

'Your parent,' she corrected herself. 'I'm sorry, child.'

The 'child' and the being sorry were the last straw. Sibli was tired of it all. She said, 'Parents is right, actually, Mrs Mason.'

The room reeked of wintergreen; the headmistress's chest must be smeared with the stuff. She twiddled a pencil and looked puzzled. She ought to be in bed.

When Sibli said she had a mother all the time – it was her 'Aunt' Aeronwy, the one who sent her those typewritten letters from Swansea – the headmistress sighed and looked at the Channel.

Sibli explained what the problem was: her father had never married her mother.

'I think, Isabel,' said Mrs Mason, 'you may be sickening for something. There are some nasty germs about this winter.'

'Sibli,' said Sibli. 'S. I. B. L. I.'

'I had better write to your father. Now, I shall ask Matron to take your temperature, and then you may be excused lessons for the rest of the day. Kindly do not speak to the other girls about who your mother is or is not.'

At lunchtime Sibli managed to get Helen on her own for a minute in the cloakroom. A tap dripped and a cabbage smell came down the stone corridor.

'What's wrong, is it your, you know, monthly?'

Sibli told her that the school had discovered she was illegitimate, and were wondering what to do about it. This went beyond a father who kept a mistress, and knocked Helen off balance.

'I'll stand by you!' she gasped.

'There's a darling,' said Sibli, and kissed her – for good measure exploring with her tongue, out of friendship; saying goodbye.

'I couldn't bear Bracing-on-Sea without you.'

'Hurry up or lunch will be over. I'm allowed to be off my food.'

Sibli took minimal belongings – coat, hat, purse, novel. The town was only a ten-minute walk. Sea, fading into horizon, was like a mood projected. At the station she bought a first-class ticket with her emergency pound note.

CHAPTER 6

Buckley & Cox, publishers, got off to a slow start. Having a printing works turned out to be less important than having manuscripts to print. Their first book was not published until the week Sibli ran away from school. Morgan had persuaded Mrs Squale, the spiritualist who had introduced him to her dubious business before the war, to write down her story. He spiced it up, called it *Confessions of an English Medium*, gave her the pseudonym 'Dora de Clancy', and put a wrapper on the jacket that said:

>How I played tricks on my rich clients!
>How the real spirits played tricks on me!
>**How romance and the occult go hand in hand!**

A brochure was printed to promote the book and introduce Buckley & Cox to the trade. Morgan did the canvassing and obtained orders for a few hundred copies, which he delivered by taxi. This was all drudgery. So was a morning at Kensington public library, making a list of publications which might review the thing. But he knew he could find respectability as well as money in the book business. Morgan, at thirty-eight, fancied reconquering London all over again.

The reviewers showed no sign of co-operating. They ignored the book. The day Sibli arrived on Morgan's doorstep, Mrs Squale's husband sent a telegram to say the law prescribed remedies for misuse of copyright material. 'Be patient and we shall all be rich,' Morgan wired back.

Having his daughter appear without notice was an

inconvenience. A woman was coming to the house that evening and had to be stopped. There would be ructions, too, unless Sibli was bundled back to school. But she amused him. A mixture of child and woman, she sat in front of the fire in his study eating toast, reddened calves showing through her school stockings. 'If you had run away a month earlier,' he said, 'you could have helped the typist send out copies.'

'You mean I can stay here and work for you? Pa, you're a dream.'

'Behave yourself. Work out your own salvation with the women. In the meantime you can live at Peele Place for a couple of days. I shall send a wire to the school and telephone your Aunt Margaret.'

'Or Ma, what about Ma?'

'You can twist Ma round your finger. Your aunt is the one who matters. Now if you want to be useful, here's sixpence to go down to the Brompton Road and buy the evening newspapers. Look for anything about *Confessions of an English Medium*.'

Squares of light in the houses excited her as she slipped through the streets. Behind the curtains, futures for everyone were on offer. The man at the kiosk was muttering to himself. Buses roared past, crammed with Londoners whose hats and eyes, as they flashed by in the dusk, were like an endless stage army of citizens.

The battle was half won. All Sibli had to do was be herself. Margaret was there within twenty-four hours, telling her she was mad not to complete her education. There was even talk of university. Sibli sat alone with her aunt in the study, pensive and affectionate, answering every question truthfully, making no fuss; just not giving an inch. She would like to live at Peele Place, but if that was not possible, would her aunt let her work in the office at Tir Gwyn? She was fond of South Wales. She would even join Ma's secretarial agency and study shorthand.

'You sound such a reasonable girl,' said her aunt,

drumming her fingers on the arm of the chair, 'but in fact you are deeply, deeply unreasonable. You have your whole life ahead of you.'

Her case was finally undermined when Sibli decided the time had come to confess to telling Mrs Mason about the skeleton in the family cupboard.

'My dear child!' said Margaret, and hugged her so close, she smelt the tiny drop of scent that Sibli had been experimenting with behind her ear. 'There is no question of the school not allowing you to stay because of that.'

But it was an obstacle. Sibli declared she was not in the least ashamed, but she couldn't bear to be in a place where shame was expected of her. The statement was unassailable. A brief telephone conversation with Mrs Mason, who spoke of 'certain matters' that would be best clarified by a 'personal interview' with Mr Buckley, decided Margaret. Isabel would not be returning.

'Sibli,' murmured her niece, and begged Margaret to let her spend a week in London 'helping Pa' before Wales and the secretarial agency, or whatever it was to be, began her real life.

Margaret agreed. Then she had to hurry back to Port Howard, where the cold-roll boys at the town's tinplate works had all taken it into their heads to come out on strike, the first unrest since the war ended. 'You'll be good and sensible, won't you, and come when I send for you?' she said, lingering on the womanly face that was pressing through the round orb of the child, the straight-severe blackness of the hair, the uncomfortable certainty in the eyes. To Morgan her last words were, 'I am trusting you, my boy. She is sixteen. It is a dangerous age.'

Sibli liked the carpeted bedroom, the generous fires, the bath to soak in behind a door with a lock on it. A week of freedom seemed a long time. Poppy, the housekeeper, took her out to buy clothes, raising doubts about various items – a long coat with a two-inch button, a knee-length woollen dress, a beret. But the money was Morgan's.

At first Sibli was content to stay in Peele Place. She combed journals in vain for reviews of Pa's book, which she read at one go. Dora de Clancy's passions were more or less genteel, some of them shared with a man called Ernest, also a spiritualist. One phrase stuck in her mind, 'I left the seance room soaked in perspiration, and Ernest smiled at me and said, "You should take a nice hot bath, my dear."' Sibli very much hoped that Ernest was meant to be Pa.

At last a review appeared. The *Daily Express* covered a page with it. Someone called 'James Dunglass, the Critic Who Pulls No Punches' devoted himself to saying the book was disgraceful. Sibli marked it savagely with a red crayon, which stabbed a hole in the headline, 'SQUALID SECRETS OF THE SEANCE'.

Her father said it was not the end of the world. 'Dunglass takes a high tone on issues of the day,' he said. 'His proprietor is Lord Beaverbrook. You've heard of him? He has come here from Canada to put us right on things.'

His coolness made her all the more upset at what he must be feeling underneath. She was amazed that this man Dunglass was allowed to toss out remarks like 'dubious moral standards' and 'verging on the indecent'. Who did he think he was? Without telling Morgan where she was going, she borrowed half a crown from the petty cash, put on her one-button coat, and set off for Fleet Street.

She re-read the article on the Underground, planning how she would ask to see Mr Dunglass and tell him in a loud voice that he was despicable. She could even slap his face. Glancing through the rest of the newspaper, she noticed a photograph of a man she liked the look of. He seemed very young. 'Stephen Davis,' read the caption, 'our war correspondent, whose dispatches on the troubles in Ireland have aroused great interest, photographed yesterday at our offices, when he was on a visit to London.' A sharp eye and thin cheeks stood out from the blur, and again she had the feeling of endless lives behind curtains that she had only to draw aside.

The district was shabbier than she expected. Sodden newsprint filled the gutters of side streets. A hook at the end of a girder lifted a reel as tall as a man from a lorry and disappeared with it through a wall. At the *Express*, revolving doors spun people in and out, and a charwoman was on her knees, mopping up muddy footprints outside the lifts. A commissionaire told her that Mr Dunglass rarely came to the office, and that in any case, no one could be seen without an appointment.

Sibli hung about outside, studying photographs that filled the plate-glass windows. Some were from Ireland – a burning police-station, soldiers with fixed bayonets guarding a bridge. She would wait for another five buses to pass. People came and went all the time. If someone called, 'Hello, Dunglass,' she would stand in his path and say, 'Cad!' Perhaps it would be at the seventh bus. At one time her life began to be governed by mysterious rules. If this stone skims three times off the sea, Aunt Margaret will invite me for Easter. If I rub the flannel between my toes nine times, I shall come top in Latin. As it happened, the pebble worked and the flannel didn't. But she sensed the beginnings of madness in such behaviour, and made herself stop.

Turning to go, she saw a slender young man crossing the pavement. He wore a tweed suit and a soft shirt, and she recognized him at once.

'Mr Davis, the war correspondent?' she said. 'My name is Sibli Rees Buckley. I'm not potty or anything.'

He was cautious but not unfriendly. He stood with his hands in his jacket pockets, head erect on a longish neck, listening to her say she was scouting for books on behalf of Buckley & Cox. The idea had occurred to her as she spoke his name; it was impossible to say which had come first, the idea or the greeting. Laughing, he took her inside, and they sat in a waiting-room with a photograph of a paper mill on the wall.

'So will you consider it?' she said.

'Consider what?'

'Writing a book for my father. About Ireland. You must know a lot about Ireland.'

'Did he ask you to approach me? Surely publishers write letters.'

'We are a very modern sort of firm.'

'What does he publish, this father of yours?'

Davis had an engaging way of gesturing with his hand, like a cat waving its paw. She said, 'Dora de Clancy, for example. Her *Confessions of an English Medium* is all the rage. Your Mr Dunglass has been pouring fire and brimstone on it.'

'And making it sell like hot cakes, I expect. Good old Jimmy.'

The thought hadn't occurred to her. A clock chimed the half-hour, a bell rang, and the commissionaire looked in and said, 'Editor's conference, Mr Davis, they would like you there ASAP.'

'So can I tell him you'll think about it?'

'I really don't know . . . I mean, Ireland,' and the paw swung in her direction.

'My father gives dinner parties. Perhaps you'd come to one of them?'

'I suppose you aren't a Fenian in disguise, with a bomb in your handbag? You have an accent.'

'It's Welsh, Mr Davis, not Irish. We live in Peele Place. Shall I ask him to ask you?'

'Tell your father I go back to Dublin in six days.'

He waved the paw and swerved away.

Pa was amused; perhaps impressed as well. He asked her what she thought her aunt would say. But he supposed they might have a few people round on Friday, now that the firm was showing promise. Within hours of being denounced by James Dunglass, bookshops had been ringing up for copies. 'Wages of sin,' said Morgan with satisfaction.

Sibli fortified herself for the occasion with a new silk dress and hair crushed to the back of her head by a man in Knightsbridge. 'I would rather keep you a week than a month,' said Pa.

The famous Virginia came, woman of unspeakable mystery, with her handsome husband Stuart, a Penbury-Holt in the flesh, a war hero.

A Mrs Thorn was there, middle-aged or more, recently widowed, wealthy, something to do with Leuchars Bank. 'I see your Daddy has gone over to rationalism,' she said to Sibli. 'He led my poor husband a dance for years with his levitations and knockings. Typical of Morgan to make money out of a change of heart. Does this de Clancy woman exist, or is she a figment of his brain?'

'My partner's life has been something of a spiritual quest, you know, ma'am,' said Johnny Cox, breaking in.

'That means Morgan will go in for religious publishing if he thinks there's money in it,' observed Mrs Thorn.

With dinner only ten minutes away, the Booleys, a Member of Parliament and his lady, another relic of pre-war days, arrived at the same time as Davis, and Sibli lost any chance of greeting him properly. He came without a partner. His black tie wasn't quite straight. His eyes glowed at her once, diagonally between the candles.

The word 'Ireland' drifted down from the head of the table, where her father was talking to Mrs Booley, who was large and wore pink. Sibli slipped into a story. At dusk, she reached a town near the border. Her lover was there. Men were hunting him. Ice lay on the roofs; the curfew was beginning.

Was Davis the right man for the part? Turned towards Virginia, now, he was telling her a story about a horse race, and she was laughing. Sibli envied her for the way men leaned towards her. Davis looked a boy beside her, boxing with his paw.

She heard her father say, 'Davis here has been reporting on the Irish troubles for the *Express*.'

'Your proprietor has some strange ideas,' said Booley, and Davis sat staring at the end of his fork. 'Ireland's soul is aflame, and killing Irishmen won't stop it – isn't that what Beaverbrook says? I agree with Lloyd George. It was Sinn Fein started it. The British Army will finish it.'

Davis didn't respond. He told a story about another press baron, Northcliffe, who, in a fit of pique, made the hall porter of the *Daily Mail* its advertising manager.

They left the men to their brandy. Virginia patted the sofa next to her and asked Sibli if it was true that she had quit school of her own accord and was returning to Wales.

'You know all about me, then.'

'Your father was talking before dinner. Stuart and I have known him a long time, remember. Through your Aunt Margaret.'

'It's funny, I can never imagine her married to Mr Penbury-Holt and living in London.'

'Your aunt and I were great pals in those days.'

'Did Henry sweep her off her feet?'

'Other way round, I'd have thought. She always held something back. I heard her say once that most men would settle for very little. That said, she quite liked men. But then, don't we all?' A door slammed and a man laughed. 'I shall get into trouble,' said Virginia, 'saying such things to you.'

Davis was in the doorway, looking towards them, but Mrs Thorn, more agile than she appeared, intercepted him. Booley came their way, scooping up Mrs Booley, grunting with annoyance.

'That young man,' he said, 'had the temerity to lecture me on the alleged brutality of Crown forces in Ireland. *Six of one, half a dozen of the other*, those were his words.'

'Mr Davis is writing a book about it for Buckley & Cox,' murmured Sibli.

'And may I ask what you know about the subject, miss?'

'Booley means you are very young, my dear,' said his wife hastily.

She walked over to Davis. 'What is the brutality?'

'You have to go there. I'm not being patronizing. Without seeing it, there's no context for the cruelty.'

'What's the worst thing you've seen?'

'It's not all horrors. Journalism never is. They make us very comfortable at the Gresham in Dublin.'

'Answer the question, Mr Davis.'

'Very well. The Black and Tans caught a republican who'd shot a baker. Who they said had shot a baker. They tied his wrists with wire and dragged him behind a Crossley tender up and down the barrack square till he was dead.'

She shuddered, at the story or perhaps at Davis. Morgan came to say that the Booleys were leaving, and a handshake from the journalist might be helpful. She turned her back so she wouldn't have to see the quarrel being buried with false smiles.

Soon they were all on the move. Davis said he would write to Morgan, but she didn't think he would. He went off in a cloak, bare-headed.

Sitting in her father's study, in the rocking-chair that had belonged to her great-grandmother Hannah, she imagined going with Davis down endless backstreets in the border town, until at last they reached an apartment looking over the rooftops. 'We are safe here,' he said, and slipped the coat from her shoulders.

'Your aunt has telephoned,' said Morgan, appearing with a cigar in his teeth. 'You are to go to your mother's on Monday. Tomorrow you are off to a matinee with Esther Penbury-Holt, whom you know.'

'No way of getting out of Swansea?'

'None. Come back when you're eighteen and we'll see.'

But she would feel then as she felt now. She rocked herself, trying to conjure up ghosts from the past. Then thought better of it, in case it worked.

CHAPTER 7

The City in raw weather breathed steam, coal smoke and the vented odours of well-warmed rooms. Big fish in silk hats glided past lesser fish in bowlers. A Rothschild in a fur coat disappeared into New Court. A Penbury-Holt in a black suit came out of Heneage Lane into Cornhill, blowing in his fists because he had forgotten his gloves.

Tom fancied a cigarette, but gentlemen didn't smoke in the street. He was on his way to Caspian Buildings and the offices of Ellis Crabb & Co, marine insurers, where the Boss, who had gone there earlier to a meeting, would introduce him to yet another City figure. He had been doing it for months. 'And this is my son Thomas, who is now with the firm.'

The firm was only Arthur, his grandfather – a three-day-a-week-man now – and Tristram, his father. The rest of Tristram's generation had hopped it, early on, Uncle Stuart into stockbroking, the late Uncle Henry into shaky business ventures.

But Tom could be relied on. Damn, damn, damn, unfortunately he could. Mounting the steps of Caspian Buildings, he stated his business, and eventually a messenger preceded him up stone steps and along stone corridors to the Ellis Crabb suite of rooms, where his father and Mr Crabb were in a snug retreat with electric radiators and steamed-up windows.

He was a figure of note, this Crabb, so Tom understood – marine insurer, re-insurer, dabbler in gold, partner in firm of stockbrokers as a sideline. Through his contacts in the shipping world, he brought business to the Penbury-Holts.

Tom knew all this from his father; he hadn't expected to go on hearing about it. But Crabb, a man in his forties, with luminous eyes and great teeth that strained against his lips, announced, 'My great-uncle (old Sir Philip Crabb, director of Leuchars Bank, you know?) was best man at your grandfather's wedding.'

'So there you have it,' exclaimed the Boss.

'We are all chips off the old block. Tom here couldn't not be a shipbroker, could you, Tom?'

'Oh, I don't know, sir' said Tom, finding something about the man that he didn't like. 'I had thought of soldiering at one time. My friend Timmy Stevens has gone for the Guards.'

'War's over,' chuckled Crabb. 'War to end wars. No enemies worth talking about.'

'With respect, sir,' said Tom, 'there are always enemies.' He resented the relationship between the Boss and bigger fish, and especially this man of teeth. It was what life in the City meant, being fulsome to those with power. 'I did think about the Royal Air Force. We saw the Zeppelin brought down at Potters Bar from the school dormitory, sir.'

'You saw nothing,' said the Boss. 'You were twenty miles away.'

'I saw the red glare, sir! We all did! We cheered like mad.'

'If he saw it, he saw it,' said Crabb flatly. 'Things are what we think they are. Tom and I must have lunch at Pimm's one day.'

'If I'm not flying a plane by then, sir, like my Uncle Stuart.'

These pleasantries went down badly with the Boss, who told him on the way back to watch his tongue. The row grumbled on through the day. They were at the Baltic Exchange after lunch, men calling figures at one another, and one of Crabb's minions brought them a profitable charter. 'You see, Tom, you see?' said the Boss.

Five o'clock came at last, but even at Liverpool Street Station the Boss didn't give up. 'Ellis Crabb is off to Berlin tonight,' he remarked, as the whistle blew. 'He is building up one of the great insurance companies of Europe. We are investing in Ellis, your grandfather and I. We have twelve thousand pounds' worth of equity in the group. One of his companies is going to invest in us. Think of that, next time you make flippant remarks.'

'I hope he's safe, Father.'

'Safe? The name Crabb has been a byword in the Square Mile for a century. You are impetuous, like your Aunt Esther. It doesn't do in the City. You will not be liked.'

'No, Father.'

'And by the way, your Aunt Esther telephoned while you were out of the office. She has invited you to a matinee and a slap-up tea tomorrow. I accepted on your behalf.'

Fires burned under arches. Canal water gleamed yellow by the windows of a brewery.

'I believe I'd have said no. Could I have said no?'

'Hardly. An aunt is an aunt, all said and done. Someone else will be there, a young friend of hers. Esther is an unusual woman, but there are things to be learnt from her.'

Tom had better things to do than go to matinees, such as shoot rabbits with a .22. He took it out on his sister Alexandra, who was miserable (a) because the Boss wouldn't take a house in London for the Season and (b) because her sister Julia had got engaged to Lieutenant Commander Sidney Rumbelow, late of the Royal Navy, now engaged in poultry farming.

'Try persuading the Bossess,' said Tom.

'You know I can't. If it's Money, her face goes all blank. You're very cruel. You could bring up Money, man to man.'

'Things are tight in business,' said Tom, 'and getting

tighter. We may have won the war, but the Germans are getting off scot-free. They say there's going to be a slump. You'll have to make your dresses last for years.'

The plump shoulders wobbled. He felt sorry for her, in the unclarified way that he felt about most females. It was true about business. And there were men starving in the England that had won the war. Timmy Stevens said an ex-colonel had been seen in Leicester Square, selling matches and bootlaces. Enemies were always at large.

At Aunt Esther's flat in Victoria there was no sign of the young friend. Esther said they were going to the Gaiety, to a new play by Maeterlinck that he must have heard of. He hadn't even heard of Maeterlinck. 'My other guest's name is Isabel,' she said, 'although I gather that nowadays we are supposed to call her Sibli. Do you have any idea who I mean?'

'Sorry, Aunt, should I?'

'She is related to the Buckleys, the family your Uncle Henry married into.'

The afternoon promised to be as bad as expected. But the girl – dropped off at the theatre by her father, a Welshman with a menacing smile – was a corker. Her ungloved handshake felt slippery, as though the fingers were powdered. Holding it would have been grand, but Aunt Esther sat between them in the stalls.

The girl began looking at him behind his aunt's head, raising an eyebrow. Some rigmarole about babies yet unborn was in progress on the stage. Small girls in their nighties who belonged in The Abode of the Children were trailing after the Figure of Joy, heavily veiled – Aunt Esther, shifting uneasily, must be regretting her choice of play.

'Mummy,' cried one of the infants, as the veil was drawn aside, 'how lovely you are!'

Sibli coughed into a handkerchief, gasping for breath. Aunt Esther shushed her. The girl sat biting her lip. Tom saw she was trying to stop laughing.

The fact that she was different to anyone he had met before took hold.

Over a knife-and-fork tea at Fuller's in the Strand, Aunt Esther spoke eloquently of Miss Gladys Cooper's acting. Sibli disagreed with her. All three quarrelled amiably about allegory in the theatre and other matters of no importance. 'What does Tom think?' Sibli kept saying. He tried to prolong the afternoon by having views on telephones and Bolshevism, but by six o'clock, sleet falling and a wind blowing through Kensington, they returned Sibli to her father's house in Peele Place.

Tom took her from the taxicab to the door. In the seconds before the maid opened it, he said, 'May I see you again one day?'

She shivered; he felt it through their coats. 'Who can tell?' she said, and went inside.

Crossing London, after he had escorted his aunt to her flat, Tom broke his journey at Leicester Square to look for the colonel selling matches on the pavement. There was only a crone offering withered blooms to theatregoers on the corner of the Charing Cross Road. He bought a handful and took them back to Old Saracens for Alexandra.

CHAPTER 8

Swansea was only a few hours away by rail, and the intended train would have got Sibli there by early afternoon. But the bindery had been working all weekend to have the first batch of the reprinted Dora de Clancy ready, and she took copies to booksellers in the suburbs while her father looked after the West End. He sent a wire to say she had been delayed.

Until the last minute she hoped something would happen — a blizzard somewhere, an accident, a death — to let her stay in London. She clung to her father as he gave her a kiss and some paper money. There was hardly anything now between her and No 38 The Strand, where Aunt Margaret's protocol dictated she should go to begin her life.

Ma was Ma, that was the guiding principle. Never mind that Ma was also Mrs Griffiths, having married a haulage contractor of that name, long widowed, in the middle of the war. Mr Griff Griffiths was a quiet, decent man with a bald head like a skinned turnip. Had he shown a weakness for skirt or bottle, or merely had a temper or been a profiteer — things that Ma might easily have overlooked — Aunt Margaret would have recognized him as an unsuitable stepfather. Instead the man had to be a paragon. He even taught a Sunday School class.

Yet he was not one of those Welsh bigots — that might have done for him, too. Things were so arranged by malign anti-Sibli forces that he kept a bottle of Johnny Walker in the kitchen and drank about an inch of it a week, and he liked going to the pictures to see Sunshine Comedies and Tales of Pathos. Nor did he show any interest in Ma's seamy past, either prurient or moralistic. So, what with Ma's typing agency (two typists), her decent husband and her decent husband's haulage business (two lorries), Ma, being Sibli's Ma (and, said Margaret, on God knows what evidence, devoted to her), was the answer.

The sooty walls outside Paddington as the early evening train steamed out had the same dismal look as the stone house in The Strand. The room where Sibli slept overlooked the yard where the lorries lived, and beyond that the quays and scummy water of the North Dock. The gulls would be conversing in short screams.

It was an Irish boat train, destined for Fishguard. At dinner an army officer tried to start a conversation, but she discouraged him with a novel.

An alien landscape slipped by. At Berlin (Swindon, in fact) mysterious lights flickered in the town. At Vienna (alias Severn Tunnel Junction) shadows on the platforms became heaped snow.

The approach to Swansea, heralded by burning clouds, was too familiar for make-believe. The officer had gone, leaving his paper, an *Express*. She scanned it for the Irish news, and found half a column under Davis's byline.

Sibli closed her eyes and imagined him in the Gresham Hotel, Dublin.

When she opened them again, the train had left Swansea and was plunging down the gradient into Carmarthenshire. Port Howard came and went, oil lamps swinging in the wind. Odd, she thought, how the world fell into line with your impulse. At Fishguard men sold her fresh tickets and said it would be a calm crossing. The purser who found her a cabin apologized for the delay – she didn't know there was a delay – and said the police had arrested an Irish crew member on suspicion of owning a revolver.

Rosslare, in the morning, was a group of sheds and a smell of fish. The Dublin train had left, and the next was not for an hour. The telephone operator at the goods office put her through to the Gresham.

They thought Mr Davis might be down at Macroom. Leisurely voices debated among themselves. Mr D. heard the news and went off, so he did. On the whole, they favoured the Macroom theory.

She didn't ask what news it was. Macroom was on the railway map, a dot near the bottom of the web. With no choice but to press on or go back to Wales, she bought a ticket and waited for a train to the south.

The journey took most of the day, crawling from one country station to another. Women with bundles peered through the window of her first-class compartment and passed on. At New Ross six policemen boarded the train, and there was a long wait. A girl with a basket walked down the platform, selling halfpenny cakes. Sibli bought one and asked if she knew what had happened at Macroom.

'Ah, they ambushed a convoy on the Cork road,' said the girl.

The police emerged, holding a man in working clothes and a muffler. Blood trickled down his chin.

No one had asked her to come.

At Cork City, where she changed trains, the station was full of military. The Macroom train waited in a bay. Young Englishmen in dark caps and officers' belts were stopping everyone who boarded it.

'Miss?' said an officer.

'I have friends in Macroom.'

'Open your suitcase.'

She watched him search it, down on one knee.

'Who was ambushed?'

He banged the clasps shut and stood up. 'We were,' he said. 'By those dirty Fenians.'

His voice was meant for the third-class passengers

as they hurried along the platform, dragging children, keeping their eyes down.

'Sorry, miss, but we lost fifteen men. They did things to the corpses.' He put the case on the train for her. 'We are posting a unit in the corridors, so don't worry.'

At Macroom it was dusk already. The town was a main street and a hotel. A man with a birthmark down one cheek, who had taken her bag at the station, went on polishing boots, leaving her to a woman behind the desk.

Indeed, she said, they had a Mr Davis. He had stepped outside an hour since.

'Two hours, at least,' said the man.

Sibli asked was there a room vacant for the night. Certainly, said the woman, since who in their right mind was visiting Macroom just now?

'No doubt the lady is from a newspaper,' said the man, finishing off a toecap with his sleeve.

She hadn't prepared herself; she hadn't thought what Macroom would be like. 'In a way,' she said.

'Miss S. Buckley, Peele Place, London,' went down confidently in the hotel register. For a half-crown deposit she got a room protected by a crucifix and a Christ with purple wounds. Damp obscured the ceiling like a rain-cloud. Sibli rested for an hour and woke with a headache. When she returned to the lobby, the man had gone. The woman was adding up figures. No, she said, Mr Davis wasn't back. He might be in one of the bars down the road, Hagan's or Kennedy's.

Lamps at long intervals broke the street into shadows. Sibli put on coat and hat. She passed cracks of window-light and a draper's with suits hunched on a wire like hanged men. No one was about. The chimney smoke smelt like rags burning. She might have been a thousand miles from England.

Her name was called, in a whisper. A figure stepped from a gap between buildings. 'This way!' he said. It was the man with the birthmark.

He had her arm before she could move, tugging her down the alley. 'Mother of God,' he said, 'if you're on that street tonight, and the Auxiliaries see you, it's a bullet first and the challenge after.'

At the far end were more figures. 'Now, you won't be harmed,' a voice said in her ear, 'but you must come with us. Don't cry out, now. Whatever you do.'

A bandage went over her eyes; strands of hair caught in the knot. Fear rose in her chest. Held either side, she was made to walk. The smell of fires was left behind. Wet grass and earth replaced it. A tree hummed in the wind. On and on they went. An owl screeched. Once the men stopped, listening. Then she smelt cow-dung, and a dog barked.

After a door there were flagstones and a second door. The blindfold was taken off. A young man with curly hair and a long mouth sat at a table, where a pair of candles were fixed in their own grease. The light reached to a figure in the corner, cradling a gun.

'Sit yourself down,' said the young man, pointing at a kitchen chair. 'What brings you to County Cork?'

She asked why it mattered. 'Do I look dangerous?' she said, and hoped Davis would be proud of her.

'We must have categories,' said the man, 'do you understand that? We must be able to say, these are police, these are military, these are judges. They are enemies, or they are harmless, or inquisitive. Or spies.'

'You think I'm a spy?'

'How old are you?'

'Seventeen,' she lied.

'They'd use anybody,' came from the corner.

'Tell me why you're here.'

'It's a free country,' she said, still having a shot at defiance.

'If the Irish were free, neither of us would be sitting here. Now, I must have an answer.'

The face had the eyes of an older man sewn into it. She

explained how she had met a newspaper reporter at her father's house in London, and followed him to Ireland.

'Who?'

'Davis of the *Express*.'

'You mean you've come to County Cork, running after a man you took a fancy to?'

'Fell in love with,' she insisted, peering at him anxiously between the greasy candles. Had saying it made it true?

'If you were my daughter...' He passed a hand over the flame. 'Tell me about your father.'

She did her best, adding, 'He's Welsh, not English.'

'So is Lloyd George,' observed the gunman.

A figure at the door said, 'Jim, we should be away.' He nodded. 'I believe you,' he said to Sibli. 'You'll be taken back to your hotel. Davis has been over at Bandon with the soldiers. He should be back presently.'

He towered over her when they stood up. Sibli said, 'Was it you laid the ambush?'

He gestured for her to go, but she burst out, 'Is it true the bodies were mutilated?'

'Lies,' he said. 'Imperialist propaganda. I give you my word. You go back to London and tell them.' He was pinching out the candles as he spoke.

She was in the parlour of the hotel when she heard Davis arrive and ask if there were telegrams. She made herself walk, not run.

He pushed her back into the parlour before requesting porter and more coal for the fire. He looked tired, almost frail. It was a boy's face.

'Are you glad to see me?' she asked.

'I'm dumbfounded.'

'I came on an impulse. Nobody knows.'

'Do you make a habit of it?'

He sat next to her on a sofa with broken castors while she described the journey. Close to, his eyes had flecks of red in the corners. She wanted to tell him everything. A heavy vehicle went down the street, changing gear, and she said, 'I have had an adventure.'

'This country is as foreign as Germany.'

'I mean, an adventure here, in Macroom.'

He listened to her story. 'A bandit having a lark,' he concluded. 'Don't let it give you nightmares. Stay here and toast your toes. I'll rustle up some grub.'

In five minutes he was back with the promise of something hot on a plate. This time he was less at ease.

'Have they found who set the ambush?' she asked.

'They'll be lucky. After an action the Fenians bury their rifles and go back to the farms.'

'The man I met said it was lies about the mutilation.'

Davis stared at the fire, fingering her hand. Tyres crunched along the street and stopped. 'All true, I'm afraid. They were bayoneted after they died, time and again.'

'But he gave me his word,' she sobbed, pressing herself against him, letting his arms draw her in.

'You should never have come,' he said gently.

At last they reached an apartment looking over the rooftops. She snuggled against Davis's shirt, wishing he would remember what her lover was supposed to say in the story, *'We are safe now.'*

'I came because of you, Davis,' she whispered, 'don't you understand?'

There were footsteps outside, and the fire brightened as a draught came under the door. Davis pushed her away as the men burst in. All she felt then was betrayal.

The Auxiliaries were polite and sympathetic. One of them bent over her and said, 'We believe it was Jim Barry, miss. He has charge of the flying column in West Cork. We want everything you can give us.'

She told them what she knew, but would say nothing more to Davis. Until then he could have slept with her. He could have been her first. She sobbed for hours, hoping he would hear and feel ashamed, while armed guards moved about the stairs and landings. In the morning she was escorted to the station and back to Rosslare.

A dream had been destroyed; for ever, she thought. At Fishguard she sent a telegram to Ma – 'I am safe and will contact you shortly.' She caught the returning boat train. But she travelled only as far as Port Howard, the town she thought of as hers.

Her feelings about Davis remained with her like a mild illness – an ache, blurred senses, a touch of fever. Her pride wouldn't let her go back to her family, whether it was Ma's sticky embraces or the intelligent forgiveness that she hoped her aunt would have ready. At least she could purge herself of the illness first. What made it disagreeable was knowing that an impulsive gesture hadn't worked, that obeying what appeared to be an unmistakable prompting from within had ended in nothing, or nothing she could lock away and refresh herself with when people asked, 'But dear, why did you *do* it?' Or when she asked it herself.

There was London, but London was risky. Melting into anonymity – said to be easy – was the last thing she wanted to do in London. London was for being visible in, when the time came. Peele Place would tempt her, and once Pa knew where she was, he would hand her over to the women. Port Howard, where the happiest parts of her childhood had been spent, was the answer. It held no threats, yet it didn't rule out the possibility of another experiment. The dark terraces and shabby tramcars suited her mood. And no one would think of looking for her there.

She did a quick turn down Stepney Street, past the market where women in men's jackets were shouting, 'Fat chickens!' and 'Clean cockles!', and found the Labour Exchange. The clerk could offer her work as a cook or a skivvy, or a typist in the patent fuel works. She might have gone for the cook, but the wages were elevenpence an hour. Did people live on elevenpence? 'All the chips you can eat,' grinned the clerk, cleaning his nails with the corner of a file card.

Behind him, a blackboard said, 'Royal Ordnance Factory. Dismantlers wanted, 19 pence an hour. Low-risk work.'

He looked at her hands and told her she wouldn't like it.

'When can I start?'

'They are old shells, mind. The older the explosive, the greater the risk. You will be asked to sign an indemnity.'

By the end of the day she was on the payroll. The munitions works was four miles outside the town, reached by a branch line. Most of it was derelict now. The dismantling was done in narrow sheds, shielded by embankments of earth, built for the opposite process, putting the explosives in. The indemnity said fatal accidents had occurred.

She signed herself Rees, her mother's maiden name, and went into the nearby village to buy some plainer clothes in a draper's on a corner, and find lodgings. A Mrs Bevan had a card in the window. She had lost her husband in the war. In bed that night, Sibli heard her talking to herself across the passageway. Furnace-light from Port Howard came through the thin curtain, and even the lumps in the mattress didn't spoil the pleasure Sibli felt at having slipped out of everyone else's life and into one that was purely hers.

Wearing white smocks over their own clothes, and wooden clogs instead of shoes, the women looked from a distance like members of a religious sect. They eyed her, saying nothing at first. The work was done in cubicles, each with a bench and stool. Narrow-gauge tramlines ran alongside. A chargehand showed Sibli how to scoop the shell and its cartridge-case from an incoming tram, and carry it carefully to the bench. She watched a fat woman open a screw with a brass screwdriver, slide out the fuse, push in a wooden plug, unclip the primer from the case, replace it with a dummy, and return the harmless shell with its bits and pieces to a tram going out.

After an hour she was held to be proficient. The important rule was not to use force. If anything jammed, you dabbed red paint on the casing and told the chargewoman, who told a man in the end cubicle, who used a vice and a drill.

Sibli didn't mind the monotony. Rain showers drummed on the tin roof; flimsy, they said, so that any blast would go upwards, between the concrete walls. A screw jammed and she tried to force it, not thinking. Her heart thumped; was she close to being herself at that moment, the real Sibli? The chargewoman grunted and sent her, with shell, to a cheerful youth in the end cubicle. He had blue eyes and said his friends called him Dai Drill. 'Only single men get to do this job,' he said, stroking the shell with dirty fingers.

The other women on the shift ranged from Sibli's age to Gran, who must have been sixty. She got to know them at dinner-breaks, the forty-five minutes when they shed their smocks, sat round in a hut with boxes for seats, boiled water on a paraffin burner, and wolfed the contents of their food tins. Her accent was too posh for them, and they wanted to know what she was doing there. She made up something about hard times in London and a family who were dead, but they weren't convinced. The older women were more sympathetic, guessing at some private scrape; it was the girls who went on eyeing her.

No doubt the attentions of Dai Drill contributed; he never lost a chance to inquire about London; once he asked what she did on Saturday afternoons, and said he knew some nice walks.

What she did on Saturdays was have a bath in the kitchen, then go into Port Howard to borrow novels from the library and look at newspapers in the reading-room, avoiding the *Express*. Davis-fever had burnt itself out, but why ask for trouble? The pure unalloyed Sibli was her aim in life.

Soon she would end the current experiment. But the shells fascinated her. She found one with the words 'Hello Mr Kaiser' faintly visible in chalk. In an hour she could clip the wings of twenty or more. Whenever a fuse jammed, perhaps once a day, she deliberately tried to force it. The fear as she put her weight behind the screwdriver was addictive, channelling itself through her nerves. After calling the chargehand, she always had to go outside and urinate. Her face burned. She felt capable of anything.

Milder weather came and she went for walks to the seaward edge of the factory with her dinner-time apple and piece of chocolate. Gaps had been broken in the barbed wire that divided factory from dunes and the beach beyond. Along the coast, Port Howard drowned in smoke. She sat in the sun, listening to the sea, imagining the voices of the men and women who swarmed here in their thousands in the war, when (Dai told her) the works was like a town, night and day.

A voice spoke in her ear. Arms held her on the sand. It was five girls from the shift, shrieking with laughter, saying it was time they gave Miss Posh a welcome.

'Pull her drawers down!' she heard.

Sibli struggled, biting her lip. Above her loomed a sturdy girl with freckles, holding a pot and a brush, dribbling red paint.

More laughter accompanied the dragging down of the garment. She tried to get her teeth into a leg but missed. Her skirt was hauled up to her waist.

'Roll her over, in the clover,' cackled the one with the paint. 'We likes to give the bum a nice colour.'

Their efforts to twist her around left a leg unguarded. Sibli lashed out with it. Freckles fell backwards and the paint spilt over her skirt. She got up slowly, holding her ankle and cursing. 'Right,' she said, 'keep her like she is. Nasty, you are, Miss Posh.'

She pushed the brush handle between Sibli's thighs. Sibli filled her lungs and screamed.

A man shouted, and Freckles yelled to him to mind his own effing business.

When he shouted again, he was close. Freckles dropped the brush and said, 'Miss Posh can't take a joke.'

The pack dispersed. Sibli made herself decent, kneeling on the sand, looking Dai Drill in the eye.

'Silly bitches,' he said. He threw down the wooden stake he had armed himself with. 'Only the rubbish work here nowadays. There was two women killed in the winter. Didn't tell you that down the Labour, did they?'

She was shaking. He helped her to her feet. 'I'll see you back to the sheds,' he said.

'You wanted to go for a walk. We've ten minutes yet.'

They went up and down a switchback of dunes. Dai Drill was nervous. The cuffs of his jacket were unravelling.

'Why are you in the munitions, then?' he said.

'For the hell of it. What about you?'

'Rubbish like those girls, aren't I? Nobody never did much in our family.'

'I think you're all right,' she said, and, stopping, put her arms around his neck and kissed him.

Not long after that, at another dinner-time, when they were walking on the dunes, she let him make love to her. Not that 'love' came into it. What she was after was the act and the freedom, and where better to assert a claim to freedom than here, on this puritanical coast, where the odds were so high against it? The act was roughly as anticipated, down to the element of brutality, the pain, the spots of blood.

Dai was a sweet boy, who seemed to know what was expected. He had come equipped with a packet of things, which caused him acute embarrassment. If it had been Davis, she would have wanted nudity and a feather-bed and a long night. But that would have been an experiment of a different kind.

On the way back she tried telling him gently that she might not be there much longer. He didn't listen at first; then was upset, saying he would smash any man who tried to take her away from him.

Dai's mood extended to the cubicles. His drill against metal gave louder shrieks than usual that afternoon. Sibli could feel the hate coming from the other girls. She would have to look out when the shift ended. Late in the day, Gran came into her cubicle to say some beggar had walked off with her jar of paint again, and could she borrow Sibli's to dab a shell.

Gran carried the rusty 13-pounder to Dai Drill. Two minutes later she was back, and the drill began shrieking.

'That beggar's still got my paint,' Sibli heard, before she was knocked off her stool. She lay in a heap, head roaring with light and thunder. They said the explosion was heard on ships in the bay.

Margaret, in her office at Tir Gwyn, was telephoned from the Castle to say a policeman had arrived with her niece, who had narrowly escaped death at the munitions works. It made no sense; a madman's message, that put her in mind of Morgan and his episodic disasters years ago, an ominous parallel that she wished she hadn't thought of.

When she arrived, her mother-in-law was giving the child strong tea and a boiled egg. Sibli had iodine on her hands, and her hair was grey with dust.

She wept when she saw her aunt, sobbing about a man who had died for her; no doubt she was having a breakdown. The phrase was a comfort, 'having a breakdown'.

'My dearest, dearest Sibli,' said Margaret, hardly able to speak. It was nearly five weeks since her niece walked out of the telegraph office at Fishguard and vanished.

'Nothing matters now the girl's back,' said Lady Mappowder, and Margaret felt Sibli's hand tighten in hers.

It was the hint of Morgan that troubled Margaret. The

demands that her brother was able to make on her went back to their childhood; she loved him, feared him and felt sorry for him, all at the same time, in ways that might soothe or stimulate her, but more often left her exhausted. Could anyone endure that all over again?

When the girl was undressed and in bed, with a fire in the grate, Margaret concentrated on telling her it was all over. But she knew that it, whatever 'it' was, exactly, was just beginning.

CHAPTER 9

When Tom joined the firm, the Boss said it would take him a couple of years to settle into City life and become 'one of us'. Tom waited confidently for this to happen. On the occasion when Ellis Crabb took him to lunch at Pimm's, as promised, the great man used a powerful phrase over the champagne cocktail. 'Fate is boldness,' he said. 'Always be ready for the moment when it comes.' Of course, the great Crabb was not suggesting he flee the City. Tom was supposed to sit tight and await instructions at 12 Heneage Lane. But time went by, and all Fate seemed to be offering was a nice oak desk.

Crabb was a man he still didn't care for, a personal view that he kept to himself. Crabb was the family's connection with the upper echelons of the City. Penbury-Holt & Co had become entwined with his group of companies, so much so that at the start of 1923 Tom's grandfather concluded it was time they called a halt.

Tom could hear them murmuring in the partners' room. The Grandfather insisted they tackle Crabb about some bonds, deposited to secure a loan, that he didn't like the smell of. Crabb was round next day with yards of explanation and a request that Tom be seconded to Caspian Buildings within a month, with a view to becoming his personal assistant – he had no son of his own.

Instantly, it seemed, the bonds smelt of roses.

'He will travel on my behalf to the great European centres,' said Crabb, square teeth gleaming with saliva. 'See morning mist over the Tiergarten, not to mention sip coffee on Lake Geneva.' In Tom's ear he whispered, 'He will have an hour to spare for the charming signoras of Milan.'

Fate was at work. Tom went so far as to think that the bold response might be to say no to Crabb. But the Boss would not have been amused. And it was excellent news about the signoras. At present he was struck with the ledger clerk, a young lady called Prudence with flushed cheeks and a high bosom, who was out of reach because the gentleman's code laid down that the females one worked with were forbidden fruit. What his friend Timmy Stevens referred to as 'a quick poke' was out of the question, even if one knew how to set about procuring one. ('Damn, damn, damn!' Tom wrote in a diary the previous summer, later destroyed. 'Timmy tells me he has had carnal knowledge with a *young pastrycook*. It is probably due to that damned uniform.')

Presently, when Ellis Crabb was the subject of widespread comment, and people (wise after the event) were saying what a shrewd judge of human nature the fellow had turned out to be, Tom wondered if he himself had been summed up in a flash, and had a weakness pandered to, by having those signoras dangled in front of him.

The first hint of trouble came when he was with the partners one Monday a few weeks later, having oysters and a glass of wine at Stone's Vaults, next door to the office. Lunch had to be compressed into thirty minutes, before trading warmed up at the Baltic. When the senior partner in a firm of rival shipbrokers barged in with a 'Mind if I join you?', nobody stirred an inch.

The Penbury-Holts had been using the same stretch of counter since the 1860s (so the story went). That made Tom's the fourth-generation foot to rest on the brass rail at the far end. Even a thick-skinned fellow like Joe Pincher must have seen he wasn't welcome. But Duck, Reece & Pincher were that sort of firm, as pushy as foreigners. They had recently moved from Lamp Alley, a seedy court in an inconvenient district, to Heneage Lane itself, better placed for the Baltic and Lloyd's.

Until now Pincher had confined himself to marching into the Vaults and waving at them across the room – 'as if,' in the Boss's words, 'it was some suburban public house.'

This time he thrust his cheerful red face at them and said, 'I thought you chaps should know I heard an odd thing this morning. One of our juniors was round at Caspian Buildings. He said Ellis Crabb was nowhere to be found, and there was a detective waiting.'

The Boss grunted and chucked down an oyster.

'Ellis is perpetually on the move,' remarked Grandfather.

'Fingers in many pies,' said Tom helpfully.

'Including the Penbury-Holt pie, they say,' smiled Pincher.

The Boss wiped his mouth with a linen napkin. It carried his name on a tab, like a boarding-school vest. He said, 'I was brought up to believe that conversation was for gentlemen and gossip was for the servants. One never used to hear it at Stone's.'

'You may hear a lot more before you snuff it,' said Pincher, and left as smartly as he had arrived.

'Man's a menace,' declared the Boss. 'Have no fear, Tom. You will start at Caspian Buildings next week as arranged. You have my word for it.'

But there were more rumours at the Baltic. When they returned from the Floor, an officer from the City Police was waiting.

Tom was a few minutes behind the others. His father had his back to the window. 'Inspector Barber has come round from Old Jewry in connection with our friend Ellis,' he said. 'Some misunderstanding.'

'He definitely hopped it over the weekend, sir,' said the inspector. 'There's been a warrant out for him since one o'clock this afternoon.'

'When you say, "hopped it" . . .' asked Tom.

'We think he went in an aeroplane from Croydon.'

'What a swine,' said Grandfather, as if a decent crook would stick to the Dover–Calais route. He added, 'If it's true.'

'Of course it's not true,' hissed the Boss. 'His uncle was on the board of Leuchars Bank.'

'Be that as it may, sir,' the inspector said, and referred to a notebook. 'As I see it, Penbury-Holt & Co has an investment that represents seven per cent of the equity of Ellis Crabb (Reinsurers).'

'And excellent dividends it pays,' said the Boss.

'You are also the beneficial owners of forty per cent of Ellis Crabb (North-West Europe). The other sixty per cent is owned by the Macedonian Petroleum Company, which is controlled by Crabb Securities.'

Tom said, 'Which owns forty-five per cent of us.'

'And appears to be bankrupt,' replied Inspector Barber. 'I notice in passing that Macedonian in turn owns a further nine per cent of Penbury-Holt, and has debts outstanding to Penbury-Holt of more than twenty thousand pounds. Ellis Crabb (Reinsurers) is also in difficulties. It owes six hundred thousand to Ellis Crabb (Argentina), which is heavily indebted to Leuchars Bank, which is also the principal creditor of Crabb Securities.'

'It goes round in circles,' said Tom.

'We can do without your contributions!' shouted the Boss, but Barber said, 'Circles is the word for it, gentlemen. Master Crabb has been robbing Peter to pay Paul for years. We don't know the half of it yet. He had a steam yacht. He had women in various places, including Paris.'

The two principals tried to brazen it out. But the minute the inspector had gone through the door, they were blaming each other. Another couple of years and Tom would have been a partner, and they would have blamed him as well.

Tom had a feeling they were finished, that all this –

brass desk-lamps under green shades, oak panelling, the founder's wall-map of the Seven Seas marked with pencil lines and names of ships – was unlikely to come his way, even if he wanted it to.

Prudence brought a query that needed his attention, but he hardly noticed the proximity of her bosom. There was too much happening. In the street, in the dusk, Pincher came out of his office. He looked up at the Penbury-Holt windows and smiled.

CHAPTER 10

'Do you think I've got a nice enough shape?' asked Helen, looking anxiously at Sibli, who was trying to stop laughing.

'Of course you have,' she said. 'It's only for corsets. I think you'll look very nice.'

'What you mean is, modelling corsets is about my level. If I didn't have a bottom I'd have a hope as a dancer.'

'I mean there aren't many sylphs around. Stop moaning.'

For six months they had shared a flat in a lapsed tenement behind Marble Arch, within walking distance of the Hermes Academy de Danse, where Helen was a student. Leases were expiring daily; soon the street would have gone, replaced by a block of service apartments. It didn't worry Sibli. She lived from hand to mouth.

She had tried planning her life, without success. The runaway-schoolgirl plan led to Davis. The regaining-her-roots plan led to home life with Mother and Uncle Griff.

She learned typing and earned her keep in the poky premises at Cambrian Chambers. During the week she lived at the noxious black house by the dock. Whenever she could at weekends she returned to Cilfrew Castle, to her aunt, who was loving but suspicious, who knew there was a man mixed up in it somewhere.

Among Aunt Margaret's plans was the getting-to-know-a-nice-crowd one, which meant supervised dances and picnics with the offspring of ambitious parents in Carmarthenshire. A few years of that and it would be provincial bliss-by-marriage. When no one was looking, Sibli accelerated the process. Margaret had the works to distract her. Aubrey's father died, which meant more distractions. For a while, unknown to her aunt, Sibli went about with a youngish country gentleman called Moelwyn whose lands included Rhydness Farm, where her father's family came from. The tenant farmer showed them a smoky kitchen and 'TB' carved in a beam. That was Tomos Buckley, her great-grandfather.

This tenuous link with her past made Sibli briefly interested in Moelwyn. A man of imagination would have used it to seduce her. But he missed his chance. His wife had been dead three years, and he told her without a smile that his experience and her youth would go well together. They watched the sun set over the Towy Valley from the leathery depths of his Hotchkiss Tourer. There was no trace of bliss about Moelwyn. Sibli, kissing him in an absent-minded way, found her clothing being interfered with. Unlike Dai Drill, with his nervous excitement, he offered only the blunt authority of a man with money. He was a dead duck. Her departure from Wales was made easier by Ma becoming pregnant. She was nearly thirty-nine. Griff got wobbly on Johnny Walker. Sibli kissed them both and wrote at once to her father to say it was too bizarre a situation at No 38 The Strand to be tolerable.

'My typing is exemplary,' she said, 'and I would love to be your perfect secretary. I promise not to be a nosey parker. Helen, my best friend, is leaving school, and her parents will let her share a flat in London with a nice girl, i.e. me. They know me well. All you have to do is write and confirm how well-brought-up, reliable, chaste, etc. I am, and we (Helen and I) will be in heaven. So how about it, dearest Pa?'

Margaret said it was out of the question. When she was eighteen they could think about it. Even that was very young for a girl to be on her own in London. Men were the problem. Margaret tried to say a few things about men.

'Men, yes, I know,' said Sibli. She had a disturbing story about being in a car with Moelwyn James, who got his face slapped for improper advances.

'You have flummoxed me,' said Margaret. 'You aren't a child, of course. I don't see you as a child. In a few years you will be a woman. I made a mistake the first time, marrying a man who seemed like a rock and turned out to be a jellyfish, because I was a modern girl and it was the sort of mistake that was waiting for modern girls in my milieu. You're modern all over again. Your mistake will be more up-to-date, naturally. It could be about not marrying at all. Who can tell?'

'So you don't mind if I go and live in London with this very well-brought-up friend as long as I don't make mistakes about men?'

'I am asking you not to go. Trying to be grown-up before it's time is not wise.'

Aubrey, seeing how worried she was over Sibli, took her away to the Scilly Isles, where a distant cousin farmed and the spring was weeks ahead of Carmarthenshire's. One mild afternoon he sailed them into an empty cove in a borrowed dinghy and made love to her on the sand, on an oilskin. 'You're a lovely woman,' he said in Margaret's ear, and kissed her thighs till her movements got sand on the oilskin. There was more of a similar nature all week. He was like he had been the first time he came on leave in the war, the Goggles who drove her recklessly around West Wales and proposed marriage while she was helping him mend a puncture. One or two of the holiday photographs she took back to Port Howard to be developed made her blush, Aubrey looked so casually possessive.

Sibli came again to discuss her future. She didn't argue, only locked her fingers around her aunt's. It was more like a handshake than a caress. To begin with, Margaret was brisk and maternal again. But her heart wasn't in it. When she said, 'You *must* consider what you want to do with your life,' it sounded merely selfish. The reproof in her voice was only a disguise for what she felt, the fear of Sibli gone, lost, finished; becoming another Morgan to tear her apart. It was Sibli's fingers that were holding hers.

Margaret detached her hand and stood up, catching sight of herself in a pier-glass, a not bad-looking woman who had recently been off with a man. She thought of Morgan and how much time she had wasted there, wanting to change the unchangeable. Why repeat that agony? 'I shall expect a bed whenever I come to London, mind,' she said abruptly. It was like doing a tinplate deal. Once agreed, you put it behind you.

Sibli touched her aunt's skirt, pressed her face against a leg, silently gave thanks. That night Margaret spoke to Morgan on the telephone. Soon after, he sent Sibli a postcard saying: 'Since your aunt agrees. Three pounds ten shillings a week.' By the summer she was living with Helen, working at Peele Place.

Sibli had grown cautious about men. She wasn't optimistic about cities, either. London was capable of solving anything, she knew, but not overnight. In the meantime she worked office hours at Peele Place, grateful to be free, to be 'a woman living in London'.

'I don't expect you to tell me about your life,' Helen said. 'I nearly died at Bracing when you left. I've told you all this, I know, but you'll have to hear it again. I couldn't stand a female near me after you'd gone. I threw myself at a boy in Carshalton in the holidays. We did things. I won't say what things. Perfunctory things. It's been perfunctory things ever since. I suppose I want to wait for marriage. But *you've* had men. I can see it in your face.'

'I had a love affair that went wrong,' was all Sibli ever gave away.

'She had a *love affair*,' Helen would say, winding a tape measure around a thigh to see if it conformed to the Table of Averages displayed in the gymnasium at the Hermes. 'Hear that, leg? Sibli knows more about love than you do.'

Rubber corsets were a new spring line in Swan & Edgar's at Piccadilly Circus. Young women who were supple and unselfconscious enough were hired by the hour to model them for lady customers.

'All part of the man-hunting industry,' Sibli called it.

She liked living with Helen, who was honest and jolly, and genuinely convinced that Sibli had the depths of character that Sibli herself saw becoming shallows as she drifted into womanhood, planless.

Men were and always would be both problem and solution. The gents' window dresser caught her unawares. He was Helen's friend, a crinkly-haired youth called Fred. Helen met him in a lift when she was on her way to the Corset Salon. Soon it was cream teas and foxtrots to the Swan & Edgar Orchestra, and roses began arriving at the Academy de Danse. Helen described his Italianate looks and saucy manner to Sibli and said he made her legs turn to water. She 'made him behave', though. Fred 'tried some funny business' in a shop doorway behind Leicester Square, and got his face slapped.

When finally he was invited to supper at the flat, Sibli had to promise to be there all the time. The rickety table had been laid for three when she returned from Peele Place that evening. In the kitchen the draining board was covered in pieces of vegetable, and potatoes like tennis balls; some smelly fish was keeping cool in the sink. A note from Helen was pinned above the stove: 'Crisis! They have found out about my Corset work. Interview with Principal at 7 P.M. Shall be late. Please entertain Fred. Bottled beer in bucket.'

He arrived before Sibli had finished cleaning the fish.

'Can't shake hands,' she said. 'You're early. I'm Sibli. Helen won't be here for ages.'

Fred sipped beer in the kitchen and watched her at the

sink. They got on. She had him slicing potatoes and finding the salt.

'Now I must go and change,' she said, and reappeared ten minutes later in a dress like a tube, with her lips reddened and a silver bracelet the gentleman farmer had given her on her wrist.

'You're a stunner,' he said, lounging by the empty fireplace.

'I'm also Helen's best friend.'

'Come out with me. I'll take you ... anywhere. Have you been to Brighton?'

'Take Helen. You're a lucky boy. She has dozens of men after her.'

Fred said they hadn't shaken hands yet, and moved closer. It was making her feel warm – his moody voice, or the look in his eye, or just the thought of experimenting with a yes to see what came next.

Handshake led to embrace. She allowed it to happen. If it had been Fred that time in the Hotchkiss Tourer, things might have turned out differently. Their faces slithered and found the right angle. Sibli's mouth tasted of gum-arabic from envelopes she had been licking all day, sending circulars to the book trade. Fred and his tongue didn't seem to mind.

His legs encircled one of hers. 'Come on,' he whispered in her ear. 'We're safe for a bit.'

'My God,' she said, 'you're a speed merchant.'

'Certainly am.'

He was loosening his tie and looking to see where the bed was, as she went to visit the bathroom.

Men were capable of anything. So were women. Until the last minute she could have done it or not done it. Sooner or later the planless woman came to every possible course of action, worthy and unworthy.

But Helen's tape measure lay on the bathroom windowsill like an admonition. 'Upper thigh, 15 inches, 12.2.23' was written on the back of a toothpaste carton. She crept into the bedroom, incensed with Fred. Rain ran down the window. He lay under the sheets, whispering to her.

Snatching his trousers from the chair, she had the key out of the lock in seconds, and secured the door from outside.

'Sibli!' he called, and his bare heels sounded on the lino. 'What are you up to? Why have you locked the door?'

'Hush,' she said. 'It's a game. I'm hiding your trousers.'

'I'll murder you!' he shouted.

After a while he gave up banging.

Helen returned at a quarter to eight. 'I recognized his type,' explained Sibli. 'I led him on a bit for your sake.' She waved the grey worsted trousers. 'You see? The man's a rat.'

She unlocked the door and threw them in.

'You rat!' cried Helen, when he came out, whistling and trying not to look red.

'Your friend has a warped sense of humour,' he snarled.

Helen was trembling, and began to cry as soon as he had gone.

'Don't be too hard on him,' said Sibli, thinking it unwise to slam the door on someone who might make Helen happy when the dream of being a dancer ended. 'Underneath he's probably a nice boy. They can't help being devils when it comes to sex.'

The comfort of friends was something. Sibli sat next to her on the sofa.

'You must hate men,' said Helen. 'They've made you suffer, that's it, isn't it?'

'If they can be devils, so can we. If I hadn't made a fool of him, I might have ended up sleeping with him.'

'Don't believe you,' murmured Helen, making herself comfortable. 'I feel better now. They aren't going to throw me out of the Hermes, either. Do you mind me snuggling up to you?'

'Not a bit.'
The sound of taxi horns came faintly from Marble Arch. Sibli stroked Helen's bosom. What were friends for?

CHAPTER 11

The success of *Confessions of an English Medium* was not repeated. The book trade, like the ghosts-and-spirits trade, was capricious. *Confessions of an English Butler* a year or two later, submitted to them in manuscript by Corker's Literary Agency, was a flop. Sibli was present when Pa and Sergeant-Major Cox were discussing it.

'You should have spiced him up like you did with the seances, sir,' said Cox.

'That was 'prentice work.'

'It made us oodles of money.'

'It's the wrong foundation to build a leading imprint on, Johnny. Moral uprightness is the thing these days. Great fat, serious, boring books. You know Barker Booley, the one they made junior minister at the Home Office? He's writing us a wholesome book about Empires and Morals.'

'You know best.'

'We shall publish the light novels as well. Refreshing tales about Britons of the new age. I have an instinct. After all, we publishers have a duty to society.'

At forty, Morgan was as restless as he had been at twenty. His life was based on guesswork. He would try anything once.

Innocuous romances kept the firm afloat. Morgan bought most of them from Corker's, books with titles like *A Cornish Maid* and *Many a Heartache*. The woman he dealt with at Corker's was Rebecca Smollett, thirtyish, with a strong-boned face, auburn hair and a body that bent nicely. After a while Morgan recruited her as his editor. She came to work early and sat behind a jar of sharpened pencils, taking adjectives out of manuscripts. She also knew where all the romantic novelists lived, and visited them in their suburban houses when they needed encouragement.

Was that the reason Pa poached her from Corker's? He used to tease her. He said her skirts were too long for a woman with such delicate calves. 'That's enough, Mr Buckley,' she would murmur, lines of fire running up her cheekbones. Probably she wasn't more than thirty-one. It fascinated Sibli to observe Pa flirt with a female, even if she was only an employee.

There were other women, she was sure. They came to the house after she had left for the day; or Pa went off for assignations. Virginia Penbury-Holt called once or twice, each time on innocuous business that left Sibli uncertain if her aunt-in-law had ever been Pa's mistress. Much as she would have liked to know, Sibli never risked going near Peele Place after hours without ample warning. A code of mutual privacy bound father and daughter together. If he had Rebecca Smollett's skirt off, even, that was his business.

Manuscripts floated in from unexpected places. Mrs Thorn passed on the opening chapters of a novel by a relative. Miss Smollett was out visiting the author of *Love in the Mist*, and Morgan gave it to his daughter to read.

'Dear Morgan,' said Mrs Thorn's letter, 'I am sure that what publishers most enjoy publishing is rubbish (otherwise why should they do so much of it?), but here is a chance to encourage a kinsman of mine called Nicholas Lambe, who has written the enclosed, and might enlarge on it if given a nudge in the right direction. He knows I know you, so I am merely the messenger. The Lambes are collaterals of my family (the Leuchars, I mean). They have more sense but less money. Nicholas lives in Paris at present on a small annuity from the bank. Who knows, he may be the new John Galsworthy. I haven't looked at it. My late husband said that reading novels made him constipated.'

A handful of pages had been typed with a purple ribbon, corrected in pencil. Sibli knew she was supposed to find a polite excuse for turning it down. It was about England after the war. Soldiers came home and cursed what they found. It sounded true. The war had meant nothing to her, but here it was, at her elbow. A Sergeant Truman said that what was wrong with England was the jazz generation – they swore, they danced, they smoked, they forgot. His wife was Jane. Jane, you could tell, had been up to something while her husband was being gassed and shot at.

'We're the jazz generation,' she told Helen, having taken the book home to read bits to her. It was only a few pages, but you felt the blood and dirt of war. In a flashback, a well-bred woman called Anna, driving an ambulance for the Nursing Yeomanry, saw a soldier beheaded by shrapnel keep running, like a headless chicken. Visiting a unit behind the lines at Ypres, with this horror fresh in her mind, she drank gin in a brigadier's office. Next minute he was trying to unbutton her tunic.

'That's *rude*!' shrieked Helen. 'Your Pa won't publish that. What happens next?'

'He hasn't written any more. I think it's beautiful. I want to know who Anna is and what Mrs Truman's been up to. It's called *Battle Honours*. I shall ask Pa if I can go to Paris and interview the author.'

She felt she knew Nicholas Lambe already, someone still young, an officer who had been through hell on the Western Front, and now was pouring out his heart in a lonely room. Her father wanted to know what Miss Smollett thought. Miss Smollett said it was a cut above *Love in the Mist* but might present problems of taste and patriotism.

'But if it's literature,' urged Morgan, 'do we not judge it differently? This may be the book that Buckley & Cox have been waiting for. I am inclined to offer him seventy-five pounds, half now and half when we have the manuscript.'

Lambe, invited over to discuss his book, seemed in no hurry to come. Sibli was tempted to make the trip herself. But the typewriter and the telephone needed her. Working for Pa, she could see what drudgery would be like if you worked for ever for someone you didn't care for, a life of tasks and wages. Even when you did care for your employer, you were still an employee.

London had lost its first sweetness. Engines thundered in the heart of everything, smoke poured from chimneys, pens scratched, typewriters clattered, legs, in the case of Helen, kicked and bent on stages: all for cash in little envelopes on a Friday. The system was astonishing. A bit of it went a long way.

Pa was an odd chap, extravagant when it suited him, mean over things like taxis for other people. Miss Smollett went everywhere by bus or tube. Sibli liked sitting in a taxi, being whisked to a destination. Against Pa's wishes, she took a trip to Camden Town not long after, to the Parenthood Clinic. The cab driver gave her an odd look. But she was only going to see someone. Esther, the unmarried Penbury-Holt who was once a Suffragette, had written to Morgan to ask if he would publish a booklet about birth control. The answer was no – did the woman think he was insane? – but Sibli said it would be kinder to tell her in person.

The clinic was between a stationer's and a pet shop, in a street where trams swayed close to the windows. The passageway smelt of urine and disinfectant. Women with babies could be seen in a waiting-room. A nurse asked her fiercely what she was doing there.

'I wish to be fitted with a birth-control device,' said Sibli, to see what would happen.

'You think you can just walk in from the street? If you are very lucky you will see a doctor for a preliminary investigation in two to three hours. Before being interviewed you will need a letter from your own doctor *and your marriage lines.*'

'In that case I won't bother. Kindly tell Miss Penbury-Holt that Miss Buckley from her publishers is here.'

Aunt Esther received her in a room piled high with cardboard boxes. She kissed Sibli on the cheek and said she gathered there had been a misunderstanding.

'I was curious as to what would happen if I wanted a pessary. I asked on the spur of the moment.'

'My dear, the women we help are poor and worn out with child-bearing. Incidentally, we do not prescribe pessaries. It is Mrs Stopes who is pig-headed about the pessary. The woman is a blatant propagandist. At this clinic we believe in the diaphragm. I would not normally discuss the matter with an unmarried woman, but I think you and I count as old friends. The booklet goes into it thoroughly.'

'My father is afraid he can't publish it.'

'Then he's a coward, like the rest of them. Is that what you came to tell me?'

'I'm sorry. He sees no reason to endanger his business for a cause he has no interest in. I have to agree with him.'

'I like honesty,' said Esther. 'I withdraw the remark about cowardice. Would you accept "self-interest"?'

'We all have that. I, you, the nurse downstairs.'

They didn't quarrel, as if agreeing that life was too short. They talked about their families. Esther asked if she remembered Tom. (Yes, his coat against hers, on a winter's afternoon.) Tom wore a bowler now and was learning to love the Baltic Exchange. And her half-brother, asked Esther, how old was he? Six months already? Sibli referred to him, it, as the Potato. Its real name was Albert. Its button-black eyes gazed on dock, rain and gullshit in The Strand. How time flew.

As she was leaving, Esther stood close to her and said, 'When the time comes for you to get married, talk to my brother-in-law Munro Parton of Harley Street. He has a gynaecological practice. They are all dinosaurs, but he's a kindly one.'

The phrase from *Battle Honours* had stuck in Sibli's brain, 'the jazz generation'. Behind darkened windows, in buildings up and down London gone black with age, the dinosaurs waited for the jazz generation to sweep them away. 'Why don't you have a lover who could take us to a night club?' Helen wanted to know. 'Don't tell me, leg, she is waiting for a rich admirer to come along. She can't be bothered with little boys.'

Fred, who had forgiven her, took them to a club he couldn't afford called the Silver Slipper, where a man with a woman's voice sang through the gloom.

Perhaps a career was the answer, but doing what? She couldn't stay under Morgan's wing. 'You had better go and exercise your charms on Barker Booley,' said Pa one morning. 'He wants someone to spend a few days in a library. Dates and quotations for his great work. I said you'd do it.'

'Doesn't he have assistants?'

'Using them for private purposes would be wrong. Booley's a stickler for right and wrong.'

The dinosaur received her in his cavernous Whitehall office. 'You must not personally be a penny out of pocket,' he said. 'One of my secretaries will supply you with authority to use the House of Commons Library, together with vouchers for two luncheons and two plain teas. A note of your bus fares, in duplicate, should accompany your dossier. By the by, Mrs Booley sends her kind regards.'

Leaving the cloakroom after her second day at the library – Booley had estimated to the hour how long she would take – Sibli saw Lloyd George in a corridor and heard a division bell. A hawk-faced Member hurried to overtake him. *If he catches Lloyd George before the bell stops, I shall find a lover within a week.* Mental imbalance again. She turned a corner, not looking back.

An April wind bent the flowers in Parliament Square.

A taxi took her to Kensington ('Bus fare, threepence'). Nicholas Lambe was there.

'This is my daughter, who is one of our editors,' said Morgan. 'We are enlightened about women at Buckley & Cox. I was explaining to Nicholas that his manuscript will be handled by our senior editor, Miss Smollett. Unfortunately she is down in Dorset today, visiting Thomas Hardy.'

Lambe looked incredulous.

'We aren't his usual publishers,' admitted Pa, 'but he's composing a new poetical drama. We are negotiating for it.'

Miss Smollett was actually at Gravesend, trying to prise the last chapter of *Her Only Secret* from its author, who lived in a boarding house and drank. What amazed Sibli was not Morgan's romancing; one took that for granted. It was Lambe. He was fifty if he was a day. It could be fifty-five. A thick, unfashionable suit in dark cloth made the hairless ball of his head look fragile, like an egg on top of a pillar.

'You are staying long?' she managed.

'I dislike London. I come here only for business.'

'You prefer Paris?'

'The lesser evil.'

'I do agree,' said Morgan. 'London is not the city she was. But we still have a fleshpot or two. I would propose that the three of us go out to dine, only I have a prior engagement with an authoress. Sibli, however, will be delighted to be your companion, I know. She is fascinated to learn more about *Battle Honours*. For example, what Anna was up to in the war.' Getting no response, he added, 'Your heroine.'

'The book has no heroines or heroes,' said Lambe. 'That is its point.'

Later that evening he came to the block of flats behind Marble Arch. The taxi honked in the street, and Helen, at the window, squealed, 'He's in evening dress. My God, he means business. Good job you're in your red velvet.'

They ate fish at Overton's, by Victoria Station. His hotel was only round the corner. Most of the conversation came from Sibli. He had nothing to say about *Battle Honours* except that he wrote occasional articles for French newspapers, and one day it occurred to him to begin a novel. He had been nowhere near the war. He spent most of it at a grammar school in East Anglia, teaching French. All this had to be dragged out of him.

'I have no time for governments,' he said over the coffee, 'or authorities of any kind.'

'That makes you an anarchist, then.'

'No time for anarchists, either.'

Men gave her appraising glances, wondering, like all men — if one believed Helen — what she looked like naked. Lambe seemed unmoved by her proximity. She tried to work up a sense of danger. Inside the boiled egg was the brain that had visualized Anna's tunic being unbuttoned by the brigadier.

The least she could do was suggest a night club. He remained unmoved, as if the band, the dancing and the expensive whisky were an obligatory last course of their supper. They were at the Silver Slipper because that was the only club she knew. Dancing, her breasts touched his shirt front a few times, but it might have been armour-plating.

Whistles blew. Policemen appeared through the smoke, and the band stopped playing. 'My goodness, a raid!' said a woman. A waitress in a spangled skirt knelt behind a table, pouring whisky down a crack in the floor.

Everyone in the club, fifty or sixty people, was taken off in motor vans to Savile Row and charged with illegal drinking.

'Exciting, yes?' she said to Lambe, when he had paid two pounds each for their bail, and they were free to go.

'Bloody madness,' he said. He grinned suddenly and yanked her against him with a rough hand-round-the-waist. But as they emerged into the street with the other night-birds, photographers' flash-lights began to pop, women laughed, men twirled silk scarves in the air and told pressmen to buzz off; the intimacy dissolved. Lambe saw her to Marble Arch and shook hands.

That seemed to be the end of him, apart from a soreness under her rib where he grabbed her; she noticed it when she undressed.

Next day the *Daily Mail* had a photograph on the back page in which she was dimly recognizable, and the accompanying report gave her name. 'If your aunt sees that,' said Pa, 'my life will not be worth living.'

He was lucky; Margaret heard nothing. Sibli half wished she knew, and thought of telling her. They could have a row about it. An evening that should have been important had slipped away unnoticed. Lambe was at the back of her feelings. Lambe had been a disappointment, but the fact remained that Lambe was Lambe – the excitement she felt when reading the pages had its origins in the mind of the creature who wrote them, and if she had failed to make contact with it, or him, the fault was hers.

A letter by special messenger surprised her. Mrs Booley sent an urgent invitation to visit the Booley house in Belgravia at four that afternoon. The silver cake-stand held a pair of rock-cakes, and a maid in a cap with dangling ribbons poured weak tea from a Georgian pot and stood mute behind the sofa in case of refills.

'We are all in trouble sometimes,' the woman said helpfully. She squatted in a deep chair, dress overflowing with high-principled flesh. 'Booley is a great admirer of your family. Your library task for him was carried out to perfection, he told me. So when he chanced on a certain item in the Northcliffe press, he asked me to have a word with you, in a spirit of friendship. You see, we know that you have no mother. I believe she died many years ago. Life at your age is difficult. But we hope and pray you are a sensible young woman. Now, I have various interests. You could fill your spare time profitably by helping me sometimes. For example, I am interviewing unfortunate girls at the Social Purity and Hygienic League at five o'clock. It is sordid work, but the League is a vital instrument. Will you come with me?'

The trap was inescapable: Pa needed Booley's book, the Booleys saw it as their duty to guide her back to propriety. Later she could make excuses. Today she would have to bend to necessity.

For a while Sibli did as required. They went to the League's headquarters, a building in Holborn with Bible texts set in the wall-tiles, and Mrs Booley saw unmarried girls from poor homes who were pregnant and receiving no help from their families. All wept, some were hysterical, one vomited in a wastepaper basket. The message for all was the same: they had sinned, they had come to the League for help, the League would save them from the workhouse at the price of hard work in domestic employment till a week before the baby was born, starting again a month later. The fruits of sin would go for adoption. Papers had to be signed. It was very businesslike.

The last girl came in. Her name was Sally Walker. Mrs Booley called her 'Walker'. She stood in front of the desk, hair clenched in a bun, the skin of her bare arms oily with fear.

Sibli had had enough. She interrupted Mrs Booley. 'Sally,' she said, 'sign nothing, have your baby in the workhouse, and go to the Parenthood Clinic in Camden Town to make sure it doesn't happen again. Ask for Miss Penbury-Holt, got it? I'll leave your name with her. There's a thing called a diaphragm. It stops a girl getting up the spout.'

How much of this Sally heard was uncertain. Mrs Booley was shouting like a man. Assistants ran in. 'Booley will be told!' came after Sibli as she walked past the Bible texts.

The evening felt enjoyably dangerous. She went to

Victoria, to the hotel where Lambe was staying. The porter at the desk regretted that women visitors were not allowed, by order of the management. A shilling, however, enabled him to make an exception for a gentleman's niece.

Nicholas Lambe was in his braces, folding his evening dress, a travelling case half packed.

'What can I do for you?' he said brusquely.

'I came to apologize for being so feeble when we had supper. I meant to tell you that reading that chapter was thrilling. They were real men and women. What could be more erotic?'

'You sound rather worked up,' he said, and left off packing.

'I was at an awful charity place earlier – Social Hygiene and all that. Enough to make anyone angry.'

'Don't bottle it up, then.'

'More than angry. Violent.'

'Violent, is it?' he said, and grabbed her arm. She planted her bosom midway between the braces. 'I have to warn you, Miss publisher's daughter,' he said, and his mouth arched against hers. His fingers were like steel, tearing at her clothes. Bruises, she wouldn't be surprised, were spreading under the skin.

He said he was catching the night ferry. But the station was only round the corner.

CHAPTER 12

Going up to the City on the 8.17, Tom turned over his *Daily Mail* and saw 'Police Arrests at the Silver Slipper.' The 'Miss S. Buckley' in the photograph was unmistakably Sibli. A braver chap, like his friend Timmy Stevens, would have kept in touch with Miss S. Buckley from the start; might even, by now, have enjoyed carnal bliss with her.

Inspired, he got the typist to do him a letter that said, '*Re* your photograph in newspaper of the 23rd inst. May I extend a cordial invitation to somewhere safer, like the Theatre.' He wrote in the 'Dear Sibli' and 'Yours sincerely, Tom Penbury-Holt,' and posted it before he could change his mind.

Diversions were in short supply at Heneage Lane. The firm was on its last legs. The great swindler, of course, had never been found. Newspapers reported Ellis Crabb in America, in Egypt, in the South Seas. The police believed he was still in Europe, but that was less fun for the journalists. The firms he had swindled wanted his blood, there being small chance of getting anything else.

City gossip soon picked out the firms likely to go under. The process took time. Some of the sinking ships were lucky. The Bank of England was said to have rescued a merchant bank. The best they got at Penbury-Holt & Co was a letter from the frightful Joe Pincher of Duck, Reece & Pincher, offering to take over the remains of the firm and employ the principals. Grandfather and the Boss ignored the letter for weeks. They toyed with selling Old Saracens and going to live in a suburb. But it would only have postponed insolvency. The Boss wrote to Pincher, and the deal was done. They had till Easter. Then Penbury-Holt & Co would cease to exist.

Tom went rowing on the lake before breakfast on Palm Sunday. It was going to be a rotten week. He thought of having a last fling and trying it on with Prudence the ledger clerk. Miss S. Buckley, needless to say, had not replied.

His sister Alexandra called from the landing stage and made him go back for her. Stepping in, she nearly upset the boat, and sat in a patch of wet that made her squeal and demand a handkerchief.

'I've hardly slept all night,' she said, as they glided towards a ball of sunlight in the trees. 'What will your job be with these Pincher people?'

Tom jerked the oars. 'Glorified office boy.'

'Is that why you're rowing round the lake like a madman?'

'I want to keep fit. I may do something else.'

'Such as what?'

'I thought of flying, but one eye is weak. I suppose I shall have to stay with the Boss. It's worse for him.'

Alexandra trailed large fingers in the water. 'I shall never meet anybody here,' she said, 'especially now we're poor.'

'Someone as pretty as you?' He hoped it sounded true.

'You shall have a kiss for that.'

She lunged forward and lost her balance. This time the boat overturned.

The week was like a bad dream. Grandfather had already resigned his partnership. The Boss sulked and wasn't speaking. Tom wished he would lose his temper just once – curse Crabb, turn the air blue at Stone's Vaults.

Everything had to be gone before Good Friday. On the Wednesday he asked Prudence if he could take her to lunch. They left the office separately and she walked docilely by his side. Her mother had asked her to buy some ribbon at a shop in Whitechapel High Street, so they had to go there first, walking eastward until they crossed the invisible line that separated City from East End.

Waiting in the draper's doorway, he watched the roaring mass of trams and brewers' drays and lorries from the docks converge at Aldgate, smoke dulling the sunlight. Asiatic seamen were arguing outside a billiard hall. A woman pushed a pram piled with firewood. As though standing at a window, he peered from one world, the City gent's, into another. Anything was possible, even carnal knowledge.

Over eggs on toast at Charlie Brown's Dining Rooms, he proposed an Easter visit to the countryside. Prudence frowned, grasping an upright fork with yolk on the end, and told him she had a sweetheart in Tottenham – should have told him sooner – hadn't meant to lead him on – hoped she was forgiven – must let her pay for her eggs . . .

Mortified, he said good afternoon to her on the pavement, and pretended he had business elsewhere.

Damn, damn, damn, he would do something with his life, if it was only emigrate to the Colonies. Had he ever made a decision that mattered? Why should he sell himself to Stuck, Puce & Stinker?

A black-and-white recruiting van for the Metropolitan Police was parked on a patch of dirty grass. A helmetless sergeant leaned against the steps, enjoying the sun.

'How would I join?' said Tom.

The sergeant looked at his suit and said, 'This ain't the Foreign Legion, sir.'

'I'm serious.'

'Well, sir, I'd ask you to spell a difficult word like "eligible" and read a line or two from a newspaper. Measure your height in your socks, make sure you was British born, and send you off with an application form.'

'I'll think about it,' said Tom, and walked away with shame burning his neck. The pattern of life was laid down. Either you were a Timmy Stevens or you weren't.

Next morning the removal men came. Half a hundredweight of contracts and correspondence books with marbled covers were packed in tea-chests. The best pieces of furniture already had gummed labels saying 'Pincher'.

Tom watched the Boss watching brass lamps being dumped on the landing. Nothing was said between them; it was still supposed to be business as usual. When the iron copy-press, unused since carbon paper came in, was being manhandled out of its corner, the mangle fell off with a crash. 'Tell them to make less noise,' said the Boss, and the head clerk wagged a finger at the foreman. At noon, Joe Pincher put his scarlet face around the door and said, 'Well, Holt, your cubby-hole at No 7 is ready, so you might care to step over and get acclimatized.'

'That's most kind of you,' said the Boss.

He took his topcoat, hat, gloves and umbrella, glanced around the partners' room, and creaked down the stairs. Pincher remained, nosing about the place. It dawned on Tom that he had just seen the end of Penbury-Holt & Co. That glance at the rolled-up carpet and the desks without drawers marked the moment of severance.

He wanted to shout through the window, 'Come back and do it properly!'

Tom clung to a table and chair. A postman came up the stairs with the midday delivery.

'It can go to No 7,' said Pincher, but Tom took the letters and muttered, 'I'm still here, aren't I?'

Pincher tapped the desk with his fingernail. 'I might as well tell you, young man, that I don't like your tone, and if I go on not liking it, I shan't be employing you. You think about that over your Easter eggs.'

Among the brown envelopes was a white one from Sibli. 'Look in one day when you're passing,' she wrote, and it would have been silly not to take the chance of putting a few miles between him and Joe Pincher. He found her eating a sandwich and writing a blurb, whatever that was.

'So we meet again,' she said.

'I've often wanted to.'

'So now we have. Do you know, they fined me two quid?'

'Were you there with a party?'

'No, just a man,' she said. 'Well, tell me about you and the family firm.'

He smiled painfully, crippled by her looks and her nonchalance.

'I read you were one of Crabb's creditors,' she said, and he began to recognize one of those modish females you read about who believed in nothing, the 'bachelor girls', thriving on the surplus of females after the war, who smoked and discussed the Sex Problem and took a cynical view of marriage.

'I'm afraid we're in liquidation,' he said.

'You mean gone bust? How dreadful. Is there anything I can do?'

'We shall manage quite well,' he said stiffly. 'We have jobs just along the street. Nobody lets you starve in the City. England's an honourable country.'

'Is it? Oh, dear!' She hugged herself, looking at him with brilliant eyes.

'Have I said something funny?'

'It was the way you said it.'

He told her he must be off.

'But you've hardly arrived. Stay and meet Pa when he comes back.'

'Thanks all the same.'

He asked about the theatre, but she said she didn't go much for theatres. She came with him to the door. The maid handed him his hat, which got in the way. Close to, Sibli's lips and skin were glazed with light, and he had a rude vision of a dark-pipped bosom occupying her clothes.

'What do you do in your spare time?' she asked on the steps.

'Play cricket. Shoot rabbits.' He saw her about to laugh again. 'Visit night clubs.'

'Really? Which ones?'

'I was in the Cursistor the same night as Signor Mussolini,' he lied (it was Timmy Stevens's story). 'We had pink champagne in a bucket.'

A woman, walking past with a child, looked back at him.

'You must be a dark horse. I like the cinema, myself. Have you seen the new Valentino? It's at the New Gallery. Matinee on Saturday.'

'Oh, really?' Before she had time to laugh, he saw what she was getting at. 'Would you let me take you there?'

'Two o'clock,' she said, and went inside.

Sibli turned up with a companion; he might have guessed.

'This is Helen,' she said. 'I couldn't leave poor darling on her own. I knew you wouldn't mind.'

Timmy Stevens would have told her to stuff it, but he felt helpless, enthralled by everything about her — scent, bosoms, straight gaze, even that deadly incipient laugh.

Inside, he put a box of chocolates on her lap. She said they were bad for the figure and passed them on to the friend.

The film as such was women melting under Valentino's eyes. After that the outing ended. 'Goodbye, we *have* enjoyed it,' said Sibli, and the two girls hurried off towards Oxford Circus.

Tom followed them, catching a bus behind theirs, then going on foot from Marble Arch. A sombre building in a side street swallowed them up. Tom hung about. When a street violinist shuffled past, coming away from the afternoon trade, Tom hired his repertoire for a couple of coins.

Faces appeared now and then, looking down. A man threw a penny.

During 'Keep the Home Fires Burning', Sibli put her head out of a third-floor window. Tom waved and was recognized. Soon he was inside the flat, drinking stale bottled beer while Sibli was changing in the bedroom, being told by the friend about the hop they were going to at the Hermes Academy de Danse.

'Shall we let him come?' said the friend.

'If he behaves,' called Sibli. 'No jazz dancing, mind, no Twinkles, no Camel Walks.'

Through the half-open door, Tom saw legs and a petticoat. 'Be careful, he's all eyes,' warned the friend.

When Sibli appeared she was tubed into shape, whorled hair like black roses over her ears. Their eyes met in the glass. 'I wondered if you'd follow us,' she smiled. 'I like to experiment.'

The Academy de Danse, with a sedate crowd twirling beneath imitation palm trees, sanctioned an arm around Sibli's waist while they danced a foxtrot squeezed out by an orchestra of four. Helen sulked at the lemonade table.

'I was hoping Fred would be here,' Sibli said. 'He's a boyfriend of sorts if she'd encourage him.'

'I get the impression she doesn't like men.'

'We are all like that sometimes.'

'Why don't we go to a night club, you and I?'

'And abandon poor darling? Look, there's Fred. He'll liven her up.'

A greasy young man hung around Helen, whose sulk deepened by the minute. Sibli went to join them, and danced with him. Tom tried to get Helen on the floor, put his hands under her armpits in a boisterous gesture, and got his face slapped.

'I know your sort,' said the MC, stalking up, 'can't keep your hands to yourself. Out.'

His sort had had enough. The double doors banged behind him. He took the stone stairs two at a time to the entrance hall.

Somebody was following.

'Wait,' said Sibli. 'Please.' She came down awkwardly, dress catching her knees. 'We'll all four go to a night club.'

'I've had enough of your friend.'

'Wait five minutes, Tom. Am I worth five minutes?'

When she returned with the others, she whispered the name of a club in his ear, and they went to the Sesame in Ham Yard. A shilling a head bought tickets for 'Bohemia tea, concert and dance'. Stooped figures were shuffling to a trumpet and a piano in a basement. A candle in a jam-jar burned on their table; there was barely room for an ashtray and four glasses. The other two were dancing.

'Some concert,' said Tom, and took a mouthful of watery gin. 'Some Bohemia tea.'

Her leg pressed against his. 'May a girl hold her father's sister's dead husband's brother's son's hand? Tell me about Thomas Penbury-Holt.'

Her attentiveness made his life seem entertaining. He was unhappy at his boarding school; a Zeppelin was shot down; Ellis Crabb lied in his teeth.

The smoke thickened and the trumpet was louder. He told her about Joe Pincher, and the lifetime of clerking to come.

'What will you do? Escape?'

'It's not so easy.'

'You can do whatever you like. You came after me like a bull at a gate. And here I am.'

'What about poor darling?'

'What about her?'

They left unnoticed. It was after eleven. In Trafalgar Square a lamp burned outside St Martin's Crypt. He kissed her for the first time in Chandos Street, in a doorway, where they stayed until a policeman moved them on.

He felt like a someone else, who never wore City clothes, who snapped his fingers at the Joe Pinchers.

She hadn't laughed at him for hours, but she did now, when he said he would do something terrible if she didn't see him again next day.

They had walked down to the river. Other couples stood along the Embankment wall, looking into the Thames. Trams ploughed over Westminster Bridge.

'I'm going to Wales,' she said. 'I am supposed to be

seeing my mother. I shall be on a train at one o'clock.'
'I've never been to Wales.'
She touched his cheek. 'Meet me at Paddington Station. Try an experiment. Try escaping.'

CHAPTER 13

Various dreams fluctuated in Sibli's head. The adoring-young-lover one came up regularly. It hadn't occurred to her that it would involve a Penbury-Holt, but since the episode with Nicholas Lambe, she had decided to take the first opportunity. It was easy enough for Helen to go on about Sibli being the sort of girl who could twist older men round her little finger. The dead weight of Nicholas on top of her was part of a wider oppressiveness that went with the secrets and habits of a life about two and a half times as long as hers. It was the spirit of *Battle Honours* she had wanted to sleep with, not the corporeal Lambe. Something similar had happened with Davis. He snared her (whether he meant to or not) with the slightly indecent glamour of Fleet Street. Of Davis himself she knew hardly anything. Poor Davis, she thought; poor schoolgirl.

Adoring young lovers were comparatively straightforward, though she had doubts about Tom's reliability. Until the last minute, her travelling companions were a man (moustache like a lavatory brush) and two women (both knitting and whispering). She amused herself wondering what the man would think if he could see through the pigskin of her travelling case on the rack, to the device wrapped in tissue paper that Mr Munro Parton of Harley Street had (after much persuasion, including tears) prescribed for her after the Lambe adventure.

Tom arrived at the last minute, sprinting past the ticket barrier as she hung out of the window and the guard fingered his whistle. Exactly as required, he conjured up that mythological figure, the man-in-love. He sprawled gasping in the compartment, a not very fresh-looking rose in his hand.

'Where's your suitcase?' she whispered.

'Must go back tonight. Boss insisted. Thinks I'm visiting the Timmy Stevenses.'

The train got up speed, and Sibli concentrated on the afternoon's task of being a woman with a pash on a man.

By the time they had the compartment to themselves they were in South Wales, stopping every few miles. Instead of leaving the train at Swansea, she suggested they go on to Port Howard, so that she could show him her favourite house, Y Plas, where her Aunt Margaret used to live.

'I must find when the last train goes,' he said. 'The Boss will scalp me.'

'I'm only showing you how to escape. You have to learn by doing it. There's no theory. Either come with me, or wait on the station for the last express back.' She pulled down the blinds and kissed him. 'People die if they don't escape.'

It was early evening when they reached the house, after walking from the station. A sharp westerly was making the trees bend, waving rooks about like black fruit on the branches, and the estuary was coiled and dark under a cloud-bank. Sibli had the key in her hand.

'Where did you get it?'

'I kept one, donkey's years ago.'

She showed him cold rooms with shrouded furniture, pressing her hand against his, and made a cocktail with crème de menthe before they foraged for tins in the larder.

'Your aunt won't mind?'

'She would if she knew but she won't.' She took a crumb of corned beef with a fork and put it on his tongue. 'There's a telephone somewhere. Ring and say you've been delayed. The last train will have gone, unless you wait for the mail.'

In the drawing-room she uncovered the piano and hit out at a jazz tune, smoking a stale cigarette from a box, hearing Tom's voice from the hall.

'I had to lie to them,' he said when he came back.

'I'm a bad influence already.'

'There's no need to make fun.'

'I'm not. I am stating the obvious. I brought you here.'

She took him upstairs to see the inlet where the water had broken through when she was a child and flooded Buckley's original tinplate works. An edge of foam glistened in the dark, beyond the trees. 'Don't turn the light on,' she whispered, and was away for a while.

When she turned back the heavy sheets, they smelt of damp and camphor. Tom spoke so gently, for a moment she was daunted. There was something hygienic about the spread-out towel (rough against her bare skin) that threatened the great event. Did she *want* a lover who did things by the book? Fortunately there was another Tom close behind who didn't speak, only burned her with his breath and tongue.

'Clever old you,' she said later, feeling at ease, as she knew she would with him.

'It's all thanks to Timmy Stevens,' he murmured, and told her how the soldier called Timmy who had been at school with him was his mentor in the matter of women.

Hearing him described, the randy young guardee, she had an image of this second man lying with them in the bed, all lips and loins. How sweet of Tom to give praise where praise was due, how modest, how decent, how naïve, how – now she came to think of it – unlike a man; how dangerous, then, to give things away that didn't have to be given.

But she was glad it had been Tom. A category had been created, men she would always be fond of.

Hot sunlight was glaring off the wallpaper when she woke the next time. Tom wasn't there. She saw him in the garden and called that she was going to bathe.

'Too early in the year,' he called back. 'You'll freeze.'

She wanted to get in the sea naked and turn blue with cold, just to see what he did. Putting on a mothbally frock from a wardrobe, she walked out in a ladylike manner, clutching the towel from the bed.

'You can't be serious,' he said, coming after her, through a gate in the wall. 'It'll be forty-five degrees, if that.'

'I believe you're the gardener here,' she said, holding the frock above her knees. 'Thomas, isn't it? Well, Thomas, when I have been for a dip, you may dry my bum with your eyes closed.'

The inlet was full of brilliant water. No one was about. A single thread of smoke rose from Buckley's Tir Gwyn works, the one that Margaret owned, half a mile distant.

'Look the other way, Thomas,' she commanded, pulling the frock over her head, and dropping it with the towel on the grass. Lapping waves bit into her ankles and made her squeal. Turning, she saw that Tom was naked, too.

'Come along,' he said grimly. 'Madam needs a bath.'

He picked her up and sloshed forward, then fell with her into the water. For a moment the cold winded them both. Then she was running back, and he was behind her, slapping her thighs and behind, shouting, 'Is that warmer, madam? Is that what madam needs?'

'Your friend has been giving you lessons,' she gasped. She leapt indoors, still dripping water. 'Treat 'em rough, I bet that's what your soldier advised.' She shivered against him, the towel around them both. 'You shouldn't have told me. Now I shall never know if it's you or him. That's what comes of being honourable.'

'I'm not, especially, so don't make fun.'

'You are, you are!' she cried, rubbing him dry, kissing his shoulder-blades.

'I'd rather be like you,' he said, suddenly gloomy, dabbing at her breasts. 'You suit yourself.'

'What is it you want to do that you can't? Leave the City? Then do it. Stamp on your bowler hat. Escape.'

'I'm in love with you, Sibby.'

'Just for now. So am I – just for now.'

'I mean for always and always.'

'You can't do anything properly, can't think, can't love, not till you've escaped.'

'I have escaped. I'm here.'

She wanted to tell him there was more to it than losing his virginity. But it wasn't a woman's job to give lectures. She liked the proud way he strutted about the kitchen, making coffee. After washing up the cups in cold water, they went back to bed.

Looking down from the terrace of Cilfrew Castle, the air was clear enough to see the trees around Y Plas. Margaret was entertaining brother Will and his family. They had come down from the Rhondda for the Bank Holiday in a motor-cycle and sidecar. A hammer and sickle were painted in red on the mudguard. Aubrey, keeping out of the way, had gone motor-racing on the sands at Pendine.

'Funny thing, I've never set foot in Y Plas,' said Flora, Will's wife.

Her daughter Nancy, who was ten, wanted to know who lived there.

'Nobody, now,' said Margaret. 'But I was brought up there. So was your Dadda.'

The purple slates were just visible. Only at holiday times was the air so free of smoke. The fine, fresh day brought back memories of the house – of her childhood, and the later years when Sibli stayed with her there, sometimes for weeks on end; the make-believe daughter it was wiser not to believe in. 'We've time to go there before lunch,' she said. 'There's a see-saw in the stables. Your Dadda and Uncle Morgan and I used to play on it.'

'Uncle Morgan,' said Will, 'once put a brick on one end, jumped on the other, and the brick went through the greenhouse. He got beaten for it, screaming that it was ballistics, he read it in a book.'

'The unfortunate Morgan,' said Margaret.

'Unfortunate be damned. He always knew what he was doing.'

Margaret drove them down in her Lagonda, letting David, the younger child, blow the horn at every crossroads. When she switched off the engine, white ghosts of dust rose around the car.

Windows downstairs were open, which meant her aunt and uncle were there, getting things ready for Theodore, who never came. Then Villette appeared from the back of the house, at a trot.

'Thank God you're here,' she gasped. 'I was going to send Abraham to the police station. There's someone inside.'

Her bun of grey hair was unravelling with agitation. It must be some old tramp, she said. Food had been eaten in the kitchen. Water had been splashed.

'Perhaps whoever it was has gone,' suggested Margaret.

'I am not stupid, dear,' said her aunt. 'Abraham and I heard movements upstairs. I am glad to see Will is here. Arm yourself with a cudgel, Will.'

The front door opened. Like figures in a dream, Sibli and a young man came out. He was carrying a pigskin case.

'Good gracious,' said Sibli, shading her eyes. 'A family get-together.'

'Isabel, you have no right to be in this house,' said Villette. 'It belongs to your Aunt Margaret and it is rented to Theodore.'

'Sibli, if you don't mind.' The girl smiled at them all and waved to the children. Abraham came round the house with a rake at the ready. 'I've been Sibli for years.'

The man looked Penbury-Holtish. Margaret realized who he was. It would have been comic if it hadn't been sad.

'We are on our way to see Mother, as a matter of fact.' She kissed her aunt. 'I thought you wouldn't mind if I showed someone the house. This is Tom Penbury-Holt,' and she put her hand on his sleeve.

'I know Tom, of course. How do you do?' said Margaret, shaking hands, feeling empty. Sibli, cool and defiant, was suddenly Morgan incarnate.

'Must fly,' said Sibli, and they set off briskly down the drive.

All Margaret's energy had gone. She saw Aunt Villette march into the house. A minute later an upstairs window was opened, and Villette's triumphant voice was heard saying that a bed had been slept in.

CHAPTER 14

The scandal had repercussions. What upset Villette was that someone had put a smouldering cigarette on top of the piano, leaving it to burn itself out in a wrinkle of scorched varnish. That was sacrilege. What upset Margaret was depravity. What upset Sibli was Tom's assumption that after thirteen and a quarter hours in bed (she worked it out) they were practically engaged. It seemed to her the foolish assumption that a woman might make, not a man. But she knew the fault was hers for provoking the situation. She had gone out of her way to find a spot of adoration, which then turned out to be less simple than expected. The Aunt Margaret problem was the most pressing. Within days she was in London, interviewing her niece in the palm court of a Knightsbridge hotel.

'Are you in love with him?' she wanted to know.

'I'm very *fond* of him,' said Sibli brightly.

'Fondness is hardly an explanation. Was there pressure of any kind? They are an artful family. I have plenty of experience to go on.'

'I invited him. That was all. He's very sweet. Did you know the family was practically bankrupt?'

'That makes it worse, if anything could make it worse. I am going straight from here to talk to your father, and then I am taking you back to Wales tonight. The Penbury-Holts must be written to and warned. They have to be made to understand there are sanctions against men who lure women into immorality. I expect he told you he'd marry you?'

'He didn't lure me,' said Sibli. 'I lured him.' Aunt Margaret had to be deterred; the truth seemed the best way of doing it. 'I have had other lovers. Don't blame Pa.'

Margaret's eyes seemed to be sinking deeper into the bone.

'You never thought to confide in me?'

'And tell you what? That I see nothing wrong in it?'

'We are discussing immorality. Who are these men? When did it first happen?'

'Long ago,' said Sibli. 'Or long enough. You must have had an inkling. That time no one knew where I was. Then.'

'Behind everyone's back.'

'Because you wouldn't have accepted it, any more than you will now.'

She knew that that was the most difficult thing of all. In an odd way she sympathized with her aunt. But there was no question of going back to Wales.

In the weeks that followed, only Helen didn't seem to mind. Others wanted her to be what she was not — 'chaste from this moment until you are married' (Aunt Margaret), 'less of a b. nuisance' (Pa, who was getting hell from his sister), 'my unofficial fiancée' (Tom, who wrote letters and sent roses almost daily).

Even Helen niggled a bit and thought it inappropriate not to make more of love when it manifested itself so agreeably. It was not that she advocated marrying the boy, good gracious me no, this was the age of enjoying yourself, of having a flirt and a carry-on. 'Twist him round your little finger, Sibby,' she said, unkind because she was innocent.

She would have been surprised to know how easily Sibli would have married Tom, or anyone, if he was like the man crossing the cobbled street with ice on his breath, in the frontier town she had never seen, where she waited in the dark. The vision was creased and soft-edged, like a document that had been in a pocket for years. She knew it by heart, one part of it to do with love, the other with danger; that was half its attraction. The man in it was a shadow. For a while it might have been Davis, but Davis was ancient history.

The fuss about the piano travelled up from Wales. Villette had noticed the mark at once. She stormed around Y Plas, noticing everything, cleaning as if the plague had been there; paying special attention to the bed. The mattress disappeared. 'Abraham took it out in the bay and tied iron weights to it,' she told Margaret. 'I knew it was what you would want.'

As for the piano, that was criminal damage. 'Forgive my saying it, dear,' she told Margaret, 'but you overlook the fact that although it is *your* instrument, a professional artist like Theodore must have it in perfect condition when he visits the house he rents from you.'

Margaret said she was not to tell him under any circumstances. The matter was closed, and a french polisher would attend from Swansea. But Villette convinced herself that the piano had gone into decline. Hints were dropped in letters to Theodore. When he didn't respond (they rarely heard from him), she waited until he came back from a concert tour of the Balkans and forced herself to use the telephone. His cousin Margaret was too forgiving, she shouted into the mouthpiece. The piano should be replaced with a new one and the bill sent to *that girl* or better still *that girl's father*.

The first Sibli heard was a note from Theodore Lloyd, sent to her at Peele Place, enclosing a pair of tickets for a recital he was giving at the Wigmore Hall. The note said he wished to discuss a 'small family matter' with her. It took some time to reach her, having been sent to Peele Place, where she no longer worked. She and Pa had agreed that her not being at the house each day would give Auntie Maggs less leverage. There was also the difference with Mrs Booley and the Social Purity lot, which might have led Booley to withdraw his great work from Buckley & Cox, but fortunately didn't. Pa forgave her. But it was somehow time to go. Sibli found a job as a receptionist with a fine art dealer in Cork Street.

When she last met Theodore, she was a child. She went alone to the recital, Helen having gone to Brighton to audition for a summer season at a vaudeville club. The music bored her but she was impressed by an ugly ferociousness about Lloyd at the piano; and, obeying his instruction to 'come round afterwards', found him in a dressing-room, rubbing white spirit on his hands.

'You were in pigtails when I was at the Royal College,' he said. 'Well, did you enjoy my playing?'

'You must be quite drained of energy.'

The reply seemed acceptable. He said it was kind of her to come, since she must have guessed what it was about, and mentioned a piano at his place in Wales, damaged by intruders.

'What does Miss Buckley think of that?' he demanded.

'Am I supposed to think anything?'

'You'd better confess!' he said grimly. He was an odd-looking man, features crammed together under a pasty forehead. 'A little bird has told me everything. Someone played the piano and left a burning cigarette on it.'

'You had better send me an account.'

'Won't do, I'm afraid. There is only one remedy,' and he massaged the backs of his hands, which were fleeced with black hair. 'You must have dinner with me at Pagani's.'

He was interesting enough to be acceptable, and there was no nonsense about walking to the restaurant, which turned out to be musty red plush and mirrors; he touched her elbow in the taxi.

'We'll find a quiet table. I want to know all about you,' he said threateningly. Then he saw a music critic called Harris, and the three of them sat together.

The men argued about modern composers. Sibli sipped champagne, watching a long table where everyone was eating soup and bread, and a man at one end was crouched over a music score, copying it on lined paper. Black instrument-cases like little coffins stood in alcoves.

A tall woman with mascara'd eyes joined them, and told Theodore that he was going to be offered an engagement to play on the wireless.

'The *wireless*, Fanny? That contraption you need an ear-trumpet to listen to? I'd rather take a piano on the beach at Southend and compete with the Thames Estuary.'

'Fanny's your agent,' said Harris, who had a beard and sad, poached-egg eyes. 'Listen to what she says.'

'The next thing your modern composers will be doing is writing concertos for the wireless. I wish they paid less attention to technique and more to what's in the damned music. I could give them a theme or two.'

He brooded, hands behind his head. 'Sibli here, who's Welsh – aren't you, my sweet? – had a granpa that a Verdi might have done something with. Not that he was anything but a typical provincial manufacturer. He would have to be metamorphosed into The Capitalist. Davy Buckley, that was his name. This Davy, this little master of a tinworks, had his throat slit one dark night by a halfwit he'd persecuted. That was before the war. He ran dying into his own works and collapsed against a furnace – tell them it's God's truth, Sibli. It was late on a Saturday night, so there was nobody about. The furnace was damned hot. When they found him in the morning, his clothes were in ashes and he was roasted. Roast man! There's a last act for a modern opera, if we had someone bold enough to write it.'

'Or cruel enough,' said Sibli, and, leaning over the table, pinched Lloyd's cheek. 'It's true that he died like that. Unlucky capitalist man! Still, he had his uses, didn't he, Theo?' She smiled at the woman called Fanny and the critic, who both looked nervous. 'The Lloyds were poor. The families were related. David Buckley bought the aspiring Theodore a piano and paid for his education.'

'There's no crime in poverty,' snapped Lloyd.

'No. No harm in a bit of gratitude, either. You'd probably have ended up teaching music in the county secondary if it hadn't been for Davy.'

Making him angry was the right idea. He was still buzzing and snarling when she asked him to call a taxi. He scowled as he said goodbye to her.

'I thought we might have had a pleasant evening,' he said.

'I thought it was *very* pleasant. I shall buy a wireless set in case you change your mind.'

Helen was desperate to meet him, but Sibli heard no more for a while and the season in Brighton took her friend away again. Helen's thighs were still too fat. The club was only paying a few pounds a week, but she said that anything was better than corsets or the back rows of choruses with unhygienic girls doing high-kicks. 'There's a comedian,' she told Sibli, 'Russian dancers, and the Heart's Desire Girls, which is four of us in special see-through costumes.'

'Really see-through?'

'It's all right, we wear undies. It could lead to high-class cabaret.'

'Or propositions from unwelcome men.'

There was a constant temptation to rescue Helen from the mistakes she was about to make. But a knowing friend was fatal, and Sibli was in the habit of shutting up. She kept away from Brighton. Tom Penbury-Holt, still trying to woo her, still working for Duck, Reece & Pincher, heard on some grapevine where Helen was, and proposed they go down to visit her at a weekend. That was easily seen through: a bed in a boarding house was what Tom had his eye on. No, no, he insisted, they would make up a party ('Safety in numbers, Sibby'), they would take Helen's Fred with them, together with his sister Alexandra and the famous Timmy Stevens, whom Sibli still hadn't met.

Still she refused. She was tired of Tom. If he had left her alone for half a year and then floated back from time to time, she might have been happy to enjoy a few hours of his company, even to take her clothes off for him. But not when he nagged her. The Brighton wheeze having failed, he fell back on a slap-up dinner with the same participants. Finally she gave in, on condition they went to a restaurant she knew called Pagani's. It was supposed to be Helen's evening off, but she didn't arrive from Brighton. Nor did the fabled Stevens appear. They were just Tom, Tom's sister, Fred (who drank too much) and Sibli; an unhappy quartet.

To complete the disaster, Lloyd walked into the restaurant, and came over to greet her. He kissed her bare shoulder. 'This is Tom Penbury-Holt,' she murmured, but Lloyd wasn't listening.

'The BBC have persuaded me,' he said. 'I am at Savoy Hill next Tuesday. I will send you a ticket for the studios.'

Tom had a fit of jealousy when he had gone. 'Our Sibli's a fast 'un,' croaked Fred, and Tom punched him in the ribs, causing him to fall off his chair. The overweight sister burst into tears. The evening ended with a swift brutality that she saw was the only way. 'We shan't see one another again,' she said.

When the roses and letters continued to arrive, she sent them back marked 'not known at this address' in her own writing.

The recital was at eight. At Savoy Hill, wires hung in thin Ts and Os above the BBC building. Sibli was vague about the mysteries of wireless. Her stepfather in Swansea had a crystal set and headphones that he fiddled with for hours.

Instead of the concert chamber she had been expecting, the invited audience gathered in a 'Listening Room'. They sat in a semi-circle on gilt chairs, facing a wooden box with fabric nailed across it. She recognized Harris, who explained that the box affair was a loudspeaker, through which the music would be relayed from Studio 3.

Sibli remarked that it would be more fun to watch him

play, but Harris explained that only broadcasting experts were allowed in the studio. Mr Reith was a martinet.

The recital began in ten minutes. Sibli went to powder her nose, then followed arrows until she found Studio 3. A card on the door said, 'No admittance. Broadcasting in progress.'

She went in. Theodore was declaring that he wanted a man from the Steinway factory, not the BBC tuner. A person in brown overalls was half inside the piano. An official was standing with head bowed. Fanny Henriques, the mascara'd agent, was holding a bowl of powdered chalk.

Theodore saw her and flexed his hands. 'What is she doing here?' he asked.

'I came to wish you good luck.'

'I am about to play. Do you think seeing my family improves my concentration?'

He dipped his hands in the chalk. The tuner rubbed the piano with his sleeve, a red light on the wall began to flash, and Sibli, escorted back to the listening room by Fanny, settled down to twenty minutes of Chopin and Grieg.

Everyone applauded at the end. Harris, though, shook his head and said he had spotted a false repetition and some inadequate phrasing.

Fanny said she hoped that Sibli barging in like that hadn't upset him.

'I had the impression he was upset before I arrived.'

'He is an artist. Everything must be held in balance. Losing his temper means nothing personal. It lets him keep his distance. The inner spirit must be inviolate.'

Harris's beard wagged in agreement. Then came more bad news. The artist had gone – left the building, walked out, cloak flying, no messages.

'Won't someone go after him?'

'Fatal,' said Harris. 'He'll walk by the river and let the night air do its work.'

Sibli had never heard such nonsense. She left by herself and searched the Embankment. Presently she found him standing by the steps to Hungerford Bridge, a silk scarf trailing off his shoulder.

'Well?' he said. 'You heard my performance. It is called loss of concentration.'

'Is talent really as unreliable as that?'

'What do you know about talent? What will you do with your life? Bear some man's brats. I hate humanity. I hate its predictability.'

She slapped his face, smiling to show there was no ill feeling, but hard enough to make his head jerk.

'Be careful,' he warned. 'I can use violence, too.' He pushed her against the side of the steps and kissed her on the mouth. 'Now call a constable and say a man who was on the wireless has assaulted you.'

'Silly Theo,' she said. 'It means nothing. You play tunes on a piano and make a religion out of it.'

She left him by the river, staring after her. When she got home, Helen was there, eating a plate of spaghetti with slices of bread and butter. Brighton had been a disaster. The comedian was an alcoholic, the Russian dancers didn't turn up, the Heart's Desire costumes smelt. 'We were supposed to get presents out of the customers,' she said. 'You know what *that* means.'

'We'll have to find you a proper job,' said Sibli, and wondered if Fanny the agent had contacts.

'Anything would do. One of the girls said the manager sends dancers off to Cairo and they're never seen again. I wish he'd send me, I said. I might as well be a white slave out there as back here.'

Visited in her office, up a back stairs behind Shaftesbury Avenue, Fanny was more friendly than expected. Yes, she knew people at theatrical agencies. A day or two later she passed on their combined wisdom: try the films. 'Films, me, never!' shrieked Helen, when told, but there was a bit more. The Britannia Picture Corporation was planning screen tests in the autumn to find British talent. Apply now, they said, sending professional photographs.

Soon after this, Theodore called at the gallery. 'I hear you have been concocting excuses to visit Fanny so you can spy on me,' he said. 'I am calling your bluff and taking you out to lunch.'

The day lengthened around them. His crushed features were both attentive and sardonic. She forgot to go back to the gallery. In the evening they were on Primrose Hill, near his house, looking over London. As the Kentish hills sank into the dark, he took her home and undressed her with his slender fingers.

It was the next day before she returned to the flat. Helen was running a wooden roller up and down each thigh two thousand times.

'Shameless huzz,' she said. 'Or is that my dirty mind? Did darling Sibby just dance till she dropped? You never tell me, do you? Always the secret. Never my total one hundred per cent pal.'

'We fucked. In the bed, on the floor, on the balcony. Theodore and me.'

'Golly,' said Helen. She was stunned. 'It's a fearful word, isn't it, used like that? You . . . fucked. I fuck, we fuck, they fuck. My father would die if he heard me. Was it nice — all that . . . fucking?'

'I'm going to bed for the day. Will you ring Daniel at the gallery for me? Say I must have caught a germ.'

'Hello, Daniel. Sibli regrets she has had a bad attack of being . . . fucked.'

'Wake me about four.'

'All right.'

Helen came with her to draw the curtains. 'I've got a screen test with Britannia,' she whispered.

'I knew you'd do it,' said Sibli, and smiled at Theodore as she began to dream.

CHAPTER 15

Lloyd was the first man Sibli went about with in public. She always called him 'Lloyd', like the red posters outside concert halls, which had 'Theodore' in smaller letters. If her presence required an explanation, she would say, 'I'm Lloyd's press agent.' The fiction had to be kept up inside hotels, where they had separate rooms, and made sorties along corridors. Otherwise she was at his side openly wherever they went.

Having a sexual relationship was flattering but not all that simple. Sibli wasn't sure what sort of a relationship it was. Did Lloyd need her more than she needed him? In bed he could be humbly affectionate, but out of it he was rough and proprietorial; he once pinched her bottom in front of a first violin.

His music, his art, was the climate she had to get used to. Enjoying a concert was easy enough. Loud brass she revelled in, also anything with strings and a sad melody. His piano-playing seemed to her godlike, less for the music than for the frenzy of his performance. Taking Helen to hear him play Mozart's A major, Sibli was angry with her for whispering, 'His head'll fall off if he shakes it any more.' Shaking his head was part of the violence that went with him (as it went with Nicholas Lambe: is that what most men were like?). Unable to plumb the music, she often caught a sense of his agony, as though he was trying to free his fingers from the black thing on four legs that was tormenting him.

What she wasn't prepared to do was let 'art' be an

excuse for trampling all over her. If he suffered because of music, she suffered because of love. The one seemed no higher than the other. He never forgot her remark, about his making a religion out of playing.

He said she pretended to be a Philistine to annoy him. 'You know exactly when I've failed,' he told her. 'When I made that *pianissimo* sound like mice wearing hobnailed boots, do you mean to tell me it passed you by? Nonsense. I'm not a fool. You sit there in the audience with your nose stuck in the air, looking bored, but *you are listening all the time*.'

She watched more than listened, seeing the despair in his gestures, or afterwards in his eyes and the broken line of his mouth; that was how she knew. And whenever he was distraught and raving, she consoled him, but only for as long as he remained on the right side of insufferable. 'You can insult me for three minutes,' went her standard warning, 'and then your time's up.'

He tried to lift her clothes and beat her with a coat-hanger when they were in the Royal Hotel at Leeds, after a concert where a wire had broken on the piano in mid-recital. She twisted loose, seized a coat-hanger of her own, and aimed at his wrist. She nicked the skin and drew blood. Another inch and it would have been the bone; he wouldn't have played for a month.

'You exasperate me,' he said, and gave the scratch an exploratory lick.

'I shall stop attending your concerts. The nervous strain is too much. Get Fanny to go with you. Take it out on her. She gets fifteen per cent of your earnings so she may think it's worth it.'

'I need you when I play,' he said, unexpectedly, holding out his cuff so she wouldn't miss the spot of red on it. With his long arms and hairiness, he looked like a wounded gorilla. 'It's you I visualize. Your face, your hands clapping.'

'Dear Lloyd,' she said, taking the arm and putting her

own tongue along the salty cut. Once they got on to love, there was no problem. 'All this little hand needs is cold water and kisses. And slipping under my behind in bed.'

Sibli let the affair reconstruct her life – if it was undemanding, why bother to have it in the first place? Daniel, who ran the gallery, told her she was too valuable to lose. He went on paying her a salary to attend viewings, take clients out to lunch and in general pop in whenever she had a minute, which wasn't often. Daniel wore steel-rimmed glasses and said she was very much like his daughter. Wisely, she pretended not to notice how often he took off the glasses to polish them, using his inspection of the lenses to look up her skirt.

Life with Helen, too, was different, now that Sibli was so often away; although she declined to live at Theo's house, as he would have liked. No one would have minded. Behind the public prudery, it seemed to Sibli, anyone who was well-to-do or an artist or a foreigner (to name a few) could be as immoral as they liked, and be forgiven by their class. But to live under Theo's roof, rather than spend nights under it, implied a contract she had no wish to make. So she and Helen still talked about men sometimes and did one another's hair.

Helen was in a threadbare show at Richmond, dancing in obscurity. The screen test kept being postponed, and when it was finally arranged, she decided not to bother because her mother wanted her to help at home for a bit, 'home' now being in Buckinghamshire. The house near the south coast where Sibli used to play sardines with Helen's cousins had turned out to be unsuitable for conversion. When the surgeon-commander left the navy, he bought a modest property in the Chilterns instead. Old Dadsie had always aspired to run a genteel hotel, and then what happened, the Mandeville Arms turned out to have furniture beetle, and they inherited a cook who drank. Old Mumsie was at her wits' end.

'They'll manage,' said Sibli. 'You go for that screen test.'

'It's all very well for you, Sibby. You sail in here, tell me what to do and sail out again. I put on three pounds last week, worrying about them.'

'It's your life. I'll come with you.'

'Will you really? That's different.'

So Sibli felt an obligation, and couldn't treat the trip as pure comedy, as she was tempted to. The studios were north of London, in Barnet. A hundred aspirants were shunted about between cold corridors and hot stages. Girls' make-up went runny. Young men boiled in their suits. An official with a trilby on the back of his head announced that a camera had broken down. The director, Mr Samauskas, would be ready for them 'soon'.

By midday nothing had happened, except that someone who might have been a famous actress was seen in a Bentley. Then the man in the hat produced a list of sixty names and said the rest shouldn't be there. The unlucky ones went away, some in tears. Sibli despaired of such meekness. But Helen was on the list. Eventually they were given bread and Bovril ('like the unemployed,' said Sibli) and herded into a shed with a cement floor and benches, cut off from the stage by a canvas partition. Arc lights sizzled like green suns on the other side. The director, a squat man with a beard and sandals, came out to say, 'I am Mr Samauskas, quietness is essential,' and vanished again.

One by one, names were called. Everyone was required to do the same, pretend to be a prodigal son-or-daughter who has returned home in debt, begging a stern parent for forgiveness. The director's voice could be heard shouting, 'Look crushed by Fate!' or 'Try to smile bravely, remembering happier times!'

Sometimes the partition trembled. How ridiculous the cinema was!

With about twenty of them remaining, man in hat announced that the director had now left for the day. 'Sorry, boys and girls,' he said, and hoped they might be invited at some later date.

'Wait for me outside,' ordered Sibli, and went behind the partition. Technicians were moving a camera that ran on rails. There was no sign of the director.

The stage extended backwards in a clutter of electric cables and properties. She saw dusty sofas and palm trees on little wheels. A man peered at her around one of the trees – creamy suit, dark eyes in a sallow face – before hurrying off.

'Are you in charge?' she called.

Behind her, the hat said, 'Leave her to me, Mr Somerset.'

'That gentleman, walking away!'

He hesitated and turned back. The face was sympathetic. He was younger than she had thought – no more than forty.

'Many are called, dear girl,' he said, 'and few are chosen.'

'It was chaos. Is it all a publicity stunt, so the newspapers will write about Britannia Pictures, scouring the country for talent?'

'You are a cynical young woman.'

Sibli had reached him. He was slightly scented. 'Please do it properly next time,' she said. 'We are all human beings.'

He was unperturbed. 'You have a trace of some accent I can't place. I pride myself on accents,' and she caught a foreignness in the voice.

'I was brought up in Wales.'

'And you wish to be an actress?'

'Certainly not.'

'They were all on my list, Mr Somerset,' said the hat.

'You had better come to my office,' he said abruptly, and led her through doors marked 'Strictly Private' to the administration block.

Silence extended around him. Typists paused, voices stopped. 'In here,' he said, pushing a door, and she saw a carpet with a dragon stretching its tail towards the window. Bookshelves covered a wall. There was no desk.

He pointed at a chair made of steel tubes, facing a battered rocking-chair where he lay back and wriggled his shoulders, getting comfortable.

'I'm Miss Rees Buckley. I came with a talented friend who has a right to be treated properly,' said Sibli, angry at his air of being inviolate. Somewhere outside, Helen was standing with swollen ankles, unhappy.

'And I am James Somerset, the chairman of Britannia Pictures. I saw at once you were not an actress. At your age they fiddle with their hair or apply too much lipstick.' He paused after each sentence, as though waiting to be corrected. 'So we are both from small countries. My family fled the year that your Queen died. I remember the black ribbons on the horses in Aldgate.'

She said, 'The rocking-chair came from wherever you came from.'

'Latvia. You are right.' His eyes seemed to float in oil. 'The chair survived. It led a charmed life.'

'My great-grandmother had a chair like it' – not to make the remark would have been to despise the workings of chance. 'I used to sit it in for hours, waiting for something to happen. I never knew what.'

'You mean the ghostly side of things. Perhaps the "something" has happened this minute. Having the chairs in common is the experience that awaited you. We must all bow to events. I shall do what I can to help your friend.'

He took her to meet a man in horn-rims ('Mr Moon, our managing director') and asked him to arrange a personal screen test for a Miss Dorkin ('a brilliant young actress, I understand').

There was even a free lift back to London in the company car that shuttled between Barnet and Golden Square, where Britannia had its headquarters.

Sibli's account of it amused Theo, who despised the cinema for its pretensions to 'art'. He said Somerset was obviously one of those immigrant Jew-boys who had anglicized himself and changed his name. 'What an intolerant pig you are,' she said sweetly, to which he replied that intolerant pigs were the ones who ate best.

When Helen returned to the studios, Sibli was with her again. This time there was no waiting about, except that Helen was an age in the make-up department. The director told Sibli that her friend had expressive eyes. It was the same man, Samauskas. 'Max Samauskas,' he said. 'Mr Somerset is my brother, only he has changed his names. If I want to make him mad, I call him Johannes.'

It was late in the afternoon. As filming began, an urgent message requested Sibli to go to Golden Square. She left Helen looking bleached under the lights.

At Britannia she was asked to wait for Mr Somerset, who was on his way from Zurich. A male secretary called Oswald, a young man with spongy cheeks, saw to her comforts and reported progress – soon after five the chairman had reached Croydon Aerodrome, shortly before six he was in the building. Dusk had come, the lift gates were busy. His presence was like a weight. Sibli was curious, as if meeting him for the first time.

The sweetish oil was still on his skin. 'I had no right to invite you,' he said. 'I have kept you waiting while I exchanged lies with bankers, sold movies that have not yet been made, and bought a hundred thousand tinpot film projectors to flood the home market.'

'As you know, Miss Dorkin is having her screen test.'

'I attach no strings,' he said cheerfully. 'You are free to have dinner with me or not.'

They ate at a restaurant in Maiden Lane. He spoke of his childhood on the shores of the Baltic, how he had embraced Englishness, how he had married an Englishwoman who thought 'Somerset' nicer than 'Samauskas'. 'I liked her to be happy,' he said, peeling an orange, while Sibli got on with her sole – he claimed to live on fruit and milk. 'It will be simpler to answer the question before you ask it. We were married in the United States. I obtained a divorce there four years ago.'

At the end of the evening his chauffeur drove them to Marble Arch. A pale hand waved goodbye. The following week Oswald telephoned with another invitation to dinner, and thereafter, at intervals, James would take her to a restaurant when she was free, watch approvingly while she tucked in to expensive food, and tell her stories of the movie business. He made no secret of his methods. Low-budget films were the best. Since the war he had cornered the picture-house business in a dozen cities; at all of them he overheated the auditoria and sold salted nuts, so that patrons would buy more lemonade and ices.

He said he had only one rule in business. 'I trust nobody,' he said. 'Except Oswald. Oswald is like my son.'

When she asked questions, he answered them. 'We were Jews,' he said. 'We came to England because we were persecuted. When I was of age, I abandoned my race and my faith. Doctrinal religion means nothing to me. I have turned into an Englishman who believes in ghosts. I like the unknown edge of things.'

After a longer break than usual between their meetings, he told her he had been to a religious house in Suffolk, Brailsham Abbey. He went there to fast and dig the garden. The monks were Anglican Franciscans. 'They are realists,' he said. On his visits he always took half a hand of bananas, 'in case,' as he explained, 'there is a demon behind the plaster that tempts me unbearably. Better to eat a banana than do something worse.'

At the end of an evening, he left her wherever she wanted to be left. If she asked to be taken to Swiss Cottage, where Theo lived, the limousine went north unquestioningly. He never kissed her goodnight.

'A man with seduction on his mind,' was one of Theo's sour remarks. Another was, 'Never trust a man who doesn't eat red meat.' As a matter of principle she continued to see James – it gave her something to do when Theo was rehearsing or with Fanny.

And Britannia was interested in Helen. First there were

meetings, then there was talk of a contract. 'I've done it!' she screamed to Sibli on the phone one night. 'They are going to pay me twenty-five pounds a week. Max – he said to call him Max – wants me to have a professional name. We've decided on Helen Honey. Great, isn't it?'

Theo dismissed her as a plump little chicken, ready for plucking. But Sibli said she was a woman with a career, and felt proud of her.

CHAPTER 16

Breakfast was when Margaret Mappowder talked with her husband. In the evenings he drifted into himself, or was closeted with his pals, if any were about, but at breakfast he was always there, calm and smart in a double-breasted blazer.

In summer he would already have ridden a horse to Furnace and the hills beyond. Now, in November, he had been pottering with one of his cars since long before it was light. Either way he liked to sit with her and gossip for half an hour. Perhaps he was reminding her that he was in no hurry to go to his copperworks, and saw no reason why her tinplate works should be more of an attraction. Didn't they both employ competent managers?

Some days Aubrey didn't bother to go there at all. So he sat with coffee and the *Western Mail* and his letters and his wife and Homunculus, the dog, teasing her with his indolence. Otherwise she would have been off to Tir Gwyn before nine o'clock. The smoke, the stenches, the hurrying men, were all in her mind when she woke; over the years she had kept a sense of anticipation. An extra half-hour with Aubrey was a small concession.

She showed him a letter from Esther Penbury-Holt, who had written to say she was about to leave for the Rhondda Valley with a Birth Control Motor Van, and would be coming on to see them at the Castle, if that was convenient. 'Minus the motor van,' murmured Margaret, in case Aubrey didn't read to the end.

'She'd be mobbed in Port Howard,' he said. 'Not that she wouldn't find customers.'

'She'll very likely be mobbed in the Rhondda.'

He folded his newspaper and glanced at the rest of her mail. 'Do I see Morgan's writing?'

She held out the letter and the printed matter that came with it, but he shook his head. 'Anything about Sibli?' he asked casually.

She said no, even more casually, adding that her brother had sent the Buckley & Cox catalogue for next year: romantic novels, a book about the horse, a collection of articles by a foreign correspondent called Davis, and ('The Publishing Sensation of 1924'), a tale of the Great War ('from the pen of a new novelist who writes with unusual candour') called *Battle Honours*.

'More lies, I'm afraid,' said Aubrey. 'It's a sobering thought, that when all of us who took part in it are dead, there will be no authentic record left. The books will be believed.' He looked at the clock. 'I'm keeping you.'

'There's no hurry.' But she was gathering up her letters.

'It's the day you put flowers on your Dadda's grave. You'll want every minute at Tir Gwyn.'

'You're right. I do work too hard. But I like the old place, so there it is,' and the words completed the ritual, leaving her free to go.

The date marked her father's birthday, not his death. That had been so fearful, the murder and the discovery next morning, that she could never bear to go to the cemetery on its anniversary in August, the time of the Port Howard riots.

Villette went with her in the afternoon, as she always did, carrying trowel and kneeling-mat. Both Margaret's parents were in the same grave. While she arranged the chrysanthemums and lilies in stone vases, her aunt attacked the weeds with the trowel, saying the council should be ashamed to charge a pound a year for upkeep.

One or two others moved about the slope. It was a raw

afternoon. Behind them the town lay in a rut of smoke. She saw Rhodri Lewis, who had been Dadda's best friend before he was his worst enemy, coming down the path.

'Fancy seeing you,' he said, as if it was an accident. 'I want you to buy the Morfa.'

Villette went back to the car. Margaret listened in astonishment as the old man insisted she must have it, that joining the two works together had once been Davy's great ambition. Now he was tired and his son was dead. He wasn't asking much money. It was keeping the works open that mattered. Margaret could make the wheel come full circle.

'If Aubrey had his way,' she said, 'I would sell Tir Gwyn, let alone take on anything more.'

All he did was thump the earth with his stick and say, 'Are you listening, Davy? Buckley's can have the Morfa.'

'While you're at it,' said Margaret, 'you might tell him what the economic situation is in Europe.'

'You'll be here to see better times. You're a young woman, *fach*.'

'I wish I was.'

She couldn't bring herself to give an absolute no. Her father and Rhodri had been close, even in enmity. In the meantime a buyer might appear. Rhodri was trying it on. He would do nothing yet.

Next morning at breakfast she told Aubrey that the Morfa was up for sale, and he said, good, that would be one works fewer when the whole town went bust.

Margaret meant to talk to other proprietors, to see if a way could be found to keep the place open. Before she got round to it, there was alarming news about Esther.

Aubrey read it out from the *Western Mail*. A motor van owned by a medical charity had mysteriously caught fire during the night at Tylorstown in the Rhondda Fach. A trained nurse wept (wrote the reporter) and said that all they were doing was supply surgical appliances for women in need. A determined Miss Penbury-Holt said that one day Science would prevail over Ignorance, and hinted that religious bigots were to blame.

'I had better get over there at once,' said Margaret. She returned to Port Howard late in the afternoon with a reluctant Esther, who was still declaring she would have liked nothing better than to wait for further supplies and hand them out in the street. Fortunately she had been in no state to do anything but lean on Margaret's arm and get in the car.

Hearing voices outside the hotel in the night, she had been in time to see petrol ignited and men running. She ran after them with a coat over her nightdress, then organized a chain of residents with buckets of water. Her eyebrows had gone, her cheeks were scorched red; she had been the one throwing the water.

Put to bed at the Castle, she insisted on writing to several MPs and the chief constable of Glamorganshire, and fell asleep in the middle of a tirade against the fire-brigade. Margaret had been looking forward to company. She invited her mother-in-law, Mirella – who lived apart in her own wing of the house, where she played Sousa marches all day and did jigsaw puzzles – to come in for dinner. Aubrey had been out somewhere all day with his racing Bentley, and she didn't see him until next morning.

It was only then she heard about the Morfa. It was closing on Saturday.

'You didn't know? Sorry, old girl. Don't get upset.'

'I am not upset,' she said. 'I am angry. This is a community. I don't like to see a hundred men put out of work.'

Half an hour later she was at the Morfa works. A train of empty coal trucks was leaving the gates. A black flag hung from the driver's cab. 'What was I meant to do?' said Rhodri. 'Go on my knees to you? The price was fair. You didn't give me a straight answer. Typical of a woman. I thought, to the devil with it. Excuse my French.'

'Tomorrow is Friday,' she said. 'Give me twenty-four hours.'

'Last shift Saturday morning.'

She went home to see Aubrey. He was in one of the garages, helping John, his mechanic, tinker with the Bentley. As a rule Margaret kept away. Everything was peaceful, wind sighing outside, engine parts on oilskin, unshaded lights making shadows. The two men were crouched by the car, talking quietly. Standing in the doorway, for a second she knew what it was like to be Aubrey, happy to be shut away from the town with his motors and dogs.

'We are just tucking her up for the winter,' he said, and followed her into the house, kindly enough, but dismayed at her persistence. 'What does Mrs Mappowder propose?'

'A consortium of proprietors to keep the place open. To help the town. I for one, Hughes at Old Castle, the Egges, you most of all. They might follow you.'

He shook his head. 'I do urge you to drop it, Margaret,' he said. 'You will only make a fool of yourself.'

'You won't contribute?'

'Not a brass ha'penny.'

'But you won't mind if I try the others?'

'You are a businesswoman in your own right. I realize I have no authority over Margaret Buckley.'

Rain, pulsing in over the estuary, closed the town in on itself. Princelings in brick palaces looked out of their sooty windows and hated the man next door. Margaret crossed and re-crossed sidings, nipped up stone steps, sat in rooms marked 'Private' where you had to shout to be heard above the mills, was listened to with respect, was even flirted with by the younger Egge. But she received no support. Hughes said it was a blessing for them all.

The lights were still on in Rhodri's office as she drove into the Morfa. Men in sweat-rags and clogs came to the open doors of the mill for air, swigging at bottles, strutting outside in the rain, perhaps for her benefit, elbowing and horse-playing, as if their right to work themselves to the bone for ever and ever was immutable.

'If I raise a banker's draft by tomorrow afternoon,' she asked, 'do I get the works? Lock, stock and barrel?'

'I suppose so,' he said, ungracious still, but red around the cheekbone. 'What does that husband of yours think?'

'That he runs the copperworks and I run Buckley's. What else would he think?'

But Aubrey kept out of her way that night, and didn't appear in the morning. She was glad; it meant that he knew.

'I am interrupting your busy life,' said Esther, propped up in bed, with a fire in the hearth. Margaret's doctor said it was 'nervous exhaustion', a diagnosis that Esther snorted at. 'Harassment by men, more likely,' she said. She had been delirious in her sleep, mumbling about Suffragettes.

Word got round the town by midday. Men going in for the afternoon shift at Morfa met the outgoing crews and marched on Tir Gwyn in a wedge of caps and aprons, drawing in the Buckley's men to share the glory.

They were all shouting for Margaret Buckley. They stood under the windows swaying like a choir, mouthing the name.

'You must go outside, ma'am,' said Trubshaw, her manager, and she went downstairs, and out to the steps.

They continued to chant, as if they weren't sure it was her, until, without thinking, she blew them a kiss, and there was wild cheering, which merged into '*Sospan Fach*'. Her tears weren't noticed in the rain.

It seemed impossible to save a tinplate works tactfully. A newspaper reporter from Cardiff was in the town before teatime. She was late returning to Cilfrew, to find Aubrey away and Esther recovered, sitting at her writing desk amid papers and ink.

They had plenty to discuss, but Margaret said little about the Morfa. Tinplate works or any works at all (she knew) were beyond Esther's range of sympathy. Men just laboured; women suffered. Easing the plight of labourers was established practice. Women were the ones without a voice.

'My family,' said Esther, when they were in Margaret's sitting-room after supper, 'think birth control too disgusting even to be critical of. If it weren't for Tom, I would barely be in touch with them these days.'

Margaret said she sometimes wondered how Tom was getting on. Behind the question, others lay unframed.

'You know he has left the City?'

'I thought he and his father were taken on by another firm.'

'So they were, Duck, Reece & Pincher. But Tom rebelled. He was being hauled over the coals for something by his new employer. He told me his exact words. He said to him, "Stuff it in your old kitbag, Guv'nor. I've had enough of Dog, Rice & Pimple to last me a lifetime." He walked out and joined the Metropolitan Police.'

Esther rummaged in a handbag filled with paper. 'When I told him I would be in Wales, he asked me to bring you something. Charlotte has been hanging on to it. You know, Tom aside, we are the most impossible family. I include myself.'

It was the silver teaspoon, former property of Henry. Margaret wondered if Tom had sent it for any reason except courtesy. Esther was watching her. Wind sucked at the chimney and drew sparks from the fire. They might have been anywhere. London, Tom, Sibli, were not far. Express trains took four hours. Remoteness was an illusion, a matter of choice.

She said, 'Do Tom and Sibli still see one another?'

'My dear Margaret, aren't you in touch with her?'

'Not really.' The words stuck to her tongue. 'The odd postcard.'

'I'm sorry to hear it. Well. Sibli broke off their friendship in the summer.'

'I feel a responsibility for my niece,' said Margaret, and hoped she was striking the right note of severity. 'Morgan is hardly the ideal father. I would like to be given some details. However humiliating it is to ask.'

'Surely you and I are old enough friends to ask anything at all.' Esther lit a cigarette and drew on it like a man. Her eyes avoided Margaret's. She said, 'What is there to say? Tom, I think, was over-keen. It is in his nature. Sibli had other interests.'

'Of what kind?' demanded Margaret. 'Older men? Married men?' Dignity didn't matter. What mattered was knowing.

'The little I know is through Tom,' Esther said, in a voice that was gentle by her standards. 'He has always confided in me. I was the first person he told about joining the police.'

'Never mind the police. What about Sibli?'

'The last I heard, she had taken up with a cousin of yours. The concert pianist. Mr Lloyd.'

The thought of Sibli involved with Theodore sank in. Even as a child he was a barbarian. She found herself shaking. 'Of all people,' she said. 'Really, I don't know whether to laugh or cry.'

'Buck up, now,' cried Esther. 'We aunts have to stick together. I know I'd miss Tom if we quarrelled. Why not go to London and have a talk with her?'

'It wouldn't be the first time. We don't see eye to eye.'

'Come back with me tomorrow. We shall have a whole train journey for discussing it. Do come.'

'Out of the question,' said Margaret, but smiling as she spoke, at Esther's simple world of solutions for everything.

'I will talk to her myself, with your permission. Young people are perfectly sensible if one takes them seriously.'

'You are a great optimist.'

'How would I ever have achieved anything if I wasn't? You think her wicked. I would prefer to reserve judgement for a few years.'

'Let me think about tomorrow,' said Margaret, but she was halfway to deciding already. It was possible that Sibli was innocent of everything but bravado. Her talk of 'lovers' was hardly evidence for a magistrates' court. 'Lovers' to lady novelists didn't imply carnal knowledge. She was a headstrong girl who wanted independence, and in pursuit of it might make herself out to be something she wasn't.

A spell was broken; Margaret was ready to make allowances for everything. On her way to bed that night, she looked in at the room under the turret where Sibli always slept. A dress hung in the wardrobe. Half a dozen novels were on the windowsill. Margaret avoided the room these days. Now, thinking of the child in bed, black curls and watchful eyes, she felt her loneliness.

On Saturday morning the *Western Mail* reporter's handiwork was all over the front page.

HEROINE OF TINPLATE INDUSTRY KEEPS
STRICKEN MILLS OPEN
REPRIEVED WORKERS SING HER PRAISES

was propped against the milk jug when Margaret came down to breakfast.

Aubrey slid it towards her and knocked over the salt.

'I admire your pluck,' he said. His handkerchief was stuck in his top pocket like the fin of a shark. 'Read about it – go ahead, you are famous.'

'Newspaper nonsense.'

He retrieved the paper. 'Listen. "A spontaneous demonstration set up a cry of 'We want Margaret Buckley!', 'Buckley' being the original name of the gallant proprietress, who responded with affectionate gestures, winning the hearts of the workmen." You meant to make history and you succeeded.'

'You knew when you married me I was a proprietor and meant to stay one.'

'I also imagined you were taking my name.'

'They were carried away. It never occurred to me that a reporter would get hold of it.'

'If you wish to be known as Margaret Buckley,' he said, 'of course, who am I to object?'

'Margaret Mappowder suits me very well.'

He read for a minute longer, then said, without looking up, 'Please don't wait if you have things to do.'

'They have to be paid at the Morfa.' At the door she hesitated. 'I have to go to London for a day or two. I shall go up with Esther later.'

'Goodbye,' he said.

The Morfa took most of the morning. Stocks of raw materials had been run down. There were ventilation problems in the tinhouse. Rainwater poured through a broken roof in a corner of the cold mill.

As soon as she could, she handed over to Trubshaw and went home, driving herself straight to the garages, where she thought her husband would be. She had been too abrupt.

A bedraggled Homunculus came out of the shed that housed the Bentley and whined at her. Bare bulbs swung in the draught. The cement floor was empty.

Mirella was playing Sousa loud enough to drown the wind. 'He has gone to Pendine Sands,' she shouted.

'In this weather?'

'He said he wanted one last run.'

The mechanic had gone, too. She went to find Esther, who was filling in time before lunch with a few letters. 'I'm sorry,' she said. 'I can't come after all. It has to do with Aubrey.'

Esther was understanding. Husbands were not her speciality. Margaret left her in charge of Hilda, the housekeeper, and drove on to the Carmarthen road as fast as she could, branching into the drowned landscapes of West Wales.

The sands were glazed with rain. She recognized the mechanic a hundred yards from the hotel. Far to the west, a flagman was visible against the sea. Beyond him again, receding wheels sent up spray that mixed with the spray blowing off waves.

The proprietor had been at the window with binoculars.

'Not ideal conditions for the measured mile,' he said. 'But your husband is a law unto himself.'

The car reappeared as a hovering whiteness. The distant flag went down and Margaret clenched her fists as a ball of water emerged, tightened, flew past the mechanic and rolled away like a diminishing halo to the eastern end of the sands, losing speed. Margaret pointed her car down the stone ramp and drove smoothly over the beach. Moving at right angles to her, the racing car launched itself on the westerly run, and she imagined she could see the goggled face as it passed.

The mechanic had a time-and-distance table under celluloid, with the stop-watch in a leather bag around his neck. He said they were timing only the west-to-east runs, with the wind behind the car. The Major was trying for a hundred and fifty. That was twenty-four seconds on the measured mile. His best so far was twenty-five point six.

'How dangerous is it, John?'

'Fairly,' he grinned. He squinted into the rain, watching for the flagman. 'Soft patches, madam.'

'How would you stop him?'

'Very pistol in my belt.'

His thumb was ready on the watch.

'Stop him, then,' she said, and got in the car.

'He'll be nearly at the flagman,' he shouted.

'I hope your pistol works.'

She accelerated to the west between two sets of Aubrey's tracks. A light burst overhead and a red globule trickled out of the sky. It was impossible to tell whether the spinning water ahead of her was approaching or receding, or even moving. She told herself it was safe anyway, that on each run he followed a separate track higher up the beach. But that meant safe for her. What if the presence of another car, or even the Very light, distracted Aubrey and made him crash?

Morgan would smile at her fears. Why think about Morgan now? Perhaps because there was nothing he wouldn't smile at. His certainty could save her from anything.

The wheels barely touched the sand. The speedometer said forty-five, but it felt much faster. She could see the flagman now, waving a red flag – at her? at Aubrey?

Then she saw the Bentley, coming over the sands in a wide arc, bearing down on her at moderate speed, its headlights flashing angrily. She flashed her own lights back, and went diagonally towards the sea, the spray thickening around her, coating the windows like gelatine.

Now he was driving alongside her, waving angrily.

The back wheels slid, and as she braked, the car began to spin. Her hands were locked to the steering. Smoke rose around her, and the smell of brakes was unbearable. Then everything was quiet, except for waves thumping the bodywork.

Aubrey helped her out of the car. Icy water soaked her legs.

'It's all right, Margaret,' he said. 'All in one piece. What happened to London?'

'Second thoughts.' She felt like crying but couldn't. 'I seem to have let everybody down, always. You. Henry, long ago. Even my niece.'

'I wouldn't lose too much sleep over her. She is what she is.'

'I was foolish to think anything else.'

'You may come to understand one another. If not – so what? We used to say it in the trenches. Everything counts, nothing matters.'

She pressed against him.

'I'm not much of a shoulder to cry on,' he said. 'But I'm always here. The world will get on without you. Let it, sometimes.'

He planted her in the driver's seat of his car, where there was a flask of brandy clamped under the dashboard.

The drink burned her throat. 'Can I be forgiven?' she asked.

'You mean for being Margaret Buckley?' Kneeling outside the car, he unfastened her wet stockings and rolled them off, rubbing her legs with his sleeve. 'You'll have a statue yet.'

CHAPTER 17

From the start of her affair with Lloyd, Sibli caught echoes of other women, a Martti from Helsinki, a Sylvia from the Home Counties, both musicians, their names let slip in conversation by Fanny. She herself was the one Sibli kept an eye on. Her black-edged eyes were deep with intrigue. Not that she expected fidelity from Lloyd. He lectured her, when they were lying naked on a sofa, about the artist being interested in only one kind of fidelity, to his art.

'What about the artist's women?' she asked him. 'Are they supposed to be faithful?'

'To his art, they are. Of course. He requires it. I require it of you.'

She found him self-indulgent when he talked about the artist. She respected the simple 'her' and 'him', as when they were on the sofa, undressed. What Theo wanted was a more mysterious 'him' for the straightforward 'her' to be bound up with; that damned conceit about piano-playing again. Mysteriousness itself she had no objection to. No doubt there was a mystery in being Theodore. But so there was in being a Sibli or a James Somerset or an anybody.

Europe, when she went with Theodore on his first major tour of the Continent, exaggerated the chaos of their life together. Fanny was there as well. She was for ever taking Lloyd aside to discuss changes in the schedule or read translations of reviews, as they zig-zagged between cities at the end of a freezing winter. Cooped up in hotels with snow still on the window ledges, they went over and over his performances.

In Amsterdam the hot-water pipes in the hall were tepid and the audience kept their coats on. Lloyd used hot flannels on his hands between items.

His Schubert, the romantic high spot that would reduce the foreigners to tears, made Sibli's face burn with its flamboyance. She was still clapping as the applause died away. A critic praised his 'distinctively varied approach'. Was that the beginning of international fame?

Audiences exuded politeness. In Geneva there were empty rows. Paris was cancelled altogether, allegedly because of a dispute in the Paris Conservatoire Orchestra. In Milan he had a row with the hotel management about the noise of trams, and ordered Sibli to give up her Jewboy. 'What will *you* give up?' she asked, but he ticked her off – more nonsense about art and artists.

Something was wrong. The critic of the *Corriere della Sera* gave one paragraph to the 'brave young Englishman'. Lloyd's confidence ebbed. Reading the signs, Sibli spoke to Fanny, who begged her to act as if the tour was a triumph. She tried to oblige, insisting they see the sights before travelling to Vienna – they wrapped up in furs and crossed a lake in a motor launch, fed elephants at the zoo, laughed at girls like skinnier Helens high-kicking in a vaudeville show. Lloyd looked at everything with a savage contempt. Fanny went on about the 'inner core' that must be kept 'inviolate'. To Sibli, a bit of violation was a way of getting closer to someone. But even in bed now, Lloyd was distant.

Snow had half melted and refrozen in Vienna. Lloyd was to play the following day. Dining with the conductor, Warburg, and other notabilities, he was told that the venue had been changed to a more modest hall. It was the influenza epidemic. Furious, he went off to practise in a piano factory. Fanny was left behind, talking to a concert promoter.

Sibli went with him and sat on a hard chair, in the shadows, watching his back and shoulders heave as if he was sobbing, fighting the music in his shirtsleeves. A watchman snored behind a screen.

Returning to the Ringstrasse by taxi in the small hours, she was unable to keep quiet any longer. 'You are a fine artist,' she whispered. 'If any of them haven't realized it, it's their loss, not yours.'

'I'm surprised you have noticed anything,' he said, as they reached the hotel. 'I have waited for one word from you. But you came with me to enjoy yourself. I quite understand.'

'I came because you wanted me. If my views on art aren't to your satisfaction, you had better find someone whose are.' Fanny was waiting up for them in the lobby. She had news of a last-minute recital in Munich, 'almost definite' if it could be advertised in time.

Outside their rooms they all kissed one another goodnight, and a moment later Sibli slipped in with Lloyd. Next door she could hear Fanny moving about.

'How can I please you?' she asked. 'Can you feel my breasts against you?'

'You've brought me bad luck,' he grunted. 'I thought I knew you. I was wrong.'

'I took Fanny's advice not to commiserate with you under any circumstances.'

'That's right, blame her.'

Sibli smiled. 'How long ago was she your mistress?'

'You'd better ask her. Poor woman, she's devoted to me.' He inclined his head, listening. 'She will be naked now. She's in the bathroom.'

Sibli sat against a pillow, the sheet held across her body.

'Tell me, Lloyd, why do you want to insult me?'

'Under the art is the dirt.'

'I thought it was the other way round.'

'You know about art, do you? You have experience, no doubt.'

'I would have done anything for you,' said Sibli.

Her instinct told her to leave while she was angry. Out of bed, she held her face against the wall, hearing the silence of someone listening from the other side, a few inches away. 'Did you hear all that, Fanny darling?' she asked loudly, and thought there was a movement. Five minutes later she was back in her room, wondering how she had put up with Lloyd as long as she had. In the morning she caught the first express out of the West-Bahnhof.

In London, she found that Helen had moved out of the flat. The wooden rollers and diet tables were gone. A note on a sheet of violet paper said she had concluded that Marble Arch was 'too, too sordid', and gave an address in Chelsea. 'Anyway,' said a postscript, 'you're never here.' But she was there now. Helen had moved on at just the wrong time, leaving the memory of her 'Oohs!' and 'Ahs!', and a dirty towel in the bathroom. A woman's presence was, would have been, a comfort; any woman. Sibli could still feel the print of Theo's body. There was an aftermath to be lived through.

A letter from her father was at the flat, too. Now that *Battle Honours* was soon to be published, he wanted to interest a film producer. Could Sibli arrange a meeting with her friend Mr Somerset?

Next morning she telephoned Britannia Pictures from the gallery, to see what she could do for Pa. The switchboard told her that Oswald had left the company. She thought this strange. Mr Somerset himself was on vacation. 'Mr Moon then, please,' she said, but he was not available.

It was as if she had been away a year, not ten days. London without Lloyd reverted to an earlier state. A coppery sun was heralding a sort of spring, and she wished she were somewhere else. South Wales, even, crossed her mind as a place to go to 'just for a day or two', as she framed the excuse. But why acknowledge a defeat when it was really an escape in disguise?

A taxi across the park and out the other side cheered her up. Tea with Helen, if she was at home, would wash away a few tears. Helen was. The flat had chrome fittings and a view of the tops of buses. A beautician was seeing to her feet. She wiggled a red toenail and said, 'Hello, darling. You're lucky to catch me.'

Some finishing-off work with oils and emery boards made conversation difficult, but Helen let it be known that she was about to start work on a picture called *Sisters Three*, to be directed by Max Samauskas himself. 'There's a very daring scene where I wear pyjamas,' she said.

'Fred will like that.'

'Sibby, I finished with Fred ages ago. Horrid little worm.'

The beautician packed her kit and departed, saying, 'Thank you very much, Miss Honey.' A No 9 bus stopped by the window and Helen wiggled her foot at the top deck. 'There are traffic lights,' she explained. 'I shall have to find somewhere else. What a bore. I expect you'll move in with Theodore permanently.'

'That's over,' said Sibli, curious to see how the new Helen would react.

'We *are* contrary, aren't we?' the new Helen said. 'I mean, you'd have been wiser to drop James. Personally I have given up men for the time being, though Max is very sweet. I don't encourage him but I don't positively discourage him, either.' She began to get dressed. 'Strange, isn't it, me advising you?'

'Tell me what you meant about James.'

'Well, he is weird and wonderful, isn't he? He goes on banana diets.'

'It was I told you.'

'You didn't tell me the half. They've had enough of him at Britannia. You didn't know? Keep an eye on Peter Moon. He and the board are doing a deal with Fox in America. Max is on their side. They all are, except that skunk Oswald, and I think he's had the sack.'

'What does James say about all this?'

'Ooh, Sibby!' said Helen, regressing briefly to Old Helen. 'He isn't there, is he? He goes off to monasteries and meditates or something.'

Sibli kissed her before leaving, her lips meeting an elasticated cheek that was telling her the old days had gone. 'I live on lemon tea these days,' said Helen at the door. Being less plump, she had ceased to be herself.

In the new London, Sibli felt almost staid and orthodox. On the inevitable journey she made to Brailsham Abbey next day, with a magazine to read on the train and a fur that Theo bought her in Amsterdam around her neck, she was merely a young woman going to visit a friend in the country. Long hedges ran into the East Anglian distance, flimsy dykes against whatever lay below the horizon. Brailsham's one taxi took her past fields of grass, across a shallow basin where a stream oozed into meadows. The driver stopped beside a group of zinc-coloured buildings under a knoll and some trees. 'Don't often get an 'oman along here,' he grinned.

The main house, small-windowed with gables, made an L against a rough cement yard. Outbuildings and allotments were nearby. Figures were at work. A rope of smoke hung from the sky with its end in an invisible bonfire. She smelt pigs.

Before there was any question of seeing James, the Abbot was sent for and she had to write a note. It was as if a woman had tried to enter the Athenaeum; men rallied to men. She wrote, 'Dear James, something urgent, Sibli.'

Presently she was led around the building. Monks stooped lower over rakes and forks. James, dressed in jersey and flannel trousers, was tending the bonfire with a stick. His bare feet in sandals were dirty.

He kept the stick between them. 'So my demon has appeared in a cabbage patch.'

She told him why she had come. He said, 'Thank you. That was an act of friendship,' and stirred the fire.

'So you knew all along. I thought you probably would. But I wasn't sure.'

'Oswald is in Berlin at this very minute, completing arrangements with Stockhausen AG that will double our European distribution overnight. Our bankers will be delighted. Mr Moon will gnash his teeth, not for the first time. But his wife is my sister, Dvina. It will all be forgotten.'

He didn't ask the source of her information. He had never seemed stranger; or more attractive.

'I've told the taxi to wait,' she said helpfully.

'There was nothing else you wanted to say? About your father and the novel concerning the war? The time isn't right to make such a movie. One day, perhaps, unless we have another war first.'

His ingenuity delighted her, if it was ingenuity. She said nothing.

'You are not going to ask how I knew?'

'You didn't ask how I knew what was happening at Britannia.'

'That was easy, my little demon. Your friend Helen Honey told you. No, I will satisfy your curiosity. I had a dream. Fasting induces dreams. A man I knew was your father held out a book to me. It was the colour of blood. I heard him say, "Out of the war to end all wars will come the moving picture to end all moving pictures."'

'I think you're making it up.'

'Remember, the ghostly side of things is our bond.'

He jabbed the stick in the earth, took two steps and kissed her mouth. It was quick but it was definitely a kiss. His breath was stale, laced with banana.

'Someone will have seen that,' he sighed. 'They stipulate no contact with the carnal world. You were an emergency, but one mustn't kiss an emergency. I shall be hauled before the Abbot and given the latrines to do in the morning. At the weekend I shall return to London. Oswald will be in touch.'

Soon after this, Sibli visited Peele Place and saw copies of Lambe's novel being sent out for review. The jackets were blood-red.

She gave a morning to Buckley & Cox. Everyone had hopes of *Battle Honours*. The typist squirmed on her seat, hammering out labels. Johnny Cox was there, sitting on the edge of a table, saying to anyone who wanted to listen that the book was very English.

'Am I right, Miss Smollett? I am not a literary man. I leave that to Morgan. What is your opinion?'

Miss Smollett said briskly, 'It may represent a new post-war genre.'

'Some people will think it a dirty book,' said Sibli. 'An interesting dirty book, mind.'

Johnny thumbed through a copy, squinting unhappily at the pages. Sibli, tearing open another package from the printing works, found herself staring at the name 'Stephen Davis'. Inside, there he was on the frontispiece, photographed at a street corner in a foreign-looking city. It brought a menstrual sensation in her belly, a flooding that wasn't quite pain.

She looked at him cautiously, trying to see what a stranger would see. 'Here is a foreign correspondent who has been to some of the most thrilling places in Europe. His sparkling style is unmatched in today's Fleet Street.' A tweed jacket hung from his shoulders like a blanket.

'Pa, why are you doing this *Dangerous Worlds*?'

'The best of his articles. I thought he was one of your heroes.'

'Is he dead or something?'

'He needs the money. He quarrels with his editors. He was in here only an hour ago.'

'He asked after you,' said Miss Smollett.

'So he did.'

It was the face of a wanted man on a poster. The head was turned, as though expecting trouble. She recognized the features and unaccountably heard the voice, but the man in the parlour at Macroom was intangible.

'He was on his way to Italy,' said the Smollett woman, 'to write about Mussolini.'

'I expect I shall bump into him one day.'

New energies were running through her life. Soon she was being invited to travel north, where the chairman was opening Britannia's latest chain of cinemas. Oswald might never have been away. He travelled with her on the train from King's Cross, telling her indiscretions about Peter Moon and Dvina.

No doubt he was being indiscreet to order. His grey eyes were like a cat's, watching her. The striped trousers and black jacket made him look older than he was. 'I owe my career to Mr Somerset,' he said. 'I would do anything for him.'

It was a dangerous sentiment. But secrets were being revealed, as and where necessary. James was drawing her into his world. She felt the fierceness of his interest.

At a mayoral reception in a blackened town hall, he took her aside and asked if she would go with him on a trip to America, leaving in a few weeks. She said yes.

CHAPTER 18

Whenever Johnny Cox asked him why they were publishing *Battle Honours*, Morgan gave different answers. It was a painful account of the Great War. Fighting men were not angels – there were certain establishments at the base camps, and unmentionable diseases, despite precautions, were rampant. Furthermore, said Morgan, quoting from a press release he had written but thought it wiser not to circulate, 'infidelity stalked the bedrooms of England while our brave boys were at the Front.' To publish an honest book was, or could be seen to be, a duty.

That was Morgan the man of principle speaking. Morgan the man of business said it would make money and might become a little classic, thus remaining on the list in cheap editions for decades. Aware that the grander publishers, the Capes and the Unwins, regarded Buckley & Cox as a very small fish, Morgan also said he would like to wipe the smile off their faces with a stylish bestseller. That was the competitive Morgan.

On one occasion, exasperated by his partner's doubts, Morgan said, 'Do you want to know the real reason we are publishing it? Because England's rulers like to impose their version of history on the rest of us. They won't like *Battle Honours*. I shall enjoy ramming it down their throat.' Sergeant-Major Cox didn't recognize how profoundly Morgan meant it.

The lawyers were not altogether happy with the book. The senior Henson at Henson & Henson said that some of its accounts of sexual relationships, though tastefully done, might be held to deprave and corrupt – the acid test of obscenity – because of a feeling that they were being approved of. 'The human race is corrupt to begin with,' retorted Morgan. When in that mood he could hear the chapel bell and see the sour green landscape of his youth, the country where he might still have been, with its guilty citizens scurrying to divine service, for the Reverend Morgan Buckley BA to toast each one on the fork of his anger. 'Purify the heart, Henson,' he said. 'The pure heart is incorruptible. Then we can all read what we like, without the upper classes having nightmares about mass debauchery.'

'Very theological, I'm sure,' said Henson, 'but we must be practical.'

'Of course we must. The book will be priced at twelve shillings and sixpence. That puts it beyond the pocket of the ordinary wage-earner. And did I mention I was a friend of the new Home Secretary?'

'The great Booley?'

'We shall be publishing his work on Empires in due course.'

'Then perhaps we should not worry too much,' said the solicitor.

Morgan approached the risks of the book as coolly as he had once approached the risks of questionable seances. More or less malign forces were at work in the universe, but they could be bluffed like everything else. Weighing up the odds did no good. God's wrath was more likely to squash the timid than the bold, that being one of God's peculiarities.

Lobbying Barker Booley was part of the strategy. Morgan sent a copy of *Battle Honours* round to the Home Office, and rang up the private secretary to wheedle fifteen minutes of his master's time. When he was granted an audience, there was something discouraging about the 'Ah, Buckley' that emerged from Booley's heap of chins and dark clothes, occupying the seat of power.

'The room suits you, Home Secretary,' said Morgan, determined not to flinch. 'You must feel a sense of history, being at the centre of things. Valuable, I wouldn't wonder, when it comes to pondering the work on Empires.'

'We have known each other a long time,' said the Minister, resting his finger-tips on the table. 'I consider it entitles me to offer you a piece of advice.' Morgan waved his hand as amiably as possible, but the voice was already continuing, 'If I were you, I would think twice about publishing a book like *Battle Honours*. Mrs Booley has read it and was shocked. She lost a second cousin on the Somme, you know.'

Morgan gave sympathetic clucks.

'Shocked. Its tone is vulgar and unpatriotic – I quote her words. I personally have not read it.'

Morgan wondered if the book had gone too far, after all. But it was a bit late for second thoughts. Nor could he dismiss the pleasure of thinking it *had* gone too far. When he spoke it was to express his deep respect for Mrs Booley, adding that one of the burdens of the serious publisher lay in plying a trade that forced him to cause offence now and again, in the interests of truth.

'Truth?' said the Home Secretary. 'That isn't the expression Mrs Booley uses.'

'But we have to be men of the world, you and I. Think of the ground that your *Empires and Morals* will have to cover. The human condition is imperfect.'

'Imperfect is not a word I associate with Mrs Booley,' said the Home Secretary, adding that he was glad the matter of *Empires and Morals* had come up, since he had decided not to let Buckley & Cox publish it.

'A bitter blow,' said Morgan, but he had been half expecting it, ever since the business of Sibli and the Purity League. 'May I beg you to reconsider?' At the same time he wanted to laugh in the man's face.

'My mind is made up,' said Booley, and Big Ben chimed in the distance.

'I leave disheartened. I hope our friendship remains as firm as ever.'

'Just remember what I said about that novel, Buckley.'

There was a sense of headmaster and delinquent that Morgan found distasteful. He had been whipped and told to go.

The only answer was the book itself. A few hundred copies were in the shops, ready for publication. The subscription libraries hesitated, waiting to see what reviewers said.

On the day, the same James Dunglass who had mauled Mrs Squale's memoirs was quick off the mark again. No decent person, he believed, would read this slur on fighting men and their wives without a shudder. Who was this Lambe person whose unhealthy fantasies debased the life-and-death struggle still fresh in all our minds? Had he fought in Flanders? Thank heaven for the other Britain, that of the millions of men and women who had kept their minds unsullied, as Arthur kept his sword Excalibur. Our nation's future depended on their moral purity.

Morgan shivered and kept his nerve. London had always been full of enemies. A telegram of congratulation postmarked Edinburgh came from Sibli. Mrs Squale sent a postcard from Leeds to say she had put her name down for *Battle Honours* at the public library.

A Notting Hill bookseller called Oscar Snell, whose father (he said) had been the Buckleys' family doctor in Port Howard before the war, wrote to ask for three dozen copies. Morgan took them round in person. The shop had a bow window like a bulging eye and not much stock on show. The bookseller was stout and rather younger than Morgan.

'As a child I frequently heard about your family,' he said. 'Your mother in particular, devoting her life to others.'

'She drank. Doctors were always being sent for. "Here comes half-guinea Snell," we used to say.'

'We have all moved on, sir. One has a hunch about a book. A novel at twelve and six about soldiers and marriages may find a specialist public.'

'Meaning what?'

Oscar Snell said that here was a case in point. They were upstairs in a cubby-hole. A lever that Morgan didn't see operated a drawer that hadn't been visible before. Snell took out a volume in a green wrapper – published two years earlier in Paris, he said, by an American lady – name of Mrs Beach – she found the Frogs more accommodating than the Anglo-Saxons – had set up shop there – brought out this novel – work of art – obscure in parts – dazzlingly lucid in others – still rare – brought into England in travellers' luggage – a copy through Dover, a copy through Folkestone – 'Hot stuff, sir,' he said, and handed Morgan a work entitled *Ulysses*, by James Joyce, adding, 'Have a peep near the end.'

The book was well-thumbed. Morgan had seen it condemned somewhere or other. It fell open at what looked like a single never-ending sentence, where some woman was brooding on men. It was astonishing; perhaps literature; undeniably obscene.

'*Battle Honours* is nothing like this,' he said coldly.

'All the same, sir, I have clients who will put it on their reading lists.'

You could never tell with books. On his way back, Morgan looked in at the West End shops, and realized something was wrong. *Battle Honours* had vanished from the shelves. Hickson refused to order more; so did Ramages. They had copies, they said, but were unable to display them, space being at a premium at this time of year.

'They have been got at,' said Rebecca Smollett. 'One can never prove it, but they have probably had the police round. The authorities are on the prowl. We shall hear something soon.' She squeezed his hand; they were old friends now. 'We can defend it as literature,' she said, and he patted her bottom and told her she was an optimist.

When Henson made inquiries, he learned there were to be charges of publishing an obscene libel, the antiquated euphemism for pornography. The enemy was at the gates. Morgan looked forward to the trial, which he would use as a platform to attack the mean-minded — he saw himself in the headlines, heroic publisher fights oppression. But there were snags.

Interviewed by appointment and charged under common law, he had first to appear before the Bow Street magistrate, who would decide if there was a case to answer. 'There will be, I fear,' said Henson, but added that his appearance would be a formality.

Standing in the dock before Sir Ernest Crampe, Morgan was uneasy for the first time. The magistrate's wing collar looked like knife points in the gloom.

Crampe had read the book and found it an insult to a civilized society. Whether a jury could be persuaded otherwise was a matter for another court. He personally had no hesitation in sending the case for trial. Looking pleased with himself, he set bail for the prisoner at twelve hundred pounds of his own, and insisted that a surety be found to put up a similar amount.

At once Henson was on his feet, objecting to these enormous sums. No good. The charge was a grave one, said Crampe, knife points threatening. Further, he understood that the author of the book lived in Paris. The next thing he would hear was that the prisoner was asking to go there.

'That may indeed be the case, sir.'

'You see, I am one step ahead of you, Mr Henson. Well, I may agree to a visit, if the passport is surrendered before and after the trip. But the bail conditions are immutable.'

In a cell below the courts, Morgan crouched against a lukewarm radiator, waiting. His own twelve hundred was in the Clerk's office within the hour. The other proved harder. Mrs Thorn, the first nominee, was dying in a private clinic, not to be disturbed. Her kinsman Lord

Leuchars, the second nominee, banker and one-time giver of seances, was out shooting, or possibly hunting.

A stool faced a wooden bunk. Its pillow, a scroll of polished wood, looked like something from a torture chamber. Time passed and repassed. The same moments repeated themselves.

Who would he boil in oil first? Crampe, relic of the last century? Or the foolish Henson, saying the bail conditions had 'caught them on the hop', as if he was the one who had to be humiliated through a long afternoon?

As the window-light grew murkier, a constable came to ask if he would like to send out for tea. Morgan told him he was waiting to be released, and where the hell was his solicitor?

'No need to use bad language,' said the constable, and the door banged shut.

Soon it would be dark outside – too dark for Harry Leuchars still to be killing things. Reluctantly, Morgan did what he had been putting off for hours, and peed in an enamel bucket without a lid.

As though that had to happen first ('Well done, God,' he would have said sarcastically in the old days), footsteps and voices were heard. The door was unlocked. Henson was there with a police sergeant. Behind him stood Margaret.

'I'm sorry it took so long,' she said. ('Your Miss Smollett's idea,' the solicitor was saying, 'tracked Mrs Mappowder down in Cardiff...')

Margaret said, 'I wish you'd named me first.'

Morgan could see everyone avoiding looking in the bucket.

'You were the last person I wanted here.'

'Time and tide, man,' said Henson. 'We had to get you out. Would have looked bad in the papers – couldn't raise bail, spent night in custody.'

Tactfully, he said his car was at their disposal, and disappeared. Margaret was returning to Wales by the next train. They headed west, behind a driver in a peaked cap.

'It's the annual meeting of the Fed. That's why I was in Cardiff. The dinner is tonight. I shall be there in time for my speech.'

'That bugger Leuchars let me down,' said Morgan.

'He may not have cared for the book. I didn't care for it myself.'

'I sent you the first copy off the press. I thought the postman must have stolen it when I didn't hear.'

Lights from the big stores flamed across them as they went down Oxford Street.

'You must have known I'd dislike it. A book that mocks heroism, because remember I'm married to Aubrey.' ('How beautiful you are, Maggs.') 'A book that talks about love when what it means is lust, that cheapens life. Someone like Anna would never condone what her brother did.' ('You must have read every word of it, Maggs.') 'And as for that Sergeant Truman, I wept.'

'You were meant to. Nick Lambe will be delighted. My angry sister came to bail me out, I shall say, because the story moved her to tears.'

They reached the environs of Paddington Station, with its cheap hotels and rubber shops.

'You're getting too old to be an *enfant terrible*,' she said. 'Why must you always ask for trouble?'

'You're so domesticated these days.'

'I always was.'

'Figure in the community as well. I grudge you none of it. We are all what we are. Sir Ernest Crampe thinks that what I am is a thorn in the flesh of "civilized society", as he calls it. He may be right. It may be the essential truth about Morgan Buckley.'

She touched his hand as the car reached the kerb and the driver jumped out. 'I am vice-president of the Fed next year.'

'None better. I shall try not to disgrace you by association. I love you deeply. Believe that, Maggs.'

She had three minutes for the train. Morgan bought her an evening paper. At the barrier he kissed her, all smiles until she was out of sight, and turned back to London and his enemies. He couldn't let her see how full of hatred he was.

CHAPTER 19

By the time Sibli heard that her father was being prosecuted he was out on bail, and they were talking about a trial within a month at the Old Bailey. The crisis appealed to her. Shocking as it was to think of Pa condemned and locked up, she imagined a hint of martyrdom, adding to his stature. A family with any pride in itself would have closed ranks against the world, not found him an embarrassment.

Her mother (life revolving around Albert, the Potato) hoped none of her Swansea friends would associate Mrs Griff Griffiths with *that man* who had been in the papers. Aunt Margaret was not much better. Sibli sent her a telegram saying, 'Thank you for standing by Pa. I am doing the same,' to which her aunt replied with a card that said, 'Your father is incorrigible, as you will learn one day. I trust you are well.'

They could do what they liked. Sibli would be at the Old Bailey with red lips and a smart hat. She didn't care if that meant missing America. 'Unless Mr Somerset intends to be back by June,' she told Oswald, 'I don't see how I can go.'

She was unable to say it to James because he was in Switzerland, fixing or unfixing something in Zurich as a preliminary to New York, which was itself a preliminary to somewhere else. Oswald purred and cajoled, murmuring about this boat and that hotel and those weekends motoring out of Manhattan to summer resorts to do deals on terraces with men called Sam and Ed. He made his employer's disappointment sound like his own, his hands made gestures that almost reached her breasts, he growled like James when he realized she wouldn't budge.

The next thing she heard was that James had sailed from Cherbourg without returning to London.

Helen found out about it, which meant that presumably everyone in Britannia Pictures knew, and invited her to her parents' hotel for the weekend. 'Now don't argue,' she said. 'You have been treated really shabbily. I am going out with a party and I shall make sure there's a spare man.'

Perhaps Helen's version had a grain of truth. James on the high seas made no attempt to reach her, though when it suited him he could send telegrams like postcards. Annoyed, Sibli dwelt on his oddities of behaviour. Reducing James to banana diets and sexual continence made him ridiculous, a revenge she hesitated to take. But a friend like that was a strain. Men were at their best when they were straightforward. She too, perhaps.

Feeling like a fling, she said yes to Helen, arriving on Friday afternoon while thunder was rumbling down the deep Chiltern valley where the Mandeville Arms stood, beyond a village, as if disowned by it.

Phyllis Dorkin was vaguer than ever. She patted Sibli's hand and said she was sorry the school had expelled her. 'Country air is a wonderful restorative,' she said, silver ornaments clinking on her chest as she showed Sibli things that ought to interest her. These included a man-trap with iron teeth hanging in the public bar, a greasy kitchen where a French chef called Bellow was eating a cake, and a mechanical cocktail-shaker that her husband had nearly got right.

The tour tired her. One minute she was saying how busy they were, the next she was a gaunt woman in an armchair, fiddling with an ashtray, waiting for her daughter to come. 'Those were happy days, when you stayed weekends with us,' she said, and sat staring into the fire.

When the chef appeared in a dirty white hat to propose *fruits de mer* and a carbonade of beef for Miss Honey and the other film stars, the woman said, 'I leave it entirely to you, Mr Bellow.'

A clock struck five and Mrs Dorkin said they would be here any minute now. Rain swept the valley, darkening the beech woods, and a maid came to ask if she should put the pan in Room 2. Mrs Dorkin told her to show some initiative, and said to Sibli, 'Blinking girls these days. The Commander would prefer menservants.'

'Is Mr Dorkin here at present?'

'Oh, he's *here* right enough. If they knew more about the working of the kidney, he might be here in more senses than just *being* here.'

'Helen hasn't mentioned he is ill.'

'She has her career. The first thing she will do when she arrives is rush upstairs to see her Daddy.'

Six o'clock came and voices could be heard in the public bar. Sibli went to her room, which turned out to be No 2, the one with the drip. A notice fixed inside the door with a rusty pin said that bed and breakfast was twelve shillings and sixpence, and in the event of fire do not stop to collect belongings.

Later there was a smell of burning beef. The lights kept flickering. Two young men arrived in a sports car, seeking a room for the night. Mrs Dorkin told them the hotel was full. They glanced into the almost empty dining-room and went away.

Of Helen and the film stars there was no sign. The barmaid in the cocktail bar, a woman with a long neck and prominent eyes, said it wasn't the first time it had happened. Sibli chatted to her after dinner. Her name was Vera. According to Vera, it was difficult for someone leading a hectic life like Miss Honey to be tied down by arrangements.

Between chats, Vera served cocktails to the passing trade, who had turned off the Oxford Road. Keeping an eye on the till, Sibli calculated that Vera was pocketing one payment in three.

Not that it was her business, any more than Mrs Dorkin was. Next day was fine, she slept late, and the shabby hotel was almost attractive between woods and fields, steaming in the sun. In London she would only sit waiting to hear from James. There were old novels in a bookcase outside her bedroom. She squatted on the carpet, reading.

A man's voice called for Helen, and went on calling. She opened a door and there was Commander Dorkin with the sheet up to his chin, eyes as lemon as a goat's.

'Don't I know you?' he said.

'I'm Sibli. We've met often.'

'You're all the same. Where is my daughter?'

'I'm afraid she couldn't get away.'

'When you see her, tell her from me that I don't know what's going on here. It needs a man. Running hotels and ships are man's jobs. If you were a man I'd ask you to stay, but men are at a premium. England's problem is a million dead in France.'

'I might be able to stay a few days.'

'But you've got a woman's voice,' he said, and drifted away.

Staying was no great hardship. Mrs Dorkin protested at first that nothing needed doing. The electric lighting was brand new, for example. Mr Dorkin had wired the place up himself. Sibli got in an electrician who said it was a wonder the place hadn't burnt down. Soon Mrs Dorkin was accepting Sibli's suggestions — a roofer to attend to the leaks, a sign on the main road pointing up the valley.

There was something triumphant about Mrs Dorkin's innocence. What, she said, if Helen did break a little promise now and then? She would soon be as famous as Mary Pickford, so it was no use judging her like other people. If you were able to defraud yourself so ruthlessly, thought Sibli, it hardly mattered what other people did to you.

She kept an eye on Vera, who had a nervous habit of stroking her throat whenever she was about to switch a banknote to her shoe or her brassiere. No doubt Mrs Dorkin would find some excuse, if it was only that staff always stole. But Sibli's interest went beyond Mrs Dorkin. She began to enjoy running the place for its own sake, finding a talent it had never occurred to her that she had, for grappling with chaos.

The accounts were not being kept properly. The first time Sibli tried to understand them, Mrs Dorkin came into the office and said she was surprised to see a young woman who had been to a good school prying into private correspondence. Five minutes later she was looking over Sibli's shoulder, saying, 'Yes, dear, but my mother used to say that a good joint of beef cost money.'

The chef was indisputably a crook. Either he was hand-in-glove with suppliers who provided false invoices, or he had buyers for surplus food. Bellow, with his rogue's smile and curly sideburns, made himself agreeable to Sibli. His hand was on her knee a couple of times. She detached it without rancour, letting him think he might be luckier one day. By not drawing back every time his garlicky breath came near, it was easier to keep an eye on the kitchen without making him suspicious.

One afternoon she even let herself be persuaded to walk up to the ridge, where the view from Brasswynd Hill at the far end took in four counties – as if it mattered. There, leaning against an ash tree, he told her his name was Henri and his father was a French count, and tried to feel her breasts. He gave up when lightly slapped, and took her back to the hotel, taking care to point out the attic at the rear of the house where he slept. Wet socks hung out of the window.

It crossed her mind that Bellow wasn't all that unattractive, as rogues often weren't. The last man she had slept with was Daniel, who ceased to be fatherly one evening after a viewing at the gallery. She could have done it easily with Henri Bellow, except that she was gathering criminal evidence against him and it hardly seemed fair. But she knew that her resistance was not clearly defined: it was merely a bias in one direction. Now that James had vanished, probably for good, she would have to re-examine the whole attractive-man question. Soon she would be twenty. That itself raised questions.

Halfway through her second week at the place Sibli went up to London to see what was happening about Pa's trial. They thought it wouldn't be before the middle of June, still weeks away. He showed no loss of perkiness. 'We are getting distinguished literary witnesses. Arnold Bennett, for example,' he said, and Sibli, her mind on other things, let herself pretend it was possible.

At the flat there was no word from James. Visiting Golden Square to see Oswald was a bad idea. She could hardly believe she was doing it.

His face held out no hope. Mr Somerset was in Atlantic City today, Chicago on Friday. No one stood still in the film business.

'I am wasting both our time.'

'Should I mention that you called?' he asked, like a conspirator, and she wondered what he was like in private, when the black clothes were empty on a hook by the bed.

'Do whatever the perfect assistant would do,' she replied, and went back to the nothingness of the Chilterns.

One could have papered a room with the bills for chops, chickens, tinned tongue, tinned ham – let alone coal, paraffin, soap. Was Henri running a shop? At the first opportunity she went to attempt an audit. She had seen him go to his room for a nap – he had winked and pointed up the stairs.

Three tons of coal should have gone into the cellar, but it wasn't there now. The torch showed a ton, at most. Sibli prowled through the kitchen. Behind a flour bin she found six tins of ham wrapped up in newspaper. Half a case of Muscadet, covered with rags and a bucket, was suspicious.

She was examining the meat safe when a man cleared his throat and she turned to see Bellow in the doorway.

'Cooking interests you, yes?' he said.

'I wondered what we were having for supper.'

'I can make you a speciality. I have the works of Brillat-Savarin in my room. Come and see. Make your choice. A swan made of spun sugar, for example.'

'What about a policeman made of tinned ham?'

'You have a fine sense of humour. But we could talk more easily upstairs.'

She let herself be led. His room was tidy, the bed covered in a blue blanket, a poster of Montmartre on the wall. Immediately, before she sat down, he tried to seduce her, hands brushing her haunches while he spoke about her virtues in a workmanlike fashion, as if he had a checklist in his head – radiance of eyes, harmony of figure, poetry of voice.

Indifference seemed the best bet. Instead of pushing him away, making it a contest, she let him paw and hiss in her ear while she studied the poster. When he looked at her suspiciously, she said, 'Finished?'

'You are the most ravishing woman I have ever met,' he said in a sullen voice. He sat on the bed and did his throat-clearing again. 'Right. Fine. You wish to humiliate me. I have my pride. I have had women at my feet, begging.'

'About the ham and things.'

'Ham?' he shouted, on his feet again. 'Ham? Good God, we are a man and woman bound by destiny.'

As he advanced on her, the door was flung open and Vera's head appeared like a serpent's on the long neck.

'Vile man, vile sod!' she screamed.

She rushed about the room, tore the poster from the wall, threw a book at Henri, shouted, 'You bitch!' at Sibli, and ran out again. The chef went after her. Sibli put the book on the bed – it was the *Méditations* of Brillat-Savarin – and followed the uproar.

In the bedroom corridor below, Bellow was whispering, 'My dove, my lamb,' and Vera was threatening him with a copper warming-pan. It caught a fire extinguisher, and the pan fell off the handle. Bellow made a dash for the stairs.

Commander Dorkin appeared in his pyjamas and said in a frail voice, 'Proceed to the yard in orderly fashion. Do not stop to collect belongings.' Sibli turned him around, and told Vera sharply to help her get him back into bed.

After that it was only a matter of threatening Vera with the police, and getting her into the office downstairs.

'I want to speak to Mrs Dorkin,' she gasped.

'Mrs Dorkin is in the garden' (netting the strawberries, fortunately, oblivious to events). 'Sit there and shut up. You and Bellow have been robbing the place silly.'

'When did he first sleep with you?'

'Weeks ago,' said Sibli, a lie for everyone's good. 'He's a rotten egg, that man.'

'I knew it. I came in early to catch him.'

'Are you married?' asked Sibli.

'What if I am? What do you know about marriage?'

'Tell me what your husband does, Vera?'

'He's a grocer.'

'So he was in it, too. Now do as I say and I won't go to the police.'

Sibli put a sheet of paper in the office typewriter and typed a confession that I, Vera Hamble, had been guilty of stealing from the cocktail bar, and had colluded with Henri Bellow in the theft of food from the kitchen.

'I want you and your romantic chef off the premises in an hour. Sign this and it'll go no further. Otherwise you know what happens.'

'You're a fine one to talk.'

'Sleeping with a man isn't a crime. Stealing is.'

Vera signed. She and the chef left together on the 5.15 bus. He shook his fist at Sibli but winked behind Vera's back. Mrs Dorkin hurried up from the end of the garden to ask what was going on. 'This would never have happened if the Commander was up and doing,' she said, when Sibli gave her a shortened version of events. 'I fear you have been precipitate.'

'They made me angry, the pair of them. Tell you what, I'll open a tin of ham and make us a ham and cheese pie. It was one of about three dishes my Ma ever learned to cook.'

They were both in the kitchen, chatting over a glass of Muscadet, when Helen arrived, bringing friends. The place was instantly full of voices and cigarette smoke. 'Right,' said Sibli, 'I want two assistants in here, a girl to skivvy and a man to be the waiter. Someone will have to run the cocktail bar.'

'Me,' said Helen, her formerly round, jolly face looking brutalized, with its eyebrows like hoops and the deep layers of make-up. 'What *has* been going on?'

'We've been waiting for you. You're only two weeks late.'

'Adrian will be your waiter, won't you, Adrian?'

A man with perfect teeth and blond curls with dressing on them smiled and sat on a stool.

'The rest of you, *out*!' called Sibli, and sent the skivvy for coal to keep the stove stoked up.

There followed the cooking of ham and cheese pies, the fending-off of Blondie, the keeping an eye on things in general. That led to the quarrelling with Helen, whose idea of running the cocktail bar was to dispense free drinks to the cast of *Sisters Three*.

'I have put a conscience box on the bar,' called Sibli, above the noise. 'Will the men please pay for drinks already consumed. Helen and I will be charging you from now on.'

They thought it was all part of the fun. Sibli laughed as

much as they did. But she was always serious about money. Objecting did Helen no good. 'This hotel belongs to my parents, who do you think you are?' lacked conviction, as did 'Your trouble is you're envious, Sibby, I'm sorry but you made me say it.' They were jolly well going to pay. Even when Sibli was foxtrotting to the gramophone, she kept an eye on cocktail consumption.

At the height of the evening, someone with mechanical skills got Mr Dorkin's cocktail shaker working. It hummed like a dynamo, churning a pint of White Lady, before sparks crackled and the house fuses blew. From the dark came a rustle of whispers. Sibli smelt hair-dressing and found herself pinned against a wall. A hand went up her skirt. 'Just like little dogs,' she said conversationally. 'I can hear you panting, Adrian. Do you have sex-dreams about things like this?' A woman laughed and the hand went away.

When the lights came on, Sibli closed the bar and sent them off to bed or sofas. Helen was too drunk to know what was happening. By the morning there was an air of apology.

'Father has been singing your praises, darling,' Helen said.

'I think he thinks I'm a man.'

'I'd get down more often if I could, but we start shooting *Happy the Bride* on Monday, and after that it's *A Woman's Heart*. They say I'm a natural, you know.'

'I'm sure they're right.'

'You know you're free to come down here whenever you like.'

'You're a real chum,' said Sibli, on the offchance that Helen would look at her and say, 'Sibby, are you pulling my leg?' But Helen's sweetness had gone, along with the wooden rollers and the Table of Ideal Measurements.

'Darling, you should have been nice to Adrian,' she said, when the cars were getting ready to leave — they were moving on to a house party in Oxfordshire. 'He'll have his name in lights in a year. I believe in letting men do most of what they like. They are the ones who run things, after all.'

'I'm sure you're right,' repeated Sibli, too sentimental about the lost friendship to want to quarrel. But she made sure that Adrian and all the other men coughed up fifteen shillings per guest for their stay – putting the price up on the spur of the moment, calculating that the admittedly mediocre breakfast she gave them of warmed-up ham and stale eggs was more than offset by the mound of post-fornication bed-linen that needed attention.

The visit had left Mrs Dorkin with ineptly happy memories of Helen, and a surprising amount of cash in the office safe. She appeared to take it for granted that Sibli would stay indefinitely. 'You have turned out to be a most competent young person,' she said, and was amazed when Sibli found a woman from the village who would come in and cook, and said that she herself would be returning to London in a day or two.

Sibli's only regret about the place was Henri, whose wicked eyes she could still see in the kitchen, fixed on her with that smiling lechery which seemed as rare in men as in women. She might just as easily have gone to bed with him as have had him dismissed. She might have managed both. A fling with Henri would have restored her to the world of men. Perhaps, even, she was lingering at the Mandeville Arms in the hope that he would look in, minus Vera, say bygones were bygones, and pluck off her clothes like feathers from a bird. The image rather excited her. When the housemaid said on Tuesday that there was a man in the hall to see her, she bet herself on the way downstairs it wasn't him. She was right. It was Oswald. He wore a leather travelling coat that must have been too warm for June. His manner was friendly but inflexible. He was to drive her to meet James Somerset. To her question, 'How did you know where I was?', he said that whereabouts could always be discovered and was she ready?

A game was being played. Sibli understood the rules without being told them. It was necessary to be swept along by events. Mundane questions were not to be encouraged.

A big French tourer was the designated vehicle. Clouds of white dust lay behind in the valley as they roared up Brasswynd Hill, blotting out the past. England was in front of them, spread out to dry under the sun in squares of green and blue.

The journey was enigmatic; how could it be anything else? London would have been too obvious a destination. There was a slow excitement about the slipping past of villages and plains. Seeing Stonehenge like broken letters on the horizon, she perceived the need to believe, when the car slowed for a turning, that James was capable of enlisting ancient monuments for his cause: that he would be waiting there with a picnic on the altar-stone. But they had only turned off for petrol.

Her contribution to the journey was to let it continue unquestioned into the south and west, on and on until they fell into the sea, or Lyonesse, or a boat waiting at a quay, or a seaplane with its engines running; anything was possible.

Late in the afternoon she slept. When she woke they were driving down a promenade. The cliffs were red. Hoses spouted water over municipal grass. Palm trees were black against the sea. Lyonesse turned out to be Torquay, its palace the Imperial Hotel. Without James the glory was fading, and James, it appeared, was still on his way. His liner should have docked at Southampton an hour before.

Alone in a suite big enough for a family, she bathed and dressed and drank white wine and took her mind off James with casual thoughts about men. The liner had been delayed. She wished the journey was still going on. There was no mystery about Torquay. A jazz band was playing, far off.

A trickle of last-light came through clouds that were taking shape over the Channel as she stood on the balcony. Invisible waves crunched on the shore; headlamps moved along the promenade; a voice came out of nowhere. It said, 'The schoolgirl used to walk by the sea and think of escaping into the world.'

She turned and saw the shape of James on the next balcony.

'I'd forgotten I told you that.'

'May I come to see you?'

'I wouldn't be here otherwise.'

He kissed her the moment he arrived, light but purposeful, smack on her lips, with a hint of tongue.

'Without my demon I was lost,' he said. 'I cut short my trip. I lay myself at your feet.'

He remained with his hands on her shoulders. They had never been so intimately alone.

'I have never inquired into your private life,' he was saying. 'You must have had admirers.'

'You had a wife, James, which is even more relevant.'

'But I gave up her particular flavour. Would you give up men for me? I guarantee my own love, my own fidelity. We have the same imagination, you and I.'

'I wonder. You've barely kissed me, ever.'

'I shall fasten my mouth on you for the rest of my life.'

That was dizzyingly erotic. 'How nice,' she murmured, not feeling calm at all.

'So – is it all right?'

'Is what?'

'To marry me, forty-two years old, who lives on fruit, who believes in the unknown?'

Once it was put to her, she couldn't live without him. 'Perfectly,' she said, and he went into the corridor and called for Oswald. Something was handed over, he took her back to the balcony, her fingers were splayed, she felt the metal slide over a knuckle. A gem sparked in a crack of light. She liked the feel of it.

'I do not believe in long engagements,' he said. 'I would like us to marry a week on Saturday.'

'How nice,' she said.

CHAPTER 20

People in Port Howard had long memories, especially people like Margaret's mother-in-law. 'I *do* hope you won't have too dreadful a time,' she said, shortly before Morgan's trial. 'You must send us a telegram as soon as you know he's guilty. Or not guilty, of course.'

Fortunately the only opinion Margaret cared about was Aubrey's and he took a realistic view of black sheep, sending her off with a kiss and a list of gentleman's requisites to buy in the West End. 'You could come, too,' she said, but he was looking forward to billiards and motor-racing. It wouldn't have occurred to him that Margaret was afraid.

London had the summer dustiness she remembered. She arrived on the Saturday. Here was Praed Street, there was the park, down those leafy avenues lay Kensington. This time on Monday it would be over.

It was hard to conjecture what their parents would have thought, were they alive – Dadda with the veins like string on his forehead, Mamma needing tonic wine by the bucketful. But at least it would have been two people more to care what happened. Brother Will was no help. 'My dear girl,' he wrote earlier from his mining village, 'you have never seen Morgan as he really is. Let him stew in his own juice. I couldn't get away from here even if I wanted to. They mean to cut wages. The ruling class has gone mad. We are all working towards a General Strike. PS, The miners have bought me a little motorcar for business. Sedition now travels up and down the Rhondda at thirty miles an hour.'

Will lived in another world. London itself was a bit like that these days, a foreign city, coloured by her fears. Margaret went shopping first, arriving at Peele Place weighed down with parcels. Morgan would be more amenable if she played the part of a woman in London to buy dresses. But her cunning was wasted. She found an agitated Sergeant-Major Cox, alone in the office with the editorial assistant.

'Gone to Paris to consult the author, ma'am,' he said. 'Miss Smollett and I are holding the fort. His daughter has been making a dickens of a fuss. She expected him at some function this morning.'

'What function?' wondered Margaret.

'Didn't say, ma'am.'

Margaret left her telephone number and returned to the hotel, to find flowers from Aubrey with a note saying, 'Chin up!' It sounded like a message to the condemned cell. Sipping whisky, she looked out on the mesmeric traffic going round and round Hyde Park Corner.

Even as children, Morgan had made her heart race with his rejection of the limits to 'good behaviour'. Banging a piano in a frenzy, he swore he was 'writing tunes' that he could hear inside his head. Often he got away with it. The ruthlessness could be childlike, or interpreted as such, a kind of innocent appraisal of the alternatives to doing what he was supposed to do.

Locked in his room for misbehaviour, he ate the first forty pages of *The Pilgrim's Progress* because he said he was dying of hunger and he had read that starving sailors got sustenance from the ink. 'The boy is out of his mind,' raged Dadda, but the boy grinned behind his back at Margaret, who stoked him up with bread and milk and sat with him for hours, both fascinated and repelled by the play-acting, but catching glimpses behind it of some torment or passion that perhaps was not contrived – she was never certain.

Aged eighteen, when he announced that God had told

him to leave the tinplate works and Dadda threatened him with a whip, he was found lying naked in a bath of icy water in the empty pickling shed on a Sunday, shuddering with cold, 'doing penance', he said, for being too afraid of the whip to defy his father and obey God's call.

'Maggs,' he would say, 'we are only a short time on this earth. We should listen to what the heart says.'

'I know your tricks,' was her stock answer, and he would smile proudly, as if they shared a secret.

Evening, when it came and there was no word from him, magnified her fears. Hyde Park Corner revolved like a toy mechanism. Had Morgan made a run for it?

The street near Marble Arch where her niece had her apartment wasn't far. Margaret had been there once. Perhaps this was the time for her and Sibli to try again. Drain smells came from an empty space where noticeboards announced that new apartments were being erected. A pub was half gutted. A crane poked over a fence. Soon there would be nothing in London that she remembered, or chose to remember.

The block she wanted was still standing, wooden buttresses against the end wall. Climbing stairs, she heard a gramophone on one landing, and on another a woman saying, 'Oh, Roger, I ask you, Roger!' from inside a flat, following her up the soapy grey stone, 'Oh, do come on, Roger!'

The electric bell of Sibli's flat was broken. Her knocks produced movements and eventually a 'Who is it?' in Sibli's voice, sounding not quite herself.

'Aunt Margaret!' echoed down the stairwell. She tried to be calm about what her niece might have been in the act of. They would never be close again; that was the awful part. Only a madwoman would have come looking for the girl.

It was a man all right. The slant of his cheeks wasn't English. He was smiling and greeting her. In the confusion she heard 'James' and 'know all about you'. Braces and bare feet caught her eye. Sibli appeared, without stockings, hair loose. A prurient vision of the two of them together blocked out everything. Margaret caught a gust of the perfume that Sibli must have splashed over her body.

'How wonderful, you arriving like this,' the girl said. 'James and I were married at Chelsea register office this morning. The only one I asked was Pa, and he couldn't be bothered to get back from France.'

'You are a shock merchant, my girl,' said Margaret, embracing her, because no other course was possible, the perfume like mashed flowers. 'You and Morgan.' She felt like a weep but reduced it to a dabbing of eyes, while the man poured champagne, from a bottle already opened, into cheap tumblers for which he apologized in a soft, accented voice.

'Do have a chair, do,' he was saying. 'I find those stairs make one puff.'

'So you and Sibli won't be living here?'

'James is buying a house for us in Highgate. We only came here tonight because ... why did we come here, James?'

'I wanted to see the famous apartment. And now I am seeing your aunt. Life is a strange affair, Margaret.'

'James loves to make mysteries.'

'They make themselves. You knew nothing of the wedding? Yet tonight of all nights, you come to the flat. We shall only be here an hour. Long enough for us to meet and hear the murmur of Fate.'

He could be as peculiar as he liked as long as he made Sibli happy. Instead of drinking the champagne, which had gone flat in his glass, he was sipping water. He took a banana from a paper bag and munched it, smiling at Margaret.

'We'd be on our way to Palestine but for Pa,' said Sibli. 'I have to stay till Monday because of the trial. It's just dawned on me, that's why you're in London. Of course. We are all rallying round.'

'Does anyone know where your father has got to?'

'Went to Paris for two days at the start of the week. I was angry with him when he didn't turn up today. But I think he's afraid he might go to prison. In which case he could have done a bunk.'

'It wouldn't be the first time in his life.'

'He thinks they're all against him.'

'He's probably right.'

'I have offered to send a private detective to the Continent,' said James.

'If Pa's hopped it, my sweet, we shall hear when he wants us to.'

There was a brisk gaiety about the conversation that Margaret didn't like. She declined Sibli's invitation to 'pop out for a meal with us this evening', which implied that the wedding night was of no consequence. After drinking the last mouthful of champagne, Margaret extricated herself from the shadowy little flat.

At least Sibli had been saved. Getting married absolved her. Bursting in on them when they were half dressed became a harmless accident. Even the hurtful fact of not being told about the wedding till after it had happened was bearable. Margaret was determined to see it as a fresh start. 'I feel lighter,' she told Aubrey on the telephone from her hotel, late that evening.

'And what's the latest on you-know-who?' Aubrey wanted to know, raising the other problem, the one that had been with her for longer, and would be with her for ever.

On Sunday there was still no news from Peele Place. That time when Morgan left Wales in a hurry and buried himself in south London, it was a year before anyone knew where he was.

Spending the day with Esther, as they had arranged, Margaret forgot him for a while. They talked about Sibli's marriage, and Esther said how fond young Tom had been of her. He was a police-constable now, doing plain-clothes work. Only a week ago he had arrested a pickpocket at a railway station. Tristram was not pleased to have a policeman for a son. In the City he kept up appearances as best he could.

News of the Penbury-Holts was always unsettling, reminding Margaret that she could so easily have been one of them for ever. A slightly different Henry would have done. Their marriage would have lasted, as marriages did. At this very moment, as Henry's wife, she might have been doing the same thing, spending Sunday with the family's toughest nut, who stubbornly refused to mellow and acquire cats and start entertaining curates to tea. But it would have been a different person listening to Esther talk about the march of women, the bat-blind politicians who were no wiser now than before the war, and, as she inevitably did after a while, the insolent doctors and clergymen who were standing in the way of progress on the birth-control front.

In the afternoon they walked down Victoria Street to Westminster and heard evensong at the Abbey, because Esther liked the choir. It was a secular outing for them both, like a walk in the park. Strolling on the Embankment, they reached a Salvation Army band, thumping away. 'Here is a shilling,' Esther said to a woman officer with a tin. 'What will you spend it on?'

'We are collecting for the League of Male Purity.'

'You'll need a lot of shillings for that,' said Esther.

As they returned to the flat, Margaret said, 'The case is tomorrow.' A police car sounded its bell and people stopped to watch it go towards the railway station. 'Frankly I am dreading it.'

'Would it help if I said I had read the book in question and found it interesting? Crude in places, I admit. But written I would say with a certain honesty.'

'The court will find it obscene. Everyone knows that.'

'Juries are unpredictable. If he believes in the book, he may change their mind.'

'He doesn't believe in anything,' said Margaret. 'I have a suspicion he won't turn up. He has been in France all week.' She hesitated. They were in the flat. Esther filled a kettle. 'I would go and ask Virginia if I thought she knew.'

'Did I tell you that she and Stuart have moved? They are in Harrow-on-the-Hill. I have the address here somewhere. Not that Stuart is often there. He keeps a biplane at Hendon.'

'You and I have never spoken about my brother and Virginia.'

'Very wise of us. In any case I expect Morgan is back in London by now.'

But at Peele Place they were still waiting.

It was mid-evening before Margaret found the house at Harrow. She waited in the big panelled hallway for her card to be taken in. An aeroplane propeller hung on a wall. 'Mrs Penbury-Holt will see you now,' the maid said.

She was shown through french windows to a garden with lawns and walls, at the end of which Virginia and a young man were playing tennis on a hard salmon-coloured court. Virginia was still slender, her hair tied back, skirt dancing as she made a savage return. The man watched it, not trying to intercept.

'Wake up,' she said, and came with him to greet Margaret. 'I believe you met my Henry at the funeral.'

He shook hands and said, 'Hello, Mrs M-Mappowder,' stammering badly. Soon he wandered off.

Virginia held her racquet in both hands, as if to stop Margaret coming too close. 'You never visited this house, did you?'

'No, you still lived in Ealing.'

'How suburban it sounds. Do you like living in Wales?'

'I've done it for long enough, I suppose I must.' She came to the point. Virginia would have heard about Morgan and the court case. He was due at the Old Bailey in the morning. Did she happen to know where he was?

A no would have sufficed, but Virginia felt the need

to be voluble. 'Why on earth ask me?' she said. 'We haven't seen Morgan for a year or more. We entertain less than we did, now that Stuart is so keen on aviation.'

'Never mind the "we". I am asking you. He went to Paris and hasn't returned. Is he coming back in time for the court case tomorrow?'

'You are persecuting me, coming here like this, you know that?' said Virginia, flushed up to her hair. 'I have had enough troubles in my life. You heard Henry's stammer. How could we have had a son like that? He played no games at school. He is trying to get himself engaged to a dowdy young woman. He won't go up in his father's aeroplane.'

'I'd think twice about it myself.'

'If I have ever done anything wrong, I am certainly being punished for it now.'

'He seems a charming boy.'

'Stuart and he don't get on.'

Her body had a stiff corseted look but above it her neck drooped miserably.

'I'm sorry. I truly am,' said Margaret. 'I only came because I'm distracted about Morgan, who is such a fool, who thinks narrow shaves are proof that Providence is being kind to him. If you don't know, you don't know.'

'He has some scheme in Paris,' Virginia said quietly. 'Before God I don't know what it is.'

So that was confirmation of disaster, of a sort. Their hands brushed as they said goodbye. Monday was going to be difficult.

She was a few minutes late, on purpose. Johnny Cox stood nervously in the lobby, wiping his face with a khaki handkerchief. Miss Smollett sat on a bench with a copy of *Battle Honours* held against her chest, like a badge she wanted to be recognized by. Henson, the solicitor, was looking at his watch.

'They sit at half past, Mrs Mappowder,' he said. 'But

technically he was in breach of his bail at ten. They will be preparing a warrant.'

'Is there no chance now?'

'I sent a man to meet the morning trains. He would have telephoned as soon as your brother appeared.'

The hall was emptying. Miss Smollett said she had seen Sibli arrive in a chauffeur-driven car. Someone (*who?*) had arranged for Sibli to sit in the court, without queuing for the public gallery. Irritated, Margaret went into the street. A late barrister ran from Seacoal Lane. St Paul's struck the half-hour. She was beyond anger.

A taxi appeared from the Ludgate Hill end. Morgan hung out of the window, waving, his yellow shirt and bow tie wildly un-English.

'Idiot,' she said.

'All well, Maggs,' he said, attempting an embrace. 'I flew in by Handley Page. Two hours and five minutes to the London Aerodrome.'

Henson bore down on them.

'Not a second to lose,' he cried. 'I shall crave the court's indulgence and get you ten minutes with counsel.'

'No need,' said Morgan. 'I am changing my plea to guilty. They won't send me to prison, then. I wouldn't like prison.'

Margaret couldn't face the public gallery. She went to the Lyons at the far end of the street. Half an hour passed. Her tea went cold and she bought another cup.

Cox and Henson came along the pavement and saw her through the window. Morgan and Miss Smollett were behind, arm in arm. There was no Sibli.

Cox began moving chairs, in defiance of the J. Lyons rules. Henson peered at the cakes as if he had never been in a teashop before.

'For heaven's sake, what happened?' said Margaret.

'Fined five hundred pounds, ma'am,' said the Sergeant-Major. 'Steep. The entire edition to be destroyed.'

'A deliverance,' murmured Henson.

'Morgan is moving to Paris,' said Miss Smollett. 'The Aeolian Press.'

'Registered in France,' added Cox.

'We might have guessed,' said Miss Smollett.

'You mean you'll live in Paris?'

'*Mais oui.* I have had enough of the mean minds of the English. *Battle Honours* will be our first publication. Accursed be the censors. A new life, Maggs.'

'Does Sibli know?'

'We had a word outside the court. She drove off in her Lanchester. We are all moving on.'

Miss Smollett was buying a cake with pink icing. Margaret felt no part of the celebration. Her brother sat grinning, his bow tie slightly askew, like a propeller beginning to turn. She knew she had lost him for ever.

The boat train from Waterloo was a minute overdue, held back for a party of nobs. Constable Thomas Penbury-Holt was near the ticket barrier, eyes open for dippers and hooks. Travellers needed to handle their wallets; that was when they were vulnerable.

A young man in a heavy suit came first, accompanying a trolley heaped with luggage. Behind him was an older man wearing a black homburg, with a dark-haired young woman on his arm. Her mouth was lightly lipsticked. Her skin seemed lit up. The guard had the whistle between his teeth. He looked. The stationmaster looked. The ticket collector looked. She was laughing. The length of the waiting train curved out beyond the canopy, into the sun and the silver rails. The police-constable said, 'Damn, damn, damn!' out loud. He moved through the crowd with burning eyes, seeking a thief to collar.

PART III

1931–1934

CHAPTER 21

Sibli believed that someone was spying on her. What it came down to was a man loitering in Piccadilly, the same man in Knightsbridge, and a car she kept seeing in her driving mirror when she was visiting a girlfriend in Wimbledon.

Tom Penbury-Holt, detective-sergeant, listened to her story. To have her step back into his life, even if it was only to ask him a favour, was gratifying. She had changed and so had he. Harder-headed now (he hoped), he made a tentative assessment: *this witness is more worried than she pretends to be.*

'My dear Tom,' she murmured, 'if you knew how many barmy characters I meet in the film business, you wouldn't be surprised at anything. One makes enemies.'

'I could say the same of the police.'

She was an attractive woman, five foot six, nine stone, dark hair, oval face, red fingernails, no visible scars, bold demeanour, pure silk stockings. The past was irrelevant. He was a police officer, doing a favour for an old friend, who had written to him c/o Scotland Yard to ask if they could meet.

He needed to know her address ('in the phone book, silly'), whether the house had ever been burgled (no), whether she wore real jewellery in the street (yes), if threatening letters had been received ('only dress bills'), how many years she had been married (six), nature of her husband's employment ('now you're being ridiculous, Tom').

He persisted, rather enjoying himself.

'Of course, Sergeant. He's a film producer, at present coping with the upheaval caused by the talkies. Remember taking Helen and me to a Valentino?'

'I have a vague recollection. Is there anyone who would want to know your movements?'

'You mean, does my husband suspect me of infidelity.'

'Does he?'

'Husbands and wives suspect one another of most things sooner or later.'

He wrote it all down. It was habit. 'Well-formed teeth. Distinctive eyelashes. Smiles frequently. Breasts approx. 37 inches.'

She was to contact him in a week's time. The man who was doing the spying sounded to Tom like a private detective. A day or two of unofficial surveillance by one of the spare men on the Flying Squad would do the trick. His pal Sergeant Swann would co-operate.

He had met Swann at Peel House, years ago, when he was still suffering from Sibli. Outside was Westminster and its slice of imperial London. Through a barred window you had glimpses of the tops of buses. Only the barrack square mattered, where they marched with shaved heads, stiff new boots and uniforms that left red marks in the skin. Tom's feet bled. He had a scuffle with an ex-soldier, a broken-nosed boy who put a dead starling in his bed and danced around the barrack-room, shouting in what was supposed to be an educated voice, 'Aeow, my Gawd, some wotter's given Penbuwy-Holt the bird.' A photograph of Sibli, wearing a bathing costume on a Welsh beach, vanished from inside the door of his locker.

His background cut him off from the rest of the class. The only one who hadn't started work at fourteen was George Swann, a clerk's son from the Midlands, who had been to a grammar school. A heavy, thick-featured youth, he was nearly but not quite as bright as Tom at arithmetic and essay-writing. His forehead went scarlet every time he was beaten into second place.

Their chief instructor was an inspector, an elderly tyrant with a silver plate in his head. One bitter morning he lined them up in a corner of the yard for Simulated Incidents.

'Who shall we start with?' he said. 'The intellectuals among us, I think. As you are all well aware, because I keep referring to it, Holt here – *Penbury*-Holt – attended an expensive school for the upper orders. So it comes as no surprise that his written work is adequate. But on the streets of a modern city, you need more than book knowledge. What is it you need, Swann?'

'Experience, sir.'

'Experience and common sense, right,' and the inspector made the silver plate squeak with his finger. 'Holt, you're on duty outside a railway station. I am a member of the public. I say to you, "Constable, I have just witnessed an indecent assault on a lady by that army officer."' He pointed at George Swann. 'Carry on from there.'

'Would you mind telling me what happened?' said Tom.

'He touched her on the hip.'

'Where is she now?'

'Buying a ticket at the window.'

'She hasn't reported it, then?'

'For all I know she's afraid to miss her train. The question is, constable, should some rascal disgracing the King's uniform be allowed to get away with it?'

'Are you sure of the facts, sir?'

'Reasonably sure.'

'May I ask where you were standing at the time?'

'Where was I standing?' roared the inspector. 'How many more daft questions are we going to have? What do you think the alleged culprit has been doing all this time?'

Tom turned to Swann, but he wasn't there.

'Flown,' said the inspector. He beckoned to the recruit, who was hiding at the rear of the squad. 'Your comrade summed up the situation in a flash, and did what a real-life molester would have done. A bunk.'

Mortified, Tom spoke to no one all day, ignoring

remarks like, 'Ecks-cuse me, sar, are you *eb*solutely certain of the feckts?'

Before lights out he was brushing his teeth when Swann came to use the next basin and said, 'There's a dog turd under your pillow.'

'I hope you didn't put it there.'

'You and I should be pals. Here, I got your girl's picture back.' It was creased. 'Some dirty sod had it in the bogs.'

'Thanks very much,' said Tom, but he wasn't interested in pals. He wanted nobody. Loneliness had a deadening effect that made things easier to bear. When the ten-week course ended, he was posted to Notting Dale station. He slept in the section house. Undressing on his first night, he heard men coughing on either side of the partitions. A newspaper rustled. Gas lamps hung from the ceiling, one to each pair of cubicles. They were extinguished at midnight. His new life began.

The Dale, a shabby quarter beyond Holland Park and the Bayswater Road, was familiar territory in a week. Streets of lodging houses and second-hand shops stretched northward to railway lines and goods yards. The white crosses of a cemetery glittered in the distance. A gasworks puffed its metallic odours over the landscape. As a district it suited Tom, one of those could-be-anywhere stretches of London, bits of ecclesiastical parishes redefined for police purposes, beyond the reach of guidebooks and gazetteers, just a place with the poor and their villains and no ascertainable history. He need never know anything about it beyond what he could see.

When he heard about Tom's old flame who thought she was being followed, George said that a spot of surveillance was okay by him. Blind eyes would be turned. They were both detective-sergeants but George had seniority. He was affably sarcastic about this evidence of Tom's interest in 'the ladies', having a sister called Eve, a not unattractive moon-faced girl whom Tom had met more than once without anything ever coming of it.

'What will she reward you with?' he wanted to know.
'A smile, I expect.'
'You single men are all the same. Thank God you've got Uncle George to keep an eye on you.'

For years after Peel House, he had heard nothing of Swann, who was posted to another division. Tom cultivated the Dale, the long folds of brick and pavement, each with its crime tucked away, and alongside it, if you looked carefully, the corresponding solution.

From plain-clothes work he progressed to CID. The duds who were going to be constables for ever laughed at his eagerness. He specialized. At one time it was bag-snatching. He calculated where the snatchers would be next. Two evenings running he hid in the yard of a pub, near the cemetery gates, where women passed, going to and from a new cinema and parade of shops. In a donkey jacket and brimless hat he passed as a victim of the Depression, humming 'Keep the Home Fires Burning', a wartime song that had haunted him at school: 'Though your lads are far away, they dream of home,' the cold rising up his legs.

On the second day he saw a figure among the graves – 'There's a silver lining through the dark cloud shining, Turn the dark cloud inside out, till the boys come home,' and he thought of Ellis Crabb living in luxury somewhere, having done his bit to disfigure the England the boys came home to.

A woman approached, the figure was at the gates, Tom hesitated, the woman screamed, and he ran across the road just as headlights flickered and a motorcar with a maniac at the wheel screeched up.

The thief, a short man in boots, was still wrestling with his victim. Shadows danced on the cemetery wall. With a yell, the thief broke her grip, and Tom leapt at him, only to be whacked between the legs by the handbag.

When the pain eased, he was kneeling on the pavement,

and the thief had turned into a gang of four men. A hand cuffed him and a voice said, 'Come along, my son. You're nicked.'

The woman was cradling the handbag as if it was a baby. 'It's all over, ma'am,' a voice was telling her. 'You can tell your husband you met the Flying Squad.'

'He's back in the cemetery,' gasped Tom. 'Ask her.'

The woman was trembling with shock. They hit him again and flung him in the back of the car. He began to repeat his name and number.

The man in the driver's seat looked in the mirror. 'Shine a light on him,' he said, and then, 'It's true. It's Tom Penbury-Holt. Christ, Tom! I'm George Swann. We were at Peel House in 'twenty-four.'

In a second they were amiable men, anxious to make amends. 'This is Dickie Sullivan, knows all the race gangs. Mush Phillips, he'd arrest his grandmother. That's Old Father Brown, consoling the victim. He's the one brings tears to people's eyes. With the end of his boot.'

They picked up the thief at the far entrance. Old Father Brown took him into an alley and punched his ribs to make him produce his cash – something over four pounds inside his socks, and more under a strip of sticking plaster in his armpit. They left the armpit money as evidence, but took the rest, and Sullivan divided it by five. Tom refused his share. The detective shrugged his shoulders and redivided it.

George said not to worry, it all went to pay informants with, so that broadly speaking it was honest. And they handed the prisoner over to Tom so he could take the credit, a gesture that George insisted on.

Thereafter they were friends. Piss-ups with Yard detectives were part of his education, George said. C8 was always looking for the cream of the divisions to work in the big motorcars – villains like the cemetery thief were rubbish when you were Flying Squad. 'I'll see your name gets dropped in the right ears,' said George, and apparently he did. There was even Eve, the sister, who taught geography and physical training out in Kent.

Life in C8 was privileged. Catching villains was all that mattered. Tom caught his share, unimpressed by the calibre of London's smash-and-grab thieves, the latest speciality. He had his eye on the Fraud Squad. Once, on late duty in the office, he used a pass-key to open up the Fraud Registry and read the Ellis Crabb files. The last reliable sighting was in Vienna, 1928. After that the file was empty. His application to move to Fraud was ignored. George said he was mad to think of it. Flying Squad had all a man desired. When Tom said you met a better class of criminal in Fraud, George didn't realize he was serious.

As for the present Sibli business, that was child's play. Mobile units led flexible lives. Tom detached a man from his car and so did George. Soon they were reporting that Mrs James Somerset had a shadow when she went shopping or met a friend for lunch. He in turn was followed to a detective bureau in Islington. His name was O'Hara. 'Keep after him,' said Tom, hoping to identify the client. But the result was a scuffle in Jermyn Street, when O'Hara challenged the Flying Squad man, who threatened to arrest him and waved his warrant card. 'Bloody fool,' said Tom, and stopped the operation.

'You are a marvel,' said Sibli, when they met briefly in a teashop. 'What would you suggest I do?'

'Lead a blameless life?'

'Or give him something to get his teeth into.'

'That's your affair, Sibby. Or ma'am, I ought to say.'

'I always liked you very much, you know,' and the red fingernails touched his sleeve. 'You think I behaved shabbily. Perhaps I did. There's no reason now why we shouldn't be friends.'

'None. Except we have our own lives.'

'Did you ever catch the man who swindled your father?'

'Ellis Crabb? I dream about him sometimes. He's in handcuffs. The Boss slugs him with a ruler.'

'You're sure to find him in the end.'

'That's a romantic view of crime.'

Tom wasn't pleased to find that she still had the same power to stir up his life. Doing her a favour had not been wise. O'Hara lodged a complaint with the Solicitor's Office. It was thrown out, as complaints always were, but Tom was implicated and had to see the Assistant Commissioner (Crime). This was Brigadier Hamilton, a sallow man with a dent in his chin who said that women were at the root of half the trouble they had with young officers.

'This person on whose behalf you risked letting a little squirt of a private detective get us over a barrel, is she your fiancée?'

'No, sir. I knew her years ago.'

'Ah. Before your marriage.'

'I am not married, sir.'

'You are twenty-five years old. You're sure you are not being blackmailed?'

'It was a kindness for an old friend, sir. Misplaced, I now realize.'

The AC(C) shuffled papers. 'You will receive a reprimand,' he said, 'and be suspended for two weeks without pay. It will go on your record, but you can live it down. And remember this. A married man fits in better with the force.'

George organized a major piss-up at the Grapes to commiserate. There was the usual ribaldry about bits of skirt. Tom put up with it. He didn't get reeling drunk. Nor did George.

'Talk to you about marriage, did he?' said George.

'As a matter of fact, yes.'

'He's famous for it. Notice the mark on his chin? They say his wife did that with a bronze Buddha when she went barmy out in India. Mind you, he's right about the Met liking men with a Mrs. Or rather, not liking them without one.'

George's wife Hilda was pregnant for the second time.

Tom, who lived in digs across the river from Scotland Yard, occasionally went there to supper. Now George had him back for a slice of brisket, and he found that George's sister Eve had been invited as well.

This time her light dress and sharp lips made her more appealing than he remembered. School had broken up for the summer. She talked about a hiking holiday in the Lakes that had fallen through. He said he was having a sort of holiday himself. Perhaps they could meet. In the background, like a chorus, George fussed over his wife, who sat with splayed legs, knitting.

Next day they played tennis in a park, and that evening he took her back to the boarding house for an hour – visitors were assumed not to misbehave as long as there was daylight. She let him kiss her, and they sat on the bed, watching sunset fill the air with scarlet smoke, like dust burning.

'George thinks you're great,' she murmured. 'He says the only question is which of you'll be Commissioner first.'

'Did he tell you I'd been suspended for two weeks? That's why I'm on holiday.'

'He thinks of you like a brother,' she said, swaying against him. 'What did you do? Something unmentionable?'

'Misused police resources for my own ends.'

'I wouldn't be surprised if George fiddles things sometimes.'

'George is a fine officer.'

'Oh, you men,' she smiled, 'you're all the same, out for what you can get. All wanting your own way. I don't know I'd trust you if you weren't George's friend.'

He liked being flirted with. There had been two or three women along the way, but none he cared about much. His career was more important. He had never forgotten Sibli's precept about 'escaping'.

Next day he said he had decided to use his enforced holiday to go to Vienna. There was someone he wanted to trace. It would be nicer not to have to go on his own.

'Separate rooms, mind!' she said.

They stayed at a hotel in the suburbs that Aunt Esther told him was popular with the English. The sleeping arrangements were not relaxed. Eve didn't believe in men taking liberties. In the mornings they met at the gloomy baths in the basement, where she outswam him every time, gliding through the water with her limbs going like pistons. Then coffee and crescent rolls, their hair still damp, and the excitement of the day ahead, in a foreign country, with a woman, even a woman who wouldn't sleep with you.

They visited the apartment where Crabb once lived, and the post office where Crabb had received poste restante letters. Tom's warrant card gave him access to a friendly police inspector, though he knew no more than was in the Fraud Squad files. But it was enough to taste the city where Crabb had lived, to examine the apartment (now occupied by a dentist) where the fugitive had looked out over railway lines to the Süd-Bahnhof.

Tom was lucky, too. A middle-aged American with a spotted bow tie and homely pink cheeks, who was staying at the hotel, attached himself to them on their last evening, and tried to sell them half an acre of beautiful Florida countryside, as illustrated in a coloured brochure. He thought they were a young English couple with money, on an illicit holiday – he chuckled about the 'naughty young people of today', and told them as a friend that any plot of land within a mile of the Dixie Highway was going to treble in value in no time.

What a shame, said Tom, they were returning to London next day. The kindly American saw no problem. Why, he planned to be in London himself in a matter of weeks. Perhaps Tom would care to leave him a trifling deposit?

It was a gamble, giving him anything, but worth a pound or two. The American duly turned up in London, and Tom was able to direct the Fraud Squad to a syndicate of loaders, selling swamp land to unsuspecting Europeans.

'You're the lad who applied to come here last year,' said the Guv'nor at Fraud. 'What were you doing in Vienna?'

Tom told him about Crabb. The Guv'nor remembered the case. 'So you're *that* Penbury-Holt,' he said. 'Let me see, you were on the carpet the other day. Over a woman, wasn't it? Fewer opportunities for skirt in my department.'

He made no promises. But George had it from a clerk on the fourth floor that Penbury-Holt would be moving soon. He saw it as defection and was hurt. His delight about Eve ('Where are you taking her next, you rascal?') was compensation. 'Just you keep listening to your Uncle George,' he said.

Tom knew it was all down to Sibli, though. She stirred a chap up and made things happen. Bloody woman, he thought, resenting her power over someone as clever and ambitious as he was. Eve, on the other hand, would make a perfectly good wife.

CHAPTER 22

Unsatisfactory as the marriage was, or became, Sibli had remained faithful for years; six, in fact. It seemed more. James's life was ruled by abstinence. His explanation was that he had no option. A sensuous nature had to be kept under control. He liked to draw attention to his diet. A sort of case could be based on the bananas. They had to be perfect — as firm as celery but moist enough to clog the teeth. When he munched them in that condition he closed his eyes, wallowing in banana. Omelettes could be used to elaborate the case. Every omelette had to have a middle that was sticky but not watery. Ten seconds either way was fatal. But when the thing was done properly, James gave groans of pleasure between mouthfuls.

A man could drown in food, he said. Still worse, he could drown in sexual intercourse. 'My little demon knows my weaknesses,' he said to her in the state-room of the ship that took them south and east on their honeymoon, establishing a theme to which he returned many times in their married life. He was easily tempted. Her naked body electrified him. If he wasn't careful, he warned, he would be in a frenzy all night. Let their bodies have all the sexual intercourse they desired, and the act would become self-destructive. Sibli learned it was no use making light-hearted remarks like 'Let's try it and see, shall we?' James would reply that he knew himself better than she did.

As with the bananas, there was a certain amount of support for his case. He was easily aroused. He had a carnal way of sniffing and snuffling. His eyes rolled and he left bruises on her skin. Afterwards he was racked with shivers. Sometimes he hurried from her bedroom, covering himself with his hands to hide the shame of another bout of arousal – except that this performance always had an air of charade, and she wasn't sure what the hands were hiding, if anything. But apart from his peculiarities about abstinence, he was a skilful lover. That, and a pride in being able to conform to a standard when she made up her mind, kept her faithful. The flirtations she allowed herself never came to much.

On Saturdays she and James might do it twice, preferably in the afternoon. It was his favourite occasion. In Latvia, in other times, there was an orthodoxy about intercourse on the Sabbath. Saturday was no longer the Sabbath for James, who was English and Protestant. But he liked to read verses from the Song of Songs. He said his grandparents would have done so before intercourse.

She always remembered one Saturday in their rooms at the top of the house in Highgate, far from servants and telephones. Greenish light fell on the walls, filtered through branches of trees. When he reached the verse about 'Honey and milk are under thy tongue; and the smell of thy garments is like the smell of Lebanon,' he produced a pair of her stockings, which he must have put there in readiness, and waved them in the air. She had been touched; even amazed, as perhaps she was meant to be.

Once she was married, Sibli no longer felt the need to experiment. Marriage was marriage, the most described condition on earth. Every possible variety had been experienced already: the sublime, the convenient, the foul, the comic. You had to hope for the best and see what yours was going to be.

Hers turned out to be well-meaning. James tried to make her happy, given his nature and the demands of running a film company when history was against him. He wept when 'dialogue movies' came in. Soon he was speaking familiarly of 'the talkies'. But the new technology gave the Americans even more advantages than they had already.

The crisis in films became a permanent feature. Sibli was allowed to contribute nothing except a wife's patience. Did he suspect boredom on her part? He must have suspected something, to have her followed by a detective. It was true that she still saw one or two men friends who had been her lovers, including dear old Daniel at the gallery, but she didn't sleep with them any more. By suspecting her of misbehaviour he put the thought in her mind.

To make things worse, he denied knowledge of any detective. All he needed to do was say, 'Yes, I had an aberration, forgive me,' and she would have been halfway to being fond of him again. That was when it occurred to her that her affection for him had been ebbing for some time.

America would be a change. Taking her there on a short business trip was a gesture. They had been happy in America on previous visits. She liked leaving Europe behind. On the boat they made love on week-nights, which was encouraging, and she had hopes for the future. Copies of the *New York Week* were brought on board when they were in the Bay, and Sibli, reading it while they waited to go ashore, saw that Theodore Lloyd was giving recitals at the Steinway Hall.

On the pier, walking to the Customs shed, James said, 'I want you to have a wonderful holiday. Oswald will look after you. He is like my son.'

'You and I can spend the evenings together.'

'Some evenings. But Oswald will plan entertainments.'

'Oh, by the way,' she said, and mentioned the recital. She was testing him. James said, 'Wasn't he your old flame?'

'A long time ago. He's more famous now. I'd be interested to know what he's turned into.'

'We shall go together and you can tell me. Better still, I will throw a supper party afterwards.'

He gave her nothing to complain of. A few nights later they listened to Theodore playing Schubert to a full house, and she tried to remember how she once felt, hearing him play when she was in love with him. What she had perceived then as the torment of an artist trying to get the better of a piano had shrunk to a severe, slightly bloodless manner. His eyes still glittered. 'Very polished,' said James, but she wondered if something had been lost. Or had the old Theodore been a trick of the light?

At the party, at Reuben's, he was as exuberant as ever. He told his host that unfortunately he saw few films, to which James replied that modern man ought to find time for new manifestations of art if he was not to become antediluvian. A film man from the Coast shouted, 'Right!' Theodore said, 'Art my arse!' and turned to someone's wife.

Fanny was not with him. His companion was an American woman with black hair like curtains down the sides of her face. Later he introduced her to Sibli, saying, 'Peggy understands nothing about music. That suits me. Art is for artists. I learned that from Sibli. She despised my art. I thought I hated her at one time. But she is unusually sensible for a beautiful woman.'

'Still the same pig, I see,' said Sibli.

'She and I are Welsh. We understand one another. I met her when she broke into my house in South Wales and did criminal damage to a piano.'

'Have you ever brought your parents anywhere to hear you play?'

'I think Bristol, once. They dislike travel. The old girl is poorly these days and the old boy wouldn't know a piano from a pilot boat. And how is your dear father? This is going to shock Peggy. Sibli's old man runs the Aeolian Press in Paris – forbidden books, printed in English.'

'I expect you buy them when you're there.'

'Under the filth is the art. Or is it the other way round?'

That was as much Theodore as she could stand. 'He likes hurting people. Just be warned,' were her last words to Peggy.

As the party ended, James told her he was catching the midnight train to Chicago. 'Something has come up tonight,' he said, refused to let her accompany him, and sent her back to the hotel with Oswald.

The suite was flooded with light, as she had left it. From the balcony she could see the reds and greens of shipping in the East River. Rain was falling. She was not tired. James's pyjamas were laid out on his bed like a corpse. The telephone rang. Oswald was asking to see her, if it was not too late.

'Of course,' she said.

He was there in a moment. The fault was entirely his. That lovely brooch, the wolf's head with diamonds, was not insured outside the United Kingdom. He had just been checking the papers.

'Do sit down,' she said. 'Those suits of yours always look as if they weigh a ton.'

A negligent clerk was the culprit, but he, Oswald, bore the responsibility. Mr Somerset gave it her only last year. The lapse was unforgivable. He would take the brooch with him now, and put it in the hotel safe.

She asked if there was nothing else; offered him a cigarette; saw his cheeks wobble as he sucked in the smoke, sitting on the edge of the club chair; wondered why he had come.

'You are like a son to James,' she said. 'He often uses the phrase.'

'He conceives the firm as a family.'

'My husband's a lucky man. What son would check insurance papers at one o'clock in the morning?'

'I have this sense of my inadequacy,' he said, and looked at her slyly through the smoke.

'Do you have a life of your own? I've often wondered.'

'I think I should go,' he said. 'It may not be safe, my being here.'

She pondered this. 'You mean not safe for me? Or for you?'

'For both of us. Please give me the brooch and I shall go.'

She proposed a theory to him. Her husband suspected they were having an affair, and Oswald had come to beg her to tell him he was wrong. 'That is a lie and a slander,' said Oswald, gazing at the tip of the cigarette. Then what about this: Oswald had been sent to see if she could be seduced. 'You are going too far, even for my employer's wife,' said Oswald. 'I am like a son, remember.'

So why was it not safe?

'Surely it's obvious, Mrs Somerset. Hotels are all eyes and ears. If someone reported me as visiting you, your husband might jump to conclusions.'

But you came, for all that.

He wriggled, bottom barely scraping the cushion. One is aware of one's inadequacies, Mrs Somerset.

The game had to be played through to the end. Sibli left him in the drawing-room while she went for the brooch; stripped naked and put on a negligee; returned with the brooch in its case, her legs and arms bare.

Jumping up, he tried not to look at her. The main beam of his gaze was over her shoulder, with quick glances downwards. 'This won't do, you know.'

'But you are incorruptible. You are like a son, etcetera.'

'He thinks I'm a robot. They all do.'

Then he made the lurch that might have been expected. She had to move quickly, to keep a table with a bowl of flowers between them.

'You wouldn't betray him,' she said. 'Unless you were following instructions. I wanted to be sure, that was all.'

'As if one could ever be sure of anything,' he said

sharply, and left in such a hurry, he forgot the brooch.

No doubt behaving badly gave clues to the state of a marriage. It made little difference whether the bad behaviour at any one time was his or hers. On the return journey to England, James kept to their quarters, another suite of rooms. Oswald and a stenographer came and went. Invitations arrived to cocktail parties. Attending one alone, a reception given by the staff captain, Sibli eyed a second officer with a beaky nose, and contemplated an affair before they reached Southampton.

Three days out of New York, she danced with the same officer at the Mid Atlantic Gala Ball. His hands felt as if they were on her bare skin, they were so fiery. In her mind she was being unfaithful already. Anger at James was at the root of it. As the band got going with a Charleston, her dress and his trousers came in for some friction. The officer's cheeks got redder.

Then she saw James, who hated dances, staring across the floor. He waved the palm of his hand.

Perhaps Oswald had been spying. A certain amount of dancing with James was necessary; she never saw the officer again. Later an odd scene took place in the cabin. Her husband wanted to have her, she wanted not to be had. He knelt before her, clawing at her underclothes, telling her that her arousal was all too apparent. It seemed to excite him. Sibli saw this as a clue to things she hadn't learnt about him yet. Was spying on her a game that appealed to him? Men were strange. Some of men's strangenesses she enjoyed, some she didn't. She said, 'I'm like ice now. Just like ice,' and he got off his knees and locked himself in his cabin.

In the Western Approaches, grey weather caught up with them. She sat on deck, under cover, with a blanket over her legs, reading a novel and drinking the steward's beef tea in a dream as the ocean slid between her feet. In theory one might seduce the captain. He had joined them at their table on the first night. He was a Texan with long legs. But it was too late. The weather smelt of England already.

Oswald brought a message from her husband. He had been neglecting her – Oswald spoke the words, avoiding her eye. He had arranged to visit the navigation bridge before lunch. He hoped she would join him. 'Please tell him I have another engagement,' she said, and slipped into the cinema to see Helen Honey in a new Britannia movie, *A Woman's Fury*.

The talkies had not been kind to Helen. Her role was a jilted typist, out for revenge. The voice sounded shrill, like a child's. A man in the audience laughed briefly. When the lights came on she turned to see who it was. He was leaving – a thin figure, the quarter-face view familiar.

By the time she caught up with him he was in the shopping arcade, looking at the men's blazers and fountain pens.

'Davis?' she said. 'It is Stephen Davis, isn't it?'

He turned and nodded. The face was darkened, almost unshaven.

'I'm Sibli.'

'So you are.'

Pictures rippled in her head. The peat fire blazed up at Macroom and soldiers burst into the room. She seemed to have forgotten nothing, especially the bitterness of knowing that Davis didn't want her, kindly offered on a plate. It was a child's bitterness. She forgave herself, not to mention Davis.

'I see your name in the papers now and then,' she said. 'You wrote a fiery article when the Prince of Wales went to Durham.'

'My editor had hopes of him and the unemployed. But he was just a boy with courtiers at his heels.' The hand gestured as it used to. 'And you went and married a tycoon.'

A voice said in her ear, 'So this is where my demon is.'

James had been shopping. Oswald the shadow was beside him, clasping parcels. 'You should have accompanied me to the bridge,' he said. 'I took the wheel for several minutes. One might set a movie on board an ocean liner.'

'This is Stephen Davis, the journalist. He used to be one of Pa's authors. I've known him for years.'

'Almost since she was a child,' said Davis, and might have been laughing at her.

'Do you write about the entertainment business, Mr Davis?'

'One of the few subjects I seem to have missed.'

'He's what they call a roving correspondent.'

'Is that a romantic thing to be, Mr Davis? Please join us for lunch. I love to hear others expound their *Weltanschauung*.'

Sibli's anger with her husband didn't go away. In the dining saloon, the pink-shaded lights on the big circular tables had been lit, it was so grey outside. Parties clustered around them, tearing bread rolls and studying menus. Davis smoked a black cigarette and asked a steward for coffee instead of a cocktail.

'The last time Davis and I met was in Ireland,' she said. 'I can't have been more than sixteen, or was it seventeen? We ate supper together by a peat fire.'

'Coal, actually,' said Davis. 'Less romantic than peat.'

'I thought Ireland was the most romantic place I'd ever been.'

'Oswald will obtain some of your articles. I shall enjoy reading them.'

Other passengers who shared the table arrived, and found they were short of a chair. Oswald told the senior steward to lay an extra place for Mr Stephen Davis, and Davis smiled and said that coffee was all he ever took for lunch.

'We seem to be two of a kind,' said James, indicating

his milk and bananas, and Sibli said she didn't think so, as she had a clear memory of Davis enjoying alcohol and red meat.

Presently the steward returned with a list and bent over Davis. His whisper could be heard, apologizing for the muddle, wanting to know where Mr Davis's usual table was.

'Table Six,' said Davis affably. 'In the Second Class, that is.'

'It makes things a little awkward, sir,' said the steward, glancing at James, who said, 'I daresay you can make an exception.'

'I shall have to see the purser. I'm sorry, Mr Somerset.'

'You have your duty.'

Sibli suspected her husband was enjoying it. 'What difference does it make?' she said.

'Ocean liners have to show profits. Mr Davis understands.'

'My fault entirely,' he said. 'I was trespassing. You have smarter shops up here, and the cinema shows the new films. I saw some real rubbish this morning, *A Woman's Fury*.'

James looked at the tablecloth. For a moment Sibli felt protective, as a wife should. 'James's company made that picture,' she said. 'I am a fan of Helen Honey's.'

'I am no film critic,' said Davis, and drank the last of his coffee.

'I have taken no offence, Mr Davis.'

'I'd better be off, all the same.'

Sibli went with him as far as the deck. Small vessels were strung out against the horizon. 'Trawlers,' said Davis. 'Nearly home.'

'Who do you write for these days?'

'Anyone who'll have me.'

'You're very self-deprecating.'

'Just honest.'

They shook hands and he seemed about to say something more than goodbye, but didn't. Dispirited, she went back to lunch and the remnants of her marriage.

James was either unaware of how she felt, or chose ignorance as the best way of coping with the change that had come over them. Any more sleeping together was out of the question. Back in London, she felt the pressure of his jealousy. One day in a quarrel she hinted at the propositions from men that she had turned down in six years, but instead of being impressed by her fidelity, or at least interested in it (probably he thought she was lying), he wanted to know what she thought about when men made advances to her.

He demanded indecent details, down to the question of whether a woman confronted with a predatory pair of trousers thought about what was inside them.

'You know as well as I, woman are as libidinous as men.'

At once he wanted to know about the second officer on the ship. Had she entertained lewd thoughts?

What they seemed to be discussing was a husband's fantasies, not a wife's chastity. After one or two conversations on these lines, Sibli found herself increasingly tempted to go out and commit some straightforward adultery. But she did nothing.

James took to pretending that he didn't mind their not sleeping together – he understood, she was learning the virtues of self-control. He went to Brailsham Abbey for a week. When he returned, with a bad back and scratches on his arms, he was still muttering about abstinence.

That night he tried to smash her door down. They might have talked in the morning, but he was off early to the studios. Her breakfast tray included a bowl of his bananas with a note that said, 'Who is she that looketh forth as the morning, fair as the moon, clear as the sun, and terrible as an army with banners? This can't go on. J.'

The bedroom door had marks on the paint where he had kicked it. A separation was coming closer. She wanted to disguise it. Telephoning Pa, with a few days in Paris in mind, she found herself being asked to go to Port Howard, where Villette Lloyd had just died. 'Theodore's mother,' said Pa.

'I know who Villette is. She's your aunt, not mine.'

'Me attending her funeral is out of the question. Your Aunt Margaret has sent two telegrams and telephoned, trying to appeal to my better nature.'

'She wants you back there, that's all. The funeral's an excuse. Come on, Pa. You might enjoy a visit.'

'Port Howard is the entrance to Hades as far as I'm concerned. I wouldn't go back to it for ten thousand pounds. No, you go on my behalf. You like the place.'

'I suppose you're consistent. I hope you're making pots of money.'

'You should see our new *Decameron* with colour plates,' and she imagined him winking at Rebecca Smollett. 'Very artistic. I shall send you one. Let's hope Customs don't open it.'

Sibli left a letter, telling her husband where she had gone, and went off to the shabby coast, beginning with a call on her mother. Approaching the house by taxi, the power station in the Strand showed gleams of light through its blackened windows. A bald man with rimless glasses stood on the steps, staring at her as the taxi bounced over the cobbles. The glance said, I shall have improper thoughts about you later.

Her stepfather was in the yard, helping a driver lift tarpaulins on to a lorry. He held his arms out sideways when she kissed him, so as not to mess up her clothes.

'Well, you're a stranger,' he said, and called, 'Albert!' to some children playing in a lorry without wheels by the fence. Sibli's half-brother ran over and greeted her. His accent was as thick-vowelled as his father's. The dark eyes were the same as hers, but there was nothing else to read into him.

Aeronwy wasn't at home. Griff washed his hands while

the maid brought tea into the parlour, then slyly offered her a measure of whisky from his bottle in the cupboard, as if it was what London visitors expected at four in the afternoon.

'Just tea,' she said.

'Your Ma has gone to Port Howard, to be with Abraham till after tomorrow. Margaret asked her to. He's not safe to be on his own. They want him up at the Castle, only he won't go.'

Albert munched cake, keeping his eyes on her. 'Is Auntie Sibli going to stay with us?' he asked.

'Not this time, Champion.'

'Just "Sibli" will do,' she said. 'We're brother and sister, you and I.'

'He knows all right, but he gets flummoxed. "Half-brother" is the puzzle, isn't it, Champion? "Which half?" he said to me.'

By stepping into the frame of their lives she became someone different. She was what they perceived her to be. Leaving the house for the waiting taxi, she could give Albert sixpence and look mean, or a ten-shilling note and look ostentatious. In the end she gave him a pound, at the same time hugging and kissing him, telling him he was her best boy; Welsh sister for a change instead of Highgate wife.

She could be what she chose to be. By the time she reached Port Howard and the Castle, the game was faster and more dangerous. All the things that Margaret wouldn't ask about lay in wait, things about happiness and husbands.

But Margaret wasn't there for the moment.

'Mrs Mappowder is still at the works, madam,' said Hilda, the housekeeper. 'There has been a difficulty with an engine. She says to tell you she will be here in time for supper. The Major is down at Pendine at present. Lady Mappowder is abroad. You have your usual room.'

The house echoed with memories. The lie of loved places

was that nothing changed. The maid ran water in the bath that was like a storage tank, testing the temperature with a thermometer. 'What clothes shall I put out for madam?'

'I've changed my mind,' said Sibli. A car was borrowed, and she drove down to Bank Cottages, the row of dwellings beyond the copperworks where Abraham and Villette had lived all their married lives. Evening sunlight coloured the estuary. As she walked up the cinder path to the back door, she saw Abraham at an upstairs window, looking out to sea. He didn't respond when she waved.

'Barmy, of course,' said Ma. 'Well, fancy you coming here. There isn't much for supper. I was going to boil a piece of cod.' A cigarette pointed down from her mouth, almost burning her chin. 'He can't be left. He's not been right for years. Not since the Joe business. He used to go out in a rowing boat and talk to him, did you know that? Villette put a stop to it. Well, it was terrible, people used to notice.'

'Does he know that she's died?'

'I suppose he must. She's at the chapel of rest, we didn't want her here. He's restless. About six times today he's said, "I think I'll go out in the boat now." I've had to keep the door locked. He's very gentle, mind.'

Sibli asked if Theodore had come down for the funeral.

'They say he's in Italy. You can't come all the way from Italy for a funeral.' Coughing, Aeronwy leaned on the sink, streaky grey hair falling over her eyes. 'Nobody would expect it.' When Sibli found an apron and said she would make supper, Ma said, 'Right you are,' and put her feet up between two chairs.

As usual her mother wanted to know about London, about film premieres and dinner parties and trips abroad. 'James must be a proud man,' she said. Sibli's 'mm' would have been enough to alert Margaret, but Mother floated away on clouds of imagination about the life she never had.

'Mind you,' she said, 'Griff is a fine man. Best of all,

he gave me little Albert.' She squinted at a match-flame, applying it to a new Craven A. 'I lost you to your Aunt Margaret years ago. Don't look, you know it's true. You always thought I was a funny sort of mother. I daresay I was. Not surprising, all things considered. So it's nice to have Albert, even if he was a bit late coming.'

The cod was ready. Dusk came over the marshes, enveloping sheds and chimneys. Sibli went upstairs for Abraham. He hadn't moved.

'It's Sibli,' she said. 'You remember? Morgan's daughter. There's some nice fish for supper.'

'Joe and me trail a line over the Shelly Pool just when the flood is coming on. You need patience. What's the hurry, Joe always says. Flats as big as dinner plates we get.'

She supposed they would put him in an institution, or move him forcibly to the Castle and hire a nurse; a locked room, anyway. Not that he was anything to her.

'I saw Theodore in America,' she said, curious to see how he would respond.

'Who's that?'

'Your son, Theodore.'

'Joe is my son,' he said. His forehead touched the pane and made it rattle. 'Joe is the world to me. Always was.'

She stood beside him, her arm around the bent shoulders. The crust of hair against the glass was as white as lamb's wool.

'His cod is on the plate,' Aeronwy shouted.

'Can you still row a boat?'

'Spot of rheumatism, that's all.'

'I'll fix something. But keep it to yourself. Our secret, all right?'

'Should be a fine day tomorrow.'

Sibli forgot about him till the next morning. Her evening with Margaret skated on thin ice. She was the nearly-daughter, the broken promise, the disappointment. When they spoke about Villette and the tragedy of Theodore's indifference to his parents, it raised the ghost of Sibli's affair with him; they soon changed the subject. James and the film industry were safe enough, but children would not have been. Sibli knew there were unspoken questions about her childlessness. Margaret had failed to have the children she wanted. Sibli, it appeared, didn't want them at all. No doubt she took *precautions*, an art probably perfected before she became a married woman. That was the way of the *promiscuous*. But these were only guesses on Sibli's part. She had no means of telling what Margaret really thought.

The funeral was at two o'clock. Margaret had to be in court all morning, presiding over the bench. She was finishing her breakfast when Sibli came down.

Aubrey, his *Times* propped against the sugar, looked at the clock and said, 'A red mark in the register for you, my girl. Your aunt has been here quarter of an hour.'

'Your uncle has been here about three minutes, so he's only guessing. I have to look in at the works.'

Sibli asked if it was all right to borrow a car again. She had some shopping to do. If Abraham Lloyd was being brought up to the Castle, so that Mother could go to the funeral, she would collect him herself.

'He won't budge. I'm sending Hilda down to sit with him.'

'I think I can talk him into it.'

'His mind has quite gone. Villette, on the other hand, was alert to the end.'

Aubrey slid a package across the table. 'Your mail, Mrs Somerset. You will observe the French stamps. A book, I would say.'

Margaret said nothing. She watched Sibli use a fruit scissors to cut the string. It was *Tales from the Decameron*, by Boccaccio. Two copies were inside, handsome volumes, with the Aeolian Press's colophon of a harp. One was inscribed: 'To Sibli, from her loving Father.' The other said: 'To Maggs, from Someone in exile.'

Sibli turned the pages. The coloured frontispiece showed a young woman kneeling under the eye of a hook-nosed Turk, face near the ground, haunches thrust invitingly under a wisp of gauze. 'Pa's going in for the classics,' she said brightly.

'If the string had broken at the post office we should have had the police round,' said Margaret.

'More fools the police.'

'The laws exist. We have to respect them.'

'Have you seen the plate on page eighty-five? Golly!'

'I'll leave you and your uncle to study them. There will be a light luncheon here at twelve-thirty. After the funeral, the mourners will come back for refreshments. Some of the Harbour Trust will be there. People from the pilotage and shipping. The Lloyds used to be quite well known in the town.'

'The men had pictures like these in the trenches,' said Aubrey, when she had gone. He turned the pages. 'A bit cruder, perhaps. Twenty years ago a man couldn't have looked at these in the presence of a woman. How things have changed. I hope you and Margaret are still friends.'

'Perhaps I should come to Wales more often.'

'It would bore you. Have no illusions. But then, you don't, do you?'

Sibli took it as a compliment. They strolled down the terraces and found the gazebo where, as a schoolgirl, she had seen Aubrey kiss his wife. Beyond the town, bars of light and mist alternated on the Bay. 'Stay a few days and come racing,' said Aubrey. 'We can touch two hundred on the sand now.'

Half an hour later she was at Bank Cottages again. Abraham had resumed his place at the upstairs window. This time he wore a pilot-jacket and a faded blue cap with a peak.

Ma was looking forward to the funeral, though worried about her hat. 'I've got this idea,' said Sibli. 'I am taking him up to the Castle – don't tell me he won't come, because he will. I'll drop you off at Morris the Realm and you can shop for an hour.' She put a banknote in her mother's handbag. 'I didn't bring you back anything from New York, so get the hat and whatever else you want. When you've finished, tell them to fetch the station taxi, and go straight up to the Castle.'

'If you insist,' said Aeronwy, peeping in the handbag to see how much it was.

All she had to do now was get Abraham out of the house. He stood holding a browned photograph in a frame. A boy with the face of a genial monkey showed sepia teeth to the camera, posed on a quay with the bows of a ship behind him.

'I just remember him,' she said.

'He remembers you,' said Abraham, and put the picture in his pocket.

'Will you trust me?'

He nodded, and followed her downstairs. In five minutes they were in Stepney Street. Mother disappeared into Morris the Realm. Trams hissed by, making sparks. Five minutes more, and the car was at Y Plas. Seagulls sat along the apex of the roof. Thistles were invading the courtyard. Through the trees, the inlet was grey and windless.

'There's a key by here,' said Abraham, and lifted a brick. He opened a coach-house where gardening tools were stored. A dinghy on wheels with the oars inside stood against a wall. They dragged it out. Through the side gate, the sea was twenty yards away.

The muddy tide was ebbing. The wheels rested in the water.

'Sure, now?' said Sibli.

'Don't want to keep Joe waiting.' He smiled at the empty boat and pushed it free. Water came over his boots.

'We need a bit of a shove,' he said, and she took off her stockings, tucking up her dress. Abraham settled himself in the bows, holding an oar to push against the mud.

Wading out, both hands on the stern, she felt the boat lighten and surge forward. She heard Abraham say, 'Morgan's daughter is who she is.'

Already he was pulling hard, long strokes that drew him away. The sound of his voice drifted back. She caught a word here and there, something about sea walls, something about 'old Buckley's'. When he was clear of the flooded marsh, in the open bay, he was still going strong, heading straight out from the land. At her feet, a crab dissolved in mud.

She no longer had a key to enter Y Plas. The house looked what it was, old and inconvenient, built for a tin-plate master, stranded now at the wrong end of town. A gap in the drawing-room curtains let her glimpse the piano, dust-sheeted in the gloom.

Parking the car near the market, Sibli killed more time in the crowded aisles, between tables laid out with the famous produce – fat chickens, green and white vegetables, live cockles, salt butter. The farm women were still outlandish, foreigners from ten miles away in men's caps and blue aprons. She remembered Villette Lloyd saying, 'Port Howard market when it's busy would be a splendid scene to paint, if the town had a decent painter. It's a big if. This is Wales so all we have is choirs.'

By the time Margaret's luncheon on-the-dot was being served, it was safe to appear at the Castle. Ma was composed inside a veiled hat like a saucepan. Her aunt's face was blank with anger. Where had she been? Where was Abraham?

When Sibli explained about the rowing boat, Margaret exclaimed under her breath and Aubrey put the water-jug down. Ma lifted her veil higher, not to miss anything. A maid served potatoes, steaming cheerfully, which no one ate in the end but Sibli. Aubrey went off to help his wife, who was making telephone calls and dispatching people. Half the town seemed to be involved – police, coastguard, the lifeboat at Pembrey, the harbourmaster, anyone with a yacht.

Sibli had her lunch, watched by Ma, who was too excited to touch a thing.

'Was he talking to himself?' she said. 'Let's hope he doesn't land up on the beach where people can see him, today of all days.'

The funeral became an interlude in the search for Abraham. From the cemetery the harbour tug could be seen off the coast, leaving coils of smoke as it went up and down, as if it was mowing the sea.

Tea was under way at the Castle before news came, brought by a police sergeant on a motor-bike. A fishing smack, on its way in to Port Howard, had found a dinghy drifting in Carmarthen Bay. They had no proof it was Lloyd's. 'This was under the seat,' he said, and produced the salt-smeared frame with Joe in it. 'Photograph of son of missing person, identified by Mrs Aubrey Mappowder JP,' he wrote in his notebook. An inspector would be up presently to take a statement. There would be an inquest when the body was recovered.

Margaret and Sibli faced one another in the Indian Room, which happened to be the nearest sanctuary when the sergeant had gone. The shutters were closed. Margaret switched on the lights. They were too weak to illuminate all the contents. The scimitars might have been farming implements. The elephant, fortified with wire, was still standing.

'Tell me exactly what happened,' said Margaret.

'I've told you. He felt like going for a row. I was doing him a kindness.'

'You must be very careful what you tell the inquest.'

'I shan't embarrass you, don't worry.'

'It doesn't seem to occur to you that what you did was wrong, morally wrong.'

'It seems to me morally absolutely right.' Sibli didn't want to quarrel, but her aunt's mouth had hardened.

'You sound like your father. He thinks he can interfere with the universe.'

'You can never get Pa out of your system, can you?' cried Sibli, her own anger stirred at last. 'You've always adored him and loathed him at the same time. A bit less of both, and you might have got on better. I don't go in for great expectations. Neither would you if you had any sense.'

'You mustn't come here again,' Margaret said, barely audible.

'I agree. It's better I don't.'

A sixtyish man in a morning coat and striped trousers appeared in the doorway.

'Oh, there you are, Margaret,' he said. 'You know, I haven't been in this room for twenty years, since the old colonel was alive. The Harbour Trust used to meet here sometimes.'

'This is Harold Egge, the chairman. My niece, Mrs Somerset.'

'Morgan's girl. I know. We know everything about Port Howard, isn't that right, Margaret?'

'I fear so.'

'I'm glad you come back sometimes. Always a welcome for you here. The Buckleys were among the founder-fathers.'

Margaret excused herself, leaving Sibli to sit on a dusty sofa with Egge. He kept his deep-set eyes on her and talked about dead Buckleys. 'Pirates,' he said. 'Interesting pirates, mind, and good for trade. Are you a chip off the old block, Mrs Somerset?'

'I do my best.'

'Your father Morgan is a colourful chap.'

'He'd take that as a compliment.'

'Tell me' – a raised finger hesitated near her breast but went away – 'is it true he sells French books?'

'They do, in France.'

'Good God!' He nodded vigorously, as if satisfied to have got to the bottom of a mystery.

Sibli had never felt more self-contained, more alone, more aware of losing James.

The police inspector came; a statement was made. 'That's grand,' he said, already rehearsing her for the Coroner, 'you were merely doing a kindness for an experienced seaman who knew how to handle a boat.'

Her cases were packed. John, the mechanic, was to take her to the station for the evening express, a story having been concocted that she was needed in London unexpectedly. Margaret had made herself scarce. Aubrey cleared his throat and rubbed his cheek.

'Why'd you do it, girl?' he said. 'Your aunt is devastated.'

'I did what was best.'

'She was very fond of the old chap. There were plans to have him up here. He could have had all his mementoes – ships in bottles, all that. There'd have been round-the-clock nursing.'

'He didn't want nurses. I let him go, that was all.'

'People can't take the law into their own hands. No doubt the inquest will paper it over, but it was a terrible thing to happen. Fair do's, Sibli, it wasn't fair to your aunt,' and she saw that all he was doing was protecting Margaret.

Leaving the house quietly looked like being difficult, until a visitor was announced. It was Theodore, all leather coat and helmet. He had driven from Dover.

'Better late than never,' he said. 'Goodness me. Sibli the ubiquitous.'

'I'm afraid we have bad news,' said Aubrey.

'Well, go on.'

'It's your father. There was an accident.'

'I let him go rowing,' said Sibli. 'He's believed drowned.'

'Poor old sod,' said Theodore, and held out his hand for the whisky and soda that Aubrey was mixing. His heavy, cramped features expressed what could have been pain or passing discomfort. He took the drink at a swallow. Margaret appeared and said, 'I'm so glad you came. There is a bed here for you, of course. My dear Theo, what can any of us say?'

John was at the door, his cap under his arm. 'Mrs Somerset will miss the train, sir.'

'Sibli is going?' said Theodore. He held her arm. 'I'll take her.'

'There is no need,' said Margaret.

'But I want to, Maggs, I want to.'

A minute later she and the cases were in an open tourer. 'God knows why I came,' he said, as he steered with one hand, putting his left arm around her shoulders. 'Some desperate long-lost guilt, would you suppose? Then I find you, of all people. Is that my just reward?'

'If you don't drive faster I shall miss the train.'

'If I turn off here it won't matter.'

He drove past a tinworks singed with flame, along the streets where she had been that morning. 'There you are,' he said. 'Y Plas. Home of the concert pianist.'

'I've now missed it.'

'Are you still an adventurer?'

The last of the daylight sank into the slates. He muttered some nonsense about the artist's need of the sensual, fumbling for the door-key like a great savage child. She waited for it to open. She had forgotten how nice it was to escape.

CHAPTER 23

The only person who accepted it all was Pa. Sibli went to stay with him while the divorce was edging towards the law courts at the letter-a-month speed of solicitors. It was enough for Morgan that her husband had entangled her with his foreign peculiarities. One had the right to be unencumbered.

He avoided all practical matters, even the nature of the deal to be struck between husband and wife. The Aeolian Press kept him busy, pumping out illicit orange-wrapped volumes for Anglo-Saxon travellers to take home, folded in with the shirts and socks. If Sibli was prepared to be the erring wife and let James Somerset be the wronged husband, she knew what she was doing. If a secret arrangement had been discussed, to settle some cash on her in return for the evidence required by law, then it was a necessary cog in the torture machine of the divorce court that the English – always the bloody English, to Morgan, cruel and hypocritical – had perfected.

Half their lives were hidden from one another. They didn't make revelations. Their intimacy lay in not interfering. Sibli assumed that Pa slept with Rebecca Smollett, that there were other women, that Virginia Penbury-Holt was probably one of them. No trace of this was allowed to show. A knowing smile would have been unacceptable.

When he went to Boulogne at short notice and was away for a night, Rebecca Smollett put out feelers towards Sibli, suggesting archly that Morgan missed life in London more than he admitted. She cited 'old friends', people like Mr and Mrs Penbury-Holt. 'You know who I mean,' she said, 'Stuart and Virginia.'

'Delightful people,' said Sibli, 'but you must excuse me,' and took the manuscript of *A Street Walker's Tale* that she was marking up for the printer, down to the other end of the drawing-room, where a wooden fan revolved in the ceiling, and she could look out on a side street being hosed down on a bright spring morning.

Occasionally she had to make trips herself, to see her solicitors in London. She had taken a flat in Covent Garden. Letters accumulated and there was always a spider in the bath.

On one visit she tried to get in touch with Helen, only to find she had left Britannia Pictures. Sibli tracked her down to a hotel in Scotland where she was making a film for Piccadilly Features, which no one had ever heard of. 'They were doing such cheap little movies at Britannia,' she said, when Sibli telephoned. 'Honestly, darling, with my reputation I decided enough was enough. This outfit is much classier. We're shooting *Maid of the Glens*. The director is a dish.'

'I'm in Paris most of the time with Pa. Bring your director over.'

'Poor darling, I should have asked about you. Everyone knows James is a pig. I knew from the beginning, but you were loopy over him and I didn't like to interfere. Good riddance, I say.'

If the old Helen would never reappear, the new one had to be taken for what she was. Sibli suggested that what Helen actually knew about James Somerset could be written on a very small piece of paper. Helen said she was not used to being spoken to like that. The telephone went dead.

In Paris, two or three personable men, apparently unattached, showed up at Pa's dinner parties. Sibli was the hostess – a role she guessed that Rebecca resented – and was introduced without comment as 'my daughter Mrs Somerset'.

No one bothered much. Somewhere there was or had been a Monsieur Somerset, but he was absent now. Men with moustaches and interesting eyes kissed her hand, gave her engraved visiting cards with telephone numbers, rang her up and suggested outings, and were rebuffed.

Until the Probate, Divorce and Admiralty Division was ready to crunch up her bones, she found it hard to settle into a normal life of assignations, if that was what lay ahead. Men were still both the problem and the solution. The only dinner-guest she might have been tempted not to rebuff was the director of a printing company, a man in his thirties called Ricard, whose long legs and nervous hands shifted about in her imagination. But he left no card and made no telephone call.

By the time the case was ready to be heard it was 1932 and she had passed her twenty-seventh birthday. Morgan made a business visit to London that week, pretending it was coincidence, but she kept him away from the divorce court. Her solicitor was all she needed.

The courtroom was dark and the wood looked dirty rather than old. All she could see of James was folded arms and a gleam of forehead. The judge had a face like a spaniel. When her letter of admission was read out, he listened with his eyes shut, savouring the words. 'My dear James,' it said, 'I am writing to tell you that I have been unfaithful to you on more than one occasion. If you apply at the Lord Warden Hotel, Dover, you will find evidence (to which the enclosed bill refers) necessary for your divorce action against me.'

The Lord Warden episode had been six months earlier. The man was hired by the solicitor. His pyjamas (blue-and-white stripes) were displayed on the pillow. He spent the night in a chair but was careful to be sitting on the bed with his braces hanging down when the chambermaid came in. She had steeled herself to do it, as she steeled herself now to answer questions and hear the judge refer coldly to 'Mrs Somerset's confession'.

'Shades of ruined women,' she remarked to her solicitor when it was all over, and James had his decree nisi. 'I suppose the papers will be full of it.'

'Don't read them tomorrow. In six months, everyone will have forgotten.'

Morgan took her to the theatre and on to supper, and returned her to Covent Garden. 'Sure you're all right?' he said. 'I still have one or two things to attend to,' and went off in a taxi to some woman somewhere.

By the morning her loneliness had gone. She went out for the papers, a pound of coffee and some croissants. She could hear the phone ringing before she reached the flat, walking slowly upstairs and reading headlines about 'A Wife's Confession'. It rang all morning.

Fanny, Theodore's agent, made a friendly call to say that life went on. Theodore rang from the north and congratulated her. Men she had half forgotten found her number. Laughing as she talked to them, she drew moustaches on the photographs of her and James to stop them looking tragic.

Esther wanted her to know that the divorce laws were a disgrace to a civilized country.

Then a foreign voice, announcing it was Ricard Barjou.

He was in London to visit a printing exhibition. Her dear father had supplied her telephone number. Lunch followed; later a play in the Haymarket. He touched her forearm in the bar. She made herself think of it as sin, just for the pleasure. The shabby red plush and gilt mouldings gave the illusion of a theatre within a theatre. Packed-in men and women swayed about, a crowd scene hinting at sexual intercourse.

She mouthed a greeting at a face she recognized, an American distributor. Ricard was uneasy, not sure what conventions were in force. His English can't have been good enough to read the London papers. 'You are not to worry,' she said, 'I do as I please.' He remained tense, nibbling his lip with wide-spaced teeth, between which were traces of saliva. His mixture of flashiness and nerves was enticing. Adultery put salt on desire; it was more exciting not to tell him the truth.

At the end of the evening, drinking coffee at a street stall, they toyed with plans. The weekend was only twenty-four hours away. 'You have heard of the English weekend?' asked Sibli. He put a fingernail in her palm.

'I fancy the depths of the country,' she said. This made him frown. March was not the month for countrysides. The nail was drawing lines again. The rooms he rented were discreet. But Sibli had made up her mind. He must find a motorcar. Then they would go away for the weekend.

'Weekends' were the new indulgence, popular and a bit vulgar, where men took girls away in sports cars, or bands of walkers set off on hikes, wearing shorts and showing thighs. Sin was hinted at in the papers. Motorcars, it stood to reason, made sinning easier for 'weekenders'. Sibli bought a spring outfit and packed a pair of walking shoes, and on Friday evening they drove out on the Oxford road, Ricard at the wheel. Rain slashed the windscreen. 'We shall be there in time for dinner,' she said. At Gerrards Cross there was thunder. He was on edge, leaving London behind. 'It's safer in the country,' she said, which only made him more nervous, with its hint of a husband in the offing. 'Every mile a mile nearer,' she whispered. 'Keep straight on. Through High Wycombe.'

The hotel was lit by a single spotlight; a wet Union flag hung above the entrance. It was a year or more since she last called to say hello to Mrs Dorkin, now a widow but keeping her head above water. 'Here we are,' said Sibli. 'Naughty weekends a speciality. The Mandeville Arms.'

'Are you my wife?' hissed Ricard. 'The hotelier will ask.'

'Smith. We had better be the Smiths.'

A man with caved-in cheeks behind the reception desk

watched them enter. 'Good evening, sir. Good evening, madam,' came from a hard little mouth. 'What dreadful weather.'

'We ask a room,' said Ricard.

'Yes, we have rooms,' replied the mouth. 'What name would it be?'

'Smeeth. We are the Smeeths.'

Sibli played with her wedding ring, hoping she looked guilty. 'There's nothing wrong with us,' she said. 'Look, we've got luggage.'

The mouth came to a decision. 'I would like a word in private, Mr Smith.'

Sibli relented; the joke was being over-extended. 'Please tell Mrs Dorkin that Sibli is here.'

'Mrs Dorkin is busy at present. My name is Herbert King. I am the general manager. Will you step this way, Mr Smith?'

They disappeared into a cubbyhole, and Sibli went to find Phyllis Dorkin. She met her carrying a vase of dead flowers. 'Oh, dear,' said Mrs Dorkin, when she heard. Herbert was her brother. Herbert's wife Ruth did the cooking. 'It all got too much for me,' she said. 'Herbert is a Methodist. He gave up a good job with the gas company to come here six months ago. He runs the place like clockwork. He won't have hanky-panky.'

The four of them met in the office. It had acquired a green filing cabinet and a picture of Jesus on the wall. Ricard was whispering that they must go back to London. Herbert, now that he knew about Sibli, wanted to make himself understood. There was the law of God, he said, playing with a pencil, and there was the law of man. Both were adamant on the subject of couples called Smith. Did they know, he continued, warming up, that proceedings could be taken against an innkeeper who let two or more pairs of unmarried persons have relations under his roof?

'Q'est-ce que?' demanded Ricard.

'We're only one pair,' said Sibli.

'There might be another. Someone more expert than you and this gentleman,' and the mouth let go for a second and smiled at the disappointed lover.

In the end he wasn't all that disappointed, Sibli slipping along the corridor in her nightie from Room 7 to visit him in Room 2.

Being quite attached to the Mandeville – if only because she had helped save it – Sibli couldn't resist having a word with Mrs Dorkin about her brother. But all she got were tears. He and Ruth were the only family Mrs Dorkin had. 'If Helen ever came to visit me,' she said, 'it would be different.'

'Things aren't any better?'

'I never see her, unless I go to London. The last time I went, she told me not to come again. The place she is living in is not terribly nice, on account of her next film not having begun.'

Sibli promised to go and see her, then put it off for days after she returned to London and Ricard went home, still believing there was a Mr Somerset in the offing; she didn't spoil the weekend by telling him about the divorce.

But it was time to think about the future. There were minor decisions to take, such as whether she should go back to Paris for the summer, which Ricard was imploring her to do, and major decisions, such as whether she should still wear a wedding ring and be known as Mrs Somerset. She thought she would, for the moment.

Late one afternoon she went to Helen's address in Soho, in Brewer Street, up two flights of uncarpeted stairs. A girl with stringy hair came to the door. There was a man in the room. The girl said Miss Honey was 'down the club, if it's any of your business.' Sibli held out a ten-shilling note and the girl said, 'The Sun & Moon in Beak Street.'

The stage-door was down an alley. She chatted to the doorman, waiting in a passageway. Feet thundered to piano music, men growled and whistled. When the doorman went back to his *Sporting Life*, Sibli slipped through the dressing-room (spotty mirrors, smell of clothes) to the side of the stage. A youth in a trilby stared at her. A row of girls were dancing an elementary can-can. All were naked except for pouches between their legs. One of the girls was plump and not kicking high enough. The bum was unmistakably Helen's.

The wisest course was to go back to Brewer Street and wait. Sibli bought an *Evening News* to sit on and perched halfway up the stairs. A pimp wanted to know who she was. A fat man asked what she charged. It was more than an hour before Helen appeared, trudging up the stairs. She wore a mackintosh with a belt and carried a loaf. Head down, she pushed past Sibli, who followed her up and said, 'Helen, it's me,' at the door.

The girl and the man had gone. The room they were in contained chairs, a table and some empty beer-bottles. A washbasin could be seen behind a curtain. A greyish brassiere dangled from a length of wire.

'If Mummy sent you,' said Helen, 'she's wasting her time. I wouldn't go back to that blasted hotel for a million pounds.'

'I don't blame you. I've met your Uncle Herbert.'

Helen put a kettle on a gas ring. She didn't take off the mackintosh. 'You can tell her I've got a job.'

'Doing what?'

'It's dancing, in a very nice theatre, till a film part comes up next month.'

She looked small and egg-shaped in the mackintosh. The stage make-up, slightly smeared, might have been an experiment with Mummy's rouge. Sibli would have cuddled her, if it would have worked.

'I want your help,' she said. 'It's to do with my career. Don't laugh.'

'I didn't. It was a pity about your marriage.'

'I could never think what it was I wanted to do. I've been working with Pa in Paris most of the past year, but it's a glorified clerk's job. It isn't life, is it? We've both had a bit of life.'

'Being famous,' said Helen. 'That's the thing.'

'Here's what I want to do. Turn the old Mandeville into a place for naughty weekends. Make people think it's *the* hotel to go to. Smart cocktail bars, smart food, smart bedrooms. A romantic welcome for old and young. No questions asked. No Mr-and-Mrs-Smith nonsense. I'm serious. One could make a fortune.'

'Sibby!' giggled Helen, in a voice she no longer used. Then the kettle boiled, and she reverted to her drawly manner. 'You don't have a hope in hell, darling, not with Uncle Herbert.' She made two cups of coffee, thick with grounds.

'He has no money in the hotel. It's still your mother's to do what she likes with. Come and persuade her to let me run it. People like Herbert run enough things as it is.'

'Don't you have anywhere to live, is that it? Has that frightful James left you in the lurch?'

'I could tell you things,' said Sibli, hoping she sounded suitably adrift; it was useful, letting people believe what they wanted to. 'But I do have a flat in Covent Garden that I'm hardly ever in. If I were to go to the Mandeville for a while, you could use the flat when I'm away. You could use it anyway. It would be like old times.'

'I like it here,' snapped Helen.

'That's up to you. I'm the one who's asking a favour.'

Helen peered at the wolf's-head brooch that Sibli realized it would have been wiser not to wear. 'I don't suppose that's real,' she said.

'Paste, of course. Worth a fiver I expect.'

'I did warn you about James.'

'You certainly did,' said Sibli, looking into the smeary eyes that told you nothing. 'So will you talk to your mother?'

'Anything to help an old friend, dear.'

Phyllis Dorkin dithered at first, but listened to her

daughter, who was apparently not living in poverty after all. 'She has a new flat in Covent Garden,' said Sibli. 'The film people are going mad about her. She'll be coming out again in a few weeks, won't you, Helen?'

'I shall try, darling, I shall try.'

A long game began. Herbert King wanted to know what Sibli was doing there. 'Having bright ideas,' she said, and suggested that one way of filling more bedrooms was to give them a handbasin or even a bath. Herbert received this with scorn. In country hotels, pitchers of water and basins were traditional. He did concede that bedrooms might be brightened up a bit. A dealer in Aylesbury sold him a job-lot of watercolours showing scenes from the Holy Land. Herbert nailed them up himself.

As Sibli had guessed, there was no money for improvements. Mrs King, who knew how to cook, said the kitchens had about two million cockroaches. Anyone could see the old range needed tearing out and replacing with electric stoves. Cupboards and larders were too ancient for proper hygiene. Sibli typed an anonymous letter to the county medical officer. A week later an inspector arrived. He threatened prosecution unless things got better.

Sibli had a plan drawn up. Stage One, kitchens. Stage Two, bedrooms. Stage Three, cocktail bars. Stage Four, naughty weekends. Stage Four was not mentioned. A substantial sum was available, seven thousand pounds, part of the sum deposited by James in Luxembourg, far from prying divorce-court officials who might be looking for collusion. In return for this, Sibli wanted a half-share in the ownership.

Herbert knew her story by now. 'I refuse to work with Mrs Somerset,' he said, addressing the ceiling, when they met around a table on a Saturday morning to discuss the future. 'I am only here because of my sister. Blood is thicker than water. However, from the gas industry I came, to the gas industry I shall be happy to return.'

But Mrs King had her eye on a brand-new kitchen with

herself as its mistress. 'I don't think we should be hasty, Herbert,' she said. 'All Mrs Somerset wants to do is make the hotel more profitable. I see no reason why that shouldn't be the Lord's work.'

Herbert was unconvinced. He wanted to speak privately to his sister. Fortunately Helen had been persuaded to come out for the day. She arrived in time to make sure Mrs Dorkin didn't weaken. Herbert didn't go back to gas just yet. The agreement was drawn up. Stage One began.

Sibli was happy there, as she had been happy there before. She decorated her room with ornaments and pictures, including a photograph of James. The more memories one could ingrain, the better. People had been coming there for centuries to make themselves feel better with hospitality. The random nature of the place appealed to Sibli, rooms and staircases slapped together under roofs that didn't match, and she was determined not to let the builders spoil it. She liked telling men what to do.

CHAPTER 24

Cilfrew Castle was busier than usual in 1932. The Fed decided it was time they had a Mappowder in the office of president, and Aubrey was told his turn had come. There was no getting out of it, short of giving offence. The South Wales Metal Industries Federation operated by wink, nod, rule of thumb, old friendships, old feuds, back rooms, firm handshakes. A knighthood was more or less guaranteed in return. It was how things worked. His own father had become Sir Lionel by the same route. You owe it to yourself, they said, not to mention your charming lady wife.

Aubrey's reluctance was met by tactful approaches to Mrs Mappowder. She wouldn't stand any nonsense from the old boy — Margaret could imagine them saying it, and was aware that one or two still called her 'The Woman,' regarding her as dangerous because she ran a tinplate works. 'Don't waste your time lobbying me,' she told the nod-and-wink brigade. 'Aubrey will do what he thinks right.'

To her relief he let his name go forward, and soon she was looking for signs that the succession of speeches, dinners and conclaves with his peers was adding something to his life. But he could turn his public style on and off like a tap. In between, his moods were the same. He tinkered with his motors and raced them, returning calmer than when he left. After these outings he sometimes came to her bed and said, 'Is it all right if I stay the night?' The Fed wasn't anything he took seriously. 'Big fish in little ponds,' he said, as long as she was the only one listening.

Family duty meant more to Margaret, who could never forget her father's angry ambitions. The stones of the old works, still visible at low tide, were a reminder of the struggle he saw himself as born to. Tir Gwyn had been built just in time, before the sea broke in. It was as outdated now as all the other mills in the town, decades behind the Germans and the Americans, but it remained an obligation, the extension of time that the living granted the dead.

She had been the only Buckley prepared to take it on, her brothers finding other careers – Morgan as a sinner in London, Will as a revolutionary in the Rhondda. There were dozens of men at Tir Gwyn who remembered David Inkerman Buckley, twenty-odd years after his death. When they saw his daughter, they saw him. If Aubrey took a less intense view of his own inheritance – the copperworks, which he rarely visited because it bored him – that made her no better than him; only different.

Halfway through Aubrey's term, the statue of General Roberts on a horse that stood outside her office building fell off its concrete plinth, which was rotting away. Old Roberts had gone black with age, the odd stone had dented him, and the horse's tail had been stolen by persons unknown on Armistice Night. Now, his head came off and rolled in the flowerbed, and a railing punctured his steed.

As the only tinplate statue in existence, as far as anyone knew, he was worth donating to the Fed's Museum of Iron and Steel in Cardiff. His face with its tinplate beak for a nose had never been up to much, and when Margaret was having him refitted and polished back to silver, she told the craftsman to be sure to give him new features in dark paint. The result was striking but skull-like.

After all that, the museum made difficulties about having him. A fawning letter of thanks from the chairman of the trustees said they would be honoured to accept her magnificent gift as soon as a worthy setting could be devised. Weeks passed and nothing happened. She sensed embarrassment. When Aubrey heard of it – not from her – he told her the trustees had a nasty shock coming, but Margaret begged him not to intervene.

'They've been discourteous to you,' he said.

'I don't want you embroiled.'

'There is a faction that has some piffling objection.'

'I can guess. It's the inscription, is it not?'

'I wish you would leave it to me.'

'It was I had the words put on, after the railway strike. After Dadda died. *Made by John Johns, who died with five others during the riots of 19 August, 1911*. Do you see anything wrong with that?'

'I see their objection. The riots were an expression of enmity, however democratic one wants to be. We all need a disciplined labour-force. Even you, Margaret *fach*.'

'Does that rule out compassion for John Johns, who never hurt a fly as far as I know?'

'I won't argue politics with you, you know that. What I will do is have the trustees on the carpet if you say the word.'

'No, thanks. If the Fed doesn't want him I'll find someone who will.'

To her dismay, the affair got into the papers, or at least the *Port Howard News*, the local Liberal rag, in the shape of a mocking paragraph about the diehards of the Fed who were refusing a statue that they had christened the First Horseman of the Apocalypse. Margaret withdrew her offer and put him back on his plinth.

It was no use expecting anything in Port Howard to change. Its works and pits and docks were run by men whose only creed was that the past was safer than the future. No doubt it was one of her brother capitalists – her money was on Egge at the Old Lodge – who had revived the Fed's memories of the 1911 riots. But if they were fossils, she might be going the same way. A small town with small ideas left little room for manoeuvre.

People still spoke of her as a model employer, with her sick-pay and production bonuses. Didn't the rollermen and their teams have a tiled room to boil tea in? What would it be next, carpet slippers for the dinner-break and toilet paper in the lavs? There was a hint of patronage in the polite enthusiasm of her peers for her compassion as a woman in a man's hard world. When it came to profits, the same cold truths blew through her premises as they did through others'. She, too, had to put hands on short-time or lay them off.

Her ambition had been to run her business on modern lines. In the twenties she looked for new markets in the Balkans and Africa. She bought bigger rollers and faster engines. Unfortunately the scale of change that was needed to compete with the world was as beyond Margaret as it was beyond Egge and the rest of the gang. Beyond Aubrey, too, not that he let it worry him. She couldn't bear to think of this familiar landscape swept away. But the result of doing nothing drastic was decline year by year for the little works. The same brush that tarred the others tarred her.

A letter from Esther, written in the spring, was in a drawer of her desk at the office, a siren song she had resisted. 'I have a proposal to make,' wrote her sister-in-law, 'which is that you and I travel to the Soviet Union this summer and see for ourselves some of the work that is being done in connection with female reproduction. I believe that a new age for womanhood is in the making there. They are streets ahead of us in matters of contraception.

'It would also be a holiday for us both. I am a tired old stick these days, I am nearly sixty-three, and I would love to have weeks and weeks of your energetic company. We could visit some imperial palaces, which I believe are preserved as museums, and pay homage at the railway station where the great Tolstoy passed away, but I am a little vague about the geography.

'You see, Margaret, you must not let yourself be tied one hundred per cent to your Factory and your Husband (who is a grand person, that goes without saying). Do not allow loyalty to entrap you. There remain worlds to explore.'

The plan was out of the question, the summer was half over, the excuses long since made and accepted, but Margaret could still hear Esther whispering from the drawer, which was supposed to hold nothing more exciting than output figures and wage sheets. Fertility in Russia was hardly the point, even supposing her sister-in-law knew what she was talking about. The point was viewing the world from somewhere other than Port Howard.

Brown smoke blew past the windows, a squall boiled in the estuary, the sun flickered on a hilltop whose green came across the water like a lamp making a signal. She had made her bed long ago. She regretted nothing – '*Nothing*,' she said to Dadda's photograph on the desk, and shut the drawer firmly.

Her secretary, a young woman called Addie, brought in a card from a visitor. Margaret read,

MR STEPHEN DAVIS

Correspondent of the *Sunday Argus*

119 ST ANDREWS HILL

LONDON EC

'On no account,' she said. 'Tell him I am sorry he's wasted his journey, but I have nothing to add on the subject of our statue.'

'He claims to have a letter of introduction from Mr Will Buckley.'

'What is it to do with *him*? Oh, very well, ten minutes. Then I'm going over to the Morfa.'

The reporter was spare, almost bony. He sat in his

trench-coat with the belt still done up, half smiling, his deep eyes fixed on her as she read the letter.

It was nothing to do with General Roberts after all. Her brother commended Davis as an impartial observer who was writing articles about the Depression. 'I have whetted his appetite with horror stories from round here,' he said, 'so try and be honest, *merched*, and don't paint him too bland a picture of your patch.'

'And how is the revolution coming along in the valleys, Mr Davis?' she asked, irritated by Will's tone.

'His miners think he'd hang a few capitalists from lamp-posts. What do you think, Mrs Mappowder?'

'He gets carried away sometimes.' She saw the need for caution. 'He believes in the ballot-box. I hope you're not going to write one of those silly articles about red flags at the pit-heads.'

'You have less poverty down here, of course.'

'We have enough. What is it you want, exactly? The Federation in Cardiff has all the export figures. We are keeping our end up.'

'I don't go in for statistics. I thought I'd write a piece about proprietors. Even those hard-faced Butes and Merthyrs your brother goes on about make a case for themselves.'

Margaret saw what he was after. 'So you can write about the socialist miners' agent and his sister who's a capitalist, and make each of us score points off the other. I wasn't born yesterday.'

'And your other brother?' he said, tapping a fingernail on her desk. 'You think I'll bring him in as well, do you? Then we'll have the bolshie *and* the tinplate queen *and* the dubious publisher.'

'That's slander.'

'I withdraw it at once.' Another smile came over his thin features, rearranging them on the bone. 'Morgan Buckley's saucy editions of Boccaccio and the Abbé Brantôme are perfectly legal in Paris. I admire his bravado. I wrote a book for him once, *Dangerous Worlds*, the memoirs of a foreign correspondent. It made no money.'

Addie appeared at the door to say the car was waiting to go to the Morfa. 'I'm not ready,' said Margaret, and asked her visitor what questions he would put if she let him, adding that it was a big 'if'.

Whether she sacked men to their face, he suggested. How long did sick-pay last? Who decided when sickness became malingering? Did theft from the works mean automatic dismissal? What if the thief had a wife and three children? What about six children, aged parents and a wife with consumption?

'You are making a game of it.'

'Or being deadly serious. Do you see your brother capitalists in the town as too hard? Do they see you as too soft?'

'No one would answer such questions.'

'Asking them is a step in the right direction.'

Margaret thought him too nice to be ruthless; behind his aggressiveness was a tendency to cough and look out of the window. In the end she cancelled the visit to the Morfa and let herself be interviewed. They kept to safe topics like welfare and medical treatment, and Davis wrote an occasional word in a notebook. Afterwards she offered to show him round the works and let him talk to anyone he liked.

Despite herself, she was flattered at the interest of a London journalist in this old-fashioned place. How gladly she had left it when she married Henry – the memory pierced her, as though everything that intervened between then and now had been a mistake.

Outside they had to wait while trucks were shunted across their path, halting and clanking and halting again. Tarpaulins, laced down, covered the boxed tinplates, consigned to Bombay. Davis stood hunched against the unsummery wind that blew grit at them.

'So you knew Morgan in London?' she said.

'Years ago. He was looking for writers, not that books are my line. He sent his daughter to Fleet Street as a talent scout. A very pretty young woman. Your niece, of course.'

An engine-whistle shrieked and the trucks stopped again. Buffer crashed on buffer down the length of the train.

'Sibli hadn't made up her mind what she wanted to do,' said Margaret.

'Did she ever tell you about the Fenians who kidnapped her in West Cork?'

'My Sibli?' She regretted the 'my'.

'They took her back to Jim Barry, who was the local commander, to find what she was up to.'

'She told you this?'

'I was there. We were both in Macroom. She turned up one night.'

'And then came back through Fishguard,' said Margaret, remembering the telegram that Sibli's mother brought round for her to see. She felt cold and betrayed, as if it had just happened.

'Very likely,' said Davis. 'Where is Sibli these days?'

'At the Mandeville Arms in Buckinghamshire.'

'That was a spectacular divorce she had last year.'

For all she knew, Davis had been Sibli's original seducer – or, failing that, the object of Sibli's seduction. Either was intolerable.

The lamp-end of the trucks receded towards the branch line and Bombay. Her engine-keeper, who had been waiting to cross from the other side, raised his oily bowler and called, 'Shocking summer, Mrs Mappowder.' The way was clear to No 1 mill, where the roller-doors stood open, and figures moved about in a twilight of smoke and sparks.

'I've changed my mind,' said Margaret. 'I'm sorry. I would rather not help you any more.'

Davis looked at her as if he had been half expecting it, nodded, and turned back to where a small two-seater was parked outside the offices, in the shadow of the famous statue. He cranked it up with a starting handle, gave a friendly wave, and drove off. Margaret stood with the wind pricking her cheeks.

She had to admit that General Roberts looked a proper death's-head. But if people didn't like him, they could look the other way. He was a permanent fixture; like her.

CHAPTER 25

Stage Two, bedrooms, was getting under way, and Stage One, kitchens, was nearing completion. Ruth King dropped ash over the stainless-steel electric ranges from the cigarette stuck in her mouth as she did shrewd experiments with the temperature, to see how it coped with pastry and pork crackling. She tried to keep her husband away from her territory by shouting, 'Kind of you to come! Would you care to sharpen a knife?' whenever he looked in.

Herbert accepted that modern machinery could do the Lord's work. He was less happy when it came to deep-sprung mattresses and private bathrooms. Sibli teased him about the moral virtues of a handbasin and a flannel, but threw in half-serious remarks about her own deplorable taste for hot baths and long telephone conversations, as if to suggest that ultimately she might change her ways. One evening, alone in the residents' lounge, Herbert offered to pray for her. 'Would you really?' she said, tugging her skirt far down over her stockings.

Her father came in useful as a mysterious figure no one knew the truth about. She hinted at his past, describing his torment as a theological student, scrubbing away sin with strong soap in the ablutions every morning, only to find himself deserted by God. 'Go on, go on!' said Herbert, but she replied that Morgan Buckley's life was an enigma; a fair comment. Men were banished from her bed these days. They were all so obvious. Even James had been obvious in the disciplines he surrounded himself with. His idea that a purpose lay behind their marriage was never eradicated, but she saw the dishonesty that lay behind these shadowy networks, supposedly controlling our lives, that Morgan (perhaps) and James (undoubtedly) believed in.

Magic was only as real as the arrogance of the magicians. Sibli wanted to shut herself out for ever from the brotherhoods and cabals that men loved to create. Even Theo had had his charmed circle of art and its perpetration, which offered a mystical excuse for being what he was, so that the applause he earned, the money he spent and the women he slept with became part of a special scheme drawn up by cosmic powers at his birth, or earlier.

There were virtues in being alone and uncomplicated. The future wasn't part of any plan to be fulfilled. Preparing for a bath – naked, thinking about being thirty in three years' time – she liked to let steam get to work on the mirror before lingering on her image and giving herself points on the beautiful-woman scale. Sometimes she got to 8 out of 10. Games were permissible, there not being anything else. Most days she was consumed with a passion to make the Mandeville in its soupy green valley a paradigm of English inns, but she knew that when it happened she would probably sell her share in it and do something else.

These days it was essential to get stars and be in guidebooks. Charming letters went to the motoring organizations. When the kitchen was fully operational – Mrs King nicely fired up with frequent snacks of salt herring and sweet sherry – and a sample bedroom with bath was habitable, Sibli arranged for an inspector to call. She made sure Herbert was off the premises, visiting a temperance victualler in Oxford. He arrived at noon, a Mr Irons in a shiny suit the colour of toast, who said he would pay for his meal, examine the facilities and depart at 2.15.

'Can't you stay a bit longer?' said Sibli, presenting herself as a woman with an unhappy past who had taken stock of her life, and was anxious to learn the difficult arts of hotel-keeping. If only she knew someone in the business who could give her some tips!

The inspector used a napkin folded like a seashell, another of Ruth's talents, to wipe his lips after an aperitif ('the teeniest cocktail on earth, Mr Irons'), and said, 'I am at your disposal.'

Lunch was a success. It was a pity there was no one else eating it. Sibli, who rejoined him as he was polishing off the marmalade pudding, even managed to smooth over the fact that for months to come, only the bar and the restaurant would be open. 'I am determined to get everything right,' she said. 'I gambled on getting an inspector who wouldn't penalize me for presumption.'

'No, no, certainly not,' muttered Irons, and wrote something on a pink form, using his other hand as a shield so she couldn't read it.

Mrs Dorkin, who did the waitressing when no one else was available, ushered in a man wearing a trilby, with a bundle of newspapers under his arm. When he saw Sibli, he took off the trilby and flourished it. Then he sat in the far corner, coughing into a handkerchief. Unless she was having a hallucination, it was Davis. The inspector had already said he preferred to take coffee at the table, so escape to the lounge wasn't possible. Head bent, her bare leg so close to Irons that she could feel the draught of his trousers when he moved, she listened with a combined nod and nibbling of her lower lip every half-minute as he told her why hotels failed.

At the same time she monitored the hallucination, who was feeding on sardines and coffee, his newspapers spilling on to the floor. 'These little blighters,' she heard him say when Mrs Dorkin returned, hoping to sell him an ice-cream, 'were somewhat bony.' The voice confirmed it was Davis.

Did some mysterious purpose lurk behind Davis, too? She glared at him and he waved back, as if he enjoyed insulting her food. The inspector was warning her about the perils of over-pricing versus under-pricing. 'They are the Scylla and Charybdis of the catering business,' he declared.

Finding it was later than he expected, Irons proposed to stay even longer, which entailed telephone calls. Sibli left him in the office and returned to the restaurant, where Davis was doing a crossword.

'I am terribly sorry we are not up to your standard,' she said. 'There will be no charge for the meal. Can I get you a complimentary brandy? Or something more lethal?'

'I thought you found honesty flattering.' He was on his feet, gaunt and a bit white around the cheekbones. 'I can't resist asking, was that the co-respondent? The man who was at the Lord Warden?'

'You aren't making me laugh, Davis.'

'I wasn't trying to. Are we supposed not to refer to your divorce?'

'There's a lot to be said for minding one's own business.'

'We are old friends.'

'We are most certainly not.'

'I see. In that case I must apologize.' He swished at flies with his newspaper, and one fell kicking in the sugar-basin. 'I presumed on – what would suit you, a long acquaintance?'

'Much better! I am prepared to meet by accident every five years or so.'

'I was in Port Howard yesterday, interviewing Mrs Mappowder. She let your address slip out.'

'That *was* kind of her. I don't particularly want people turning up to see me, Davis. Now if you'll excuse me.'

She went to visit the kitchen with the inspector, managing to pluck the cigarette from Ruth's mouth and throw it through the window while he was admiring the stoves. The Davis business rankled.

Inspector Irons examined the roller-towel by the sink, looked inside the refrigerator, and was asking about the septic tank when Mrs King shouted, 'Kind of you to come!

Would you care to sharpen a knife?', and Herbert appeared in the doorway, carrying a case with the stencilled message, 'English Fruit Wines (Non Alcoholic)'.

He insisted on marching in front of her and Irons as they toured the inn, flinging doors open with a bang and bowing obsequiously, and was persuaded to leave them only when Sibli said she smelt burning from downstairs.

'I sleep in here,' she told the inspector, showing him her bed with its cream nightdress folded by the pillow. 'This gives you a better idea of how we plan to furnish the rooms.'

The pink form fell on the carpet, and as Irons stooped to pick it up, she was on the brink of closing the door behind them and starting an experiment – in bribery and corruption, not sexual relations, which were incidental.

The inspector's face was red as he straightened up. Would the wages of sin have been three stars or no stars?

The door stayed open. But she enjoyed the knife-edge.

When Irons had left, she looked for Phyllis Dorkin, and found her drinking tea in the residents' lounge with Davis. Not only had he not gone, he had asked about a room for the night. This was obviously out of the question. She sent Phyllis on an errand, explained convincingly that the plumbing wasn't up to guest standards, and got rid of Davis, though not before establishing why he had been in Wales, and hearing that he had met Will Buckley as well. She learned that her uncle would be the next Member of Parliament for his valley, when the present one died, which was expected to be soon.

Davis had continued to come down in the world. His motorcar was small and had dents.

'I shall give a party in the autumn, when I'm back in town,' she said, as he was cranking the engine and she was thinking how tired and on edge he looked. 'Should I send you an invitation?'

'You can reach me at the *Sunday Argus*.' He shook hands with her and said, 'Goodbye, old acquaintance,' as if it was he had got the better of the encounter, not her.

Dust shimmered in the afternoon sun when he had gone. In the office she wrote, 'Dear Mr Irons, I do hope you enjoyed your visit.' A film-star photograph of Helen stood on the desk, signed, 'Sincere best wishes from Miss Helen Honey.'

Sibli had sent a letter and then a telegram to the Sun & Moon, asking her to pop out and stay with her friend, who was still fond of her. But Helen didn't come.

CHAPTER 26

London, the other life, was still potent. Never mind men, who could be found anywhere, but just *London*, its night clubs and teashops, the galleries, the parks at dusk, and Kensington, unchanged from Sibli's first memories of it – Morgan country, full of promise. She left behind a tarted-up Mandeville Arms, to which the inspector had awarded a single star, and came back to the flat in Covent Garden with its mound of letters, and autumn winds rattling the windows. She supposed it was home, and wondered if Helen might be persuaded to leave the smelly attic in Brewer Street and join her. But Helen had gone away; to Paris, someone thought.

It was the season of parties. Having hired a maid-who-cooked called Em, a Scots girl with big bones and a face like raw beef, she gave women-only lunches where she presided in bright silk dresses with her wedding ring still in place, and let her guests know how fond she still was of James, how glad she was to be free of him.

Dvina Moon, James's sister, came uneasily, spying her out. A film publicist's wife said that Mr Somerset was refusing to make movies with divorces in them, an unlikely story. Fanny Henriques, who was still Theo's agent, had them in fits about mad artists with temperaments; she didn't include Theo.

To her supper parties Sibli invited the same women with their husbands or lovers, and extended the range, looking as far afield as Harrow-on-the-Hill, where Stuart (war hero) and Virginia (woman of mystery) accepted but never came. The Penbury-Holts had always intrigued her, with their soft skins beneath the bourgeois carapace. Tom she would have liked as a guest, but Tom was married (she heard from Esther), busy being a detective.

The Greek pianist and black trumpeter Sibli hired for her occasions played, on the whole, to her film-business and art-gallery friends. Davis got his invitation but didn't bother to reply. The last she heard of him was his articles about South Wales in the grip of Depression. He mocked the bosses, even Aunt Margaret, reserving his sympathy for the poor. A sentence stuck in her head: *The miners squatted in silent circles like black Buddhas, waiting.*

Occasionally she heard voices from Wales. Now that Sibli was free of marital obligations (her mother's phrase), Aeronwy was expecting a trip to London, expenses paid, and Sibli thought that if she had to be Lady Bountiful, she might as well do it properly, and have Griff and Albert up as well.

They came at half-term; Albert wore the cap and tie of the local grammar school. Meeting them at Paddington on a raw October afternoon, she waited till they were in the taxi before disclosing that the nice clean hotel in Bayswater where they were heading was for Griff and Aeronwy only. 'This one,' she said, eyes on Albert, 'is coming to stay in Covent Garden with me.'

'He can't possibly!' cried her mother, and the boy himself frowned at Praed Street and a shop with whirling sprays and elastic bandages in the window.

'You and Griff will have a holiday with nothing to worry about. I shall get to know Albert.'

'He'll be better with us, won't you, love? You can see your sister every day.'

Sibli might have been trying to kidnap him. She put her arm around Albert's shoulder and said there was a very jolly Scotswoman called Em who made the best chipped potatoes in the West End. Em obviously came as a relief; she didn't sound like divorcées and loose living. Some folded banknotes changed hands, pressed into the palm of Mrs Griff Griffiths's glove.

'You look,' said Sibli, standing on the pavement outside the Park Towers Private Hotel, 'as if I was the gypsies come to steal him. We'll be over to see you tomorrow evening.'

'He'll be fine, won't you, Champion?' said Griff, and Sibli guessed that he was the one who would really miss Albert.

Hands waving diminished and they were alone. Albert stretched his legs and pushed his cap to the back of his head. Being manly suited him, if he could keep it up; his comic was in his fist, slowly disintegrating.

'Is it far, Sibby?' he asked.

'A mile or two. Is this your first time in London?'

'Is Hampton Court London?'

'Sort of.'

'I went there on a school trip once.'

The bell of a police car made him blink. In the turbulence around Seven Dials he slid along the seat and she saw damp comic-stains on his palm. It might have been kinder to leave him with his Ma and Pa, except that she itched for an Albert experiment, as there had once been Isabel experiments, long ago. The dull backs of his boots looked forlorn, preceding her up to her flat. Was there an Al slowly ripening inside Albert?

With Em, everything proceeded smoothly. 'The boy is dying of starvation and wants his tea, ma'am,' she announced, before the boy had been to wash his hands, and her raisin-bread and cakes helped cushion his shock at finding he had brought his father's pyjamas instead of his own; there had been some hasty repacking on the pavement in Bayswater.

Albert's room was at the end of a corridor. The flat was large. 'Done up for a banana importer, so they say,' said Sibli, showing him the room, which had a bed, a wireless set and the rocking-chair from Rhydness. 'The chair's your

Uncle Morgan's, strictly speaking,' she said, 'it has a history,' but he wasn't curious. He lay on the bed with the door open, listening to Radio Normandy.

Outside, footsteps echoed along the street. The red D of a theatre sign was visible down an alley. Sibli answered telephone calls and made them, saying she was sorry, she was busy, she was entertaining her brother. 'Pull the other one, dear,' said a man who claimed to own a night club. From Albert's room came the stirring theme-tune of 'Mr Fang, Oriental Master Crook', brought to you by the makers of somebody's stomach powder.

Sibli changed to dark skirt and dark stockings, told Albert they were going places, replaced his blazer with a fisherman's sweater, threw his cap in a drawer, walked him into the Strand and on to a bus, and set off on a guided tour. She remembered when she was his age longing for London like she longed for puberty.

Albert sat with his hands in his lap, as though he was still listening to Radio Normandy. What caught his eye were sleeping birds on ledges, in the shadows behind the red neons at Piccadilly Circus. It was hard work, showing him actual sights. He stared at the West End without comment or questions.

The Zoo next day had some of the same anti-climax. The place was his choice. Albert mentioned vultures in passing and then seemed bored when they reached them, flapping on bits of tree. Of the morning Sibli remembered only the smoking turds of an elephant and a snake's head striking at glass.

In the cafeteria she tried to get him to talk about himself, but heard nothing his parents wouldn't have told her. Behind the sprout of black hair and the vowel-mashing accent, Al stayed in hiding, if there was an Al.

Taking him to a news cinema in Baker Street spelt failure. They watched baseball, boxing and a ship on the rocks ('Are you enjoying it?' 'Yes, Sibby, it's very interesting'). A professor rose majestically in a balloon. A storm blew roofs off in Australia. 'We can go if you like,' she said, and they left as Herr Hitler, a minor German politician, was feeding what looked like jam sponge to a dog.

Returning to the flat via tea at a Corner House, it was dusk already. The landing smelt of cheap perfume. 'There's a lady and gentleman in the sitting-room,' said Em.

It was Helen, fleshy about the hips and wearing a typical spotted frock, hopping around and introducing Emil, a thin sallow man with a wrinkled forehead. He looked kind; they stood hand in hand while Helen wiggled an engagement ring and described how they had met in Brussels, where she was dancing. This was closer to the old Helen than Sibli had seen for years, though Emil, pressingly foreign in his manner, spoke unsettlingly about 'the blonde goddess' and 'the sex-appeals'.

So that was that. Helen would marry the heir to a chocolate factory – if Sibli had heard right – and live in Brussels, conceiving Anglo-Belgians. Explaining things to her brother, Sibli thought what a sad phrase 'in school together' was. 'You've heard of the film star Helen Honey?' she added. 'This is her.'

'A girl needs to settle down,' said Helen.

'As I begged of her, though no man is second to me in appreciation of her *re* the movies.'

It was time for Mr Fang, Oriental Master Crook. Albert retired to his wireless while Em served cocktails. The young lovers – Emil was no chicken, but probably the right side of forty – were staying at a quiet hotel in Kensington, quietness and greenery being what the Belgian liked best about London and indeed England, of which he had rosy views. They had been touring by motor. 'We were in Buckingshire, which I believe is known as Beechy Buckingshire,' he remarked, and Helen murmured, 'Later, Emil, later,' and said to Sibli, 'God, I was beastly about your divorce. I ought to be sent to bed without any supper.'

'It didn't matter.'

Emil needed to use the telephone and was installed in Sibli's bedroom.

'He's jolly busy, he has all these business interests,' explained Helen, and wanted to know about James and if she had found another man yet. Her own life had resolved itself with Emil Cammaerts. The Sun & Moon was a bad dream. They stretched out on a sofa from opposite ends with their legs up, their calves in contact, talking about men as creatures one could do what one liked with, pretending about them as they used to in the old days.

Albert appeared and asked if he could go outside to explore. He had a school scarf coiled around his throat. Pleased at his initiative, Sibli told him to stay between the angle of Southampton Street and the Strand, and watched him from the window go along the well-lit road towards the church and the dark façades of the market. Opera-goers were about, making for Drury Lane. Thirty minutes, she had told him; he had a luminous watch.

Emil's voice murmured on behind the closed door. Sibli poured wine and returned to the sofa. She started talking about the Mandeville Arms, and felt Helen's leg stiffen against hers.

'I wanted to have a word with you about that,' said Helen, 'the fabulous things you have done to it, which Emil says have put thousands on the value.'

'Interested in hotels, is he?'

'He knows all about property.'

'And chocolate.'

'You mustn't laugh at him, Sib, or I'll die. He's a fabulous businessman.'

The Mandeville was to be sold. Mrs Dorkin had agreed, Mrs Dorkin had signed a transfer of the property to her daughter. Monsieur Cammaerts was obviously a fast worker. Sibli stretched her legs and smiled and drew the facts from Helen, who kept saying they should wait till Emil was there to explain it all.

Presently he was, his voice gone hoarse with telephoning.

'Investment matters,' he confided, but was happy to put Helen's best friend ('as she has often told me you are') in the picture *re* the Mandeville. His portfolio was such that English country hotels did not fit in. Mrs Somerset's most kind investment of seven thousand pounds would be returned with interest calculated at a generous four per cent.

Trying to sound respectful of his expertise, she asked if she might be compensated for the time and energy she had expended. Emil thought about this, stroking Helen's arm, and said he was sure they could reach some arrangement. In any case, the securities she would receive in repayment of her seven thousand were those of an investment group with interests in the Congo, their value increasing in leaps and bounds on the European exchanges.

'I had a friend who said one should always ask if shares are quoted in London.'

Helen said, 'Honestly, Sib,' but Emil was visibly amused by such conservatism.

'I was thinking of cash, you see,' said Sibli.

'*Cash?*'

Someone was knocking at the front door.

'Cash is dead wealth, it is no use to anyone except to pay the dressmaker, Mrs Somerset. Allow me to explain the technicalities,' but he had made hardly any progress before Em was showing Aeronwy and Griff into the room.

Everyone talked at once, 'What a surprise' and 'We were getting worried' and 'Monsieur Cammaerts is from Brussels,' followed by Griff's 'Where the sprouts come from'; his hat had left a red ring on his skull.

They would have telephoned but the line was always engaged. Ma looked suspiciously at the remains of cocktails. Albert and Sibli (she can't have forgotten) were expected at Bayswater; a special cold-meat supper had been ordered. But Sibli had forgotten.

And where exactly was young Champion?

There was no easy answer. Ma dragged the curtains

aside and said he might be lying dead somewhere. Helen and Emil departed, Sibli promising to be round first thing in the morning to conclude the discussion. Griff hurried into the street and Sibli sent Em after him in case he got lost.

An hour and a half had now passed since Albert went exploring. Ma was stretched on the sofa, saying her heart was giving out. When Em and Griff returned with a constable, who wanted a photograph of the missing person, Sibli left Em in charge and went out with her stepfather.

A lorry piled with boxes of vegetables came up Southampton Street. A metal shutter was raised with a clatter and a light came on in an office. Soon the market would be open, jamming the roads with lorries and porters.

Down-and-outs were queuing for soup and bread outside the church. The Salvation Army captain had seen no boy. The church steps smelt. Griff said, 'Not your fault he disobeyed his sister.'

'Nice of you to say, but I'm afraid it is.'

She tried the Strand, where she had taken Albert to catch the bus, and they walked to Trafalgar Square. Nelson was floodlit; he seemed to be falling sideways out of the sky.

Sibli remembered the birds asleep that her brother had commented on. 'Let's try here,' she said, and they found Albert by St Martin's, face upturned, studying the ledges. He was working his way round the square, having counted a hundred and ninety-seven pigeons and two hundred and forty starlings so far.

'You're a bad lad, Champion,' said Griff, without rancour. 'He'll have to come back to the hotel with us now. You know what his Ma's like.'

So there might be an Al after all, even if the boldest thing he did was give people frights by studying wildlife and buying saveloys and tea from a stall with the florin that Ma insisted he carry in an envelope, along with five sheets of toilet paper and his address. But Sibli knew she had failed to understand him. An opportunity had been lost. Walking back, she asked Albert to name a single treat he would like before they returned to Wales. Visit a newspaper, he said promptly, and have his name cast in metal, so he could stamp it on things.

When they had all been sent back to Bayswater in a taxi, Sibli tried to reach Tom at Scotland Yard, but the night desk said there was no one in Fraud at this hour. Her suspicions about Emil Cammaerts were for Helen's sake more than hers. Next day she made him a proposal, offering to buy the hotel herself, but only on condition she dealt with Helen – at this point still in bed, Sibli having arrived before nine o'clock with the intention of getting him on his own.

His response was predictable. Helen the rosebud understood nothing of finance. 'No doubt she would sell it to *you* for a sing-song,' he said, having apparently revised his ideas about Mrs Somerset's grasp of business.

'She'll sell it to me for a fair price less the money I am owed. Incidentally I shall guarantee that her mother can go on living there. If you sold the hotel, would you insist on a similar guarantee?'

'There is no need. She has her brother, the sainted Mr King. He can look after her.'

'I doubt it. I shall see what Helen says.'

As Sibli expected, this didn't go much beyond 'I love him' and 'Don't be horrid.' Another muddle had arisen to plague Helen Honey and threaten her happiness. For the moment Sibli did no more than paint a vivid picture of Mrs Dorkin destitute in a bedsitter with mice ('Oh, Sibby, Emil's not like that!') and leave her offer open.

Meanwhile she got hold of Tom and talked to him in an interview room at the Yard, suggesting he make an inquiry or two about Emil Cammaerts.

'Have you forgotten the last time you asked me to help?' he said, unexpectedly smart in grey suit and striped tie.

'That was different. All you have to do is ask your

friends in Brussels if they've heard of him. Dear sweet Tom. Is it true you're married?'

'Dear devious Sibli. Yes it is. I'll see what I can do, but no promises.'

Davis was easier, when eventually she managed to reach him at the *Sunday Argus*, and she was invited to bring her brother to the offices at five o'clock on Saturday afternoon. But when Sibli arrived at the Park Towers to collect him, Ma and Griff were ready as well, waiting in their coats and hats. Albert's hair had been cut short. Flanked by his parents, he had the air of a prisoner under escort. Since leaving Covent Garden, he seemed to have spent his time at museums.

On the other side of London, Davis took the visitors in his stride when he greeted them in the tiny front hall, shooing them up stone steps and along corridors with dusty boards underfoot. It was a small, old-fashioned newspaper, distinguished and hard-up.

Poking fun at the premises, he said they were what one expected a backstreet factory to have been like in Dickensian times, making soap or patent medicines. The chemical smell was printing ink. He whisked them through the editorial department. Ma kept telling Albert to stand up straight and listen, and he might learn something.

In a room labelled 'Sub-editors' men languished around a brightly-lit table. A shape moving behind frosted glass – it appeared to be eating a sandwich – was identified as the editor, Hector McInch.

'He has just agreed I can go to Germany for the elections,' Davis told Sibli, while a woman in a white coat was showing Albert the wire-room machines, chattering with messages.

'Better than Wales,' she smiled, and he said, 'Come to Germany with me. We're acquaintances of long standing, after all.'

He was leaning against the corridor wall, arms folded, a glitter in his eyes that could be mischief or ill-health.

'I don't think that sounds very sensible.'

'You never struck me as going in for sensible behaviour. Can I ask a personal question? Do you enjoy troubling men?'

'I didn't think I troubled you. I asked you to a cocktail party and you couldn't even be bothered to answer.'

'Loud voices and bad music. I never quite picked up the habit.'

'You *are* an arrogant chap, Davis,' she said, as Albert and his parents emerged, and they all moved down a floor to the noisy printing works, where type was being banged and squeezed into frames by men in aprons, and the boy was led to a machine to have his name cast in metal by a typesetter, crouching in his bucket seat.

The printer asked him something, speaking in his ear because of the din, and Albert murmured back. Levers moved, the hot slice of metal with raised letters along one end emerged, Albert wrapped it in his handkerchief. Then a copy-boy came to say that Mr Davis was needed upstairs, and Davis had them shown round to a printer's café next door, where he would collect them in half an hour, when the presses were ready to start.

Ma wiped the seats with tissues from her handbag before anyone could sit down. Albert sneezed while they were waiting for tea from the urn, his mother said he was catching cold and where was his handkerchief, the line of type fell on to the marble-topped table, Griff picked it up and pressed it into the palm of his hand, Ma said, 'Have they spelt it right?'

She lifted Griff's hand to look and screamed, 'Wicked boy! It says Albert Buckley!'

She slapped him and he fell on the floor. 'Leave him, Ma,' said Sibli, and stepped between her mother and Albert, who had crawled under an empty table. A printer whistled and another called, 'Now then, you ladies.'

From Ma came, 'Buckley, indeed. I've had enough trouble with Buckley.'

From Griff, 'Fair do's, the boy only does it because his sister was a Buckley.'

Sibli said it would be wise if she and Albert went for a stroll.

'He doesn't belong to you, so you give him here.'

'Come on, Albert.' Sibli rescued the line of type, and they walked down the backstreet to the greenish lamps of Queen Victoria Street, and little Blackfriars Station across the road with the names of destinations chiselled around the entrance, *Dieppe* and *Paris* and *Berlin*.

'Too near the ground for birds to roost in,' she said. 'So what's all this about Buckley?'

'I thought you'd understand.'

'I do.'

'I wish I was Buckley like you. I wish Uncle Morgan was my Pa. Since he was *your* Pa and Ma was *your* Ma, and now she's *my* Ma...' His eyes were raw, spilling tears. 'I asked Ma once and she said I'd have to wait till I was grown-up.'

'You ought to have asked me. Or I ought to have told you without asking.' They stopped on the bridge. A tug was going down with the tide, its fierce red and green eyes receding. Here beginneth the first lesson. 'Ma was a Miss Rees from Port Howard, lived with her mother, fell in love with your Uncle Morgan, had his baby without marrying him: me. Morgan ran off...'

Going back, she was glad to see the tears had been replaced by curiosity. 'Was all that really true?' he said.

'I wouldn't have told you otherwise.'

'Did Uncle Morgan talk to the spirits?'

'He said he did. But that's something else.'

In the press room, men shouted and a bell rang. Ma sulked, scowling at the rollers. As they began to turn, Davis said, 'I meant it about Germany,' and Sibli shook her head.

Soon the roaring was too loud for speech. Al had his hand in his pocket, where the line of type was.

CHAPTER 27

Keeping an eye on her investment, Sibli borrowed a car and drove out to the Mandeville, only to find that Helen was there. She was alone, Emil having gone back to Brussels on urgent business. Drive and garden were thick with leaves. Herbert had quarrelled with the builders, and no work was being done on the bedrooms.

'The sooner it's sold the better,' said Helen, who was in a dressing-gown and had the day before's make-up on her face. 'Aunt Ruth is drunk in the kitchen. I've told her she'll have to go.'

'Her cooking is one of the few assets this place has got. You'd better let me take over for a bit.'

'So you can ask for more money. Emil says that a woman in business is worse to deal with than a man.'

'What a nice compliment. I didn't know he had it in him.'

'You took against Emil the minute you saw him. Just because you married a foreigner doesn't mean they're all the same.'

That seemed a good moment to start being stern with Helen, but a bracelet clinked and Mrs Dorkin appeared holding a dead mouse by its tail. Mentally, she seemed to be going the same way as the commander.

'Hello, dear,' she said to Sibli, 'Helen doesn't mean to be cross with people, do you, dear?'

'Take that disgusting thing away.'

'He was in the larder. Naughty little boy, now he's dead. Helen's only upset because of the policeman.'

'*Mother!*'

'Put the mouse outside with the compost,' said Sibli gently, then she sat Helen down by a lukewarm radiator and dug out the story.

A detective constable had called to see Emil in Kensington. While the man was waiting downstairs, Emil took his passport from the dressing-table, helped himself to the pound notes in Helen's handbag, spoke of 'a misunderstanding' that would be fully explained when he sent for her within twenty-four hours, and disappeared down the fire escape. That was days ago. She had no address for him in Brussels. The hotel bill hadn't been paid; Mrs Dorkin had lent her the money.

No more was heard of Emil, except that Sibli was again in touch with Tom for explanations. Monsieur Cammaerts had convictions in Belgium for fraudulent conversion, and a year earlier had been questioned about share-pushing in Manchester, though never charged. Sibli repeated it all to the victim.

Helen was persuaded to move into the flat at Covent Garden. She was pregnant, with a craving for chocolate that made her weep when she thought about the chocolate factory – which, like everything else about Emil, turned out to be non-existent. 'We have both let men ruin our lives,' said Helen. Sibli humoured her by pretending to agree.

One afternoon, when they had spent hours cooped up in the sitting-room with chocolates and cocktails, she had the un-Sibli-like feeling that it was true, that without the strong brick walls of men their lives had collapsed on themselves into a mess of femininity. Em coming in with the afternoon mail broke the spell with her red working-woman's face and the brisk soapy odour of her clothes. But for a moment Sibli knew what it was like to be Helen.

'Listen, darling,' she said, 'you have to make a decision pretty soon.'

'Not today, Sibkins.'

'You've heard me talk about Munro Parton. He'll look after you when baby comes. Or doesn't, if you see what I mean.'

'There's my career to think of. It isn't fair, Sibby,' and she stirred the violet creams with her finger. '*You* don't go round getting pregnant.'

'I'm hardly a model for anyone.'

'I don't want the little beast. Do you think I ought to?'

'I'll take care of you either way,' said Sibli, the impartial friend.

Sweat shone on Helen's forehead. She said, 'If it was a girl I'd call her Isabel,' and, 'Oh God, I'm going to be sick.'

Helen was persuadable in either direction; that was the problem. Sibli set out in the following days to be rigorously impartial. 'You are my dearest friend,' ran the argument. 'All I want is your happiness.'

You wish to have the conman's child? Maternity skirts, nurses, bassinets, baby-clothes, rattles and perambulators will appear as though by magic. Munro Parton will see it enters the world unobtrusively. Then it can be adopted. It can even be kept.

You prefer not to have it? My hundred guineas will guarantee the alternative Munro Parton, a nursing home outside London up a drive screened by pine trees, minimal pain and then baskets of grapes, plus professional advice on how best to avoid begetting another of the little blighters, men being such unreconstructed beasts. But you must decide. I shall do nothing to influence you.

Approaching in the taxi not long after, Sibli was only mildly surprised to note the drive and the pines, much as she had imagined them. A Novemberish wind off the Thames estuary sighed in them as she mounted the steps and felt herself observed. The matron said that Miss Dorkin had been suffering a little discomfort, nothing of any consequence, but the resident doctor was with her, and perhaps Mrs Somerset would wait in the waiting-room.

Walls lined with books deadened the sound. A telephone bell rang far off. Among the reading matter was an old *Sunday Argus*, with a Davis dispatch from Berlin that she had missed. It had his usual touches — ruined gentlefolk eating beans by candlelight, stormtroopers rattling moneyboxes for Nazi Party funds, the doddery President Hindenburg being hoisted into a carriage by his aides and his hat falling off. She could hear Davis's voice behind the words.

'Miss Dorkin is ready for you now,' said a nurse, and Sibli, entering a room that looked across Kent to a line of sea, dumped her fruit and flowers (fresh from Covent Garden) and cradled Helen, who wept and shuddered in her arms.

When the spasm subsided and Sibli was perched against the pillow, stroking hair and holding a hand, Helen said, 'It was what you thought best, wasn't it, Sibby?'

Sibli nodded. 'Mind you,' she said, 'I did mean to be impartial.' But there was a secret bias in everything one did.

It was a gloomy week, making her unusually glad to hear from Davis when he returned to London. He telephoned to ask if she could read German, having brought back some Nazi speeches that needed translating. When they met she thought him changed, unless it was her. His head was full of what he had been seeing; his preoccupied air reminded her of the Davis she first knew.

She found a friend of a friend who would do the translating. Davis handed over the speeches in a teashop, and said he supposed she hadn't bothered to read his articles. 'They sounded like you,' she said, 'or you sound like them. Whichever you prefer. I liked the bit about the thousand naturists at dawn, saluting the flag.'

'Germany's no joke,' said Davis. 'To hear the Nazis talk, you'd think they won the elections. They're a murderous crew. McInch wouldn't print some of the stuff I sent him.'

They met once or twice — for a cheap meal in Bloomsbury, to see a Russian film. He avoided talking about himself. After the film they walked to Oxford Circus, and he hailed a taxi for her; the tube would do for him. It wasn't easy to picture him in a suburb, in a house with a family.

'Where do journalists have their nests, Davis? Edgware? Ealing? Richmond?'

'Anyone would think there's a mystery. Jump in the taxi. I'm coming as well,' and he told the driver to go to South Kensington.

They passed the half-lit edges of the Park and crossed the Brompton Road border to where genteel lives went on behind curtains. She was on the run again, slipping through nets of unknown streets in a city she didn't know, danger waiting in figures outside pubs or black closed-up motorcars. Neither spoke as they crept into shadowland, until Davis said 'Peele Place' to the cabbie, and she shivered, seeing ghosts.

The house they stopped at was Morgan's. A light shone over the front door.

'Home,' said Davis. 'I thought you'd have known.'

'Pa lets it to Americans. He has done since he's lived in France.'

'Not the top floor.' He had a key in his hand. 'I use the entrance at the side and the back stairs.'

'So you and he are friends.'

'He published my book, that's all. I bumped into him in Paris. He wasn't asking much rent.'

'I used to live on the top floor.'

'I know. I found a hairpin once, in a vase.'

She followed up the long staircase, which had been reconstructed to bypass the second floor and the Americans. On the landing, now Davis's entrance hall, a note reminded him of pickled pork in the larder.

A daily woman cleaned and cooked. 'This is the bit visitors see,' he said, and the square room with heavy curtains was more or less as she remembered, except that now it was bleak and disordered, like a hotel room about to be vacated.

Her bedroom had turned into a study, with a cheap desk where the bed had been. Here she had lain having thoughts about Davis, the back of her neck in roughly the same place as a stack of old *Sunday Argus*es, hips pillowed in the region of the Remington portable, toes in the space now occupied by *Bradshaw*, world gazetteer and *Who's Who*. Past and present hung together.

In the sitting-room she scrutinized his shelf of books while he poured wine from a half-empty bottle with a patent stopper.

'To our long acquaintance?' he suggested, but she didn't feel like pleasantries.

The house had too many ghosts. She sipped the blackish wine and put down the glass by a tattered *Red Badge of Courage*. 'Will it be all right if we sleep together now?' she said.

CHAPTER 28

Remaining single might have jeopardized Tom's career, but love came into it as well. Eve was eminently lovable. With her supple limbs, tennis-ball breasts and general glow of health, all thanks to years of PT-mistressing, she promised a lifetime of keeping up to the mark.

Pre-eminently, she was a wife who understood, as demanded by the life a police officer led. 'My little sister will never give you a moment's trouble,' George Swann once assured him, and, roughly as George had forecast, Eve gave up her job and devoted herself to Tom and the house with bay-windows they rented in Battersea, facing a market-garden and a power station.

When his work took him to the City, Tom felt that, after all, he had not strayed so far from the life that once seemed inevitable. His old impatience with the customs and disciplines of the Square Mile, when he hated the daily journey to the poky offices in Heneage Lane, had dwindled. At times he even had twinges of regret for the fine figure he might have made as the partner who brought new blood into the Penbury-Holt partnership. Now, wearing a well-cut suit, he could still drift down Lombard Street on the tide of brokers, disguised as one of them, the unknown spy in their midst.

Sometimes he waved his warrant card and entered the Baltic Exchange for a chat with the Boss, who was still employed by Duck, Reece & Pincher as a shipbroker, and was still paid a comparative pittance. The Grandfather was dead; of a tired heart or shame, depending which version you preferred.

The Boss had never forgiven his son for joining the police, and Tom would never have gone there in uniform. They talked about the Bossess (she now devoted herself to church missions), or the Slump (the Boss knew a stockbroker who had shot himself), or even the ancient Ellis Crabb saga (the Boss still listened for City rumours, which were invariably false); Crabb was the closest they ever got to Tom's career at Scotland Yard.

To Eve the Penbury-Holts were fascinating, and she would find any excuse to bring them into the conversation. The more Tom said they were an ordinary middle-class family, his branch of which had fallen on hard times, the more she wanted to know about their former glories, or, in the case of Stuart the aviator and Esther the eccentric, the glories that were still to be seen.

One evening early in 1933, Tom was studying a street map and other documents on the dining-room table, where he worked when he was at home, when Eve came to stand behind him and asked if they could do something special for his birthday in February.

'I never plan my birthday,' he said, straining his eyes under the yellowish lamp as he tried to find Gorak Street. 'I might not even be free.'

'I wanted it to be a surprise, but you hate surprises.'

He found a Nowak and a Gondzik. 'I suppose we could have George and Hilda here.'

She put her brown arms around his neck. 'Or we could do something with your family.'

His finger lost its place and he said, 'Damn, damn, damn. Can't you see I'm working?'

'What's it a map of?'

'I can't tell you that.'

'It's Warsaw, it says on the top.'

'There are certain gentlemen who would very much like

to have that information, so I want you to forget what you've seen.'

'Oh, lawks,' said Eve. 'I'll go away, but how would it be if we celebrated your birthday at the ancestral home?'

He found Gorak Street and ringed it with red crayon. 'Look here, Eve, I've told you often enough, Saracens is four flats nowadays and the Boss lives in one of them.'

'So it's one quarter of the ancestral home. You ought to care about tradition.'

'You mean snobbery.'

'Please don't call me a snob,' she said, and went back to the kitchen, leaving Tom to wonder fleetingly if he should have known more women before he settled down with Eve. The thought was soon lost amid the ramifications of the Polish Horse Dealer's Fraud inquiry.

This had lasted for months already. The dealer, a familiar figure at auctions in south London, was suspected of smuggling forged currency into the country. The information came from another Pole, an illegal immigrant who lodged at the horse trader's house, and was threatened with deportation unless he co-operated. The Illegal was a Flying Squad informant. He produced forged dollar bills, and told George Swann that sidelines in Polish bonds and British insurance stamps were also on offer from the printing press in Warsaw.

The Flying Squad could have kept the case for itself. But George – like Tom, an inspector before he was thirty – said they were family, weren't they? Anyway they needed someone who could pass himself off as a bent stockbroker, wanting to do business in forged securities, and able to talk convincingly about seven per cent Polish Stabilization Bonds. Carrying a wallet stuffed with banknotes to flash when buying drinks, Tom met the horse dealer at a railway hotel and gave him an order for bonds and stamps. That was weeks ago. The Illegal had gone to Warsaw. He might even be dead by now.

Tom had proposed going to Warsaw himself, but the

Yard was suspicious of foreign police. 'We want the flies in our web, not theirs,' said George.

So Tom waited and studied railway timetables, had talks with the Bank of England printing department, and made inquiries about Gorak Street (where the forgers were reputed to do their engraving) in the guise of a solicitor trying to trace a legatee. Crime was something to take seriously. Working late at the Yard one night, Tom was down in the basement, searching for files. His cuffs were getting dirty; he wanted his supper; a rat was playing games behind a wall. Partners at Heneage Lane (or anywhere else in the Square Mile) were never at the office a minute after 5 P.M. They whisked themselves away to freedom, just as Timmy Stevens (last heard of selling American motorcars in Monte Carlo) had done with his entire life.

Damn their eyes, they were just businessmen! A brilliant young detective, on the other hand, was a servant of society. He liked the phrase; he thumped the wall and the rat shut up. Climbing the long stone steps he decided that his generation was beginning to see things with the same clarity that had ruled in the war. After the lackadaisical twenties came the new-broom thirties. One day the Boss would grasp it. Tom said a cheerful 'Good evening' to the night constable and walked home under a dull red sky, arresting vagrants with his eyes.

A week or two before his birthday, his sister Alexandra came to the house on a Saturday afternoon. He was at Battersea library, looking things up in a Polish-English dictionary, and found her with Eve when he returned, their faces flushed from the sitting-room fire.

'To what do we owe the pleasure?' he said, narrowing his eyes detective-like at her uniform of black skirt and severe hat (eats too many sweets, an office-worker, virginal, hopeful), and giving her a peck on the cheek.

'Can't a sister visit a sister-in-law?'

'One looks for motives. One is trained.' He smiled; he

had a sense of humour. 'One thinks of reasons why young Alexandra on her afternoon off suddenly decides to come Batterseawards.'

'Oh lawks, he's going to arrest you.'

'Some plan to do with my birthday. Am I right?'

'If it is, it's more than you deserve,' said Alexandra. 'You've become an old grump. You never call to see me.'

Eve went off to the kitchen to make tea, leaving the two alone by the fire, whose comforting effect was heightened by the view outside, winter allotments under the clouds.

'I've hardly seen you since the wedding,' said the young woman. 'I have had an assistant under-manager called Ronald buying me flowers and *silk stockings*. I know, I know, that comes under the Bossess's heading of things a young lady should send back.'

'Did you?' He yawned in the shadows.

'Yes,' she said sadly. Then she giggled. 'What about your Mrs Somerset?'

'Less of the "my" Mrs Somerset.' He stared at his fingers, held out against the flames. 'I was sorry to see her ruined like that in the divorce court. It's very un-English, letting a wife take the blame. But his real name was Samauskas. They were immigrants from Russia.'

'Still,' said his sister, eyes wide with mischief, 'Mrs S. was a fast little piece, was she not?'

'Who is that?' asked Eve, coming in with a tray.

Alexandra became busy, making room on a table. 'Nobody, really. A sort of friend of the family.'

'Do you mean the woman who married Tom's Uncle Henry and then left him? The one who lives in Wales.'

'That's somebody else,' said Tom. 'She's a Mrs Mappowder, a Miss Buckley as was. Mind you get it all down on paper so you won't forget.'

'He makes fun of me and your family, but the Swanns aren't half as interesting. Should I know this Mrs S.?'

Tom sat with his hands behind his head, watching Alexandra keep out of it. Icing gleamed as she sank her teeth in cake. Sibli was as distant now as the partners' room in Heneage Lane. She belonged to the same era as Ellis Crabb of the saliva'd teeth. She was just a photograph in his mind. 'It's a Mrs Somerset, who was in the papers last year,' he said. 'She had an unfortunate divorce.'

'I read about it,' squealed Eve. 'He was in films. So *that's* who Family Friend is.'

'In a manner of speaking. I knew her years ago. She was a Miss Buckley, a niece of Mrs Mappowder.'

'Oh, Tommy! Tommy-Tom-Tom!' Eve was kneeling by his chair to pour. In her excitement, tea splashed his shoe. 'I shan't pry. Never pry with a man, Alexandra.'

'Her father is Morgan Buckley, who nearly went to prison once. That's true, isn't it, Tom?'

'Pornography, no less.'

Eve nodded, working things out. 'Margaret was the one who married Henry, yes? Henry was the hero in the bombing raid who died of his injuries.'

'Er, more or less,' said Tom. 'Though I've always thought that what he really died of was a broken heart.'

'Miss Buckley didn't break your heart, I hope?'

'Nothing was ever proved,' he said lightly, and one of Timmy Stevens's obscenities about the ephemeral nature of cunt came appositely to mind. 'The Buckleys are a family to steer clear of, is all I want to say.'

When the matter of Tom's birthday came up, he accepted, with good grace, the way in which the family dinner party that Eve had been coveting at Saracens – Saracens, Flat No 1, that is – slid into place. Alexandra had organized it with Boss and Bossess. Aunt Esther, who had taken up motoring, would drive Tom and Eve out there. The whole family would be in attendance; 'like old times,' said Alexandra. Eve was radiant, and the little circle of Penbury-Holts drew closer round the fire, wasting no more time on the Buckleys, the enemy.

That concluded the birthday discussions as far as Tom was concerned. The Horse Dealer affair came to a head, but not until the day before his birthday. A telegram from Warsaw said the Illegal would be on the same Hook-to-Harwich ferry as two businessmen, travelling with samples of cloth in cabin trunks. It meant hanging around the quays at Harwich to see what turned up. The detectives left London the day before; Tom assured Eve that he would be back within twenty-four hours.

It wasn't his fault that no one suspicious was aboard the first ferry to arrive, and that another message came from Warsaw soon after to say the businessmen would be a day late. He had to send a telegram to Eve, 'Delayed overnight.'

George was there with his own team of men. George didn't send telegrams. 'The ladies have to learn patience, my old son,' he said.

The second day passed with freezing winds and false alarms. The midday ferry was delayed by heavy seas. It was getting dark when it came up the river. Presently the Illegal was seen in the queue at the Customs shed. He nodded towards two men in overcoats, and Tom sent a boy with a second telegram for Eve, 'Delayed again, go without me.'

George, the senior officer, wasn't having their visitors grabbed at Harwich for Customs to get the prizes, or worse still the local plods. The luggage was glanced at on the bench, the businessmen strolled through to the platform.

George and his team shot off by road, boasting they could beat the train to London, which didn't leave for half an hour. All Tom had to do was make sure the Poles were still sitting comfortably when the whistle blew. Later, returning from the lavatory, he saw them playing cards, and said, 'Good evening' to the priest wearing a clerical collar who was standing in the corridor, who was really his sergeant, a dodge suggested by George.

This was the stuff, he thought. No birthday treat as a child provided anything half as satisfying. Nonchalantly, he read his evening newspaper, glancing at the northern suburbs, where lights began to cluster, feeling himself one of the avengers that England needed. Polish villains were even more villainous than the home-grown sort. Invisibly ranged behind him he sensed the vast complexity of the State, urging him to stop the rot.

At Liverpool Street Station they all hurried over the platforms, the quarry impeded by luggage, the pursuers slipping ahead to the taxis. No George was at the barrier, no unmarked cars in the yard.

Tom's taxi with four men on board was pulling out to begin the last leg of the chase when he saw his brother-in-law's vehicle appear on the wrong side of the yard, and George jump out and peer helplessly at the stream of taxis. Another second and he would have missed the kill. Tom got out as the cab slowed to turn into the main road, nearly went under a lorry, and ran back for him.

They managed to catch up with the taxis. 'Thank you, my boy,' said George. Tyres hissed in the wet, the street lamps had haloes. The convoy stopped at the Rathbone Hotel. Presently the visitors were in the lounge with the horse dealer, drinking whisky and laughing. The trunks had gone upstairs.

George was magnanimous, saying it was Tom's collar, that he'd have missed it but for him. The arrest seemed to happen in slow motion, the mud-grey faces, a cigarette stubbed out, a bottle of ginger ale knocked over. 'No trouble, if you please,' said Tom. 'We're all going up to your room.'

The cloth samples in the trunks were genuine enough, but false linings were soon detected, crammed with packets of bonds and folders of employment stamps. George flung an armful on the bed and told a constable to start counting. Turning, he slipped a wad of stamps under his coat. He saw Tom had seen, and winked.

Tom pushed him into a tiny bathroom and locked them in. The other was laughing. 'Perks, my boy,' he said, jammed up against the bath. 'This is worth a few quid to some juggins.'

'Do put them back, George, so we can have a nice clean case.'

'Clean as a whistle, my boy. You haven't seen a thing.'

'Unfortunately I have.'

'Don't be daft. I'm Uncle George. You're married to my sister.'

'Hand them over. I mean it.'

They struggled between the fittings, wrestling clumsily, and the stamps slid into the lavatory.

'Now they're no use to anyone,' said George, and pulled the chain. 'What am I going to do with you? We aren't moral theologians. We catch thieves. There's an entitlement to gravy and always has been.'

The day was compromised. The elation went away. Tom continued working as long as he could, till the three men had been charged, statements taken, telegrams sent to the authorities in Warsaw. For the first time he thought about Eve and the birthday party, not sorry to have had such a good excuse for missing it.

He would make it up to her somehow; in any case she would be having a lovely time at close quarters with the in-laws. Perhaps they would insist she spend the night there. Sleeping alone didn't bother him; on the contrary, he could rise early and leave for the Yard at seven without bothering about tea in bed and kisses. Not that he didn't find her lovable.

From the road the house was in darkness, but when he let himself in he saw a light from the kitchen, and was astonished to find his Aunt Esther there, sitting with her knees almost touching the coal stove, reading a book.

'It seemed wiser to call off the celebration,' she said, drawing on a cigarette. 'Your mother was very understanding. Eve and I have had a nice quiet evening here.'

'I'm surprised she didn't wait up for me.'

'She was very tired. I think she worries when you're away.'

'Eve?' he called, wagging his finger at the ceiling. 'Really, that girl has to pull her socks up. We can't ask Mr Criminal to keep conventional hours. Take today. I'd been at Harwich watching the ferries . . .'

His aunt boiled a kettle while he gave an account of the operation. Her only response was to say, 'So we can all sleep safe in our beds now,' when they were drinking tea.

'I expect you are pulling my leg. You have to admit that catching forgers is better than not catching them.'

'I am delighted to see you doing so well,' she murmured. 'Your present by the way is out at Saracens, gold cufflinks inscribed with the crest of the Metropolitan Police.'

'Thank you, Aunt, very kind indeed.' He kissed her cheek, dry and unpowdered.

'Eve thinks you'll be a chief superintendent before you're forty.'

'Eve thinks it because I think it.'

'I hope she occasionally has thoughts of her own.' A tram went rattling down the high street, far off; coal settled in the stove. 'Try to make her happy. It's what Penbury-Holt men are not very good at, I'm afraid.'

This was going a bit far, even for a peculiar aunt whose peculiarities were well-known. He said, 'Do come off it, Aunt Esther.'

'No, Tom, you listen to me. I was dismayed to hear Eve say in all seriousness that your Uncle Henry died of a broken heart. Now, if there was any broken heart in that marriage, it was Margaret's. I don't like to hear a friend maligned. Henry was my brother, but the less said about him as a husband the better.'

'Eve is for ever asking about the Penbury-Holts.'

'Then tell her nothing or tell her the truth.'

The rebuke wasn't called for. What a cheek, he thought, at the same time keeping cool. Aged relatives had this tendency to mistake one for a young person. 'I do hope

I'm not being called to account,' he said. 'I shouldn't like that much. However, these are trivial domestic matters.' His coolness seemed to him masterly. 'All I'd say is that the Penbury-Holts owe nothing to the Buckleys.'

'You sound just like your father.'

'Well, I'm sure that's a compliment. The Boss certainly had no time for the Buckleys. Morgan was a scallywag.'

'And now to crown it all, Sibli has been in the papers.'

'I say nothing about her.'

'It was she who broke your heart,' said Esther gently. 'I was always sorry about that but I never managed to say it.'

'It's ancient history.' He rattled the stove. 'I think I shall now go and see Eve is all right.'

'That's the wisest thing I've heard you say. I shall walk to the high street – I didn't bring the car. The trams are still running.'

He saw her to the door. His aunt looked smaller and squatter than ever. 'By the way,' she said, 'Eve has some news for you.' She raised a man's umbrella and opened it with a grating sound.

'About what?'

The umbrella moved away. 'About babies,' came from under it.

He locked the door and went slowly upstairs, saying, 'Damn, damn, damn,' under his breath.

CHAPTER 29

For a man in his situation, Davis didn't own much. A couple of suits and a faded dinner-jacket were the backbone of his wardrobe. The prints of village life had been on the walls since Sibli's childhood; he hadn't even added a school team photograph or a mother.

A tin alarm clock by his bed was the only timepiece. Cigarettes lived in their packets, as did sugar and coffee, his staple diet, and the ashtrays were saucers with burns. Even the bathroom contained nothing more personal than a safety razor, a toothbrush and a cake of soap. When the time came, Sibli had no trouble finding room for standby supplies – make-up, bath salts, stockings.

Discovering Davis was a slow process. It was like sleeping with a man without a past. What had he done all these years? (He told her he was thirty-seven, which made the Davis she first knew no more than twenty-five.) Not having possessions could be his nature or it could be a ruse. Sibli, back in the world of men, was ready for anything. He didn't seem to be concealing a wife and children, though he did mention an Italian woman he lived with for a couple of years.

As a lover he was nervy and playful, inclined to laugh at his bony frame, 'my carcase', and her well-packed flesh, 'your irregularities'. She wasn't sure she trusted him. He would suddenly fall asleep or yawn or do something disharmonious, like commenting on the sweat on her belly, or telling her a funny story about McInch while his hand wandered over her breasts. Some nights his coughing fits made the bed shake; he described them as 'hereditary', and could be awake for hours, sitting in an armchair with a blanket around his shoulders, scribbling in a notebook.

Not that Sibli was there every night, or even most nights. She had her own life. Davis was a thread running back into the past that it amused her to explore. Had she just met him for the first time at somebody's party, mooching about in his dinner-jacket and clip-on bow tie (it lived in the same drawer as his socks), she would have found something oppressive behind the bravura. Nor did she like the sound of that cough.

Then there was the poker school. Having a key, she looked in one Sunday, after lunching with friends in Chelsea. Cigarette smoke was filtering out to the stairs. Davis and three men were sitting around the dining-room table, clutching cards. They stood up to be introduced but didn't leave the table and their money — Rabin, a dark-featured American who wrote for the *Chicago Tribune*, Pugh, a football correspondent, and the chief sub-editor of the *Argus*, a man with bristly hair called Shorrock.

'It's a hell of a good game just now,' said Davis, transferring his own whisky to a cup with dried coffee stains in it, and offering her a measure in his glass, as if he wanted to make her an honorary member. She didn't take it.

'From the smoke you've been here all day.'

'Since eleven PM last night, ma'am,' said Rabin.

Davis patted his pile of coins and pound notes, which was larger than anyone else's. 'We slept for three hours when it got light,' he said.

It was a cold day at the beginning of March. The only heating in the room was a small electric fire. Sleet fell between the window and the chimneys opposite. Unshaven men playing cards didn't bother her (they might even interest her), but Davis's ready acceptance of squalor did. Her chatty 'Pigsty is the word that springs to mind' produced an echo from Rabin, who said, 'Ma'am, you're right.'

In the kitchen, among dirty plates, she made herself tea.

Was there any point in Davis as an object of desire?

The man with bristly hair appeared and said the session was over, that Stevie, as they called him, had gone down smiling, having raised the stake to a level beyond his means on what turned out to be a dismal hand, and was now writing out IOUs for painful amounts.

'Just as well he'll be in Berlin to make some nice expenses,' he added.

This was the first that Sibli had heard of another trip to Berlin. She poured boiling water over the debris in the sink and said her goodbyes. Davis, the rat, had one of his coughing fits – perhaps rats could provide them on demand – and she left Rabin opening a window and telling him to get a lungful of air.

Two days later Sibli was answering letters after breakfast when Em announced the arrival of Davis. In his old check overcoat he looked gaunter than ever.

'I'm going abroad,' he said, sounding almost apologetic, for Davis. 'McInch the Miser is convinced that Hitler is about to become a sweet-natured democrat, now he's in the driving seat. So I'm sent there for a month, which is all he can afford. Second-rate hotel, and cables to go overnight where possible.'

'Off you go then, Davis.'

'I meant to tell you earlier, but it was a matter of finding the right moment. I thought this time I might persuade you.'

'I always admire a man who keeps trying. Unfortunately I'm going to Paris to stay with my father.'

'You didn't like the poker game.'

'I didn't like one of your friends telling me about Berlin before you did. Send me a postcard.'

'If you change your mind, here's my address.' He scribbled it before kissing her cheek. She made a point of not taking it to Paris.

Life with Morgan was as agreeable as ever. His affection was undiminished as long as his affairs were not interfered with. Only Sibli, he felt, never judged him, and he could tell her what he was up to – or, where appropriate, not tell her anything at all – without losing her sympathy.

Rebecca Smollett, his business confidant, was reliable enough with the books and magazines he handled, even in what he called his 'Black' department. Black material went beyond the stuff on sale downstairs. Rebecca ran an efficient mail-order business. The timid spinster had grown into a secretive middle-aged woman who took five years off her age and had the knack of making Morgan feel he was a young devil again, violating a pure female; her auburn hair was tawnier and thicker these days, expensively packed around the brows, and she edited stories of amazing rudeness without flinching.

She knew there were other women. But they were rarely seen and never threatened her. Morgan had a theory that jealousy held in check acted as a stimulant to the injured party, who even worked better as a result. 'I've seen Rebecca smouldering when she imagines I am romantically interested in someone she suspects is half her age,' he told Sibli one evening, going back in a taxi from the Moulin de la Chanson. 'As if I would be, at my time of life.'

'As if.'

'When roused she'll tear through a manuscript in hours. And spice it up in the process.'

'Do your steamier books get into England?'

'I prefer *avant-garde* to *steamier*.'

'So do they?'

'Very much so. Anglo-Saxon countries are where we do best. It's where the State wants God to be a moralist, never mind the fulcrum of eternity.' His dark head, greying above the ears, reclined in a corner. Pa's voice always soothed her, even when he was talking gibberish; not that God was necessarily gibberish. 'The Almighty there comes down to a man in a black hat with a telescope, surveying sweaty humanity as it tries to enjoy itself, and shouting at it to stop. Or so I've seen it said.'

'By whom?'

'Nicholas Lambe, since you're asking. He writes brilliant forewords for the classier end of my market. How dare anyone talk of smutty books when the binding is immaculate and the Abbé Fournier or Dr Cyrus M. Mortimer DSc introduces it with a thousand words of really excellent prose.'

'Those are his pen-names?'

'Good, aren't they? Don't sound so disenchanted. Nicholas needs to keep himself going while he writes his sequel to *Battle Honours*.'

'He should have finished it by now.'

'Call and see him one day. He has a second-floor apartment he can't afford, not far from where we've just been.'

'I might.'

They reached the Aeolian Press, where the window-display downstairs featured a jungly interior of greenstuff and branches, from which hung bunches of orange-coloured books. An impudent poster in the paws of two stuffed monkeys announced, 'Les Fruits de la Littérature'.

'I've been seeing of another of your old authors,' she said. 'Remember Stephen Davis?'

'Burned himself out too young.' They were in the lift, trundling upward. 'His book didn't sell, either.'

Davis didn't matter. She had plenty to do, shopping, going to galleries, meeting some of Pa's friends – a *directeur* in a police department, a woman who sang in cabaret, a professor of divinity, all part of Morgan's network. Ricard was away.

Max Samauskas, James's brother, heard she was in Paris and telephoned her. He was setting up a film with French locations, and Sibli went with him and his wife to the races at St Cloud, where she won sixty francs and then lost them again; too much like Davis.

A *Sunday Argus* or two were on sale on Mondays. When she had been in Paris three weeks she bought one and read Davis on the new Germany. He had stood outside the

Garrison Church in Potsdam, at the service to inaugurate the first Reichstag of the Nazi Party. 'They've been down to the vaults,' an excitable Communist told him. 'The Generalfeldmarschall' – the old President, Hindenburg – 'has gone and stuck a wreath on Frederick the Great's tomb. That's it. Hitler has got the old fool's blessing. They will be rounding us up in a week.' Davis had seen a man hanging from a lamppost in a suburb. No one went near. When the police came, they threw the corpse on the back of a lorry.

'Yellow journalism,' said Pa. 'How can he possibly know what's going on in Germany?'

It was true that the French papers were cautious, and the London *Times* – which Morgan subscribed to because he used it for coded advertisements in the Personal column – was writing respectfully of Herr Hitler and his progressive policies. The fate of Europe was impenetrable; the answers to Davis ought to be easier, but it wasn't clear that she would gain anything by looking for them.

Nicholas Lambe was on her list of diversions. Sitting straight-backed with his arms folded in the Café de la Paix, where they met in mid-afternoon, he looked more like the bald-headed colonel in *Battle Honours*, who liked to slip a hand under his driver's khaki skirt, than the man who conceived him.

It was years since she read the book, but she remembered its half-hidden theme, the eroticism of war, and told Lambe how badly she thought the courts had treated him. He sipped a pink gin and said nothing. A new generation of the British would discover him, she said, once they did away with censorship.

'Some bloody hope,' said Lambe. 'It's no use Morgan sending you round to butter me up. I know what he wants. Sex on every page.'

'Not if you don't want to write it. Why should he? He isn't a fool. He can easily find hacks who'll write yards of it. You're supposed to be writing the peacetime sequel to

Battle Honours. He wouldn't be human if he didn't want some fucking in it now and then, that's all. The people in the book wouldn't be human if they didn't want it, either.'

'How nicely you say it,' said Lambe sarcastically. 'It isn't a word that women are supposed to use. I have endeavoured to make them use it in the novel. They refuse. Even the whores refuse.'

'So at least the book's got whores. I'll tell Morgan, shall I? Since you seem to think I'm here on his behalf.'

'I thought it was obvious. Not having had the pleasure of your company for many years.'

'You've got the pleasure of it now. There is no ulterior motive, I assure you. I really did admire *Battle Honours*. I was the first fan you ever had.'

'You flatter me. Not for the first time.'

'You mean going to see you in that hotel in Victoria.'

He didn't reply, which was sensible of him, and they arranged to meet later. At seven he collected her from the apartment for an early dinner; Morgan was out, and Rebecca could be heard typing with two fingers.

An evening with Nicholas Lambe was added to all the other evenings that accumulated by the age of twenty-nine. He was not a boring man, but she would have welcomed more about his unfinished saga and less about a long-dead wife and a boat-building son in Suffolk. Lambe minus books didn't count.

She let him take her dancing in Montparnasse, at the Michel, which only the French ever visited, so he said. Max Samauskas was there with a party of English. When she introduced him, Lambe said, 'How clever of you. You have scored a point,' and hurried her away.

'You realize he used to be my brother-in-law?' she said. 'They might yet make a movie of *Battle Honours*.'

'I expect nothing.' He tried to get an arm into the sleeve of his overcoat, swaying against her on the pavement. 'I don't even expect you to come back to my apartment.'

'That's a relief. Come to Morgan's for a nightcap.'

She heard voices and smelt Davis's cigarettes as they entered the flat. Hot breezes came from the fan; the steam pipes were scalding. Davis gave them a sideways stare from the sofa, where he was talking to Rebecca.

Morgan got up to greet them, breaking off conversation with a man in steel-framed spectacles, sitting with a briefcase at his feet, who nevertheless continued to talk, waving a photograph and saying in a high-pitched voice, 'A man wearing women's underwear is a political offence to them. Human frailty, as is obvious, is never attractive to dictators except as evidence of the fallen world they have come to rescue. The Weimar Republic –'

'Herr Professor K. K. Haeckel of Berlin,' said Morgan, and the monologue paused. Wet eyes blinked at her. 'This is my daughter, Mrs Somerset, and a very old friend of hers, the brilliant novelist and essayist Nicholas Lambe. What a gathering of talents, eh? It was your Steve Davis who brought the professor to safety. He had with him nothing but the clothes he stands up in and his unfinished autobiography, which we shall publish to international acclaim, next year I daresay.'

Johnny Cox, the faithful aide, and Yvette, the skinny Frenchwoman he had married, stood ready with a tray, from which they handed round food and drink. 'Langoustines on toast?' he said, and Sibli wondered if Morgan was turning Sergeant-Major Cox into the butler, and his wife into the cook.

'As I was telling you, the Weimar Republic had many faults, but it provided useful outlets for sexual idiosyncracy. The new regime will inhibit them, which may be disastrous for Germany. The middle classes –'

'Fascinating,' said Sibli, without halting the flow, and moved towards Davis. She noted the stained shoes and smoke-laden clothes; the eyes with bloodstained corners were a new feature. 'You've had an adventure,' she said.

'The bell rang and there they were on the doorstep,'

said Rebecca. 'I had better see if Dr Haeckel wants to send any more telegrams. Excuse me.'

'I thought journalists didn't meddle, Davis.'

'He runs a thing called the Institute for Sexual Behaviour – trust the Germans. He's also a Jew. There are fears they'll be stopped from leaving the country.' He offered her a cigarette, although he knew she didn't smoke, and she wondered if there had been a woman in Berlin. 'I was asked if he could travel with me. Your father's version is more colourful.'

'Why not take him to London?'

'He prefers Paris. Besides, I knew Morgan would like him. They'll either make each other rich or get arrested.'

Lambe joined them. He was drinking whisky now. 'That German refugee,' he said, 'has just informed us that even the pervert has his dreams.'

'I've heard worse epigrams,' smiled Davis.

'We aren't talking about epigrams. Haeckel's briefcase is full of photographs for which I imagine one could be arrested even in France. He's a raving queer. Or perhaps a transvestite. Or both.'

Sibli was curious; she asked what the pictures were.

'He's just been gloating over a Prussian officer in dress uniform from the waist up, and women's underclothes lower down. I prefer not to go into detail. But I find it unwholesome, and I've told him so.'

'For a man who wrote a novel that was banned,' said Davis mildly, 'you're surprisingly touchy.'

Lambe flushed. '*Battle Honours* described the emotions of war as they really are. That's why they banned it, my friend.'

'And sex.'

'Are you trying to put my novel in the same category as that German filth? I'm no prude. Am I a prude, Sibli?'

'I don't think anyone suggested you were.'

Bringing Lambe home had been a mistake, but Davis wasn't helping. He said, 'Haeckel is certainly a homosexual. He also has dirty fingernails and bad breath, and he never stops talking.' Davis kept his voice low; Haeckel droned on, the fan whirled overhead. 'He doesn't appeal to me either. But he thinks we ought to tolerate what he calls the darker side of existence, and I think he's right. It's the kind of toleration England lacks, more's the pity.' He turned to Sibli. 'If I were a novelist like your friend here, I'd try and be less bigoted.'

'But you're not a novelist, that's the whole point, you're a bloody journalist!' roared Lambe, and Morgan, as if he knew exactly what the argument was about (and perhaps did, thought Sibli), jumped to his feet and announced they were all going out to the street fair in the Place d'Italie. After all, it was barely midnight.

'We shall visit the tent celebrating Woman,' he said, in the rich, fraudulent tones that he never used on Sibli. 'Ten unforgettable minutes is what the fat lady with the microphone promises, for a mere fifty francs. Dr Haeckel will lead us there, won't you, Herr Professor? You will tell us what makes voyeurs of us all –'

'Speak for yourself!' snorted Lambe.

'– and how we all hide secrets in our corruptible hearts. They tell me there are exquisite *tableaux vivants*, The Midnight Swim, The Naked Idyll, Secrets of Lesbos, Diana the Huntress. Not to mention a turn called Rosie and the Snakes, and finally Woman herself, a bit of fluff called Conchita, dancing to a gramophone and throwing her nightie at the audience.'

Morgan touched a switch near the door. The lights went out, except for a lamp with a red shade on a table. Shadows lurched across the wallpaper, and Sibli recognized the style that had given Pa his stature in the world of spirits, leading people on with his nonsense. Haeckel was through the door already, escorted by Rebecca. Yvette laughed softly. Lambe was struggling with his overcoat again, and Sibli helped him.

When she looked for Davis, she couldn't see him. Then

he appeared framed in the doorway for a second, his hat on his head, something in his hand. Outside, he wasn't with the group waiting for the lift. Footsteps came from the stone stairway, and she ran down, calling after him.

In the street, where she caught up with him, he had hailed a taxi. His suitcase was already inside.

'Aren't you coming, Davis?' she said. 'Please come.'

'Your novelist needs you.'

'Now who's being touchy? Where are you going?'

'London. I'll take a train to Calais and catch the first boat. You can always come with me, if you want to.'

'I will if you wait till tomorrow. Tomorrow, I promise.'

Ten yards away, Morgan stopped a taxi. 'Professor Haeckel's party, this way!' he shouted.

She heard Davis say, 'Gare du Nord,' and felt her heart beating. She didn't see his face at the window.

Heading for the Place d'Italie, she found herself pressed against Lambe. She took his hand and thrust it savagely between her legs, but he was too far gone to notice.

CHAPTER 30

That summer, for the first time, the Mandeville Arms showed signs of life. No one questioned Sibli's authority now. She persuaded Helen to run it, after quarrels.

It was a calculated risk. Herbert King had to be demoted; he solved the problem by disappearing to a beach mission on the Isle of Wight, or, as his wife told people, 'Mr King has gone to Sandown to meet his Maker.'

Helen, nervy after the nursing home and almost as thin as she had always wanted to be, began by wearing unsuitable dresses and avoiding the guests. Sibli got her into deep-coloured blouses and pencil skirts, and told her to be visible at all times, though she had to amend this when Helen, gaining confidence, began flirting with husbands.

'Disastrous, full-stop,' said Sibli. 'You pay attention to the *wife*. For the man you remain inscrutable. Then they'll both want to come back for different reasons.'

'How boring, dear,' said Helen, but did as she was told.

Sibli wondered how many one-star hotels there were in the south of England with decent facilities and a cook who knew about mayonnaise; hundreds, probably. She advertised in a guidebook and *The Lady*, hoping to attract a few of the new motorists who sped up and down the Oxford road, who might like to break their journey in this byway down charmng Chiltern valley, newly-decrtd rms, excllnt cuisine.

'What happened to the jolly weekend idea, no questions asked?' said Helen.

'We have to see if the place works on conventional lines.

I haven't forgotten, but we want the roses-over-the-door lot first.'

It was clematis, not roses, a pink film clinging to the bricks. On fine days the new gravel drive and forecourt sparkled like salt. Mrs Dorkin weeded the flowerbeds, kneeling on the rubber mat Commander Dorkin had used; sometimes she ran grim-faced through the hotel, killing wasps with a rolled-up *Daily Telegraph*.

A trickle of guests came for one night or two. A honeymoon couple stayed briefly, betrayed by confetti in a shoe, and spoke in whispers. A family of four, bespectacled parents and two bony girls, were there for a week; at the end of each afternoon they brought back fungi and butterflies from the beech woods and Brasswynd Hill, where they had picnicked on ginger beer and Mrs King's pies. These were idylls, lives seen detached from whatever it was that would make them like all other lives, yet consistent within themselves.

Sibli spent much of the summer at the hotel. One night she dreamed that Davis was there on his honeymoon. She followed a trail of confetti to his bedroom, and heard them laughing behind the door.

Since the spring, and her return from Paris, she had heard nothing of Davis. She forgot about Davis. She refused to have anything to do with a man who expected a woman to run after him. If he was still drawing false conclusions from her behaviour at sixteen, a bottled-up ex-schoolgirl mad with fantasy, so much for Davis as a man of the world.

Davis in fact was stone dead. He had died in Paris, or even earlier, at the poker party. He was the sort of man who always let you down, not so much a betrayer as a not-botherer.

When Will Buckley, her uncle, rang up and mentioned the name 'Davis', she felt like saying, 'Who?'

It was autumn again, the time of year when people telephoned to pick up threads after the summer. Sibli was back in Covent Garden, leaving Helen at the helm. Uncle Will the socialist wasn't the sort of man to care about threads. She hardly knew him. But he was a Member of Parliament now, a name in the papers. Sibli had seen the result of the by-election that followed the death of the sitting MP, and sent a telegram.

'So what do you think of a Buckley in Parliament?' he asked.

'We shall be a respectable family yet.'

'Not by the time I've finished with the worshippers of Mammon, the coal-owners and the poor-law guardians, not to mention the Ramsay Macs and Neville Chamberlains. I shall mince them up. Now, I am in the process of finding my feet in café society. If you were to help me meet one or two folk, I wouldn't forget it. I believe you know that journalist Stephen Davis who came to see me once . . .'

'You must have been talking to Pa,' she said.

'There's quick you are, *merched*!'

'I thought you and Pa never spoke.'

'Time to forget fraternal quarrels, I told him. He was most helpful. He gave me names – the odd publisher, a banking family, a couple of peers, a leader-writer. He said you and Davis were old friends. You were on my list in any case. They say you do a lot of socializing.'

'I thought you were supposed to be smashing the system.'

'From the inside, *merched*, from the inside.'

Sibli's role was apparently the social butterfly, even the well-connected harlot, though she suspected that behind the blustery charm her uncle was making shrewder appraisals, more worthy of the Buckleys. His categories didn't bother her. Her own were flexible.

He hoped that she could invite Davis and a few others from Fleet Street or the arts to dinner, along with wives or whatever, so that he could meet them informally. The details were up to her.

An effort had to be made. Blood (she told herself) was thicker than water. 'I'm sure something can be arranged,' she said.

Davis having been pronounced dead, she wanted to think she was resurrecting him purely as a favour to the new Member for Rhondda North. When she found that Davis had moved out of Peele Place and couldn't be traced, she had to go looking for him. It got harder to tell herself that she was only doing it as a duty.

The *Argus* was unhelpful about his current address, telling her to write a letter, which would be forwarded. What could she say? *Dear Davis, Come to dinner to meet my uncle, the new MP. Love, Sibli.* That would give the wrong impression. So would anything she might write. When she telephoned he was never there. Humiliated to be doing it, she visited a public library to look at *Argus*es since the spring. They came by the month, fixed to wooden binders with flexible brass pins that turned outwards and threatened the fingers. She saw that the late Davis had been in East Anglia, reporting week by week on 'The Condition of the Rural Labourer'.

Unwillingly, she ran her eye down columns of text. He had seen pigs who looked happier than men, he quoted chunks of Cobden and Richard Jefferies, he reported Davis-like encounters. Talking to women under a canvas lean-to as they sheltered from a thunderstorm, in a corner of a field that stretched to the horizon where they were picking swedes, he argued with a farmer who arrived on horseback and accused him of trespass and fomenting strikes. Enraged, the farmer stepped up to the lean-to and fired his shotgun in the air, causing the horse to bolt. The sun came out, the women went back to picking swedes. The farmer was last seen chasing the horse.

The rural articles had ended weeks earlier. She saw nothing else by Davis, except a short feature about Sylvia Beach, the Olympia Press and other avant-garde booksellers in Paris. A paragraph devoted to Mr Morgan

Buckley said he was a former preacher who left Britain on account of its hypocrisy, following the prosecution in the twenties of the famous novel *Battle Honours*, by N. Lambe. Mr Lambe was described as 'an elderly author, still struggling with the sequel'. The article was signed, 'By Our Special Correspondent', but she guessed it was Davis.

Sibli's hands were grubby and she had a scratch of blood on her thumb where a pin had caught her. Indifference hadn't worked, after all, and she went to the *Argus* office and asked for Shorrock, the sub-editor.

He was all solicitude, taking a pencil from the clump in his breast pocket and writing Stevie's address on a scrap of newsprint. It was only round the corner from the *Argus*. Stevie was unwell with one of his coughs.

'I thought he might have gone back to Berlin.'

'Oh, no. No, no, no, no, no. Not Berlin.' Shorrock took her into a corner where he could whisper. 'They had bitter battles in the spring, he and the proprietor. His copy was cut. I cut it myself, as instructed. Stevie thought of resigning, but as he says, he's already resigned from most of Fleet Street. And whatever Stevie says about him, McInch is more critical of Mr Hitler than most of his ilk. Did you read Lord Rothermere the other day? He doesn't believe in Nazi atrocities. "A few isolated acts of violence", according to his lordship.'

She found the lodgings up a staircase, above a printing shop, with Davis typing at a yellow table, offering her an armchair (sagging bottom) and a pot of coffee (boiled on a gas ring), asking if she had just returned from Paris. That wasn't any of his business, so she told him it had been a busy summer and left it at that.

A square of sun came through a skylight, illuminating the shabbiness. Downstairs a Linotype machine clinked like coins being counted. There was no satisfactory way into a conversation. 'One of Stevie's coughs' suggested a sick man in his pyjamas, who could have been sympathized with, but the only sign of ill-health was a bottle of medicine and a spoon; meanwhile the black cigarettes were going strong.

'You may have seen that my uncle won the Rhondda North by-election.'

'He'd have had a job to lose it, with a thirty thousand majority. No offence. The miners give safe seats to people they trust.'

'He's no chicken as you know, but he does have ambitions. I shall be giving some dinner parties and inviting you. I assume he's a cause after your own heart. That was all I wanted to say. You don't have to come, Davis.'

'I enjoy meeting socialists. But most of them soon learn to guzzle the champagne.'

'What do you expect them to do? Drink tea with condensed milk and wear dirty boots? The first time I saw you at a social occasion, when you came to dinner at Peele Place in nineteen twenty-one, you wore a black tie, and I seem to remember a cloak as well. It was nothing to do with the kind of journalist you were.'

'Fancy you remembering that cloak. I thought it was very classy. I've got fewer illusions now.'

'So you live in a slum and feel superior. Is that it, Davis?'

'It's cheap and I'm trying to economize. I've been taking flying lessons for months. It cost more than I thought it would to qualify.'

'You've done it already?'

'Last week. A man from the Air Ministry comes down. You fly five figures of eight and land within fifty yards of a mark.'

'How many yards were you within?'

'Forty-nine.'

Davis was all mysteries. He talked about having flown as a Lufthansa passenger from Berlin to Munich, which hardly explained the sudden urge to become a pilot. Many men (Theodore Lloyd, for example) were 'romantic' or liked to present themselves as such. Davis always struck her as being the opposite. He made no attempt to present himself as anything, unless the unvarnished no-nonsense reporter was itself a trick of masculinity, performed with intent.

'If you're doing nothing,' he said, 'come down to Croydon on Thursday. I'm going on a cross-country.'

'By yourself?'

'Unless you come.'

It was insultingly casual. If she hadn't happened to call, there would have been no invitation, to fly in aeroplanes or do anything else.

Her ex-husband would say that the accident of her calling on Davis in time to receive the invitation was itself part of a more comprehensive chain of accidents whose ultimate operations were revealed only to those of the highest sensibility. The answer, owing something to James, was to make no decision, to say, 'Goodbye' as lightly as he had said, 'Hello', to float away from the dispiriting room – she could hear the typewriter thudding before she reached the bottom of the stairs – and wait to see what Fate dictated between then and Thursday.

On Wednesday evening it sent a telephone message that Em told her about when she returned from a party. Helen needed her badly because unexpected guests were coming for the night, an overflow from Lady Somebody's hunt ball. Faced with tricky decisions, James used to fall back on his banana diet and wait behind a locked door for inspiration. Sibli chose a hot bath with a slosh of perfume, and soon decided to take no notice of Fate. An overnight telegram to the Mandeville said, 'Leaving at dawn for unpostponable engagement but you can do it standing on your head.' By nine she was at Croydon.

A clerk in the aerodrome office looked approvingly at her leather motoring coat (tweed jacket and skirt underneath) and directed her to the private pilots' chart room, which turned out to be a hut with a coke stove and drawers full of maps. It was unoccupied. A slate on the wall had columns headed 'Pilot' and 'Flight Plan'. A single entry had been chalked in, 'S. Davis' followed by 'Port Howard, Carms (direct) & return, late PM.'

A minute later he appeared, carrying two flying helmets and a long coat faced with motheaten fur. Irritatingly, he had taken it for granted that she was coming. Port Howard was 'just about right', a morning's flying to the west, land on the sands, an afternoon's flying back to the east.

'What's the farthest you've been, Davis?'

'Until you get your "A" licence you can't go more than three miles from the aerodrome.'

'So today you're going two hundred. What happens if the tide is in when you want to land?'

'It won't be.' He was selecting Ordnance Survey sheets mounted behind celluloid, and signing for them in a ledger. 'Low water is one o'clock. The Met Office says a weather front will reach the far west later on, but we should be home by then. I've organized cocoa and bars of chocolate.'

The aircraft he had rented for the day was behind a hangar, a sturdy Handley-Page biplane in blue and silver. A mechanic was standing on a block of wood by the tail, oiling a control wire and making adjustments to a pulley. A flap was said to be not quite right, and a bolt would be replaced, as soon as Stores could find the right one.

Sibli was tempted to say, 'That's my motorcar over there. Let's go to Brighton for the day. Much more fun!' She curbed her impatience while the mechanic fiddled away, and Davis brought a pair of gloves and a blanket to put round her legs. A blanket meant he was trying. Eventually the bolt arrived, but it was after eleven before everything was ready. As they walked to the plane, the sun was turning white.

Tucked into her separate cockpit behind Davis's, connected to him with a voice-pipe in her helmet, she heard him say, 'Switches off. Suck in,' and saw the mechanic swing the toy propeller. Her experience of flying was limited to trips with James, in powerful aircraft that had armchairs bolted to the floor. What she felt was curiosity more than fear, directed at Davis more than flying.

The engine roared, a man waved a flag, and they rumbled across the grass and were in the air almost at once. Sibli could hear the wheels spinning underneath as they passed over a bungalow with a smoking chimney.

The maps were her job. Davis had drawn a pencil line through Reading, which he expected to reach in twenty-five minutes. 'Richmond Park!' came down the pipe. 'Dead on,' she shouted back, impressed at how easy it was. Steamy balls of cloud appeared below them, and she lost the Thames. But the line on the map went comfortably through Reading.

'Are you commissioned to write articles?' she shouted. 'Is that why we're here? "How the aeroplane will change our lives", sort of thing?'

'I happen to like flying.'

'We're all grist to your mill, Davis. I saw what you wrote about Morgan. And my friend N. Lambe.'

'Tell me if that's Reading. We shouldn't be there yet.'

Sibli saw street patterns and a river on the right. It was difficult, through goggles and steamy clouds.

'It's Windsor. There's the castle.'

The pencil line didn't go through Windsor. Davis talked about not allowing for drift, and changed course. When they struck a patch of turbulent air that made them slew and fall sickeningly, he said he was going up another fifteen hundred feet. The clouds ahead were thickening into a wall of grey.

They flew above them, in sunlight, but cold crept under her thighs, however hard she tugged at the blanket. When they had been in the air an hour, a gap in the cumulus showed villages strung out along a road, and green swellings in the land, marked here and there with white.

'Could be chalk downs,' called Davis. 'What does the navigator think?'

'Is your air speed still a hundred and five?'

'I doubt if it's more than ninety.'

'You might have told me.' The gap closed while she was recalculating their position. Since the amount of drift was guesswork, she thought they might be over the Cotswolds. But in that case it shouldn't have been chalk.

'I would say we're lost,' she said. 'Shall we look for somewhere else? Bristol would be nice.'

'Tell me about Lambe' seemed to come through the tube, and when she ignored him he asked again. 'I want to know what attracts you to him, that's all.'

She said that even if there was a short answer one could shout down a voice-pipe, she had no intention of giving it, and would they not be better employed establishing where they were?

'So you don't deny it?'

'Deny what?'

'Being attracted to him.'

'Think what you like. Has it ever occurred to you what women want? Of course it hasn't. You're a disaster, Davis.'

Her mouth was dry with shouting, her eyes hot under the goggles. 'Davis!' she said hoarsely in what remained of her voice, but the tube was dead. She had the illusion that the back of his helmet was really the front, that he was looking at her through pin-holes in the leather.

The engine spluttered and cut out, and the plane tilted forward. Air whistled, something creaked in the wings, the nose dropped further. They fell through cloud, unstoppably now, the mist driving into her mouth till she could taste the water. She tried to scream, 'Why, Davis?' but it came out as a whisper.

As the plane burst from the clouds, it was almost a relief to see the fields where she was going to be killed. Cattle stood in them. She shut her eyes and waited. When the engine restarted she opened them again and saw the horizon sinking as the nose came up.

The voice-pipe hissed and Davis said, 'I was getting

disoriented. Had to come down quick. Tricky business. Couldn't talk. Put a cork in the pipe. My apologies.' They banked over a railway line. 'The weather front came sooner than they said. Let's forget about the west and go back the way we came. I'll fly due east.'

'Do what you like, Davis.'

The cocoa was lukewarm in her flask, and the icy cubes of chocolate had no taste. London was an easier target to aim at. They skimmed along under thinning clouds, picked up the Chilterns, saw the northern suburbs sprawled in a haze.

'Shall we find somewhere to land?' he asked. 'Have a late lunch? I'd like to think we were having a proper day out.'

'Just keep us alive.'

Chelmsford had a landing ground, but somehow they missed the town. His gloved hand drew her attention to the coastline, and beyond it the North Sea, patched with sunlight. It was well into the afternoon. An estuary was visible.

'Crouch?' he called.

'Blackwater, I think.'

'We don't have all that much petrol. We might make Croydon.'

'Let's not try. Land down there,' she said. 'I can see grass inside the dyke.'

The nose dipped and he came down low over flooding sands, turning back towards the grass, which was mercifully short, and a row of huts up against the dyke.

The scene enlarged itself at terrifying speed. Rabbits scattered as they bumped on the turf, the aircraft beautifully trim for a moment until a wheel went into a hollow, causing a wing to scrape the ground. Wires twanged apart. They came to a halt, lopsided.

Sibli opened her eyes to see holiday shacks in the lee of the dyke, their blistered planks in blues and greens, iron chimneys sticking out of iron roofs. No one appeared.

Davis helped her from the cockpit. They weren't dead after all.

The huts all had names, *The Nook* and *Lazy Days* and *Tropicana*. He studied a map while she looked through windows. 'The village is a mile and a half,' he said. 'They're sure to have rooms.'

'Wonderful, and you can get a poker school going in the bar. We might as well enjoy ourselves while we're young, mightn't we, Davis?'

'Laugh away. No doubt I deserve it.'

'You certainly do.' Through the window of *Tropicana* a cactus, a coal stove and a teapot were visible, and she couldn't help thinking of Brighton. Even the patient tea-dancers, twirling at the Metropole, seemed enviable. She wanted Davis to suffer as she was suffering. 'You were a fool, staying above the clouds for so long,' she said, and he muttered that it was good practice for night flying, and peered with her into *Tropicana*.

'There's a tin marked "Tea",' he said.

'Who comes here?'

'Eastenders with a bit of money and a car. Nudists. Cranks. Retired burglars.'

'We could boil a kettle. I'm dying of cold.'

The key was under a bucket. The season was over; no one would come to the coast till spring. The boards creaked and there was sand on the linoleum. It was almost a bungalow, with beds and a kitchen and paraffin lamps. Davis sniffed around. He found a pressure-stove and trimmed the wick, tasted water from the rain-butt, opened a tin of condensed milk, made the tea. 'A place of our own,' he said, blowing cigarette smoke at the ceiling.

'The quicker we get back the better. It was a mistake, my coming today. Everything you and I do turns out to be a mistake. Never again. I've learnt my lesson.'

The queer Davis smile came and went. 'I wanted to liven things up between us. You're a very ungetattable woman.'

'That's your problem. Others are able to solve it.'

'Including N. Lambe, I expect.'

'You've got him on the brain. When you were trying to kill us earlier you wanted to know what attracted me to him. I suppose the answer is that he wrote a book I found erotic.'

'Another randy artist,' said Davis glumly. 'I knew, but I wanted to hear you say it.'

He sounded like a different Davis, one she might be drawn to. The sky was darkening. The rabbits were back. A gull perched on the rudder of the plane. Davis stood in the doorway, listening for the sound of a vehicle.

'Nobody'll come,' she said, adopting the fate-and-mystery approach, lighting one of the lamps, waiting for Davis to start putting a foot wrong in his usual way. He closed the door and watched her, not speaking. She filled a stone hot-water bottle – the summer visitors to *Tropicana* were realists – and put it on a mattress. Thin blankets and a pair of sheets were in a wooden box. She tied back her hair and made the bed. 'What's for supper?' she called, and he rummaged through cans.

Behind the hiss of flames was a deeper sound that could have been a vehicle, until she realized it was the sea, outside the dyke.

'Was my name in the flight plan?' she asked, when they were eating sardines and corned beef.

'As Mrs Somerset, yes.'

By now, he said, the authorities must have declared an emergency at Croydon. Phone calls would be made to police stations along the route, asking for reports of a crash or a forced landing. The story would get into the papers – 'Mrs Somerset Missing on Mystery Flight', he suggested – but thought the item too late for the editions that went to Wales.

'What about your next-of-kin?'

'Rabin at the *Chicago Tribune*.'

'It was a serious question.'

'I have a married sister in Yorkshire, but they see the

early editions, too. We can still find that pub, if you want to. There's a torch in the plane.'

'I'd rather stay.' She touched his hand. 'Let's go and look at the sea.'

The blackness was intense, and Davis used the torch to guide them as they scrambled up the grass. Waves were tumbling against the stone face. A wind hummed in their ears and he held her against his bones.

'Which way is Germany?' she said.

He pinched her nose and pulled her head to the left. 'Straight ahead of you. Why?'

'I should have gone with you. I shall, next time.'

'If there is a next time. Dear old McInch doesn't trust me with the Germans.'

They turned back to the lighted box of *Tropicana*, and when the door was locked and the faded curtains drawn, she undressed in front of him, watching his face, being as deliberate as she could; not that there was much scope for modesty.

'Do I please you?' she said.

He nodded and let her open his shirt and touch his nipples. In bed, with the stone bottle cooling at their feet, she felt she was about to be had for the first time by Davis, not (roughly) for the fiftieth; her vague mathematics was mixed up with the smell of his flesh and the flickering of his tongue. Were they being honest with one another at last? She knew this was a dangerous proposition and might be nonsense, but it was the one that fitted her mood. In the end it was only mood that mattered.

They became two other people, the Davis and Sibli who might have existed long ago but never had. They made love and talked in between, Sibli mostly listening, Davis laughing at Fleet Street, at English politicians, at the Nazis, at himself; once, in the small hours, wind rattling the windows, he whispered that he had wasted his life, that journalism was a fraud, that it left wickedness untouched, the corruptions of England as much as those of Germany.

'But it did occur to me,' he said, levering himself on to an elbow for another of his poisonous cigarettes, 'that if I was suddenly converted to Hitlerism, enough to be persona grata, I might get another crack at Berlin. Only this time I'd wait till I was clear of the place, then write a devastating book. That might be worth doing.'

In the morning they slept till nearly ten o'clock. Both were anxious to get back to civilization. They left a pound note in the tea-caddy and replaced the key under the bucket. Then they set off for the village.

CHAPTER 31

Davis was stubborn. He clung to his frowsty habitation around the corner from St Paul's as if he wanted to demonstrate to Sibli that for all the intimacies and confessions of a love affair that had finally got going, he reserved the right to be a man living in a hole in the earth, insisting she crawl in and lie with him if she really loved him.

It would happen unexpectedly, after days of living like normal people in her flat. They would be out late at night. He would steer them in the wrong direction. Her 'Oh God, not there again,' became part of a game. The dark stairway, the dripping tap, acted on him like an aphrodisiac. 'I like the dirt,' he said to her once, which made her think of Theo. His hands were all over her before they were through the door. In the morning there was no cupboard of make-up and perfume, not even a pair of stockings. He wanted the room left bare and primitive. Her underclothes smelt of sex, and she suspected he enjoyed hearing her wash herself in lukewarm water with a cake of red soap. She knew she should never have put up with it.

To an extent, Davis at close quarters was not unique among the men she had slept with. He could be rough, thoughtless, difficult. The difference with Davis was the nature of his confessions.

His history tormented him. In the past it had not occurred to her that anything ever tormented Davis. His self-sufficiency was part of his attraction. His need now to confess his weaknesses made him irresistible in a different way, one that demanded a sympathy she had never been asked for by anyone.

Over the years, he said, he had achieved nothing in Fleet Street except a reputation for being awkward. 'Balls,' she would say, or words to that effect, and wrap up the words with kisses, but he was better informed than anyone else on the subject of Davis. The hard young man who was acclaimed as the clever journalist had been a dissident from the beginning. In his heart, and in print when he thought he could get away with it, he questioned the fine motives that people in his articles put forward. At the same time he was questioning his own motives, and inevitably he had to question the motives of the proprietors who owned the newspapers that paid him his salary.

The process was self-destructive. The hard middle-aged man found he had outmanoeuvred himself. At his blackest he was left with a gallery of figures who all had feet of clay, whether they were ostensibly heroes or villains. Any solution, if one existed, had to come from outside the existing system. Thus his apparent interest in socialism and the hard-done-by generation – whether in a Welsh mining valley or the Suffolk countryside – whose popular leaders went on about the coming storm. But he was not political by nature. Sibli saw that romantic acts were what mattered to him. That sentence he wrote about the miners squatting like black Buddhas, waiting, was his image of the poor ready for the spark of revolution to fall. 'Whichever way you turn,' she read in one of his notebooks, 'you are always facing East,' but he wouldn't have dreamt of joining the Communist Party or even of taking its grey polemics seriously.

Socializing meant the Covent Garden flat, and Davis in his seedy dinner-jacket. They were there on the occasion, not long before Christmas, when Davis, plotting to get back to Germany, remarked across the table to his proprietor that Hitler might have something to be said for him after all, at which Uncle Will pointed a fork with half a potato on it and said that unemployed miners were already drilling on the moors above the valleys, ready for the day when the fascist upper classes, aided and abetted by the placemen of Westminster and naïve journalists like Davis, tried to ram dictatorship down the throats of the British. 'Would you say Stalin was a dictator?' asked Davis, to keep things on the boil, and McInch tapped the table approvingly; by the end of the evening the ticket to Germany was perceptibly nearer.

They spent Christmas at the Hotel Mandeville, as Sibli now called it. Helen kept it ticking over. Herbert King had returned with the winter, but at that time of year there were few guests and the damage he could do was limited. He spoke of going back to the gasworks and lay-preaching. 'I think you're wise,' said Sibli, Ruth having told her that nothing would move her from her kitchen and that if Herbert went, he went alone. One wet morning in December, Herbert announced after breakfast that they were all in line for hell-fire, and left for good.

Helen, restored to her plump-chicken look these days, wore skirts above the knee and talked about maturity, which she claimed to have reached. She nailed up slashes of holly and taut paper-chains, hung lanterns that dripped grease from trees outside, and advertised a Christmas Eve dinner in the local newspapers; a voucher entitled each guest to a free cocktail, wittily christened 'Emil's Blood' in memory of the Belgian. Two unmarried girls from her Britannia days were invited to stay, along with their men friends.

Helen had met Davis once or twice already; now she said she looked forward to getting to know him properly. After the Christmas Eve dinner, when everyone was dancing to gramophone records, Davis insisted on partnering Mrs Dorkin, and Sibli found herself dancing with Helen. 'I think your Stevie is a wow,' said her friend. As they passed behind a pillar Helen whispered, 'You still love me a bit, don't you?'

'I love you a lot.'

'Just like the old days,' murmured Helen.

Christmas Day was frosty with an east wind, griping in the chimneys. It brought problems in the shape of Davis's chest, which laid him up in bed. Mrs Dorkin remarked helpfully that the Commander used to say one heard coughs like that in the tuberculosis ward. At night, Sibli let him sleep alone, confining herself to an adjacent bedroom, where she left the door open.

She had dozed off when she heard the door click shut. The room was in darkness. A hand touched her through the bedclothes and Helen said, 'It's only me. I knew you'd be lonely.' A naked leg tried to get in. When Sibli told her to go away, the body fell like a log on the bedclothes and Helen's slurred voice said, 'Sibby, I do need you.'

'You've nearly fractured my wrist,' said Sibli, but she wanted to be kind. 'Look, dear,' she said, 'there's a time and a place.'

'I know he's very sweet,' the voice said into the blanket, 'but you don't want to make yourself cheap. There was a lot I could have said when you were in the papers. 'Mrs Somerset's Aerial Adventures' and all that. Really, Sibby! But Helen forgives you if you love her.'

The leg tried to get in again. Sibli put on the light and Helen began to cry. At the same time Davis started coughing. Sibli went to attend to him, and when she returned, the room was empty.

The incident wasn't repeated. Helen drank too much, and managed to be rude to Davis. Perhaps it was only to be expected. The holiday left her white-faced, chain-smoking, dieting furiously. When they left, Sibli made sure she had a key to the flat. Helen must come whenever she liked; she could just walk in. The idea was to follow this up with messages of encouragement, insisting she visit London more often, but it was a difficult time. Being in love wasn't conducive to selflessness. Davis needed nursing for weeks; it was February before he was back at work.

Germany loomed up. The management of the *Sunday Argus*, which meant McInch, still dithered about sending him to Germany. As Davis explained, the staff was small and most of the newspaper's columns were filled by specialist writers ('the windbag brigade') who rarely stirred from their booklined studies in the south of England. To have a Davis at all was an indulgence.

A long interview with Hitler appeared in a London newspaper in February. As a result, McInch wondered if there was any point in wasting good money on sending a man to such a well-behaved country. Davies said the proprietor read the good tidings aloud to the editorial meeting.

The article was 'Hitler's Momentous Talk to the *Daily Mail*'. It had a genial Führer declaring how 'peacefully minded' he was, and assuring England that the Nazis were not being beastly to the Reds (although, as Davis remarked to Sibli, most of the *Daily Mail*'s readers wouldn't have cared if he boiled them in oil and threw in the British socialists as well). Why, asked Hitler, should his forces bother to attack these dissidents? It was true that the Communists had been well equipped with rifles and ammunition. But they decided not to use them because they were so impressed by the Nazi arguments.

'For "arguments" read "terror",' said Davis. 'I managed not to laugh, and then I said, "Please sir, Mr McInch, should one not be following that up by seeking further evidence of Mr Hitler's peaceful-mindedness?" It worked. We go a week on Monday for a minimum of three months. That should be long enough for me to get what I want for a book.'

'It'll finish you with the *Argus*.'

'It'll finish me with Fleet Street.'

'You can always live on me,' she said. She wasn't worried about their future. The future was whatever happened next with Davis.

While Sibli was getting ready to leave – Davis seemed

to do no preparing, except to spend more time with his German dictionary – she visited Mrs Moon, to see what they were saying in Hampstead about Germany.

'I know all about the so-called reign of terror,' said Dvina, 'but Jews do make a speciality of being persecuted. *You* couldn't say that but *I* can.'

She felt sure that Hitler was doomed already. The army and the industrialists were losing patience with him. 'The English are very popular there,' she told Sibli. 'You and your lover will have a wonderful time.'

Plump and voluptuous, she was curious about Davis, who bothered her. With Sibli's connections it would be easy to find a satisfactory second husband. But Sibli wasn't prepared to discuss Davis.

The Moons' house in St John's Wood, half a mile from the road where James still lived, brought back echoes of Sibli's marriage. Bells rang, tradesmen delivered flowers and packages, a well-waxed car was always waiting in the drive. The streets kept their distance.

That life was in the past for ever. In bitter weather she went shopping for woollen vests that would keep Davis's cough at bay, and a stock of his pungent cigarettes that would make it worse. Returning to Covent Garden in the middle of the afternoon, she found a bowler hat and rolled umbrella in the hall, and heard angry voices. Helen, half dressed, was in the spare bedroom with a middle-aged man. He was in his shirtsleeves, adjusting his braces. Helen squealed and pretended to faint on the bed.

Unhurried, the man moved on to his striped tie. 'Your friend agreed a price and now she wants more,' he said in a cool, starched voice, smiling at himself in the mirror.

'How wicked,' said Sibli, and had the wallet out of his jacket, draped over a chair, before he could stop her.

His 'I shall have the police here in three minutes' was calm enough, but the nicely shaven cheek was flushed. An assistant secretary in a government department, at a guess, or even a permanent under-secretary, occupying the flexible hour between lunch and his desk.

'I doubt it.' Sibli extracted the banknotes, which included a fiver, and picked up a lighter from the dressing-table. When the man took a step towards her, she jerked the flame in his face. He stood rigid, watching her set fire to the money and drop it blazing into an ashtray. Helen hugged her bare legs and shivered.

'Just to help you on your way,' said Sibli, and preceded him to the front door, where she flung wallet, bowler and umbrella down the stairs; the hat was still rolling as he pushed past her, saying, 'Fucking bitch' under his breath in the crisp upper-class voice.

Sibli would have enjoyed herself, but for Helen. Helen had planned it for Em's afternoon off. Perhaps there had been other such afternoons. She made it worse by swearing he was 'an old chum', that she had been 'touching him for a loan', that 'things got out of hand'.

'How long have you been doing it?' asked Sibli.

'What do you care? As long as I run the hotel and leave you free for lover-boy.' Helen was bent over a suspender, twisting to look down the seam. 'I could rot there with Mother and Mrs King.'

'We shall get things organized this year. I shall spend more time there. We'll have a proper staff. I promise.'

Helen swayed about, squirting scent on her thighs, peering in the mirror, reddening her lips. 'I want you to be in love, really I do. I care about you more than anything and all I do is be horrid.' She looked sideways at her bosom. 'I want you both there for ages in the spring.'

'As soon as we're back from Germany.'

'So you're definitely going?'

'Come on, Helen, you know we are.'

'Soon, I expect.'

'The day after tomorrow.'

'That's great. Give Stevie hugs and kisses from me and I hope he gets to interview Herr Hitler.'

Brave Helen, having replaced grousy Helen, said her goodbyes and left, presumably for Buckinghamshire. Twenty-four hours later she was desperate Helen. Mrs Dorkin telephoned to say that her daughter was travelling to Hamburg, to a bar-revue where she had worked before. 'I didn't know about that episode,' said Sibli. It was the Blue Sleeve, said Mrs Dorkin, and please could Sibli do something?

The best Sibli could do was speak to Mrs King and tell her that she was in charge. After that it was all railway stations and steamers. They went via Paris, where Davis wanted to consult K. K. Haeckel, now living in an apartment of his own, about opposition groups in Germany.

Sibli had arranged for Morgan to give her lunch. Waiting for him to return from a meeting, she looked at a set of galley proofs on his desk. They were case histories of men and women with curious tastes in sex, ranging from the painful to the unhygienic; all came from the Haeckel Institute in Berlin.

Engrossed in them, she didn't notice the approach of Rebecca Smollett, who leaned over her and said, 'May I take those, please?'

'Golly,' said Sibli, 'let me finish this one about the woman and the camel. Do you think it's true?'

'It is a scholarly work, intended for the medical and legal professions. May I, please?'

'When I've finished. Do you publish much stuff like this?'

'We have a medical division. I have asked your father not to leave things lying around. I am not to be blamed if people look at them and take offence.'

'I'm not offended, I'm fascinated. What countries do they go to, these medical books?'

'Anywhere that will let them in. We are an international business,' and Rebecca smiled proudly; even her breasts seemed enriched these days, like her auburn hair.

Morgan made light of Haeckel when he and Sibli were

having lunch at an American-style restaurant, calling him a harmless old buffer with pious hopes for mankind. 'Pornography?' he sniffed. 'Well, he has letters after his name. His institute contains brain-tissue from perverts. He had a conversation with Freud in nineteen twenty-six. I think you can trust the Aeolian Press to negotiate the narrow line between science and filth.'

'Just be careful the English police don't come after you one day,' said Sibli.

'If they do, you will be able to intercede on my behalf with that Penbury-Holt detective. And talking of your friends, you might warn Stephen Davis to take anything Haeckel says about a man called Miros with a pinch of salt.'

'Who's Miros?'

'Some phantom figure. K. K. believes in a secret army of anti-Nazis controlled by a mastermind, preparing to seize power. It's pure fantasy. I'm sure Davis has more sense than to dabble in all that, and if he hasn't, you can persuade him.'

An American hurried in with his wife, wiping snow off his spectacles. A few seconds of freezing European wind blew in with them, and a memory stirred, of the cityscape she imagined once, with icy roofs and a man in danger.

'You're very concerned about Davis.'

'Not in the least, I'm concerned about you. Davis is a come-down after James Somerset. But I suppose you know your own business,' and she said, 'Yes, Pa, thank you, Pa,' to shut him up.

A day later they were in Berlin, at a new hotel like an office block off the Kurfürstendamm. She tried to see the city as a tourist. The trams worked, the pavement ice was well salted, a taxi-driver gave her a flower, she got lost in the Karstadt store, a black-uniformed young officer tried to pick her up at the Radio Tower.

Davis was busy at ministries and the foreign press club. From the tower she thought of him down there somewhere, having a bite in a café while he studied his phrase-book, ready for an interview with a civil servant who probably spoke English anyway. For all she knew he was renewing his acquaintance with the mistress he might have in Berlin. A window far off glinted in the watery sun and she speculated about Davis lying in bed, sharing a cigarette with a woman she would never meet, looking out and seeing the tower against the sky.

It was then the officer spoke to her. He faltered when she said she was married. Her lie didn't sound like a lie. She longed for Davis and feared for his safety. 'Where would you take me, anyway?' she asked, and the officer said promptly, 'To a tea-room, Fräulein.' He bowed and went away.

If there were dangers in Berlin, they were biding their time. Davis said the propaganda ministry had forgiven him for the hurtful things he wrote the year before. He had even been allowed a glimpse of Dr Goebbels at the morning press conference. To begin with, McInch would get a study of German youth. Davis was finding out about blood oaths.

The hotel bedroom overflowed with booklets and typed articles from the department of youth, all translated into good English. But when they were in bed, Davis locked her hand in his and said, 'Did you see all those mad-eyed Hitler photographs in the shop windows?' Davis's skin was always colder than hers. She hugged his thin shoulders but he wanted to talk. 'They say dissidents have started to disappear. First there were kangaroo courts in workplaces, handing out floggings. Now the security police come up the stairs at three o'clock in the morning and make them vanish into thin air. There are special prisons for them. So they say.'

'Who's they?'

'People without names.'

'Is Miros one of them?'

'No such person.'

'But you don't hear about special prisons at the propaganda ministry.'

'True,' said Davis, and told her that what you heard at the propaganda ministry was that two women of fine old Prussian families who ought to have known better than to spy for the decadent Poles had had their heads chopped off at seven that morning at Plötzensee Prison by an executioner wearing a frock coat and a cocked hat.

Davis's article in the following Sunday's *Argus* brought a friendly letter from the youth department. Sibli wondered if the authorities were really so naïve. 'They are very arrogant, which comes to the same thing,' he said. Sibli had no objection to double games and the danger that went with them, but she wondered if Davis had something more on his mind than gathering clandestine material for a book.

Espionage occurred to her. She dreamed about the executioner at Plötzensee; he leaned on his axe to peel a banana, and she saw that under the comic-opera hat it was James. Next day she said, 'No one's been asking you to spy for your king and country, have they?' His 'Don't be silly' proved nothing, like his 'No such person' about Miros.

In between Davis's interviews at Reich ministries and the university (he had moved on to education now) she knew he had other meetings. One evening a ticket to Falkenberg, in the suburbs, fell out of his German dictionary, and he grabbed it from her, before remembering to be casual. All she could get from him was routine denials, as if someone had warned him. When she asked if he had a lady friend in Berlin, he said, 'Only you.'

Soon after, he announced they were going to Hamburg, where professors and institutes would occupy him for several days. He had told the education ministry that he wanted to broaden his picture. Where better than a cosmopolitan seaport, with English widely spoken? She could find Helen, he said, and see some of the night-life.

They were to catch an afternoon train. In the morning he asked if she fancied a visit to the Haeckel Institute. They walked to the Tiergarten, which the institute overlooked. It was March, but there were flurries of snow. Davis gave no reason for the excursion. Two men in black raincoats stood under trees on the edge of the deserted park, watching them go up the steps.

A young man with a broken nose answered the bell. Davis introduced himself and said, 'You must be Kurt. I know about you from the professor.'

Kurt waved them in and slammed the door.

Packing cases stood in the cavernous hall. Two men in aprons were carrying a plaster-cast of an enormous pair of buttocks down the stairs.

'We are taking precautions,' said Kurt. 'The less we leave in the building, the better.' He wiped his nose. 'I apologize for the cold. We are unable to get coal delivered for the boilers.'

Davis made notes, nodding sympathetically as Kurt described the records beyond price that they hoped to send out of the country. 'Here is one at random,' he said. '*A Case of Pseudo-Hermaphrodism in a Bavarian Village*. Could you both take some files under your coats?'

'More than my job is worth,' said Davis, 'but you can rely on my understanding.'

There had been rumours that some of the files concerned senior Nazis. 'All lies,' said Kurt. 'You must tell the world that we are scientific, not political.'

Shouting was heard in the street. The branched light bulbs went out, leaving hall and staircase in gloom.

They went upstairs to a room with a balcony, overlooking the park. Military bandsmen on the back of a lorry began to play, not quite in tune, and another group of men in black coats emerged from a car and looked up at the building. Students arrived in a bus, some with swastika armbands.

Kurt opened a window and shouted, 'We have done

nothing wrong!' but the discordant music drowned his voice. 'I am not afraid,' he said. He was shaking. When he telephoned the central police station, they told him to put his complaint in writing.

Eventually the music died away and the soldiers produced a sledgehammer and broke down the door. Students ran through the building, throwing books from the windows, to be shovelled up and loaded on the lorry. A woman knelt weeping on the floor. The men in black took their time over papers and photographs; what didn't go to the shovellers was put aside and neatly parcelled. One of them examined Davis's press documentation. 'You have the possibility to inform the English of the good work the German youth are undertaking, in cleansing out the Bolshevik and homosexual filth,' he said.

Sibli heard Kurt scream, 'They are taking us away!'

Davis went on scribbling. He didn't look up.

Afterwards the scene kept flaring up in her mind. The Hamburg train was warm and clean. Snow flew horizontally past the windows, and when she had been sick in the lavatory, she stood in the corridor with her forehead against the icy glass, Davis hovering and whispering reassurances. 'We have to get out of this insane country,' she said, knowing he wouldn't go, that she couldn't leave him.

One of his chills would come in handy, but he wasn't even coughing. 'Couldn't you have a touch of pneumonia, Davis?' she said, when they were in the dining car, and he was typing a dispatch for McInch. He pushed the sheets towards her. The scene had been made to sound dark and menacing but somehow inevitable, as if history would excuse the men who had done it. 'Clever swine, aren't you?' she said. 'I suppose the Nazis tipped you off. Building up trust – is that it? Dangerous game, Davis.'

Hamburg was the same game, three hours distant. The cobbles shone with grit and ice. In the dusk, Sibli looked for swastikas but saw only electric signs and a statue of

Bismarck. 'I suppose Hamburg was your idea,' she said, when they were in their big polished room at the Lloyd-Hotel. 'Is it where Miros lives?'

'Is this a Professor Miros who's an educationist?' said Davis. 'I must interview him in that case.'

'If you got on the wrong side of those people we saw today, you wouldn't last two minutes.'

'I'm an accredited correspondent of a friendly State. Let's enjoy ourselves. Shall we go out on the town and see if we can find Helen Honey?'

'She can wait till tomorrow. Take me somewhere nice for dinner and bring me back to bed. I don't ask for much. Just stop me shivering, Davis.'

She saw them as two of a kind, wanting to be in love, never quite sure if they were. Their joint secrets had been let out of the bag, or had escaped from it somehow. They accepted one another. His cold streak remained a matter of pride; she was still the free woman with an interesting past.

What they might become had hardly been touched on. Was Hamburg the place to discuss it? Was anywhere? Awake in the middle of the night, she climbed on top of him and made love half asleep, passionate but languid, the gas-fire hissing behind her, the air chilling her breasts, and in the distance the melancholy blasts of ships' sirens from the Elbe. Snuggled against him afterwards she said, 'Would you like to marry me one day, Davis?'

'I should need a room with an unmade bed to escape to. A cold-water tap for you and no clean stockings.'

'I might want a child.'

'Did you know they start apprenticing small boys to be Nazis when they're six?'

'Don't change the subject, you bastard,' she said sleepily, but drifted off in his arms without resentment. No one could tell what they would become.

CHAPTER 32

Next day she told herself not to be a fool, that Davis knew what he was doing. An official from the university collected him at the hotel before nine o'clock, and Sibli was left to see Hamburg by herself. She was going to be on her own until the evening.

Sightseeing didn't appeal to her, though as a gesture she took a taxi around the edge of some frozen lakes. A couple of hours at a Turkish baths followed by some shopping made her feel more at home.

Unwisely, she tried a cinema that was showing a 'masterpiece of the New German Cinema'. A Teutonic woman with staring eyes rallied a medieval city against the Vandals and died wielding a sword as victory was won. When Sibli came out of the cinema, the street lights were on and snow was starting again.

The thought of seeing Helen cheered her up. Taxis knew where the Blue Sleeve was, not far from the Elbe and the old harbour. Its respectable façade was manned by a whiskered doorman, but nothing much was happening at seven in the evening.

Getting to see the manager, Herr Bucher, was easy enough. Thin and bald, he took a quick squint at her fur coat and gold earrings, wrote down Davis's name and newspaper, inquired about the weather in England and the King's health, and begged her to wait in his office until her friend arrived. This week, he explained, Miss Honey was being a hostess, not a dancer.

Left alone with a magazine and a box of cigarettes, Sibli could hear him shouting at a girl because her feathers were drooping. A pianist plonked away, rehearsing sentimental tunes.

Helen, when she appeared, said, 'Thank goodness you aren't cross.'

'I gave up being cross with you long ago.'

'I had to get away, you see,' and Sibli kissed the hopeless face with its hopeless eyes in their dark sockets of make-up, and offered the management's cigarettes.

'He gets them especially from Egypt,' said Helen, 'and keeps them for business clients.'

'Then they're sure to be good.' Sibli lit one with a brass lighter in the shape of a schooner and put it between Helen's lips.

'How do you come to know Otto?'

'I don't.'

'*Mein Gott!* is all I can say. It's typical of you. He treats women like dirt, but you get round him at once. Has he asked you to sleep with him yet?'

'I told him I was here with a famous British journalist, so perhaps he won't.'

'He will. Have you left Stevie in Berlin?'

'We're both here while he does some interviewing. You and I can spend the evening together.'

'You'd best abandon me altogether,' said Helen. 'I'm happiest leading my own life. You may think I'm deplorable but I quite like me, and me is what I understand. I know this place is foul but it doesn't pretend to be anything else. I was here for two months the last time, dancing.'

'Why Hamburg?'

'It was where the agency sent me. Better than Brussels, I can tell you. I nearly went to Algiers once. English girls are so popular, English *roses*.' She looked down at her bosom. 'This time I'm putting it all in the bank,' she said, as if that explained everything. 'I work at least six nights a week. I might go back to England with hundreds of pounds.'

'I'll tell Otto we are having a reunion.'

'But Sibby darling, I can earn twelve marks just on drinks.'

'All right, we'll pretend I'm a client and they can sell me the watered whisky instead. I don't have to drink it, do I?'

Helen said she had never heard such a ridiculous idea, but Herr Bucher was amused, and put flowers for them in an alcove where hot air came out of a grating.

'Perhaps you would care for a bottle of iced champagne,' giggled Helen, when they were settled, and other girls were eyeing them. The dresses were short, with wired bodices that stuck out in front. Half a dozen men were there already, brought in by taxi-drivers or shipping agents, blinking at the warmth and the bosoms. Blue and silver curtains shivered on a stage.

'That would be delicious,' said Sibli, and put her hand on Helen's. The pianist played 'Tipperary' in their honour, and the manager sent over a dish of olives with his compliments. Helen crammed three in her mouth and said, 'These will go down as miscellaneous refreshments, two marks.'

'What happened to the dancing?'

'Otto thinks I'm too fat. They used to make you do it naked. It was pretty frightful. The Nazis stopped all that. They said you had to wear something down below. They're very clean.'

She pressed her leg against Sibli's and said how amazing it was that Fate had brought them together like this, sending Davis to Hamburg. The room where she lived was described, the occasional men she took there who 'meant nothing', the landlady who looked the other way, the smoky stove, the lingering smell of herrings when the wind blew from the fishing quays. It was a sort of life, buoyed up by Helen's conviction that the sleaziness wouldn't last for ever. 'Let's pretend Stevie's in Berlin,' she said. 'We've never been together in a foreign country, just you and me. You can come back to my room and we can talk about the old days. Stevie won't mind. I expect he's found some night-birds to play poker with.'

Days seemed to have passed since Sibli saw him walk off in the morning. Anxiety over nothing she could identify ached at the back of her mind. Watered spirits arrived and Helen washed them down with stuff that sparkled dubiously, while Sibli pushed her own drinks out of sight in the alcove after taking a sip. Otto sent crackers and cheese with his compliments ('Supper, twelve marks,' whispered Helen), and the curtains shivered as cabaret time approached.

Girls were engaged with businessmen and ships' officers in the poorly-lit alcoves. To a ripple of applause, a saxophone tried to sound sultry, and Otto, wearing a dinner-jacket, parted the curtains to announce the hottest show in town.

Lights went out, leaving a glow from the stage, where a bare-breasted young woman in a skirt of feathers, presumably the one who had been shouted at, sang throatily about a faithless man. Presently she writhed a bit and let the skirt fall off. Men leaned forward to stare at her belly and the cardboard star glued on below.

Someone pushed against Sibli, and Davis said in her ear, 'I've brought a friend. No questions. Talk later.' Miss Feathers was displaying her rear view, where another star wobbled. Davis's friend pushed past Sibli and sat next to Helen. A round face was visible, with a peaked naval cap and what looked like carroty hair over the ears. He greeted the women in German. Otto himself brought them a bottle of so-called Deutscher Sekt, and said he was delighted to see they had made up a foursome.

After Miss Feathers the Blue Sleeve Girls went into action, kicking legs of different lengths to a trumpet and drums. Having Davis beside her made Sibli contented and sleepy. 'I love you,' she whispered, and Davis pulled her close, as if he meant to kiss her. But it was her ear he wanted. 'Listen,' he said, 'his name's Walter. Met by arrangement. Problem with police. Nothing serious. Tip-off they were coming. Not a criminal. Got out back way.'

The stage trembled as if the flying legs were too much for it. Sibli had to strain to catch the telegram-voice. 'Needs somewhere for night. Hotel not safe. Thought of your friend. Can you persuade?'

She had half a mind to say, 'Davis, you must be mad,' but his manner didn't encourage argument. 'I'll try,' she said, and when the dancers thundered off for a breather and the lights came on, she took Helen to the Ladies.

The cloakroom was empty. Washing her hands, Helen looked in the cloudy mirror and said, 'I bet you anything, that red hair's a wig.'

'His name is Walter.' Through the wall the piano tinkled. 'He needs somewhere to go tonight. Will you be a sweetheart and put him up? His creditors are after him or something. Or his wife.'

'I suppose if he's a friend of Davis . . .' Helen giggled. 'Does he take his wig off in bed?'

'I don't think you need worry about sex.'

'Better sex than politics, I say.'

When the cabaret resumed, Walter seemed half asleep, but his eyes kept turning to the door. On the stage a girl in a bathing suit did acrobatics, a comedian made a joke about circumcision, the Blue Sleeve troupe reappeared and stamped about. 'Get Helen to sit on his knee,' whispered Davis, and dragged Sibli on to his. They were two drunks having fun with women.

It was Sibli who had a word with the manager and said the men insisted on borrowing Miss Honey. Twenty-five marks changed hands.

The apartment was five minutes by taxi. 'This building,' said Helen, and they stopped where an illuminated globe with the figure 6 in black hung over stone steps. The roof shone with ice, as it used to in Sibli's dream. The snow had given way to clear skies, glowing with light from the quays to the south.

As Helen had warned, a woman with keys came out to look at them. 'These are my friends, *meine Freunde*!' sang Helen, swaying against Walter as they went up the narrow stairs, while Davis gave Sibli's bottom an ineffectual pinch through her coat.

In the chilly apartment, embarrassment set in. 'God, I'm drunk,' said Helen, and locked herself in the bathroom. 'Very kind ladies,' said Walter, and Sibli thought he looked terrified. He was young and rather ugly; the wig didn't help.

'Where will you go tomorrow?' asked Davis. The man whispered something, but his English was evidently as poor as Davis's German, so Sibli had to translate. It boiled down to 'Someone will contact you soon' and 'Sailing-ship basin.'

They were all drunk, but Sibli wondered if Davis was only pretending. He reassured Helen that everything was 'under control', that all she need do was 'trust us till tomorrow', that if anyone came to the door in the meantime, she should 'rattle the bedsprings and sound as if you're making love.' Helen giggled at this.

Back at the hotel with Davis, it was less funny. 'We shouldn't have involved her,' said Sibli.

'She picked him up in a club. She could hardly be arrested for that.'

'So is he Miros?'

'He's a Communist, he's a wanted man. He was someone I had to meet. I wouldn't have seen him again. I think he was about to leave the country. But they came after him.'

'What do they know about you?'

'Nothing, or they'd have been waiting for me here.'

An alarming thought occurred to her, that Davis was enjoying himself. He had found an excitement that kept cynicism at bay. The man in the wig mattered to Davis because he was a life in danger. It was the threat of violent means and ends that attracted him.

Romantic heroes didn't appeal to Sibli. The Davis she liked better was the one who had doubts, who needed comforting about his past, whose essence lay in his vulnerability. But you couldn't select only the bits of people that you found attractive. If she liked what she discovered about him yesterday, she must endure what he was up to today and hope for the best tomorrow.

A few things were explained as they lay in bed, question and answer.

When did it start? When he was first in Germany. Who had approached him? A man whose name he wasn't told. What had Haeckel told him? Names; dreams. Was there going to be an insurrection? No hope. Then what was the point of meeting Walter, or anyone? They were a network; they had stories of torture, of prison-camps behind barbed wire.

Where were he and Walter when they learned the police were coming? A lodging house across the Elbe, in Wilhelmsburg, near the big shipping basins. Where did Davis keep his notes? It was all in his head. What would happen tomorrow – or today, it was after midnight? No doubt someone would contact him. What would happen to Walter? No doubt someone would decide.

Why is your skin so warm for once? Nothing, a touch of fever.

Is all this what you wanted? Yes.

Unable to sleep herself, she watched Davis's narrow features in profile against the pillow, and the flush burned into his cheek. Her bedside lamp shone on the novel she tried to read without success. Coughing, he was half awake at times; she gave him water and spoonfuls of the medicine he carried.

Illness solved everything. The hotel doctor would come, prescribing rest and nourishing food, even insisting on a holiday in the south. Miros, Walter and the other ghosts could fend for themselves. She had no sympathy for Walter, whose hideous wig seemed to condemn the whole network: if that was the best they could do, how could they expect to outmanoeuvre the State? Her compassion was reserved for Davis.

Around dawn he slept heavily, with only a fluttering in his eyelids to suggest that an inner Davis was active. A bout of coughing as the hotel began to stir gave her further grounds for hope, but when he opened his eyes and heard what she had to say, he smiled, shook his head at the word 'doctor' and went to shave.

They were downstairs having breakfast when his name was called, and he went into the lobby, where Sibli saw him talking to a bedraggled woman in a coat down to her ankles. Presently he returned to say he was taking the visitor to Helen's apartment. And after that? 'I shall keep my *Argus* appointments as if nothing has happened.' So Walter would be off their hands? 'I expect so. I'm sure so.'

Sibli said she was going with him, but he told her she must stay at the hotel in case there were messages.

'I don't like orders, Davis.'

'I'm safer without you.'

His coat went over his shoulders. He and the woman went through the revolving door. White fog hung in the street, and a man was chipping ice from the tramlines.

Leaving instructions that she was to be told of any phone call or letter, she went back to their room and lay on the bed. It was the wrong time to leave him, or she might have gone back to England then. Who did Davis think he was? She began making a list of his deficiencies, the mock-heroics, the awful cigarettes, the pathetic wardrobe...

When Sibli woke it was after two in the afternoon, and she thought someone had just knocked at the door. No one was outside. She brushed her hair, trying to stay calm. How could she have slept for so many hours?

The air was still foggy. Surely by now Walter had been spirited away? Davis was safe in some academy, pretending to listen to a pedant's monologue, drawing stormtroopers and Hitler moustaches in his notebook.

Another hour passed. She went downstairs and found the manicurist idle in her salon, a stout woman who said that Germany made the best emery boards in the world, and applied a dark red varnish that wasn't the one Sibli wanted. She accepted it without complaining.

Fog had thickened and lights were on throughout the hotel. People hurried through the revolving doors into the foyer, expanding into the warmth as they opened their coats and greeted friends.

At the magazine booth she read day-old headlines in English newspapers. Then a page was calling her to the telephone.

'All well?' said Davis.

'What about you?'

'I'm in a post office. Can you come round to Helen's?'

She said she supposed so, clicking her dried-blood fingernails on the ledge.

'Nothing to worry about. I'll be waiting.'

The taxi crunched over ice and grit, the driver grumbling at the fog. The globe that said 6 threw its yellow light on the steps; the day was over already. Walking upstairs, Sibli heard the rattle of landlady's keys behind her. She didn't look back.

The air in the apartment was thick with cigarette smoke, suggestive of poker and all-night sessions. Helen, who answered the door, had an air of excitement; she wore a tight dress and had plastered herself with make-up. Davis was at the window. 'Won't be long now,' he said, coming to kiss Sibli, and she saw to her dismay that Walter was lying on a couch, apparently asleep, the wig still in place.

'I thought it was over and done with.'

'He's leaving the country. It's been arranged.'

'But Davis, they can't even arrange a proper disguise.'

'They're more competent than you think, otherwise they wouldn't have survived as long as they have,' he said, and Helen broke in, 'All it needed was a spot of glue.'

Davis folded his arms, trying to be hard-headed Davis. 'A taxi will be here at six-thirty. That'll get him past the police controls at the dock gate, with us providing a distraction.'

'Why have you mixed Helen up in this?'

'She's got a mind of her own, thank you,' said Helen. 'I think it's very clever. Walter is the one who drives the taxi. Davis is taking an English officer back to the ship, and we're the girls who've had a drop too much, come to join the party.'

'It isn't a game.'

'Quite right,' said Davis, 'it's a cause, not to mention a chapter in my book,' and Sibli knew he wasn't going to change his mind.

She heard the details in silence. The 'English officer' was the second mate of a coaster who was being paid to take an illegal passenger. It left the Sailing-ship basin for Dublin on the next tide. Davis would wear Walter's cap and coat to drive the taxi out again; he would use a different gate, but in any case the police didn't look twice at a taxi with a couple of women returning to the city.

'If you were caught,' said Sibli, 'they might do anything.'

'Deportation, that's all. But I won't be.'

Walter sat up and stretched. He came over to shake hands with Sibli and make a speech. Your friend, he said, is a great Englishman, and this will not be forgotten. Spoken in German, it sounded formal, like a citation. Do not be afraid, he said, we shall never require a service from him again. 'One time I meet you all in England,' he concluded, in English.

His stocky figure had a melancholy look, and when he winked at her and pulled the cap over his orange curls, Sibli winked back to keep up his spirits.

She cornered Davis in the kitchen but at the last minute couldn't bring herself to quarrel. Misguided enterprises had appealed to her in the past; this one, however flawed, would have to take its course. She put her arms around him and they stood by a greasy stove that smelt faintly of gas, not saying anything. Her heart-beat calmed down. Suddenly she was sure of success.

In the living-room, Walter was poring over a street map. The last minutes flew by. Helen rinsed her mouth with whisky to help her act the part.

'Taxi come,' said Walter from the window. Sibli saw it at the foot of the steps, and a man walking away.

They went downstairs noisily. This time there was no landlady. Walter sat behind the wheel, the other three scrambled in behind. He drove slowly to the next street, where a man in a short naval jacket waited under a street lamp, rubbing his gloved hands together. The man spoke briefly to Walter, then joined the others. 'I'm Foster,' he said. 'What the hell's all this?'

'English friends of mine,' said Davis. 'We've come to see you off.'

Helen put her hand around the seaman's neck. He was fortyish, with small eyes and sparse hair. 'Only pretending,' she murmured, and kissed his cheek.

They snaked across a junction where trams with clanging bells bore down on them, and disappeared into more backstreets. The fog was at its thickest as they approached the Elbe. At a cobbled bridge it swirled like steam. Then the taxi dived off to the right, rattled over sets of railway lines, and began to crawl alongside the blank wall that enclosed the harbour area. '*Eine Minute*,' said Walter through the speaking tube, and Helen dutifully clambered on to Foster's lap.

Davis stroked Sibli's hair, and she put her head on his shoulder. She saw a gap in the wall and a lighted window. Helen began to sing, out of tune:

Oh I do like to be beside the seaside,
Oh I do like to be beside the sea...

A hand rapped on the window and the cold air rolled in as Davis wound it down. His other hand was on Sibli's breast. Helen sang,

Oh I do like to stroll along the prom prom prom
Where the brass band plays tiddly-om-pom-pom.

The policeman was middle-aged and wore rimless glasses. He shone an electric lantern on Helen's thigh where it showed above her stocking, on Davis's hand, on their faces. '*Wer geht wohin?*'

Foster produced crumpled documents. 'Vessel *Mull of Kintyre* at berth No 4, in Segelschiffhafen. These are my English friends.'

'Isn't he lovely?' shrieked Helen.

'*Bitte*,' said the policeman, and jerked his head for them to proceed. But someone shouted from the police post, and a second man came over to the taxi. This one was younger. His face was expressionless.

'Hello, I'm a film star,' shouted Helen.

'*Steigen Sie aus, bitte.* Get out, please,' he said, and Sibli felt Davis's hand tighten on her arm. 'No women.'

'We're English,' said Helen, 'and we'll do what we want.'

'You'll do what you're told.' The voice was cold and precise. The two women got out. He waved the taxi on.

'What are we supposed to do now?' asked Sibli, ready to be angry but knowing it wouldn't help.

'What whores always do. Keep walking and hope you get picked up.'

He turned away. They kept to the wall. Sibli's legs were shaking. 'We did it, we did it!' whispered Helen, but all Sibli could think of was Davis changing places in the dark, having to return by himself. The fog muffled everything, footsteps, rattle of cranes, chorus of sirens. Presently an empty taxi leaving the harbour picked them up, and took them to the hotel.

'I'll stay with you till Stevie gets back,' said Helen. 'The Blue Sleeve can do without me.'

The hotel was busier than ever. At Helen's insistence they went to the dining-room, after making sure the head porter knew their whereabouts. Sibli watched her gobble up meat and vegetables but could eat nothing herself. Dreams of frozen rooftops and the hunted man meant nothing; they would vanish the moment she saw Davis.

After an hour she knew something had happened, but it was as long again before she was asked to go to the general manager's office, where a man in a raincoat who said he came from the police commissioner's office was waiting. She knew she was about to be arrested, but it didn't matter, as long as she could see Davis.

'Fräulein Somerset,' said the official, 'I deeply regret that I have bad news for you. Your friend Herr Davis has met with an accident.'

She heard 'stumbled on edge of dock' and what sounded like 'afraid he is dead'.

The rest came back to her later – may wish to return to England immediately, all facilities at disposal, British Consul notified, expressions of profound sorrow.

Later still, the ship's wake creamed away into the greeny-black distance. It was another dream. She knew Davis had been murdered, she knew it would never be proved. Helen gripped her hand as they stood by the rail, perhaps in case she tried to jump when the German coast was no longer in sight. But Davis wouldn't have approved; there was no escaping Davis.

PART IV

1934–1936

CHAPTER 33

The past receded, Davis with it. Memory was something, but not much. The real Davis had no coherence. Living, she felt herself go the same way, lacking bonds between one bit of her and another. Were they edging towards reunion in some other continuum where streams of electrons joined like water and ran into an eternal sea? The thought wasn't religious so it must be mad. Presumably it was in order to have mad thoughts about the dead.

The horror was Davis in bits, each with a label in her memory — scrutineer's glance, bony nose, cigarette-stained finger; the habit of persistence, the light behind the eyes; his breath, his skin. Dear Davis, she thought, I should have made you marry me, I should have had your child; a Davis-child had been known to appear in her dreams, but usually she managed to wake herself before she saw its face.

One form of self-help was telling people she wanted justice. It wasn't too successful. The Foreign Office, where an assistant secretary listened to her in a room with a ticking clock, said that if half what she alleged was true, both she and Mr Davis were guilty of conspiracy against a friendly State, and those who played with fire should not be surprised if they got burnt.

When she attacked his ministry (citing cowardice, hypocrisy and stupidity, to be going on with) he closed his eyes, murmuring that he was making allowances, dear lady, for your condition. He reminded her how helpful the

German authorities had been. They had even sent over the post mortem report by diplomatic bag. She wasn't authorized to see it, not being Mr Davis's wife, but a translation had been passed to the sister in Yorkshire.

Sibli read it after the funeral at Harrogate, where the sister, a capable woman called Harriet, had marshalled a husband and half a dozen relatives for the occasion. The document was on her kitchen dresser and bore a smear of marmalade. It reported death by inhalation of water, alcohol in the blood and no marks on the body consistent with violence.

Sibli used her story to batter other listeners. The *Chicago Tribune* printed a short piece by Rabin, Davis's poker-playing friend, headed 'Mrs Somerset's Tale. Friend of Dead English Newsman Accuses Nazis of Complicity in Harbour Tragedy', which was followed by copious denials from Berlin, and a statement from the British Consul in Hamburg that praised the Germans for sending the coffin back to Dover free of charge. No one called Foster, the English second officer, could be traced. 'Walter' might never have existed. No doubt Foster was a policeman and 'Walter' was dead.

Fleet Street listened with half an ear, noting familiar ingredients – 'well-known divorcée', 'colourful life', 'dead lover'. One front page had her photograph; another had Davis as well. There was some toying with rumours of skulduggery, but no one wanted to take up a cause that the government disowned. McInch said he had a duty not to prejudice the liberal voice of the *Argus*, founded 1799, by trawling these murky waters. A late, brief obituary appeared the following Sunday about a 'lone wolf' of The Street who relied on 'quirky insights', and once wrote a book. For some reason it was reading about the book that broke her heart.

Her best bet should have been Will Buckley MP, who boasted that he knew the way Europe was going. His invective fell on fascist lackeys – Hitler's, Mussolini's –

and he began by promising Sibli that he would lay the facts before Parliament and the British people.

Sadly, as he put it, he had to reconsider. The facts as disclosed by Sibli might, if aired, damage the Left as well as the Right. Socialists in Britain needed public sympathy. Their defence of an eccentric journalist who was in Germany ('about which, I recall, he held equivocal views'), in the company of a woman who had been in the papers ('I am saying what others may think, not what I think. I am your uncle'), might backfire.

The more brick walls Sibli encountered, the more determined she grew to demolish them. She was young; she had years to do it in; she wouldn't rest until Davis was vindicated. If she wrote a book, her father could publish it. 'Gladly,' said Morgan, 'but will anyone read it when I do?'

Davis became an obsession; she couldn't let him go. When Oswald called at the flat one day, and sat on the edge of a chair twiddling his hat in his hands, she hoped that Britannia Pictures wanted to base a film on the life of a journalist who died fighting for what he believed in. Oswald said merely that Mr Somerset would like to have a meeting with her.

For the occasion she wore discreet mourning and some pearls that James once gave her. A car collected her from Covent Garden and drove her, oddly, to a merchant bank in Bishopsgate. There she was taken to a poky room on the second floor, where James stood with his back to the door, looking out on a square of City grass with a bench and a pigeon-stained statue of Hermes.

When he turned, the face was older. 'I am profoundly sorry,' he said. 'I met him once, on board a liner. You have taken it to heart. I can see it in your eyes.'

The rocking-chair was in the corner, and she guessed he no longer had an office at Britannia. He retained an interest in the company, he said, but his life had moved in other directions. Economic theory and the re-establishment of gold as a universal currency were the channels for his energies. He liked the solitude of the bank, evolving ideas that could reach as far ... as far ... (he let the words hang) as government circles.

'You wanted to talk to me,' she said, and saw a banana skin in an otherwise empty wastepaper basket.

'Someone in Whitehall told me that you were trying to pursue your friend's case. I can understand your feelings, but it is a labyrinth.'

'Are you trying to stop me, too? I thought you were offering to help.'

'I know your nature. You have a strong will. But nothing will be achieved.'

'Do stop pontificating, James.' She stood up to go. 'Tell your friends in Whitehall I shall harass them for years if I have to.'

'We are both from small countries, remember.' He came around the empty desk. 'The English had no time for us when we lived like pigs in the East End. My revenge was simple. I became rich. Now I am becoming influential. Find a revenge that makes you happy. That's all I say, my ex-demon. The dead require only to be remembered. Use your talents for the future.'

His eyes held her for a moment. She kissed him and felt grateful. He had freed her from something.

'I suppose,' he said, walking her down a vaulted corridor, 'you wouldn't come back to me?'

'Never.'

The car was waiting; she returned to Covent Garden, thinking about revenge, not seeing much prospect of it if she gave up fighting for Davis. Revenge *was* Davis. On the face of it James had told her two contradictory things. So was he a wise man or a charlatan with a golden tongue? Or could he be both at once?

Sibli kept the campaign going. Volleys of letters were directed at British politicians, European socialists, American newspapers. But she returned to the Hotel Mandeville and made it her base. Decline had set in again. Helen was there, too, grumbling about the guests. 'Remember the naughty weekends we used to talk about?' said Sibli. 'Perhaps we should give them a go.'

Nothing mattered now; they could try anything. What was this 'society' that one shouldn't offend against? Few of her letters received replies, and then all they offered was sympathy. Meanwhile the Nazis murdered Dollfuss, the Austrian chancellor. Germany was rearming. There were new dramas in the world. One dead journalist was soon forgotten.

'I feel like an outlaw,' Sibli said to Helen one morning in late summer, the beech woods full of murderous birdsong. Helen nodded and said, 'Goody, so do I.'

'Let's make fools of them. You know, *them*, the ones in authority who tell us how to behave. Let's have girls on tap for well-off men with motorcars. Charge high prices. Make a fortune. Laugh at all the pompous prigs.'

'Sibby!' squealed Helen. 'You can't!'

But Sibli had glimpsed what James meant by revenge. After that it was only a question of working out the details.

CHAPTER 34

Port Howard's history of poverty and strikes didn't prevent the place celebrating George V's Silver Jubilee in 1935 with as much enthusiasm as if the King-Emperor in person was going to appear miraculously in the town and stand there under the grimy banners, casting rays of glory over the citizens.

The pageant was held at the Castle in May 'by kind permission of Major Mappowder' and so was the bonfire in the grounds at night. Margaret had chaired the organizing committee, planned the pageant, paid for the costumes and the band, and even persuaded young Egge at the tin-stamping works (old Egge was dead) to donate one tin mug, stamped with coloured picture of King and Queen, per child of school age.

At the Mayor's Parlour in the evening, where the nobs were having supper before going up to the bonfire, Margaret announced her intention of handing over Y Plas to the borough, together with adjoining land that she proposed to lay out with public gardens and swimming baths. Everyone banged the table and drank her health; the news was round the town in an hour.

There was no point in keeping the house. Theodore had given up his lease, and Margaret never went there. Had things turned out differently, the person to give it to might have been Sibli. The long silence between them had deepened over the years. Margaret broke it when she heard about Davis's death. The newspaper headlines were painful ('well-known divorcée' hurt her most), but she wanted to go to Sibli, to be at her side; or, to be honest, she wanted Sibli to come to Port Howard, to be at hers. As it was, she sent an affectionate note; waited for weeks; in the end received a printed card acknowledging sympathy, with 'Thanks' scrawled at the bottom.

The town kept Margaret almost as busy as the works. She had no wish to eclipse her husband. But she knew that when people spoke of what 'the Castle' was thinking and doing, nowadays they meant her rather than Aubrey. His father had been a figure on the bench, famous for summary judgements. Aubrey endured it for a few years in the twenties, then resigned abruptly. She was the JP in the family. The week after the pageant she added to her popularity by refusing to fine men who defied a new byelaw that forbade bathing in the New Dock. She said it was safer than the river. A crowd was waiting to cheer her when she left the courtroom. Aubrey, as contrary as his wife in some ways, said, 'Well done, old thing,' and went off to Surrey with his Bentley for two weeks' racing.

While he was away, an officer in the town's yeomanry battalion visited the Castle to ask if his engineers could set up a 'sound-locating unit' in the grounds, overlooking the sea, for a couple of hours on Friday evening. An RAF night bomber from Wiltshire would be over Port Howard to give the unit practical experience of detection, and the Castle, being elevated, was the ideal place for their equipment. There was no reason to object. Margaret invited Albert to come over from Swansea to see the fun, which amounted to an aircraft droning above the clouds, and twelve men on the lawn with dials and headphones, while cranking a strange device to and fro, like a pair of dinner plates upturned to the sky.

When Aubrey returned and heard about the exercise, he said it was a disgrace. Bombers? Ready for another war? He would have sent the yeomanry packing. What was Margaret thinking of? She told him not to be so childish. He told her she was too anxious to be thought well of.

Usually their differences evaporated, but the quarrel lingered. It got mixed up with her giving Y Plas to the town, a gesture that irritated Aubrey. Perhaps he thought she was hinting that he give away a few acres, too.

'When I close the copperworks,' he said, 'I may let the council have the site for playing fields. That is, if they pull down the buildings at their own expense.'

'Why make yourself out to be some sort of tyrant? The Mappowders have been here two hundred years. You know you've no intention of closing the works.'

'Haven't I? I am the last Mappowder to grace this town with his presence, am I not? There are no little Mappowders after me. So I need hardly worry about the family name. *You* can always revert to being Margaret Buckley after my time.'

The pain of her childlessness was easily reawakened. Aubrey's remark turned the knife. So, for the same reason, did the impending transfer of the Buckley home, stirring up memories of the family and its generations.

Having put off the necessary visit to Y Plas – to make an inventory of the contents in case there were items that her brothers or their children might like to have – she had finally brought herself to devote a Saturday to it. The day before, Theodore appeared out of the blue. A large motor-car trundled up the drive to the Castle and out of it came Theodore, his half-French wife Estelle (Margaret had heard about her), a fat child of six months called Maurice and a uniformed nursemaid.

'We are touring Wales,' he announced. 'Estelle wishes to see precisely what grime her maestro sprang from. I may say we have been to Normandy to see what grime *she* sprang from – she is a soprano of some distinction – and it was composed of butter, Calvados and cow manure in equal proportions. Can we stay a night?'

Next morning a visit to the site of Bank Cottages, long

demolished, where Theo had been brought up, was disposed of in twenty minutes. 'That's the Bay,' he explained to his wife, pointing over the fields, 'where my wicked cousin Sibli sent my old man to his death in a rowing boat when he was widowed.'

'Is that true?' Estelle asked Margaret.

'The girl thought she was doing him a kindness. She didn't mean him to die.'

'Fortunately the murder squad was never called in.'

On the way back they came in sight of Y Plas. If Theo wanted his piano, Margaret said sharply, he had better hurry up and remove it. 'Her father lived there,' said Theo, 'an ironmaster with a heart of stone – or gold, I'm supposed to say, because he paid for the little pianist's lessons. A madman killed him, Estelle. Someone should write an opera about the craziness under the surface of little towns like this, waiting to burst out like pus.'

Estelle asked if they could go inside. Why not? A key had to be collected from the woman in Ship Street who went in once a week to dust and set mousetraps. The house smelt like a cave, filled with underground air. It had gone downhill quickly once there was no longer a Villette to use her sacred substances, the sugar-soap and black-lead and Duraglit, doing her duty by the Buckleys. Mirrors had clouded, walls darkened.

Estelle paused in front of pictures, a cracked canvas of fishing boats running before a gale in the estuary, a steel engraving of a tin works; deferential to other people's lives, in contrast to Theodore's proprietorial air, kicking up the carpet and leaning against door-posts, as if he had sucked Y Plas and its history into his wake.

Rummaging in an upstairs drawer – she was making a start on the inventory – Margaret came across a photograph album that had probably lain untouched for thirty years. 'This is Theo's mother as a young woman,' she said, and saw him glance over his wife's shoulder at the slim, angular girl with puzzled eyes.

'She has a sensitive mouth,' said Estelle.

'We were always told she had an artistic nature, but everything took second place to the children – to Theo, anyway. She had a hard life.'

'Unlike her sister, who was smart enough to marry Margaret's father. The fact is, Villette was a drudge by nature.'

'What an ungrateful man you are,' said Margaret.

'Sibli once made the same accusation.'

Margaret used a notepad from the drawer to jot down particulars. She moved into the main bedroom, the one with the great brass bed. One wardrobe, one dressing-table, two stools, one chest, one divan, one gilt mirror. Was it from this room that she had looked at the flooded marsh with Sibli, the child? She opened a shutter and saw Estelle walking by the shore.

The bed creaked and Margaret turned to see Theo sitting on the edge.

'So here we have the engine-house of the Buckleys,' he said, tapping the counterpane with a finger. 'This is where you were all manufactured. I can almost hear old Davy heaving and grunting. No doubt his generation went about it as enthusiastically as mine does – or yours, come to that.'

'It's no use you trying to be clever with me. I've known you too long. You are just my cousin – my objectionable cousin, which is how you force me to think of you.'

He smiled. '*I* admire *you*, all the same. You're a paradox, Margaret. Half of you is a worldly woman. The other half is a moralizer. It thinks I'm a monster and Sibli is a harlot. Well, I have to admit, she does have leanings in that direction. I only hope you feel more charitable towards her than you do to me.'

'Did she ask you to say these things?'

'Good heavens, no. But we stayed a night at her place on the way down. It's the Hotel de Mandeville now. A bit of French has crept in. She told me that what she really wanted was "Hotel de Dream", after an establishment she read about in Florida. But that was a bit explicit for the English countryside. Discretion is Sibli's watchword. It's very tastefully done.'

His ugliness and coldness were part of his power. Where did such natures come from? Margaret changed the subject by telling him he was lucky to have found a wife like Estelle, but he persisted with some nonsense about smartly-dressed girls at the hotel who wore wedding rings and dined with men in the restaurant, before slipping out to one of the bungalows in the grounds. Margaret went on with her inventory. 'Alternatively,' said Theodore, 'they may go off in a motorcar and book into someone else's hotel. Or just stay in the motor. As her jolly friend Helen says, there are enough lonely spots within half a mile of the Mandeville to hide fifty cars.'

Margaret wrote '1 green carpet, worn at bedside' and shut the notepad. 'We had a Peeping Tom up before the bench last year,' she said. 'I felt sorry for him. He was such a *dirty* little man.'

'I'm only the bringer of bad news, my dear cousin. You are the head of the family. Who else should I take my malicious gossip to?'

'You could keep it to yourself.'

'We should be friends, you and I. You must visit us in France one day. We have bought a place near La Rochelle.'

How dangerous it had been to let herself think, even for a second, that Sibli could be a surrogate for the child she never had. Y Plas was where this ghost-child made its home. No doubt that was the true reason for her reluctance to get rid of the house. The child called from the garden and lay dreamily in the bath. It ate jam on its finger and read forgotten novels in the library. It was an echo of Isabel, that was all. She would be glad when Y Plas had gone.

Estelle came in to say there were wild raspberries in the garden. The house was locked up again, the Lloyds continued their tour of Wales, a baby's rattle they left behind at the Castle was acquired by a housemaid who was in the family way. Margaret said nothing to her husband about Sibli and the hotel. The story might be true; it was best forgotten.

Port Howard's chimneys went on pouring smoke into the sky and justifying the town's existence. It was there, in the indifferent heart of furnaces and the long patience of machines, that Margaret was able to renew herself. Would her father have known what she meant? She liked to think she was the true heir to David Buckley.

By the end of the year there was one problem less. Aubrey, drifting further into himself, away from the public life of the place that was also Margaret's life, was offered a knighthood 'for services to industry in South Wales'. At first she was afraid he would reject it, as he had come to reject so much since the war. He kept the letter in his bathroom and read it each morning when he was shaving. Water splashed it and blurred the signature of the panjandrum in the Cabinet Office who said he had one week to decide, and don't tell anybody – on pain of execution, no doubt. 'Sir Aubrey,' he repeated over breakfast, three mornings running, fingering his moustache. 'And his Lady.'

The idea tickled him. He replied at the last minute to say thank you, and went to Buckingham Palace in March for the investiture. King George had died in the meantime, his place being taken by the popular but rather wan young Edward, Prince of Wales.

'What did he say to you?' asked Margaret when they were leaving the ballroom in the crush of new knights and their families.

'He said, "Aw, Port Hard, passed through it once on a train, y'know." I daresay he'll improve when he's been King a bit longer.'

'Is it only old men who get knighthoods?' Albert whispered to Margaret. Encased in a blue suit that set off his red cheeks, he was already as tall as his aunt.

'Albert!' she said. Then she added, 'You may be right.'

A family for investiture purposes was limited to four. Margaret had insisted on taking two children, so they would remember having seen a king. Albert was her choice. Aubrey's was Emily Mappowder, a daughter of his younger brother Victor, who worked for a bank in Toronto and was in London to set up a European branch. Emily and Albert burst out of the Palace ahead of them and ran across the courtyard to find their parents in the crowd.

Family gatherings delighted Margaret. She made the most of the illusion – Griff in the unnecessary morning dress that Aeronwy (long fur coat, hat like half-hearted turban) had insisted on, placid Victor with his excited wife Cynthia, their two younger children quarrelling in Canadian accents, Albert silent at Emily's chattering, and Elizabeth, Aubrey's unmarried sister who had come up from Worthing, determined to get into the middle of the group photograph, Palace windows in the background, that would be framed in drawing-rooms for ever.

A modest reception followed at Brown's Hotel, where Esther (who refused to stand outside palaces) was waiting for them. 'I have some bad news,' she whispered to Margaret, when everyone had a glass of champagne. 'Stuart has had a terrible flying accident. I only heard last night. He is unconscious and they may have to operate on the brain. Virginia is at the bedside.'

Cynthia Mappowder stood listening, anxious to know who Stuart was, who everybody was. Esther was still providing her with a brief genealogy of the Penbury-Holts when Margaret saw a figure at the door. It made straight for her. 'I don't believe it,' she said, and Morgan put his hands on her shoulders and said, 'Hello, Lady Maggs. I had to come over. I am delighted. No honour was ever more deserved.' Under his breath he added, 'By you, that is.'

'I shall never get you all sorted out,' squeaked Cynthia,

and Morgan stuck his dark, preacher's face close to hers and said, 'Just as well, dear lady. Heaven knows what you might discover.'

Albert's cheeks looked red enough to blister. Morgan boxed at him playfully, shook hands with Griff, kissed Aeronwy, who made a hissing sound, and had a few words with the new knight before returning to Margaret and steering her into a corner.

'His father had one, so why shouldn't Aubrey, I suppose. But I suspect they were thinking of you as well.'

'We shall quarrel if you go on about it. I'm sure there is plenty of fault to be found with the honours system. But I'm very happy for Aubrey, and that's that.'

'Admirable Maggs! I see Will and Flora aren't here.'

'Flora wrote to say she was sure I'd understand. You didn't even acknowledge the invitation.'

'I thought I'd make it a surprise. In any case, I wasn't sure until the last minute that I could get away.'

'You've heard about Stuart?' she said.

'It was in the *Continental Daily Mail*.'

'How is Virginia taking it?'

'How should I know? Wicked Maggs, what are you suggesting? If I have a minute I might take her flowers and be sympathetic, as long as I don't have to rub shoulders with too many Penbury-Holts.'

'Is he going to die?'

'I hope not. I mean, I'm sure not. It was only a little accident. He's not much over fifty. Younger than me — younger than you.'

'I'm getting to be ancient,' she said.

'You mustn't say such things,' and he seized her hand and held her fingers to his lips, so that for a second she got a gust of the unadulterated Morgan, sweet and paralysing, before she became aware of Albert, watching intently from the other side of the room, and told her brother to stop playing the fool.

'Cruel Maggs! Anyone would think it was a game.'

'You haven't spoken to Esther,' she reminded him, and presently Esther had joined them and was giving a detailed account of the wind conditions and faulty aileron that had conspired to make Stuart's aeroplane turn over as it landed.

Trays of food circulated. Victor proposed a toast to 'Sir Aubrey', and Aubrey fiddled with his moustache and said it was Margaret they should be toasting, which they did. One of Cynthia's children was sick. Esther was praising Russia to Elizabeth, who wasn't listening. Margaret saw Aubrey take out his watch. Looking for Morgan to say they must catch the three o'clock from Paddington, she realized he had gone, and had the old feeling of being let down.

When they reached Port Howard, Aubrey growled at the mixture of rain and smoke that swirled around the car as they were driven up to the Castle. 'Do you ever feel you would like to live under blue skies?' he said. But it was just one of his moods.

That night he tapped on her door and asked if he might come in. She lay in his arms, the pyjama trousers he had kicked off scrunched in a ball by her feet, and he told her he had plans.

'Tell me,' she said, snuggling against him, hoping they were plans that would shift the new Sir Aubrey into the limelight, and her out of it.

'I've reached a decision about the copperworks. I'm closing it before the end of the year.'

'You can't. You mustn't, Aubrey.' She sat up, feeling as desolated as if he had confessed to having a woman on the side. 'I didn't marry a man who ran away from his obligations.'

'Fiddlesticks.'

'Two hundred men out of work isn't fiddlesticks. Go away, please, I don't want you in my bed.'

'You're behaving stupidly,' he said. But he got out and strode to the door.

'I'll buy the works myself,' she called. 'If you won't keep it open, I will.'

'Over my dead body.'

The door banged. A moment later he had to come back for his pyjama bottoms. Margaret brought them up on her toe. She was unhappy for his sake. But ready to fight.

CHAPTER 35

Sibli woke from a dream about Davis. It was seven in the morning. A door slammed and a car drove off from a bungalow, the sound fading quickly. Inside the hotel, water gurgled, bolts slid, stairs creaked. Em appeared with a pot of tea and ran the bath, and when Sibli had soaked for ten minutes, the bed was made and her clothes laid out.

As usual it was wholesome grey costume and plain blouse, plus spectacles in tortoiseshell frames to give a touch of severity. As Helen once said, she would have gone down well in the staffroom at Bracing-on-Sea. Her appearance, like the hotel's, told the middle-class visitor to expect competence and civility; after that, the blazing fires, hot water, fresh eggs for breakfast and reasonable prices only confirmed the first impression.

A doctor and his wife, returning to London from a medical meeting in Oxford, had looked in for dinner the previous evening, on a friend's recommendation, and decided to stay overnight. Sibli chatted to them when they had eaten breakfast, and said that, yes, the ham was home-cured.

'This place is a real find,' said the husband. 'Though if you'll forgive my saying, Mrs Davis, we appear to be the only guests.'

'It's still rather early in the year. We had some couples in for dinner, as you saw. I must admit, we have our bad patches. If I didn't like it here so much . . .' Sibli gestured at storm-swept beeches through the window. 'I'll tell you a secret. I'm blessed with a dear father who lives abroad, who helps out now and again.'

The doctor looked embarrassed. His wife said, 'So Mr Davis . . .'

'He's dead. There you are. I've told you the story of my life, I can't think why. Sympathetic faces, I suppose.'

'We shall certainly pay a return visit,' said the doctor, and Sibli went off to the Sanctuary with the slight feeling of relief that she always experienced when she spoke about Davis's death, even in the meaningless terms of a polite conversation.

'The Sanctuary' was Helen's word for the hotel office, to which she and Sibli alone held the keys. Helen was back from the bungalows with Friday night's takings. They were quite healthy, ends of weeks being a time when men who set out to deceive their wives could more easily create excuses.

'Sixty-two pounds,' said Helen. 'Together with seven shillings and sixpence which had fallen out of some chap's trousers on the floor.'

They did the calculations in their heads, it being a rule of the place that as little as possible be written down. Twenty-one pounds went back to the three girls who had been working. The rest had to be banked, which was Helen's job. As usual she was in a hurry – Matthew, the new acquisition, was coming at eleven – and as usual Sibli had to insist she take the standard precautions, and Helen left in a bad temper.

The car zoomed off. Sibli stayed in the Sanctuary, writing letters. Banking the cash was a ritual. They kept accounts under false names in two towns ('I suppose we are the bad girls of Bracing-on-Sea,' said Helen). At Aylesbury, Helen breezed in as Mrs Davenport-Guest and put most of the money into an account called Rural Markets Ltd, 'a sort of co-operative among smallholders,' as she explained to the manager. Rural Markets didn't keep the money for long. Once a month it all went to a nominee account at a Paris bank – 'Some of us are interested in buying property in France,' explained Mrs Davenport-Guest. In Henley she became Mrs Carstairs and followed similar procedures.

The scheme wasn't foolproof, but it would take a bit of unravelling. Occasional letters arrived from a 'proud' or 'adoring' or sometimes 'anxious' father, enclosing substantial cheques to help with 'your brave little enterprise'. Sibli paid these into her genuine bank account, and was careful to keep the letters as evidence that they weren't ill-gotten gains. Not all the money returned to England. A core remained in France, where Morgan played with it on the Bourse to his daughter's advantage.

All this was crime; she and Helen were criminals. It was not permitted in England to organize the sale of sexual favours. Sibli found this absurd. Laws against immorality had been unworkable throughout history, so the State settled for the next best thing and interfered with the financial arrangements. It was a crime that hurt no one, a mere technicality, though Pa (when he first heard of the scheme) said sternly that running a house of ill-repute was generally understood to be a sin as well as a crime, and he hoped Sibli wasn't serious. When he accepted that she was, he still didn't like it. 'If it's money you need...' he said. But of course it wasn't.

The last letter she wrote was prompted by an item in that morning's newspaper, which said that the well-known stockbroker and pilot Mr Stuart Penbury-Holt, who had been seriously injured in an air accident the previous week, remained in a coma and was not expected to recover. 'Dear Virginia,' Sibli wrote, 'I have only just read of your husband's accident. Please believe how sorry I am. I send you my sympathy and my love.' Compassion came easier these days.

Matthew arrived for Helen, looking like a studious schoolboy, with his steel-rimmed spectacles and weekend blazer. Sibli referred to him as 'the boy solicitor'; he was in love with Helen. He waited for her in the residents' lounge and read the *Daily Telegraph*. When she returned, Helen came straight to the Sanctuary.

'I shouldn't have been horrid,' she said. 'It's two years to the day. I didn't realize till I was at the bank.'

'It's all right. I'm glad you remembered.'

'Will you come out with us? We're going to see the new Clark Gable. Back in plenty of time.'

'Thanks, I'll be better off here,' said Sibli.

In the dream she was trying to have a photograph of Davis framed at Harrods. It was in a *Daily Express* of 1921, when he was reporting from Ireland. The assistant said, 'It's ridiculously small, it would look quite wrong in one of our frames.' 'You silly rabbit,' said Sibli, and took the newspaper away. Then she was in Morgan's rocking-chair, the one that had been his grandmother's. When she looked closely, the picture was only a smear of printers' ink.

The two years felt like twenty. But at least she had done something with them.

The bungalow idea came from Matthew, who was one of their pieces of luck. Sibli had decided to buy a couple of flinty fields, bordering the hotel on its unwooded side, for the sake of privacy. The first solicitor's brass plate she saw in High Wycombe announced an important-sounding partnership. The leading partner was in court. He turned out to have only one associate, a lanky son who spoke knowledgeably of 'current land values' but flushed easily. He was eager to do the work, and came to look at the fields, staying to drink her whisky (which went to his head) and meet Helen. He boasted of the money he meant to make but didn't see how he could in his father's practice. His name was Matthew.

Sibli gave him other bits of business, and, when the blameless father offered his personal supervision, declined with thanks because they got on so well with the son. Matthew lived with his parents in a Chiltern village. Soon he was finding excuses for escaping to the Mandeville. Helen thought him a scream. One wet Sunday she took him to her bedroom. Soon after that he was brought into the joke of starting a brothel in the English countryside, which was how it presented itself at the beginning. The bungalow plan – staff quarters well away from the house, where naughtiness could flourish out of sight – was merely the joke taken a stage further.

In the early days they couldn't gauge what the demand was going to be. To meet it, whatever it was, Sibli set strict criteria. '*Not* all breasts and lipstick,' she said. 'The sort of girl I want can appear at the hotel in a cocktail frock and look like somebody's fiancée. If she speaks badly she'll have to learn to keep her voice down.'

Helen recruited the first of these paragons before there was any work for them. Brigit was a Midlands girl she had met in Hamburg who now sold cigarettes in a night club in Brighton. Carla, once a starlet at Britannia, had sunk ('Or risen,' said Helen, scornful of her acting abilities) to being sketched wearing corsets for newspaper advertisements. Sibli put them on the books as maids. She was halfway to being a procuress. The word had an uncompromising ring. But there was no turning back.

The police were another unknown quantity. A Mr Swann who turned up one morning gave her a bad moment. 'Am I speaking to *the* Mrs Somerset?' he wanted to know.

'As it happens I'm *the* Mrs Davis. Who are you, exactly?'

He held up a police warrant card, and she saw he was a superintendent. She blinked at him through her spectacles, trying to feel calm. But he only grinned and said he knew who she was, she was Sibli. He was George. He had a sister who married his old pal (and hers), Tom Penbury-Holt. 'So you see,' he said, 'I have heard much about you. When I first knew Tom we were at the old Peel House, back in 'twenty-four. He had a photograph of you in a bathing suit that was much admired.'

'I shall have to watch my step,' said Sibli, falling into a routine for men with paws at the ready. She didn't mind as long as the paws kept their distance. George settled down happily with a glass of gin, boasting about Scotland Yard. Thieves in motorcars were making a nuisance of themselves in the Home Counties, where country houses were no longer remote. He was setting up a new burglary squad. Thus his presence in the Chilterns, where he remembered that Tom had spoken of Sibli and the Mandeville.

'And do they have children?'

'A boy, and another baby on the way. Strange to think you might have married him. Would you have liked being a policeman's wife?'

'Would he have liked being a hotel proprietor's husband?'

George thought that very droll. He found room for a second gin; told Sibli she was a grand woman; said the air out here was like wine. As he was going he remarked on the brand-new 'de' in front of the gilded 'Mandeville' on the wall. 'Very French,' he said.

'One has to be competitive,' said Sibli, and pointed to workmen in the field. 'We are building new staff accommodation, do you see?'

She made him promise to come back soon ('Bring Tom, bring your wives') and dine as a guest of the house. 'Thank you, I have no objection to accepting the odd favour,' he said, a remark that stuck in her mind. But she heard no more.

Her only other contact with the law was a visit from the local constable, a mild-mannered officer, who found a couple of non-residents drinking after hours in the bar and ticked her off. He came by occasionally, PC Peter Whelm, puffing after pedalling his bicycle up the lane from the Oxford road. He had known Commander Dorkin, and always had a chat with Mrs Dorkin, who was either ignorant of what was going on at the hotel or pretended to be. She had Helen's company, which was all that mattered. Slow-moving PC Whelm, with his 'Plenty of peace and quiet up here, ma'am,' was comforting. It was Swann, with the knowing look in his eye, who sometimes recurred to Sibli as a fleeting anxiety.

Progress was swift. Men – men so inclined – were able to sense the availability of skirt. Word got round. It was the era of the roadhouse, the bypass and the commercial traveller in his Austin Seven. Two girls weren't enough. Sibli and Helen travelled to London to visit a café off Monmouth Street, near the club where Helen used to perform, the Sun & Moon, in search of dancers who might remember her. Girls, said Helen, met there in the early evening to gossip and drink tea.

They chose the wrong evening. A girl who had seen a mouse was abusing a waitress who said she was a liar; rain and dirt blew in from the street; a crooner was moaning on the wireless. Seeing no one she knew, Helen led the way to a table at the back of the narrow room. The women she spoke to ignored her. 'What cows!' she whispered to Sibli, and a man with pale eyes appeared, leaning over them, cutting his fingernails with a penknife.

Sibli said, 'We were just going.'

'Not yet you aren't,' he suggested, and a paring fell in her saucer. 'Strangers stick out like sore bums here,' and he giggled at his joke.

It was a disconcerting world to be on the edge of. Getting up was difficult, he stood so close. Steam hissing and the rain outside were the only sounds.

Then a sharp female voice said, 'I've seen you, haven't I? Ages ago, the Social Purity place. You spoke up for me.' She pushed the man aside. 'Put that thing away, Dino, you'll cut yourself with it one day.'

Sibli saw a thin, personable creature in a squashed hat. It was the girl she once told not to submit to Mrs Home Secretary Booley.

'You were Sally, weren't you? Sally something.'

'Sally Walker, madam. I did like you said.'

All Sibli remembered was being enraged and wanting the girl to stand up for herself. The Booley programme would have involved birth, shame, adoption, chastity and domestic service. What had the Sibli programme involved?

They moved a few streets away to the back bar of the Café Royal, where Sally drank a cocktail and told them her story. It was quite short: the baby died, she worked in a shop, she drifted into clubs. That was life, she seemed to say, it wasn't Sibli's fault, it was the kind of thing that happened.

'I bet she's on the game full-time,' said Helen, when the girl had gone to powder her nose.

'Is that a reason for recruiting her? Or not recruiting her?' Sibli wondered how Davis would have measured Mrs Booley's solution against hers, in terms of human happiness. The surviving bits of Davis didn't contain such information.

She recruited Sally, anyway. The girl showed no surprise, except that she said, 'You too?' when she realized what she was being offered. It was more money for less work, with plenty of free time to go up to London. At the de Mandeville she proved cheerful and inventive. But knowing her story proved a nuisance, since it made Sibli feel responsible. She got to like her, another complication.

There was no more slumming after that. Sibli went to see Fanny, who was still Theodore's agent, with plans to bring culture to the small hotels of southern England, a cause, she said, that had occurred to her at the de Mandeville. She envisaged a bureau for supplying out-of-work women possessed of artistic inclinations. They could spend a season as waitresses or receptionists at country locations, entertaining the guests between times; anything from arias to tunes on a ukelele would do. A small commission would be paid.

Fanny was amused, and supplied the names of unemployable artistes. Perhaps she had an inkling of what was involved. Sibli increased her staff by two restless women in their twenties, a mischievous jazz pianist (Beryl) and an almost beautiful harpist (Françoise), who were willing to be temporarily diverted into sin.

Approached in the right way, there was never any shortage of women. Nor, as the de Mandeville's reputation grew, of men.

Helen returned promptly from seeing Clark Gable. The hotel was busy all evening, the bungalows active half the night. Next day the takings were a pleasure to count.

A lazy Sunday was in prospect. But Matthew, due before lunch, failed to appear. Instead he telephoned, very agitated, asking Helen to meet him at a hotel ten miles away. When she returned, she was agitated, too. On his way to the de Mandeville, he had noticed a burly man in labourer's clothes coming out of the wood. The solicitor, who had seen him more than once in court, recognized him as a police sergeant. He kept going, sure that the hotel was being watched.

Within a day, Sibli thought so herself. There were lights in the woods after dark. A man was seen trying to peer through the curtains of bungalows.

They knew what to do, as Helen reminded her: 'We said we'd close everything down for a month, longer if we had to.'

But that was before they had a thriving business to ruin. Sibli had Sally in to the Sanctuary and talked to her about the way a London *maison* did things. The answer was that money changed hands and worked wonders if, a big if, you knew the right detectives.

Sibli walked in the squelchy orchard while she had a think. Hotel linen fluttered on the line. Sunlight illuminated Brasswynd Hill and flashed on something, possibly binoculars; she knew the uncertainty would finish them off, if nothing else did.

It took her all day to track down Superintendent Swann,

insisting she speak to him personally about a country house burglary. His voice came on the telephone late in the afternoon. He was in Surrey, thirty miles away at Guildford police station.

'I hear you've had intruders,' he said.

'It depends what you mean by intruders. I wondered if we might meet, but not here.'

'My wife is used to my long hours. There's a new roadhouse on the Bath Road out of Twyford, going west, the Ace of Diamonds. What about seven o'clock?'

Helen was reluctant to be left alone, but Sibli pointed out that they were unlikely to mount a raid in her absence. She met George in the Highwayman's Bar. It had chains, Ye Olde Gibbet (ceiling-high, with hooks to hang coats on), horse pistols and prints of coaches being robbed. Lilac menus the size of calendars were in evidence. George said the sweetbreads were much admired.

'It's kind of you to come, but it can't be a long evening,' said Sibli. 'We have Peeping Toms in the grounds. That's the problem in a nutshell. What does one do about it?'

'Inform your local PC. I was on the beat when I last had one of those. It was in Harrow, lady complained she'd seen a man up a tree. We found he'd built a proper little platform opposite her bathroom. We never caught him, but we saw a lot of her bathroom,' and his eyes narrowed at a leggy girl who came in with a sunburnt man. 'Much used by the villainry, this place is.'

'I wondered if there was any other advice you had.'

'I don't know yet what it is you want.'

'I've told you.'

'It doesn't sound the whole story. You wouldn't bother me with it.'

'Why, because I'm a worldly divorcée who can take care of herself? That isn't necessarily the case. He's been seen near the staff bungalows.'

'Is that so?' George Swann had a protective air that she found encouraging. 'Could it be that you're frightened of a particular man, someone you know? Ex-lover, ex-husband? Don't forget, it was I helped Tom, that time you were being followed.'

'You've got a good memory.' She contemplated Ye Olde Gibbet, which looked suspiciously modern. 'I'd like to be frank.'

'Good girl,' and he touched her knee; they all reached the knee in the end.

'If a person were to tell you things that involved breaking the law – not a very important law, in some people's estimation – would you have to report the matter?'

'It depends. I might have problems if this person told me she'd poisoned someone. Armed robbery, too. Demanding money with menaces. High treason. Stealing the Crown jewels. But by and large,' and a thick finger drew surprisingly feathery circles on her stocking, 'one knows one's friends.'

Sibli saw the point of no return. She saw, too, that George's manner invited conspiracy.

'Let me ask you as a friend,' she said, and the chasm was at her feet. 'Do you know of any reason why the Buckinghamshire police should be interested in the de Mandeville?'

'None at all. So what is it that's upsetting you?'

'I wonder if I'll regret this,' she smiled, and told him about the girls and the bungalows. She left out nothing except Matthew.

He listened with eyes half closed, as if he were at a concert. When she had finished he said, 'You mean to say that you have got a disorderly house going half a mile off the Oxford Road? You know what you are, Sibli? You are a tonic. I take my hat off to you.'

'I assume I'm not under arrest.'

'You are not. Go back to the hotel and I'll make some inquiries, then talk to you on the telephone tomorrow. In the meantime, don't worry. Carry on as though nothing had happened. What are your busy nights, Fridays and

Saturdays? If a raid is coming, that's when it will be. Leave everything to George – Uncle George, your Tom used to call me.'

After that, it was surprisingly simple. They met again next evening. George had been busy. Her fears were correct. The hotel was being watched, and was due for a visit on Saturday. A local man had started the process (that innocuous Peter Whelm, thought Sibli), and it would be dangerous to interfere now. The raid would have to take its course. In the meantime two or three girls could be sent up to London, and those who stayed must be busy at waitressing or playing the harp or whatever. Incriminating items at the bungalows should be disposed of. 'Things of a pictorial nature,' he said helpfully. 'Objects connected with discipline. Even the humble rubber goods, if available in bulk. Naturally, men must not be hanging about the place with expectations. Put the word out on the grapevine.'

'Could the police have sent someone in already, pretending to want sex?'

George thought this unlikely. 'Confucius he say, police officer in bawdy house with trousers down makes poor witness in court. Go on as near to normal as you can, make sure there's some innocent to-ing and fro-ing to the bungalows, keep any stray men happy with free drinks, and you'll be all right.'

'What happens in future?'

'By a happy coincidence, an old friend of mine is in a position to make decisions pertaining to vice in your local force. I'll see what his price is. A monkey is probably the going rate, that's five hundred pounds. Then you can enjoy the security you ought to have had in the first place.'

'And you?' asked Sibli.

'It'll be enough to see an old friend of Tom's happy. Now, let me tempt you to the sweetbreads.'

George made no other demands. The raid took place and was satisfactorily chaotic. Sibli made a point of being nice to Peter Whelm, who was among the squad of men who came pouring up the drive in motorcars, and went away in them an hour later.

Business continued as usual. Aeronwy had one of her fits of depression brought on by life in Swansea, and came to stay at the de Mandeville, where she spent most of her time in bed, drinking tea and smoking and talking to anyone unwise enough to look round the door. Sibli found it easier to tolerate her mother these days; was even fond of her, as long as she came in small doses. Albert was one of her themes. She was very proud of him, and said his father couldn't wait to have him in the business, the day he left the grammar school.

'He *must* go to university,' said Sibli. 'I want something better for Albert than lorries. Griff can afford it. Tell him I said so.'

'You sound like your Aunt Margaret.'

'Don't tell her that.'

Aeronwy found time to suck a toffee to destruction between Craven As. 'She's not well, your aunt,' she said. 'She had a dizzy turn when Albert was there.'

'Give her my love. I'm afraid I can't see us meeting.'

One of her mother's cigarettes nearly burned the hotel down, but at last she went.

It was a month before George took delivery in the Sanctuary of a small brown-paper parcel, on its way to his friend. They chatted over a cup of tea. Tom had recently been made up to Superintendent – 'four months after me,' smiled Swann, and said she might be amused to know that Tom's department at present was Vice. 'Then Murder, if he's lucky. But Tom's a bit pure, that's his trouble.'

Sibli took this as another of George's hints. Since he was at the hotel, she suggested, was there nothing she could arrange for him?

Come to think of it, he said, he had never seen the inside of one of the famous bungalows.

In that case, who would he like to show him round?

Carla, who was nearly a film star once? Françoise, who wore a long white dress when she played the harp?

She had an even better idea. What about Carla *and* Françoise?

George Swann taken care of, Sibli returned to the Sanctuary. The afternoon post had arrived, with a reply from Virginia. 'You were most kind to write,' she said, 'the more so since I failed to write to you at the time of your tragedy. Why are people not more kind to one another? Your letter has made me feel both ashamed and grateful. There is absolutely no hope for Stuart although he hangs on grimly as he did in life. I hope that we might meet one day in the future.'

Sibli pencilled 'Pa's mistress' on the letter and filed it away under 'Personal'.

CHAPTER 36

Morgan had little to do with authors, who reminded him of human frailty. They were always pleading poverty, cadging advances, promising manuscripts that arrived a year late, expecting their rubbish (even rubbish about breasts and kisses) to be treated as holy writ, drinking Aeolian Press sherry, pinching Rebecca's bottom. Fortunately she knew how to deal with them, the big-stick approach tempered with morsels of carrot. This left Morgan free to be a brooding presence. He was the one who studied markets, cultivated dealers, made sure the hot stuff filtered into America and England and South Africa. When he did see an author these days it had to be someone exceptional: Professor K. K. Haeckel, for example.

Rebecca had three items for the morning meeting.

'Item One. *The Apotheosis of Miss Skinner*, by Arthur Appledene. There is an unfortunate misprint on page twelve.'

Copies of the orange-wrapped title, newly in from the printer, lay on a low marble table, next to the jug of *citron pressé* and Morgan's Egyptian cigarettes.

'I have already had words with the typesetter, sir,' reported Johnny Cox.

'Does it matter?'

'I leave you to decide,' said Rebecca. '*A wicked light shone in Cynthia's eye. Lying back with her dress disarranged, she displayed her silken logs.*'

'Cheer up. It might make someone laugh. And the next business?'

'Nicholas Lambe is anxious to see you. He is confident of finishing the novel by the end of the year if he receives a further advance.'

'Nick has been about to finish it for nearly a decade. Why should we believe him now any more than last year? If he's desperate, get him to write a couple of Arthur Appledenes.'

She sighed. 'Last item. Professor Haeckel's proposal to write *A Sexual History of Modern Times*. I feel strongly that we shouldn't encourage this until he has completed his autobiography. Of which, I have to say, there is no sign.'

'It may turn out to be roughly the same book, but "modern sex" sounds better. We shall have civilization is in decline, da-da, mankind must have a sexual revolution, da-da, chapters about the tragedies of the wedding night and the perversions of English public schools, da-da. I can see it now.'

'To my mind he is a boring little man with nasty habits.'

'Poor persecuted Haeckel. What does Johnny think?'

'Bit above my head, sir, that stuff.'

Rebecca had her fiery look. 'You want to dress up Haeckel's hysterical ravings as science, am I right? Or psychology. Psychology, I expect.'

'Think of the potential for intellectual respectability.'

'Everyone will see through it. At least our spicy fiction doesn't pretend to be anything else. I am proud of our fiction.'

'Rightly so,' said Morgan. 'You are one of the finest book editors in Europe. I think that's all, Johnny,' and Sergeant-Major Cox left them alone in the study.

'I know my views count for nothing in this firm,' said Rebecca. 'I have made my bed. I must lie in it.'

She was too valuable to lose, though Morgan sometimes wished she had found herself a nice Frenchman. 'Haeckel's manuscript will need brilliant editing,' he said. 'I shall be relying on you.'

'I am not interested in smutty textbooks.'

'But you'll do it for me. Say you will, little tiger.'

'I am not your little tiger these days,' she said, but when he came round and stooped over her chair, rubbing his face against her tawny hair, she didn't object. 'I daresay I will have a look at it in due course,' she murmured.

'Come and sit on the sofa with me.' He led her by the hand. 'I thought we might go away for a few days, you and I. Stay at a village in Provence where I'm thinking of buying a house. Will you come?'

She nodded, collapsed in his arms. After descriptions of the house and the vineyards he whispered that he had a secret to share about K. K. Haeckel. His *Sexual History* was already written. He was arriving in person with the manuscript at noon. The book would be rushed out by the autumn. She was the first to know.

'I should give you a black eye.' She spoke without conviction. 'I should have gone back to England years ago.'

'Little tiger!'

Morgan's affection for her was genuine. It was not of the intensity she wanted, but it never was, with women. She was a sensible creature. By the middle of the morning, when Oscar Snell, the London bookseller, looked in on one of his continental trips, she had come to terms with Haeckel.

Snell could be relied on for sly jokes and gossip. This time he told Morgan that the book he had once seen in Snell's hidden drawer, the notorious *Ulysses* by the notorious James Joyce, would soon be openly on sale in England. 'It is now a work of art, my friends, rude words and all,' he said. 'The authorities have turned themselves into literary critics.'

'We have the American courts to thank for *Ulysses*,' said Rebecca.

'But England is definitely changing. There is a new pocket magazine, *Men Only*, a lively little thing with nice articles and stories, but here and there a *nude*.' He produced some copies from a paper bag. 'It's most tasteful.

Still, despite the shadowy bits, one can tell what it is, which is what men are not supposed to want to look at unless they are married to it or it's art.' He peered at the magazines through half-rimmed spectacles that made him look like his father, the doctor. 'See here, if Miss Smollett won't be offended. Coloured drawings of females partially attired, certain areas concealed by a parasol or a book. Which tends only to emphasize their nature. So is this allowed to be art, too?'

'Ten years ago the police would have seized them,' said Rebecca, peering over his shoulder.

'Exactly. Now here they are, in a magazine that has advertisements for motorcars and shaving cream. One ponders these things.'

Morgan brushed them aside. It was stuff for schoolboys or young men with spotty skins, however disguised. 'One of these days,' he said, smiling in Rebecca's direction, 'I may close down the Aeolian Press and return to London publishing.'

'Excellent, excellent. We all have our roots, my friend. As you know, I still visit Port Howard from time to time to see my aged mother. She told me on my last visit about your sister's gift to the town. You know of it, of course?'

Morgan nodded. He had asked Maggs to send him a photograph of Y Plas when it was razed to the ground so he could exult over the ruins, but she didn't oblige. What he hadn't known until Oscar Snell told him was that the copperworks was closing, and Margaret was trying to organize a consortium to purchase it.

'They talk of nothing else,' said Snell, and the phrase brought the place back in all its awfulness, belching chimneys, dirty river, crooked streets – did the piss-pot lady still make her dawn collections? – hideous chapels, fly-blown shops, cramped lives and futile merchant princes. He heard their voices and smelt the stink of industry. Then Professor Haeckel was ushered in, clutching his black briefcase, and the nightmare went away.

Haeckel had been in Switzerland, writing the book. The manuscript was tied with green ribbon, but there was no question of his handing it over until he had expounded its themes with the help of diagrams and photographs. He continued to do this through aperitifs and a buffet. Everyone was expected to listen. This included Johnny Cox and his wife, and even Hélène, the maid, who had taken Haeckel's hat and coat.

Hélène was invited to sit alongside him on a sofa, where he munched vol-au-vents, causing showers of flaky pastry, and used her as a demonstration model whenever he referred to the sexual sufferings of the proletariat – 'Like this young woman from the land of nowhere,' he would say, or, more provocatively, 'This young woman could tell us stories of men's embraces if she chose.'

The telephone rang and Morgan retreated to his study. K. K. Haeckel's squeaky voice in the distance, describing the difference between a transvestite and a hermaphrodite, sounded like a gramophone being played at the wrong speed.

'It's me,' said Virginia.

'Hello, darling. How is he?'

'He died a quarter of an hour ago. I'm still at the hospital.'

'Very sorry to hear,' said Morgan. He had rather counted on old Stuart getting better.

'What am I to do?'

'Do?' The question was too broad for a quick answer. There was an uneasy sense of plans reshaping themselves. 'Be brave. Grit your teeth for the next few days. The funeral will be hard going.'

'You don't intend coming?'

'Be reasonable, my love.'

'So what am I to *do*?'

'What everyone expects, be Stuart's widow. Never mind the difficulties in your marriage.' ('Difficulties!' she said.) 'We've discussed this often enough.'

'It's different when it happens.'

'Things usually are. I shall be waiting for you. But there's no hurry.' He had to sound firm as well as kind. No woman in his life had endured like Virginia, but Virginia in the open was going to be different from Virginia in secret. 'Upsetting the family won't do any good. In time we can be together.'

'You make it sound like years.'

'Do I? There are people here. High-level discussions are going on. We can talk again later. My shoulder is always available to cry on.'

'I'm not your sister, you know,' she said bitterly, and rang off.

Professor Haeckel was still spouting. Morgan stretched back in his chair. It was the wrong time of day to think about solutions. Warm air filtered through the shutters. He dozed, and dreamed he was preaching a sermon to a vast hall full of Penbury-Holts. A voice was heard, bellowing from outside. Could it be God?

Morgan woke to hear uproar from the drawing-room. Rebecca appeared as he stood up.

'Nick Lambe is here,' she said. 'He has been drinking.'

'Who let him in?'

'He pushed past Hélène.'

Lambe was waving one of Haeckel's photographs and shouting, 'If God had meant us to be perverts he'd have made other arrangements for procreation.' His jacket had stained armpits and his face was purple.

'Someone offer him a vol-au-vent,' said Morgan.

'You publish this man's filth but the real writers can starve. You're a charlatan.'

K. K. Haeckel was unconcerned, his greasy spectacles regarding the intruder. Johnny was whispering to his wife. Hélène had scampered off.

'Go away and finish your novel like a good boy,' said Morgan, which made Lambe lurch at him with strangling gestures. The publisher stepped aside smartly, only to catch his foot on a rug and lose his balance. Lambe swayed over him. Morgan rested on his hands and knees, saying, 'Help, help' in a discreet sort of way. It reminded him unpleasantly of an incident at Margaret's wedding, when he was subjected to physical violence.

Johnny had seized the absurd Lambe from behind. Yvette threw a glass of Perrier in his face, and he was manhandled out of the apartment, shouting threats.

'Perchance I shall write a new chapter,' Haeckel was saying. 'The Angry Heterosexual, Enemy of Progress.'

'No time for that now,' said Morgan decisively. He took the green-ribboned manuscript and handed it to Rebecca. Lambe could still be heard, shouting in the street. A day that promised well had gone astray. Very likely God was trying to tell him something.

CHAPTER 37

Margaret saw the Penbury-Holts as an unlucky family. They lacked feeling, which had been at the root of her own troubles with the one she married.

She sent the usual condolences to Virginia and received an acknowledgement weeks later from the other Henry, the elder son, the one who had been a disappointment. This took the form of a printed card, rather more elaborate than Sibli's, stating that 'The burden of Mother's grief makes it impossible for her to reply personally to the many hundreds of friends who have written following the tragic accident to Stuart.' It sounded like an admonishment.

She and Virginia had been the young wives recruited to the tribe before the war. That dead-and-gone period was one Margaret preferred to forget, but Virginia's bereavement brought it back — not that Margaret had much time available for idle thoughts during the drizzly Port Howard summer. Aubrey was implacably opposed to her. The copperworks was his; a man had the same right to shed the burden of an ageing business as he had to throw away a suit or have a dog put down. Even if she succeeded in forming a consortium that had both the cash and the will to keep the works going, Aubrey had made it plain that he would refuse the offer. He told her she was misguided; she had a bee in her bonnet; she was like her father, who nearly ruined himself with grandiose ideas.

'There is nothing grandiose about keeping people in work.'

'You are doing it because you are Margaret Buckley. No more and no less.'

Virginia used to say, 'Men, don't talk to me about *men*.' Some covert understanding had existed between her and Margaret about the fleshy tribe who must be deferred to, but whose rule was not without absurdities that could be laughed at. Did all daughters-in-law have this comradeship? Virginia was the more spirited one in those days. Her hints of a grosser, more predatory interest in sexual matters alarmed the softer-skinned Margaret, whose only aim in that direction was to be decently productive.

What was that picture of the brothers wearing the unflattering bathing costumes of the time, standing with their arms on one another's shoulders on a deserted promenade? Virginia had laughed at their ugly bodies and said something about being free of men – hadn't she flapped her arms and giggled about being free like a bird? As if anyone was ever free.

Margaret and her husband had a truce in September, when Aubrey's brother the banker and his family came from Canada, and there were excursions to castles and beaches. Late one afternoon the women and children came back from a visit to St David's and the cathedral. Aubrey was on the terrace, taking tea with a man in a linen suit and a stout woman. It was Munro Parton the surgeon and his wife Daisy, the Penbury-Holt daughter – *Dippy Daisy*, melting a little in some unexpected sun.

'What a surprise,' said Margaret. 'It must be all of fifteen years.'

'Parton is a fisherman,' said Aubrey. 'He wants to try the Towy next year so I've pencilled some dates in my diary. Why haven't we had these splendid people here before?'

'Why, indeed,' smiled Margaret, wondering what had happened to make her persona grata. She had always felt sorry for Daisy, who was puffing and blushing now, and entangling herself in an explanation of why they were there.

'There was a family matter that Daisy wanted to raise with Margaret, when she has a minute,' explained the sensible Munro, and presently the two were in Margaret's sitting-room.

Mrs Munro Parton sat straight and solid, overflowing from the chair a little. Her feet were splayed, as if they meant to march off in opposite directions. 'Virginia's Henry asked me to come,' she said. 'They've all asked me.' Beef-red features quivered; the family face had been unkind to her. 'Tristram sends his best wishes.'

'It must be serious if Tristram approved your visit.'

'I am glad to be here, you know. I have often meant to write.'

Margaret stopped herself saying that in that case, it was a pity she hadn't. She leaned forward encouragingly. 'Come along. We are friends.'

'Are we?'

'Of course we are.'

Daisy looked at the carpet. 'Your brother Morgan has enticed Virginia to Paris. They are living together.' Her voice sank so low, it could barely be heard. A steam-whistle shrieked far away. 'Henry has been to France. But your brother is guarded. There is a non-commissioned officer who has a revolver.'

'I'm not his keeper,' said Margaret, with more vigour than she intended.

'He might listen to you. Henry is distraught. He took a horsewhip with him, fully intending to use it.'

The room was unusually airless. Margaret got up to open a window. 'I'm all for a family that thinks about honour, but aren't horsewhips taking things a bit far in this day and age?' Deep breaths did nothing to alleviate the tight feeling in her chest. Giddiness made her grip the sill. 'I make no defence of my brother,' she said. 'I see no need to.'

'Is there something wrong?' Daisy was on her feet, her arm around Margaret's shoulder. 'You sound peculiar.'

'I have these turns sometimes. It's nothing. Thank you.' The shakiness had nearly gone. 'I was about to say, surely Virginia is old enough to look after herself?'

'She is under his influence. The bereavement has been too much for her.'

'What does Munro think about it?'

'He has never had much time for my family.'

'I agree, families are difficult. You had better tell Henry and Tristram that I listened to what you had to say, and leave it at that.' Margaret rang for the housekeeper. 'Now that you're here, can't I persuade you to stay the night?'

'I'd love to, but we have to get on.'

Strolls in the gardens followed, and a men-only look at Aubrey's motors in the garages, before the Partons drove away, hands waving from the Rolls-Royce.

Only when they were off the premises could Margaret admit to herself how angry she was with Morgan. He was beyond the beyond. Alone with Aubrey, she told him that when Victor and family left, she intended going to Paris. In all the years her brother had been there, she had never visited him. Instead they met in London when he came over. Going to Paris would have been too much of an acknowledgement of his shady activities there.

'I'll drive you up,' he said. 'But will you do something for me? Go and see a doctor when you're in London. Munro Parton had a word with me, concerning your bouts.'

'I wish Dippy Daisy would mind her own business. I've seen a doctor.'

'Provincial quack. Munro has given me a name in Harley Street.'

'They all scratch one another's backs, these specialists.'

'You're not indestructible. I am asking you to see him.'

'I'm sorry. Of course I will.' She thought how settled and *commanding* he looked. But she meant to get the copperworks out of him, if it killed her. 'I can tell you now what he'll say. Come to terms with your age. It's what they all say.'

In the event she wasn't far wrong. She sat in the consulting-room at eleven in the morning, having her heart listened to and her legs tapped with a rubber hammer by another of the fraternity. It was the blood pressure that bothered him. He had Aubrey in so he could say it again. Steps could be taken, a diet prescribed, a holiday taken, nervous tensions avoided – 'You mean come to terms with my age,' said Margaret, and caught her husband's eye.

The Paris trip, she made out, was a holiday in itself. Aubrey suggested he travel with her, but she didn't want him there, making her feel even more awkward. He talked about going south to one of those places that people went south to, Biarritz or Nice. 'We'd both hate it,' she said. 'Why not wait for me in London and drive me home?'

He kissed her from the platform; the smell of tobacco and tweed suit stayed with her as she found her seat. 'Come back safe,' he said through the glass, and stood with his hand raised, watching her go.

Paris was dreadful. At first she was alone with Virginia, Morgan having had to 'slip out for a meeting'. No doubt he was scurrying down the back stairs as she was going up in the lift.

'This must come as a great surprise to you,' said Virginia. She wore a black dress and a touch of eye-shadow. The ghost of her beauty was still there. 'The children were upset at first. But they only want my happiness.'

'It's Morgan I've come to see,' said Margaret.

'He has been wonderful. We've been friends for years – I don't mean *intimate* friends in that sense. He was always someone I could talk to. Life with Stuart wasn't exactly a bed of roses, any more than yours was with Henry. You don't mind my alluding to Henry?'

'Not if it makes you feel better.'

'I've done nothing to be ashamed of. My worst enemy couldn't say that. It was six weeks after he died before I came to Paris, and don't forget, Stuart had been in a coma for ages before that, and might as well have *been* dead. It's easy enough for people to criticize.'

'I assure you that I'm not.'

'How much longer was I supposed to wait? Nobody thinks of *my* predicament. What do people expect, that I should climb on top of a bonfire like one of those Indian women and go up in smoke? Or jump under a railway train? Would that do? I don't think you have any right to be censorious.'

'We were like sisters, you and I,' said Margaret, but Virginia was already saying, 'One is entitled to a little happiness, is one not?'

Margaret heard Johnny Cox along the corridor. As she left, 'Life is short enough, God knows,' followed her through the door.

He was in his cubby-hole, a box with a desk, talking to a youth with comb-marks in his hair. Cox was like another version of her Trubshaw, loyal and long-suffering. Pretending to tidy the desk, he covered a hefty orange volume with a file. 'I heard you were here, ma'am,' he said. 'May I say what a pleasure it is to see you in Paris. This is the Lady Mappowder, Alexander. You will have heard of her. She is sister to the proprietor.'

'I'm Snell,' said the youth. 'Father is an antiquarian bookseller.'

'Is that the Port Howard Snells?'

'You've got it!' said the boy, who turned out to be Morgan's new editor, the old one, Miss Smollett, having recently departed.

'Reached retirement age,' said Cox, as though he felt an explanation was needed.

A door closed somewhere in the apartment. 'That may be him now,' he said, and went in search of Morgan.

'I'm learning all sides of the business,' said young Snell.

'We have an excellent autumn list.' He uncovered the fat orange book. 'This was edited by my predecessor. It's what the trade's been waiting for. Have a gander.'

She had time to read the title, *A Sexual History of Modern Times*, before Morgan appeared. He slid the book out of her hands. 'One of our medico-psychological works,' he said. 'For sale only to the profession.'

'Surely not, Mr M. The print order –'

'Shop talk!' cried Morgan. 'We keep shop talk for meetings,' and shooed the juvenile away. 'Well, Maggs, we must celebrate. How many times have I implored you to visit us? Are we what you expected? We are famous in our way. You should hear the comments we get from the Anglo-Saxon tourists who visit our bookshop downstairs. They find it very refreshing. We like to think it's the respect for freedom of expression that John Milton wrote of in the *Areopagitica*.'

A mild headache that had been troubling Margaret all day throbbed harder in her temples. 'I can do without your old nonsense,' she said.

'Shall we go and join Virginia? She feels – wrongly, I know – that you are judging her. I have told her, there is not a drop of rancour in Margaret's body. Margaret, I said, is a saint.'

She reached past him and closed the door. 'I think Virginia's having a nervous breakdown.'

'We all have our ups and downs.'

'You've ruined her.'

'*I've* ruined *her*? I wanted her to wait six months at least, but no, she had to come rushing over, practically before Stuart was in his grave.'

'When did you seduce her, twenty years ago? Twenty-five?'

'I'm very fond of her. Maggs, don't condemn me because I loved – what does the poet say? – not wisely but too well.'

'Stop acting. We all knew, and she knew that we all

knew. Don't you think she found it humiliating? That she wanted to escape from it?'

'She wasn't a schoolgirl.'

'No, she was a decent married woman who got dazzled by your second-rate charms.' She thought her head was going to burst. 'You're a wicked man. I've always pretended you weren't, but you are.'

He frowned and made m-m-ing noises through closed lips. 'What denial can I make? If you think it, in your heart, then you're probably right. I – am – a – wicked – man. Maggs says I should wear the penitent's sheet, so wear it I will.'

'You'll do nothing. Silly speeches is as far as anything goes with you.'

'If harm was done, it's too late to undo it now. If I told her to go back to her family, would that achieve anything? What can I do to make amends? See more of you, perhaps. Learn more from you.' He snapped his fingers and gave her a kiss. 'I know! I shall revisit Port Howard. In future I shall come and see you, what, twice a year? Regular as clockwork.'

Despite herself, Margaret thought how much she would like that. But she mustn't be so easily swayed. 'Promises!' she said.

'I'll begin this year. Before the end of nineteen thirty-six I shall arrive in the old town. That'll give the local gossips something to talk about. Or will that be difficult for you?'

'I shall survive. Morgan, is this a solemn promise?'

'As solemn as I'm capable of. I will be there.'

'Good. I look forward to seeing you. On your best behaviour, mind. You must bring Virginia as well.'

'A new era!' he said.

He had plans for her stay in Paris, but she left almost at once. She had said what she came to say. When they met next it would be in Wales. 'You are on probation, my boy,' she said, and he answered, 'Maggs, you are incomparable.'

In the street, waiting while he found her a taxi, she was amazed at the orange pyramid of *Sexual Histories* that filled the shop window. Her headache was better.

CHAPTER 38

The Vice Squad was a stepping-stone for Tom. Before it came Personnel and after it he anticipated Murder. Fraud was ancient history. A man had to move around, to see and be seen. His career was gathering momentum.

The Commissioner had him in for a chat, early on an October evening, some months after he went to Vice as the Number Two.

'Are you enjoying it?' asked the Chief.

'I think I've found my feet, sir.'

'No one enjoys Vice much. It sounds exciting but it ain't. You'll be aware of the special problems. We aren't purity police — more's the pity, I daresay. We live and let live where immorality is concerned. To some extent prosecution is an arbitrary matter. Thus an officer exercises choice. Thus he is exposed to certain temptations. Thus . . .'

Red and white lights trembled, caught in the river as a tug and its barges pushed eastward against the tide. Tom had let his attention slip, or he would have been aware of nothing beyond the hunched figure with its back to the dark window. He sat forward with concentrated deference, trying to act as if he were being told something new. These days the rising man needed to study careers and their history; he could have told the Chief the going rate for bribing a constable or an inspector, and how it had kept pace with the cost of living since before the war.

The Commissioner switched on the desk-light. The dent in his chin looked as if it reached to the bone.

'I keep an eye on your progress,' he said, and glanced at a file, open in front of him. 'I am glad to see you've become a family man.' He turned a page. 'I remember our little chat when I was AC(C). You were at a crossroads. I hope I was of some help.'

'Your advice was crucial, sir. I never looked back.'

The sentiment appeared to find favour. But any pleasure Tom felt in his performance had faded by the time he was back at Vine Street with Carter, his intelligence officer, who had news of a mobile brothel (a converted furniture van) that was said to be offering short-times in the King's Cross area.

'Photographs? Statements?'

'Rumoured sightings, Guv'nor.'

'Don't waste my time with it.'

The AC(C)'s reprimand was the only time Tom's career had faltered, and who had been to blame for that? He resented being made to remember Sibli. Not long before, George Swann had done it in his friendly, tactless way, at a family do. The new baby was being christened Tristram, at Eve's suggestion; she had no time for the Georges and Bills of her own kinsfolk.

George, quaffing beer and fending off children as they rushed around the garden, mentioned that he had bumped into Mrs Somerset at a hotel in the Home Counties. 'A charmer,' he confided, and Tom said, 'A femme fatale if ever there was.' That night he made love to Eve. It was the first time since Tristram was born. She gasped a bit and held him tight. As marriages went, theirs wasn't at all bad.

Now, after being reminded of that damned reprimand over that damned woman, he had the same shameful urge to reassert himself with Eve. He took a shilling box of chocolates home to Battersea and she ate them at one go when Tristram and his brother Horatio were finally asleep, and she was reading the estate agents' details of semi-detacheds in greener districts that she was getting excited about. He felt comfortable with Eve; surely that was the point of a marriage?

But he seemed doomed to keep encountering the Buckleys. The woman Carter brought to see him soon after wasn't herself a Buckley. She was tall and in her forties, her intelligent features marred by a small, bitter mouth. Carter said that she claimed to have information about pornography, but refused to speak to anyone below the rank of superintendent. Like many police officers, Carter was no match for righteous middle-class citizens, especially if they were women. Tom didn't let himself be patronized – had no need to, being middle class himself.

'It's Mrs Smollett, I believe?' he said.

'Miss Smollett.' The correction came out as a hiss. 'I am Rebecca Smollett and I have been employed for some years by a publisher called Morgan Buckley, whose imprint in this country was Buckley & Cox. In Paris, where he now resides, it is the Aeolian Press. I was his editor until earlier this year, when I decided to return to this country.'

'May I interrupt you?' he said. 'I have a feeling that what you are going to tell me is important. It would be useful to have an informal note of our conversation. May I send for our Miss Martin?'

'Of course. One hears of matters that are sometimes not acted upon by the police. I am choosing my words carefully. The more that is written down, the better.'

'You are very well-informed, if I may say so,' he murmured.

She was very angry. He knew at once she was a woman wronged. It was in her over-powdered face and the corseted jut of her breasts. Wronged women made poor witnesses at a trial; jurors didn't care for a cold recital of facts, hinting at malevolence. What they were good at was informing, raking through their memories with iron claws.

'You say "distributors". Could you be more precise?'

'Certainly. In New York, an antiquarian dealer, Galaxy,

No 1200A Madison Square Gardens. In Madrid, Don Manuel Orti, Calle de Sagasta. In London...'

Miss Martin's pencil caught the rhythm from Miss Smollett's voice, and she smiled once or twice, as if sharing a secret between spinsters that meant bad news for men.

'Does the title *A Sexual History of Modern Times* convey anything to you, Superintendent?'

'Aeolian Press, published last month, on Customs & Excise "A" list. We seized three copies in a routine raid on a Paddington bookshop.'

'You regard it as obscene?'

'Obviously. Aeolian Press stuff is risky, but the Director of Public Prosecutions is broader-minded than he was. This is in a class of its own. The stuff on perversions is extremely explicit.'

'You found the plates shocking?'

'Deeply.'

'I believe photographs of pubic hair and ladies' parts are taken very seriously?'

Miss Martin's pencil flickered across the pages. 'Very,' said Tom, reflecting that one of the three copies, briefly left on a desk in the back office at Vine Street, had had the best illustrations removed with a razor blade. It was the constable who left the book unattended who got the reprimand.

'So you will prosecute?'

'The Director will consider it seriously. But what's the use of clobbering a little Cypriot with a kiosk in Praed Street? It's a case of sledgehammers and nuts. If more copies have got in, we should like to find a major outlet.'

'At least twelve hundred copies will be here by now. The name I gave you, Oscar Snell...'

Tom listened attentively. He called Carter in and they both listened. They wanted to know if Morgan Buckley ever came to London.

'Now and then. I have seen him nervous of arrest, but

he had a fancy woman here. She joined him in Paris recently, so he no longer has that motive.'

At 'fancy woman' Miss Martin's pencil danced. Tom said, 'And would you know his movements?'

'I might receive information. He has another address in France that the Sûreté may not be aware of, a house in Provence. The village . . .'

It was all very satisfactory. Miss Smollett, whose eyes had become brighter as she talked, went back to her bedsitter in Kensington. Miss Martin said she would stay late to get the interview typed up. Tom discussed surveillance with Carter, and booked a call to the Sûreté's liaison officer. 'There was a prosecution in the twenties involving Buckley,' said Carter, and Tom said, yes, he knew.

On the bus going home that night, stuck at roadworks on the Embankment, he daydreamed about the case. Buckley was at his mercy, red-handed in London. The beauteous Sibli was there – *her* again, as if he hadn't banned her from his brain years ago. She pleaded with him for her father's freedom. 'My dear girl,' he said, shaking his head. Next moment she took her clothes off. She wept, naked. Who would know, anyway? Her pubic hair was plentiful but trimmed, as he remembered it. *By what right did he remember it?*

The remembering was corrupt. How would it look in his file? 'A senior officer who could be assumed to have some experience of women, he was like putty in the hands of his former lover.' He seemed to be ruined already. Then the bus jerked forward and he was the incorruptible Penbury-Holt again, going home to his wife and sons.

Preparations were made. A warrant was signed for Buckley's arrest. Tom went to Paris and talked to the liaison man, and they drove slowly past the Aeolian shop in a taxi. The French were theoretically helpful, but they always failed to be as outraged by pornography as the British were. Tom himself didn't rise to outrage, but that was irrelevant; the system demanded that lines be drawn and individuals crushed now and then in the name of purity. Meanwhile the most the French would do was 'keep an eye on him', unless warned of his imminent departure for London, when they would tail him to the coast or the airport.

But Morgan Buckley gave no sign of taking risks. Weeks passed, Snell Antiquarian Books was left unraided, Miss Smollett's statement stayed under lock and key in the Vine Street safe.

Eve was drawn to a delightful property ('Tall Chimneys') having spacious garden (mature apple tree) in favoured Dulwich avenue (excellent buses). They went to look at it on a Saturday afternoon. A fence sagged; a shed door banged in the wind. 'I really like it,' said Eve, and another piece of the future fell into place.

CHAPTER 39

Women were too much in evidence at the Mandeville. Sibli needed a manager, or perhaps just a man. Apart from a head waiter and Sidney, the gardener/porter, the staff was female.

'Why don't you two get married?' she asked Helen one Sunday, when all three were relaxing in the Sanctuary.

'That's a tactless question,' said Helen.

'Is it, Matthew?'

'Er, not at all. No.' He sucked his pipe. 'We plan to, of course.'

'I thought perhaps you could do it right away and become the manager.'

'She's only being mischievous. We can always advertise.'

'But would I trust whoever answered the advertisement?'

'A man couldn't run this place half as well as you do,' said Matthew. 'I mean it. The way you handle the young ladies.'

Helen listened to him with her round-faced, blissy-eyed look. Amazingly, she was the Helen of Bracing-on-Sea again. Sibli had even heard her address a cream cake when she thought no one was about, telling it not to think it was irresistible, because it was about to be sprinkled with rat poison and thrown in the bin. What was it like not to change – or, having changed, to revert to what you started with? Sibli felt pity; then a touch of envy.

'Did you tell Carla about that scent she's started

drenching herself in?' It was a bring-Helen-back-to-earth question.

'Mm. She says . . .' Helen whispered in Sibli's ear, 'She's got this new theory that men have a funny smell. She wants to drown it.'

'Tell her two drops behind the ears and the same on her legs if she must. Or else.'

'I think you'll have to tell her, Sibby.'

'I'm going to France for a few days at the start of December. You might as well start practising.'

Her life was impermanent. The revenge phase was over. The authorities had been mocked. Civilized men in pin-stripe suits rolled up in nice motorcars and ate expensive food in the restaurant. Then they scurried off to wooden shacks in a field and spent even more.

Sibli tried to spot clients from the grander professions. Erring manufacturers with Birmingham number-plates, reps and bagmen hurrying for a quick sin before they reached Gloucester, brought small satisfaction. It was the thin-rolled umbrella, the dark suit, the well-kept hair and hands, that made her hope that here was the head of a government department, or a major-general in mufti, or a judge with powers of life and death.

Once or twice, talking to the girls, she heard scraps of evidence. A man with sallow features had mentioned Whitehall. A suit had a Savile Row label. The rest was imagination. Yet the principle of mockery remained. Sibli stood apart, deriding the shabby system of justice that policed private lives but showed no interest in how Davis died.

In Paris she met Ricard Barjou, who counted as an 'old friend' and who sometimes wrote to her with glimpses of his life – a business trip to Milan, the birth of his son. He signed himself 'Meester Smeeth'; his letters were undemanding. Now, he took her about and they slept together. He spoke of Christmas with his family, and bought her a drawing of a cat by Picasso; it didn't look much like a cat.

The city made her sad. She slipped through its layers of dirt and beauty, unaffected. She was a woman away from home, escaping from what was itself an escape; the chain of escapes was never-ending.

Pa she saved for the last day, to cheer her up before she went back, but he was not at his best. Virginia, as Sibli half expected, was with him. She looked gloomy and didn't say much. No one mentioned the absence of Miss Smollett.

The phone rang continually. Copies of their autumn bestseller were in demand all over Europe, explained Pa. He said they thought of going south for Christmas.

'You don't think Virginia would prefer London?' asked Sibli, but Pa rapped his knuckles on a copy of *A Sexual History of Modern Times* – the apartment was littered with them – and said England was difficult at the moment.

There had been a promise to visit Aunt Margaret, but just at present he found that impossible. Sibli was given no details.

On the way back she paused in London to go shopping and attend a party the Moons were giving. She went straight from the station to the flat in Covent Garden, unvisited since early summer. Mail was redirected by the Post Office, but some circulars were on the mat. A handwritten envelope caught her eye. Inside was a note from Esther, hoping this would interest her, 'this' being a pamphlet.

Printed on greyish paper and stapled together, it announced its subject as *Chemical Birth Control. A Plea to Parliament, the Medical Profession and the Pharmaceutical Industry*. It seemed unlikely to find many readers. 'As a result of a visit to the Soviet Union,' it began, 'I have been made aware of the great interest being shown by their scientists in the development of a substance that could be ingested by women, for the purpose of preventing pregnancy. It is a little-known fact that a compound known as "Infecundin" was experimentally used in Vienna in 1932. A substance found in barren cattle . . .'

She must be nearly seventy, thought Sibli; one of the forgotten army of Suffragettes, destined to be one of the forgotten army of birth-controllers as well. The address on the letter was unchanged. Later, tired of the crowds in Knightsbridge, Sibli took a taxi to Victoria and climbed two flights of stairs.

Esther answered the bell. She had ink on her chin. 'My dear child,' she said, 'you must be psychic. I need to know your father's address so I can send Virginia a seasonal present. I hear she's unhappy.'

'I saw her yesterday. I was in Paris.'

'I suppose I should blame your father, but what's the use? My family has plenty of unhappiness of its own.'

'But you keep busy,' smiled Sibli, looking around the musty living-room, where a typewriter stood next to a loaf, and dusty books covered the sideboard. 'I have been reading your latest pamphlet.'

'You might draw your uncle's attention to it. He is supposed to be a socialist and receptive to new ideas. I made sure that every Member of Parliament received a copy before the summer recess, but to date I have had no response.'

'You never ask for contributions. Am I allowed to make one?'

'People's commitment is what I want, not their money. You're very kind. A secret benefactor in Wales – I leave you to guess who she was – paid for my birth-control van years ago, but it wasn't a success. I do best what I've always done, drip, drip, drip away at the stone. I'm having a flag day to buy stamps, so I can circularize every doctor on the register. Two hundred pounds or thereabouts. You could help with that.'

Sibli thought of saying, I'll write you a cheque. But she guessed that Esther wouldn't want it. She wanted the hard labour, the street corners, even the averted faces, without which there was nothing to win over.

'I could bring some helpers from the hotel. They'd shift a flag or two.'

'Now that *is* an offer. Saturday week, the last Saturday before Christmas. It will be quite like the old days.'

The Moons' party was dull. James was there, accompanied by a young woman wearing a brooch of jewelled holly. 'Season's greetings, my dear,' he said to Sibli.

Helen met her at West Wycombe Station the next morning and gave a glowing report. Hotel busy, bungalows busier. Oh, and Carla had been rude to her, so she sacked her.

'She must have been very rude. What about a replacement?'

'She hasn't actually gone.' Helen turned off the A40 and just missed a tractor. 'I wanted to frighten her.'

'You don't sack people and then unsack them.'

'That's right, find fault with me. I thought I was doing well, but I was obviously mistaken.'

'I'll talk to her.'

Six days absent, and anything might have happened; Sibli supposed she had got off lightly. The hotel was clean and polished. Mrs King, no fool behind her blowsy manner, knew how to keep order. Sibli checked the invoices, read the letters, visited the bungalows, told Carla to behave. At dusk the orange floodlights came on. Was the de Mandeville, then, to be the rest of her life? Being away from it encouraged speculation. But she had been glad to return.

An owl screeched in the wood. Helen, at reception, had just told Sidney to show a man in a muffler to his chalet. 'I forgot to tell you,' she said. 'Aubrey Mappowder telephoned yesterday. His wife is ill.'

'Was it urgent?'

'He didn't say so. Actually, I think it was the day before yesterday.'

The number was engaged. It was late in the evening before Sibli got through. Aubrey's voice was flat and tired.

'Margaret has had a stroke,' he said. 'She's quite comfortable.'

'You mean she's better?'

'Not exactly.'

The significance sank in. Sibli wanted to ask how badly her aunt was affected, but she guessed that Aubrey had told her as much as he wanted to. She asked if Morgan knew.

'Certainly. It was the day after you were in Paris.'

'Is he coming?'

'He says it's not possible.'

'I'll see if I can change his mind. I'll come down tomorrow.'

'I'm glad,' said Aubrey, and Sibli tried not to read anything into his gladness.

Johnny answered the phone and barked at her politely. 'Gone to Provence, worse luck,' he said, 'along with Mrs Penbury-Holt. The telephone has not been installed there yet.'

'I need the address to send a telegram.'

'Your father is acquainted with the situation. Under the circumstances, ma'am, I think it best if you trust me, Johnny Cox, the old comrade.'

His manner hinted at conspiracy; she didn't press him. In the morning she caught a Welsh train at Reading. It was a Friday. Helen and Mrs King were left to cope with another weekend.

The estuary and its smudged air unrolled. Aubrey had sent John to meet her. She asked about Margaret as they drove down Station Road – there was a ridiculous tube that communicated across the glass panel – and his hollow voice came back, 'I hear her Ladyship is improved today.'

A trolley bus went by, flashing sparks from the overhead wires. A modern town was trying to be born, without much success. Blackened stone and raw brick stayed sullenly the same. On the hill, Cilfrew Castle preserved its dignity at the end of the drive, the fake turrets falling towards her as clouds streamed in from the bay. A car with a pennant was leaving, and John saluted. 'His worship the Mayor,' he explained, opening the door for Sibli, and she hoped Margaret was sitting up in bed.

'Any improvement?' she said, as Aubrey came down the steps.

'Something happened this morning.'

Margaret had been unconscious from the start. He led her upstairs, telling her about the Harley Street man who had been down the previous day. Specialist and GP had consulted in the library before giving a lengthy opinion that boiled down to the next seventy-two hours being crucial. There was a degree of paralysis.

In the long corridor they passed the room that Sibli used to sleep in. What did the place always smell of? Cold stone, lavender soap, smoky fires. Nothing had changed. A nest of brimming brass scuttles waited in an alcove outside Margaret's bedroom. The door was open. A nurse, stiff-aproned, sat with a book in her lap. Coals hissed in the grate.

The marble head was deep in the pillow; the marble lips were set firm. A faint coloration showed under the cheeks, and the nails of the folded hands above the eiderdown were pink; almost pink.

'Hello, Aunt Margaret,' Sibli said, while Aubrey warmed his hands at the fire. He kept his back turned while she spoke again, and bent over the bed to squeeze the dry fingers. The nurse had left the room.

He said, 'She spoke early this morning. They washed her and gave her glucose, then I sat here on my own. I read her bits of the *Western Mail*.'

'What did she say?'

'The quack was curious to know. I told him it was too faint to make out. He said not to pin too much hope on it, whatever it was.'

'What did it sound like?'

He poked the fire with his toe, and flames lit up the

room. 'She said, "Goggles." It was her name for me, when I knew her first. Motoring goggles, you see? She hasn't called me that in twenty years.'

'So she knew you.'

'Or she was dreaming. I like to think it was dreaming.'

That was a useful way out, thought Sibli, possessing no useful way of her own. My dear wife/aunt/sister has fallen asleep. When she wakes, trumpets will sound, and (assuming these are earthly trumpets, not celestial) reconciliation will reign. Sibli saw herself and Margaret together, in some convalescent climate, Alps or vineyards in the offing. One or other of them was murmuring, 'Faults on both sides.' How simple and satisfying. How improbable, too, however close they were once. The happiest memories were the cruellest.

She made herself useful, seeing the visitors who called with letters and cards. Unasked, the housekeeper had ordered straw to be put down on the gravel to deaden the sound of wheels, a custom that had mostly died out with the war. 'More work for someone, picking it all up,' grunted Aubrey, who divided his time between the sickroom and the garage where he was fiddling with a gearbox. A magistrate and an editor arrived together, busy men with thick accents, angling for news of Lady Mappowder's condition. 'We are very optimistic,' Sibli told them. A tinplate proprietor with whiskers brought a handful of hothouse flowers and boasted that his uncle had saved David Buckley from bankruptcy in 1909. 'Amazing how envy lives on,' she said sweetly.

A man in his thirties with scarred hands, wearing a best blue suit, brought a letter signed by her workers at Tir Gwyn, respectfully hoping that Margaret Buckley ('as we always think of her Ladyship') would soon be restored to health. He was Benjamin Howells. When he said he was related to the Johns family, Sibli knew there was something she ought to remember.

'Before your time, ma'am,' said the man. 'Well-known

martyrs in the town, the Johns. John Johns was shot by English soldiers in the strike of 1911.'

'The one who did the General on his horse in tin-plate?'

'And had his name on the plaque. You've got him.'

'What happened to it?'

'Still down at the works.'

He hesitated as he was going. 'Excuse me asking, but who should I tell the boys I've been talking to?'

'Who do you *think* I am?'

'Well. Morgan Buckley's daughter, I *think*.'

'That's right.'

'Famous woman, you are. The boys won't believe it on the afternoon shift. Honoured, I am.'

She smiled back. 'Honoured I am, too.'

Esther sent a telegram to the Castle, as did Dippy Daisy. Will Buckley arrived in the flesh in the early afternoon. Sibli, at the window of her room, saw the station taxi grinding up the hill and wondered who was in it. The fire had been lit for her, and she had retired after lunch for half an hour alone. Wind rattled the window and a draught she remembered from childhood stirred the curtain.

She watched the taxi and half expected to see Pa step out, but it was the wrong brother. He had come down on one train and would go back on the next. He was due to speak in a debate on the Means Test that evening. 'They are many, we are few,' he declared. 'But I have some sharp arrows up my sleeve.' Four years in the House of Commons had turned his conversation into rhetoric.

He shook hands with Aubrey, looked at his watch, kissed Margaret's forehead. Going downstairs with Sibli, he asked where Morgan was.

'On his way here, for all I know.'

'He'll have some excuse trembling on those equivocal lips. He should have been a Tory politician, our Morgan.'

'I don't think you know much about him.'

'I knew what Morgan was like before you were born,

merched,' he grinned, and jammed a working man's cap on his head for the ride back to the station.

Aeronwy was expected in late afternoon, bringing Al as soon as he was home from school. By half-past three it was getting dark, and lights were on throughout the house. When Sibli was called to the telephone in Margaret's sitting-room, a maid was drawing the curtains. A desk-lamp shone on unopened letters and family photographs, and Sibli saw one of herself, at the back, half hidden; in disgrace.

The operator said she had Paris on the line. It wasn't Pa. Through the mutterings of the French telephone system the voice said, 'knickers and lamb, knickers and lamb.' Then the other voices died down and she heard, 'God-dammit, *Nicholas Lambe.*'

'How unexpected.'

'It's about Morgan. Is he there?'

'No. Should he be?'

'Are there policemen hanging about the place?'

'Not that I'm aware of. You'd better tell me what's happening.'

'He might be arrested if they know he's in Britain.'

'If that's true, he's presumably aware of it himself.' She lifted a corner of the curtain, but there was only the empty terrace and a light flashing in the bay. 'What are you telling me?'

'Warn him when you see him. The Smollett woman knows something. She tried to pump me on the telephone. I wouldn't trust her.'

'I wouldn't trust anyone.'

'Your father and I are old friends,' he said, but an enemy would say the same.

When he had rung off, Sibli studied a Bradshaw. It was out of date, and in any case there were too many Channel ferries. He might come in a plane, but where would it land?

She walked outside, saying she needed a breath of air.

The weather was restless, gusts of wind and low cloud threatening rain that didn't come. Presently the station taxi arrived again. Standing in darkness at the end of the terrace, Sibli waited to see who would get out. It was Aeronwy and Al. The boy bounded up the steps. She heard coins clink and her mother saying to the driver, 'Here's sixpence for yourself.'

The front door shut behind them. Sibli went on walking up and down, trying to be logical. If Pa was taking precautions, would he arrive at the station? More likely he would get out at Swansea. Or come by car, approach from lanes behind the Castle and walk through the paddock and kitchen gardens. If the Buckley ingenuity had saved her at the Mandeville, wouldn't it save him in Port Howard? He might not even be coming.

Someone screamed in the house. By the time a maid opened the door, the housekeeper was coming downstairs. 'Her Ladyship has gone,' she said. Her voice followed Sibli up, repeating it to others.

Aeronwy was the source of the scream. She stood chattering with grief in the corridor, attended by Al in his grammar school blazer. Seeing Sibli, she said, 'There will never be anyone to replace her.' It was almost a shout.

'Go and sit down and have a glass of water,' suggested Sibli.

'She waited till Albert was here. They can do that, you know. He hadn't been in the room two minutes before she passed away. She idolized that boy.'

Nurses were already preparing to lay out the body. Sibli glimpsed false teeth in a basin. How terrible it was; how little she could comfort Aubrey, or herself.

'So that's that,' he said. His arm trembled on Sibli's shoulder. 'I'm sorry Morgan wasn't here.'

The four of them gathered in the library, where trays of sandwiches were ready. The doctor joined them when he had certified death. Telegrams had been sent. Aeronwy snivelled into her smoked chicken. 'All right?' Sibli said to Al. He nodded, pale but calm; he looked more than fifteen.

Aubrey put his glass of whisky down and said, 'There's something I want to say, before witnesses. Over the past year, Margaret tried to persuade me to keep the copperworks open. I refused. In memory of her I now intend to do so. Buckley's will be maintained as before. I shall make a public announcement tomorrow.'

Sibli thought it would be hard for her to make amends as neatly as that, if at all. She longed to get back to the de Mandeville, hotel of dreams, with its Gershwin tunes on the restaurant piano, women in red skirts, men coming to the boil. Never mind Al, her protégé. Never mind Pa, who was sure to hear that Margaret was dead, and stay away; one of the telegrams was to Johnny Cox.

Aubrey told her she was welcome to borrow Margaret's car and return it at the funeral. She was free. She could be at the hotel by midnight. Before leaving she went back for a last salutation. The nurses had finished. Aeronwy came after her, propelling Al towards the bed.

The marble Margaret had gone, leaving a mask on the pillow, already losing definition. Sibli was aware of a vehicle and men's voices outside. Perhaps the Mayor was back. Thuds on the front door suggested he was drunk.

'Kiss your Aunt Margaret,' Aeronwy was instructing Al. 'Your sister will do it first.'

'I think not,' said Sibli. From the window she saw a policeman's helmet below.

Draughts blew through the corridor suddenly. Two figures wheeled into sight, marching side by side. One was a large man in a trilby hat. The other was Pa. Light caught metal between their wrists.

'Were you with your aunt when she died?' said Pa.

'Not in the room. What's happened?'

'Oh, miscarriage of justice.'

'Don't approach, madam!' warned the trilby, as she went to embrace him.

'All right, Harkness, it will be in order for Mrs Somerset to kiss her father,' said a voice. It was Tom, raincoat swinging open, Aubrey close behind him.

'Gales in the Irish Sea,' said Pa. 'And then these oafs. I'd have been here in time, but for them. I believe that that Smollett woman's to blame.'

'Your famous author – you'll know who I mean – telephoned to say that she knew.'

'Did he, now?'

He jerked the escort forward, towards the room where Margaret was. Aeronwy stood in the doorway. 'Handcuffs, there's nasty!' she croaked. 'Come away, my boy.'

But the boy stood his ground, making way for Pa and detective to pass, then following them into the bedroom.

Tom, the rearguard, was brusque and cool, eyes meeting Sibli's. Aubrey had turned away, pretending to study a painting of infants and a spaniel.

'What will he be charged with?' she said.

'Publishing an obscene libel. Conspiracy to corrupt public morals.'

'What could he get?'

'Eighteen months. Two years.'

She made an effort, just in case it might help Pa in some way she hadn't thought of. 'It was kind of you to bring him here,' she said. 'Where was he arrested?'

'Four miles away. Burry Port railway station.'

He, too, was swallowed up by the room. They were all in there now. The horror drew her to the door. Morgan was on his knees by the bed, Harkness stooping over him at an angle, as if he had a deformity of the spine. The detective's hat had fallen off and lay on the carpet.

'It will be a funny world without you, Maggs,' the voice was saying. It was quiet, almost conversational. 'Where have you flown to? You were the only woman I ever loved. My dear, dear Maggs,' and the voice nearly broke.

Sobbing noises came from Aeronwy. Tom had joined the figures at the bed, making a group. They might have been three brothers locked in grief. A key came from Tom's pocket. Harkness straightened up, rubbing his wrist.

What Sibli noticed was the way young Albert tensed, as if he was expecting the prisoner to make a run for it. He kept looking at her, and back at Morgan. But they both knew there were men downstairs in the hall. There was nothing to be done.

Morgan remained on his knees. He was now able to lean over the body, hands either side of her head, handcuffs hanging from one wrist. Harkness was rubbing his back; perhaps lumbago was why they released Pa, not compassion.

Sibli watched him kiss the fallen mouth. 'Goodbye, sweet Maggs.' He stood, holding out his wrists. 'I'm ready.'

The steel clicked back around Harkness's wrist. It was all over. Except that as they moved to the door, Pa's face crumpled and he gave a fearful groan. 'Oh, my Christ!' he said, and pressed his free left hand to his belly, doubled over and gasping.

When Harkness tried to yank him upright, the prisoner fell on his knees again. This time the detective went down beside him. Now they were two brothers praying.

'Oh, Christ!' said Pa again, massaging his abdomen. He was chalky white and sweating.

'What is it, man?' said Tom.

'I shall be all right,' came out in an agonized voice. He and Harkness started to rise together, only to end up on their knees again as another spasm went through Morgan. The sweat was running off his chin. He gasped something to the detective.

'What's he saying?' asked Tom.

'He says it's his bowels, sir. A lifelong condition.'

'The emotions,' said Morgan, speaking like a man in agony, 'always defeat us.' He hung his head, and a sharp breaking of wind was followed by a prolonged rattle of flatulence, accompanied by groans and a beating of his forehead with his fist.

Harkness turned his head away, looking disgusted. Aeronwy left the room. Tom was bright red. 'Take him to a WC,' he ordered, and the escort got Pa on his feet. The nearest facilities were down a side corridor, a dead-end. Aubrey pointed the way; his cigar blazed angrily. A small crowd watched Morgan, groaning and bent nearly double. Maids hung about with unnecessary buckets of coal. A constable had come up from the hall. Al loitered in the distance, where the blind spur ran off the main corridor.

Was it all a performance? If so, how and why? Offhand, Sibli couldn't recall any 'lifelong condition'. But what did she really know about Pa?

Prisoner and escort had disappeared. So had Al. Sibli went in search of him, and saw the handcuffed pair as they reappeared from the spur. More groans and flatulence could be heard. At the end of the passageway, the closet door was open.

'Sir!' called Harkness, and Tom hurried up. 'What is it *now*?'

'WC too small, sir. Physically impossible.'

'Handcuff him to the pipes and stand outside the door.'

There was no sign of Al. She joined Aubrey and said she was sorry about Pa. 'An enigma, your aunt always called him,' he replied, and she said there was no better way of flattering Morgan Buckley.

They were discussing the funeral when bangs and shouts were heard. Harkness appeared in the corridor. 'He won't open the door, sir.'

'Break it down, you idiot!' shouted Tom.

'Opens outwards. It's very thick. I think I've done my shoulder in.'

Water was pouring from under the door. The constable was ordered to lie on his back and kick the bottom panel out. When he succeeded, he jumped up, his back sodden, shouting, 'He's gone, the window's open.'

The crowd heard and a maid giggled.

Sloshing about in water from the torn-off pipe, Tom could be seen peering over the sill. 'Bit of a ledge!' he shouted. 'There's an open window – one, two, three along.'

They rushed about, but there was no Pa. Inquiries as to why the window of an empty room, that couldn't be opened from the outside, should have been unlatched, giving Morgan an exit to another blind passage and thence (presumably) the back stairs, made no headway. Members of the family had been visible throughout, as far as anyone could remember. Only Sibli remembered the absentee.

For the next hour, everyone was herded into the drawing-room – except the handyman who had to repair the pipe – while police reinforcements arrived and searched house, roof-spaces, outbuildings, grounds. Superintendent Penbury-Holt would have kept them there half the night, but Aubrey got on the phone to his solicitor.

Upstairs the graven image of Margaret was still potent, waiting to be processed into memories, though not just yet. Aubrey had lit two candles and put them on the dressing-table. The fire was smothered; the door closed.

When Sibli had gone with him to arrange the room, a constable was sent to keep them in sight. He had a quick look under the bed as they left. But Sibli already knew that Pa was clear of the house. Al had told her in the drawing-room, when everyone was still rushing around. 'At the works,' he breathed.

The outlines of the escape could be guessed at – opportunism, quick thinking by Al, down the back stairs, through the kitchen gardens, into the lanes. Very likely a bicycle would be found missing.

Money was going to be needed. Sibli had some bungalow cash that needed spending; Aeronwy's handbag, turned out when she wasn't looking, yielded crumpled fivers, smelling of face-powder; Aubrey lent her something in case she had to find accommodation on the way. It came to a bit more than thirty pounds.

Penbury-Holt himself searched the car she was taking. However hard he tried, traces of Tom-the-lover would be left, if she knew where to look. 'Y Plas, the old house, has been knocked down, did you know?' she said. He didn't reply, only cautioned her about the penalties for aiding and abetting. She could expect to be stopped on her journey. She was free to go.

No one followed her. She left the car in a street near the station, where the policemen in the yard wouldn't see it, and set off along the rows and terraces, towards Tir Gwyn and the sea, where rain would soon be blowing in.

'The works' could only mean one place. Hunted, in a town he no longer knew, Pa would find a shed, a hut, a piece of tarpaulin.

Lamps on the tops of tall poles heralded Tir Gwyn. As a girl she went there often. A locomotive chuffed in the sidings. Wind stirred dust, ash, an acid smell. Rollers thudded, out of sight, and through a gap between enormous doors, she glimpsed figures doing a fire-dance amid whirling sparks.

Methodically she explored the darkened perimeter, trying to see the place as Morgan saw it. If he hated Port Howard, then the cavernous brick halls with their dirt and heat and smoky grinding-down of the human spirit would be the inner vortex of the nightmare.

A derelict stone building with smashed windows looked a candidate. She took a step inside the entrance. Something scuttled away from her feet; the blackness smelt of a void in which generations of men and machines had turned to dust. She called, 'Morgan!' two or three times, but she knew that an hour inside there would have driven him mad.

She had to find him before it rained. Coal bunkers failed her; so did drums of chemicals, leaking under a corrugated-iron roof. Halfway around the site, where it was open to the marshes, she found him in a timber store. He appeared grasping a length of iron. Pa with a weapon was more comical than terrifying.

'Put it down,' she said, and heard the handcuffs, jangling from the other wrist.

'I wouldn't want them to win.'

'They won't.' She handed over ten pounds, keeping the balance for bribes.

'The spirits were busy tonight. I could hardly have done it on my own.'

'You couldn't have done it without Albert.'

'There may be an affinity between him and me. It may have been my seed that impregnated his mother. In a psychic sense, I hasten to add.'

'Never mind that.'

The ten o'clock hooter was almost due, signalling the night shift. She told him to wait.

'Drinking water would be useful,' he said. 'I did try puddles, but they're worse than you expect. I'm exceedingly thirsty.'

'I thought you were dying.'

'Oh, that. The body will oblige with most things, if you really need it to.'

A woman in a hat and fur coat at a tinplate works had to make sure she wasn't seen. Waiting in the shadow of the office building, while men carrying mess-tins began to drift in from the town, she called to the first likely candidate, a boy who ran from the rolling mill, quick off the mark, the moment the hooter sounded.

He dodged past the incomers as they tramped three and four abreast.

'What's up, then?' He was about Al's age, but smaller, greasy cap at an angle.

'Important message for Benjamin Howells. Do you know him? He's coming off the afternoon shift. Here's a pound note to look. You'll have two more when you bring him back. Not a word to anybody.'

Three pounds was a man's weekly wage. The boy vanished, weaving among the opposing currents of men, until she lost sight of him. Minutes passed. Latecomers hurried in, over cinders and grass. The crowd had thinned out.

When the boy reappeared, Benjamin was behind him, strolling with his tin under his arm. A thin hand came out for the money.

'You keep your mouth shut, you understand?' said the man.

'Yes, Mr Howells.'

'At your service, Miss Buckley. I know that's not right, but it'll do, won't it?'

'I desperately need your help,' she said, and told him the truth. He listened in silence. 'His only crime is the books he publishes,' she said.

'We've heard about those. My brother-in-law's a lay preacher. Very hot on sinful literature, he is.'

'I must get him away. I've got twenty pounds here and I can get more tomorrow.'

'They say Morgan hasn't set foot in the town for years.'

'He only came because of his sister.'

'How is she?'

'Bad news, I'm afraid.'

'Passed over, you mean?'

'Earlier this evening.'

'And nobody thought to tell us? *Never mind them – they're rubbish.*'

'I'm sorry. I've no right to ask anything of you.'

'It's hard to believe she's gone.'

Sibli had one more try. 'I'll give you a hundred pounds,' she said.

'We all have our price, don't we? Especially the poor. Dear me, a whole hundred pounds, that will buy anybody. There's women down the docks in Swansea will sell themselves for a shilling.'

'Yes or no?' she said, tired of this Welsh debating society.

'I'll get him away. But keep your money.'

She told him where Pa was, and that he needed water. And a bolt-cutter, she added; a bolt-cutter would come in useful.

The thought that Benjamin might suggest a ship terrified her; she saw Pa's body floating in the dock, as she had seen Davis's in nightmares. But when he returned, in twenty minutes, he had other ideas.

The solution was a nice rail wagon. A man could lie down in one, between the boxes of tinplate. Benjamin, checking consignment tickets in the sidings, had found a loaded train of tinplate going to the Far East via Avonmouth docks. It went off to the main line early next morning. There would be some shunting at Bristol later in the day. Mr Buckley could hop it there.

They got him into a wagon near the middle of the train. Fifty yards away a locomotive hissed and jabbed at another line of trucks. 'I'm much obliged,' said Pa from under the tarpaulin. Benjamin had brought him a quart of ginger beer, a heel of bread and some cheese. The handcuffs had already parted for the bolt-cutter.

'Outside Bristol cathedral, seven o'clock tomorrow evening,' said Sibli; it was the only meeting-place she could think of. 'It'll be my friend Helen, in case I'm being watched. She'll have more money.'

She took off her fur coat, which had the rest of the cash in the pocket, and stuffed it under the tarpaulin.

'Oh, ta,' said the voice. 'I've been thinking about Lambe. *He was the one*. He told the Smollett woman and then got cold feet and phoned you.'

'How did Lambe know?' She was beginning to shiver.

'Little Hélène is sweet on him. She could have heard. Who can you trust?'

'Me,' she said, and put the rope through the eyelet, so he would be able to tie the tarpaulin flap from the inside.

Benjamin escorted her through the alleys. His jacket was round her shoulders. There was no one about. The street with the car was deserted. Rain had begun to fall. She found a leather coat on the back seat, and pulled it on gratefully. When she turned to say goodbye to him, he had gone.

During the journey she was stopped twice by police, at Swansea and Gloucester. It was out of her hands now; she wasn't optimistic. But Helen returned from Bristol the next night to say he had been waiting for her, looking a bit dusty but cheerful enough.

Sibli was back in Wales, for Margaret's funeral, before she heard from him again. Crowds followed the hearse and filled the cemetery, swept by mist from the bay. She saw Benjamin Howells in the long line of mourners who filed past the grave. He raised his hat.

A telegram addressed to her was waiting at the Castle when they got back. It originated in Paris and read, 'Buckley 1, Penbury-Holt 0.'

CHAPTER 40

On the Saturday before Christmas, Sibli took four of the girls, half the total, to London to sell flags and go shopping afterwards. They all wanted to come; she had to pick names out of a hat. The chosen were Carla (minimally perfumed); Beryl (the one who liked jazz); a new acquisition, a stocky blonde called Daphne, and Sally – this last was a cheat, Sibli having surreptitiously marked her slip to make sure she was in the party.

Esther had a licence for a pitch near Oxford Circus. 'Motherhood Clinic, NW1' was printed on the tins and paper flags, even Esther having to concede that 'Chemical Birth Control' had little hope of success in Oxford Street. She spoke vaguely of helpers at work in the suburbs. Sibli thought it likely that the six of them formed the entire fund-raising force, but if so, it did nothing to diminish Esther's confidence.

'You stand *thus*,' she said, striking a mildly aggressive pose, 'weight on the right foot, head cocked, smile on face, flag and pin at the ready. Do not rattle the box. The police prefer us not to. Remember, if a man catches your eye, he is lost. Women are less susceptible.'

Margaret's death had affected her deeply. She didn't go down for the funeral: 'All those Welshmen in black,' she explained, 'all those depressing hymns. I'm too old to need reminders. I am glad to hear about the copperworks. Margaret knew what she wanted. There will be thousands of Margarets by the time you're my age – millions, perhaps.'

Of Morgan's escape she knew nothing. Newspapers had

carried no reports. But she had a piece of news about Tom. There had been 'some calamity' at work, and Eve said he was unlivable-with.

The flags sold better than Sibli expected. The girls worked hard, distracted only by a jeweller's shop with a window full of cheap rings, draped in tinsel and dominated by a photograph of a film-starry man with a moustache who gazed into a woman's face, above the words 'MAKE 1937 THE YEAR SHE SAYS YES'.

'Stop goggling, girls,' Esther commanded, and moved them along the pavement. 'You are much happier as you are, single and fancy free. The waitress and the chambermaid are important members of society, and don't let anyone tell you differently.'

Sally caught Sibli's eye. Like the others, Sally was less keen on selling flags to women, but pounced on men, especially those on their own. Sibli saw Beryl stroke a naval officer's lapel. He put a florin in the box.

By half-past twelve every flag had gone. Esther stowed trays and boxes inside a vast canvas bag and led the party into the nearest pub, where they fed on meat pies in a snug screened with etched glass, and Sibli insisted they drink champagne.

When they were leaving – Esther to take a taxi home with the boxes, the others to visit shops – there was a brief delay while Esther begged string from behind the bar to mend the handle of the hold-all, tearing under the weight of money. When they emerged, a police-constable was arresting Sally, who had gone ahead.

'Didn't do a thing!' she was complaining. 'Tried to sell a bloke a flag.'

'You were importuning him for an immoral purpose. The only flag was in your coat.'

'That was the one I was selling him.'

'Come on down the nick or I'll do you for obstruction as well.'

Sibli began to speak, but Esther was quicker.

'Do you know who I am, constable?'

'I can't say I do, madam.'

'I am Miss Penbury-Holt, and this young woman has spent the morning raising money for a charity of national importance.' She tore open the hold-all and rattled a box under the constable's nose, at the same time producing her permit. 'Here is my authority. We are in this together. Would you like to arrest six respectable women, constable? Why stop at one?'

He was hesitating. 'It looked to me like undue familiarity. There may have been a misunderstanding.'

'I have been dealing with policemen's misunderstandings since I was in the Suffragette movement, before you were born. Now, do you wish all six of us to accompany you to the station? We will certainly liven up your Saturday.'

He was only a boy. Esther still had the collecting box in her hand. 'I'm sure it's a good cause,' he mumbled, and put in sixpence.

Sibli found her a taxi. They waved her off and walked down Oxford Street, laughing.

PART V

1940

CHAPTER 41

In the overbright June afternoon, the occasional band of cloud passing over the sun woke Sibli with its shadow. She was lying on a blanket between the hotel and the orchard, wearing a bathing suit, suncreamed legs and arms outstretched. Every time her eyelids flickered, Helen, sitting in a deckchair and watching her closely, started chattering again.

This was annoying but inevitable. A month earlier, as the German armies started spreading over Europe, Matthew volunteered for the Bucks Light Infantry. On his first leave, a weekend pass from a depot twenty miles away, he and Helen were married by special licence. Their honeymoon was a night in London, after which he returned to his unit. Helen's marriage was now of two days and a bit's duration, as she kept reminding Sibli, describing herself as the 'soldier's bride' who (she sportingly admitted) was 'like thousands of others', though she couldn't help wondering if 'all those other girls are going through what I'm going through.'

Beyond the hedge, which had grown to a satisfactory height and density, a gramophone in one of the bungalows was playing a song about apple-blossom time, just audible.

'If the Germans invade, Matthew will be in the front line. He's like that,' said Helen gloomily. The sun was blazing again but Sibli gave up trying to sleep. 'He'll do something brave and be killed, silly ass.' Helen ran her hands down her dress. 'Do you think I got pregnant on Saturday?'

'Bit early to tell. Is it what you want, the hero's child?'
'No need to sneer, Sibby.'
'I didn't mean to. We shall all be looking for heroes.'

A recent letter from Aeronwy said that Albert was war-mad and not working as he ought for his Higher School Certificate next month, which would decide whether he went to university. The town was full of excitement after a German plane flew over the docks at ten o'clock in the morning, so low it almost hit the cranes, machine-gunning and bombing. Aeronwy claimed they had a broken window and she smelt the gunpowder. Even worse, it led to Albert announcing that he meant to be a fighter pilot.

'A rumour has reached me,' she went on, 'that you are intending to buy a farm in Carmarthenshire. I wonder you have not told your mother about this. If we are to have bombs raining out of the skies in Swansea I hope that Albert and I will be able to go there where it's safe, I do not think my gas-mask is working properly, our air-raid shelter has got mice, every time the sirens go I feel poorly. Griff has to stay for the business, but I could look after the farm for you, assuming the rumour is true, but I cannot imagine what you want a farm for.'

The Swansea gossip machine hadn't yet identified the farm. It was Rhydness, the property that Morgan inherited from his grandmother, and sold to finance his life in London before the war – the war they couldn't call 'the War' any more, the next one being well under way.

Buying Rhydness was a response to uncertain times. Sibli managed to get some of her French investments back to London. One day she would give the place to Al, if he lived that long; if they all did.

Streaks of white across the sky passed above the cloud-strips and at right angles to them, 'vapour-trails', the new phenomenon.

'Ours or theirs, do you think?' said Helen, for the umpteenth time.

'I'll get Em to make us some tea.'

'Matthew thinks Hitler will invade almost at once. He says Dunkirk was all very well but they don't have a single machine-gun at the depot. You're not to tell a soul.'

Sibli heard a motor-bike on the road and thought it might be a telegram about Morgan; the authorities still favoured the telegram. She pulled a dress over her head and went into the hotel.

Since Paris fell and France capitulated, she had been trying to get information from the Foreign Office. But they were inundated, and had little to tell anyone. James, who might have helped with his contacts, had gone to spend the war in California. He was a Jew, or the Nazis would have him down as one, so she couldn't altogether blame him.

An army captain and a civilian were at reception; a motor-cycle and sidecar could be seen outside.

'Captain Wiggins, War Office,' he said, a cheerful man with a ripe-tomato nose, 'and this is Mr Sparrow, from the county council. I wonder if we could have a word.'

'I was ordering some tea. We can have it in the lounge.'

Captain Wiggins had a file of papers, some of which slithered on the floor as he sat down.

'More haste, less speed,' he said.

'Are we in a hurry, then?'

'War's on, I suppose we must be. Nice place you have here. Bungalows in the grounds, I gather.'

'Perhaps you'd like to stay to dinner. We keep strictly to the food regulations, of course, but I expect the kitchen can find us something tasty.'

'I only wish I could.' He took a slice of buttered fruit loaf as soon as Em appeared with the trolley and chewed it with satisfaction.

'This is your sole residence, Mrs Somerset – Davis? – I'm confused.'

'It is.'

'Ah.' He searched his file. 'You are down here as owning a flat in Covent Garden.'

'Does it matter?'

'In a general sense, no. In the particular sense of our visit, it does, rather. You see' – he reached for more fruit loaf but changed his mind – 'under provisions of the Emergency Powers Act, I am afraid we are going to have to have this whole bally place for the army.'

'The Act of 22 May ult.,' said Mr Sparrow, 'not that of 24 August, 1939.' He sat back looking pleased with himself.

Captain Wiggins was eyeing her legs. She ran a hand through her hair, still warm from the sun. 'What does the army want to do with it?' she said.

The captain shook a finger, as though at a saucy remark. 'Not allowed to tell you that, unfortunately, but it would be a reasonable guess that a headquarters of some kind is envisaged.'

'How soon?'

'The advance party will be here on Wednesday. Mr Sparrow will attend tomorrow with one of my colleagues for the purpose of signing an inventory.'

'I can't do an inventory in twenty-four hours. I need more notice. Also I have a staff to think of.'

'Hitler isn't giving *us* much notice,' said the officer. 'Fortunately you personally have a flat to go to. You must warn your staff of the need to be over the hills and far away by 07.00 Wednesday. My friend here may be able to help with emergency billeting.'

'For one night only,' said Mr Sparrow.

They zoomed away, leaving a haze of dust. Nothing had changed. Mrs King had her feet up in the kitchen, nodding over a glass with a smear of sherry in it. Helen was waiting for her tea, fingering her breasts. The gramophone played on in the bungalow. Sibli had a desperate feeling of loss at the thought of an enterprise built up over years wiped out in five minutes, whatever was said about compensation. Yet she had a sense of being carried along by events, reshaping lives that liked to think themselves free but were always constrained by other lives, interacting out of sight. Captain Wiggins and his diktat was only an extreme example of the process.

Everyone was summoned to the dining-room to hear the news — Mrs King, the bungalow girls, the head waiter, Sidney, three straight maids and the barmaid. Helen, who knew already, was sulking in the Sanctuary. Mrs Dorkin, who didn't entirely understand, had joined her, wearing her dressing-gown, and was talking about the late Commander's experiences at the Battle of Jutland.

There were a few tears; expressions of anger; excitement; apprehension; resignation. Sibli promised everyone a bonus on top of their wages, and started work on the inventory.

Around eight o'clock she paused and poured herself a gin. Helen was looking after the handful of customers, the last they might ever see at the Mandeville. Outside it was still warm. Long shadows were growing out of the trees. To the south a vapour-trail fell apart in strands of pink.

Sally, who was helping with the inventory, came out to find her, and put her arm on Sibli's shoulder.

A man was pushing a bicycle up the road. Something odd about him resolved itself into the combination of black overcoat and summer's evening. He was almost at the gates before Sibli recognized him.

'It's my father,' she said. 'Go and put a bottle of bubbly on ice, quick.'

He was not in a good temper. 'Physical humiliation,' he said, 'is the Lord's preferred solution for keeping the human race on its knees.'

'Why are you wearing that overcoat?'

'It has special characteristics.'

It was so heavy, she could hardly hold it. 'There must be something in the lining,' she said.

'There is,' and he put his finger to his lips.

When the gold was locked in the Sanctuary, and he had spent a while snorting in a bath, he was more like Pa. He

FEB 1996